····Chasing

The···

····Truth

A Novel

by
Barry Lee Davies

PublishAmerica
Baltimore

First printing

ISBN: 1-4137-1714-4
PUBLISHED BY PUBLISHAMERICA, LLLP
www.publishamerica.com
Baltimore

Printed in the United States of America

This book is for my wife, Shirley Davies. Her infinite patience, encouragement, love, and faith made it possible to complete this book.

And to my mother, Thelma Davies. If God has a plan on how to be a loving and caring mother, then he must have given it to her.

The characters mentioned in this book are fictional. The Police Departments of Abbotsford and Vancouver are very real, however, and the author acknowledges and salutes the dedicated men and women working within those Departments.

The world relies on the dedication and professionalism of the men and women of the United States Armed Forces, and although the characters are of the author's imagination, capabilities such as *Echelon* and the ability to listen in on *any* electronic communication, exist.

•••CHAPTER ONE

With the stench of stale urine still burning his nostrils and his ears still rebelling against the loud obscenities directed towards him while in the cell area, Craig Fletcher walked out of the elevator and into the first level garage area. Carrying the booking sheet in one hand and brushing the dust off of his leather jacket with the other, he looked down the length of the garage and saw his partner talking to a uniformed police member; his short frame was animated as he talked. Feeling impatient, he pushed the elevator button and bellowed in protest, "Tom! Let's go! I want to get the hell out of here."

The elevator door opened and Craig stepped inside and turned around in time to see Tom Gifford slip in a patch of oil as he high-tailed it for the door.

"For Christsake! You can get killed in this bloody place," Tom said, as he jumped into the elevator.

Pushing the button for the third floor, Craig turned to his friend and smiled. "Tom, you're thirty-six, and getting fat, bald, and ugly. You never exercise, you eat and drink everything you want, and then you worry about a little patch of oil doing you in. I'll be damned if I know what Jo-Ann sees in you."

Tom laughed and wiped the hair from his forehead. "A little bald spot in back, is all; I do all right. Look, it's getting late, what say we go for a drink?"

"See, there you go," Craig said as the elevator stopped. "Always thinking about your stomach."

7

The two of them stepped into the third floor detective office with Tom still insisting, "We could go to Chung Ling's for Chinese."

Craig was tempted because he didn't want to cook for himself, but he didn't want another late night. "Not tonight, Tom, probably tomorrow. I've got to get home."

They weaved their way between the desks as they entered the office, Tom starting to get on Craig's nerves with his insistence. "What the hell you got to go home to? Since Jennifer moved out a month ago, you haven't gone out but three times. It's just a drink and supper for cryin' out loud."

Craig's desk was in the northeast corner, and as he sat down in his chair he looked at the pile of paperwork with disgust. Looking around the room, only Art Campbell was sitting at his desk talking on the phone. The big forty-five year old redhead was chewing the hell out of a pencil.

Campbell put the phone down and, knowing he craved one of his cigars, Craig asked, "What's the matter, Art, can't you light that thing?"

"Humph. Easy for you to say, you're not the one going crazy. I can taste it! I can even smell that sweet aroma."

Both Craig and Tom laughed, with Craig still ribbing Campbell, "Sweet aroma my ass, put a match to that pencil and it would smell the same as your cigars. Better in fact. I bet you ten bucks that Betty doesn't allow you to smoke in the house."

"Big deal! I'm quittin' ain't I? Too damned expensive. Damned government taxin' the hell out of everything good in life."

Tom piped up, "First time I ever agreed with the government. Think of it as the government doing you a favor. No, better yet, thank them for doing *me* a favor."

"I suppose you don't have any bad habits. Leave me alone to suffer in silence," Campbell gruffly replied.

Craig turned his attention from the two men and looked out of his window towards downtown; the rush-hour traffic moved in spurts. He thought of the people who didn't have to rush home, and who were window-shopping or walking around Stanley Park. He remembered the times that he and Jennifer spent walking the sea wall, eating french fries wrapped in old newspaper, and just sitting and lapping up the sun.

He missed her! He missed being with her and he missed talking to her. She had moved out a month ago, telling him to get his act together. She had said she was tired of his indifference to his family. He could still hear her telling him that she could put up with the shifts, the disappointments, or even his bitching, but not the indifference.

8

The truth was he wasn't sure what his own problem was. He was beginning to hate the job because of the loss of time with his family, and then he would turn around and take it out on them. He missed his eight-year-old daughter too. Lorraine didn't understand a damn thing about the whole mess.

Craig looked around the detective office and saw that the other two men were busy, and picked up the phone to call her. He was halfway through punching the buttons when he hung up, knowing he couldn't say what he wanted from his desk.

Looking out the window at the traffic volume, Craig knew he had to get the hell out of the building. He'd had enough for the day.

"You thinking of that wife of yours again?"

Craig looked at Tom and sat up to his desk. "None of your damn business."

"I thought you said you wanted to get out of here? We've got the paperwork on that jerk downstairs to do."

Craig rubbed his face and was suddenly tired of the whole merry-go-round of locking them up and letting them go. He stood up and looked across at his partner at his desk. "How about you finishing up for me, Tom. I'm bushed and want to get going."

"Fine." Tom threw his pen on his desk and leaned back. "But you better not let Wong catch you leavin', you owe him a couple of hours already."

Craig smiled and crossed two fingers together. "Inspector Wong and me are like this."

"Sure, with you on the bottom if he catches you."

Hugh Wong was in charge of the detective branch. At forty-nine, he was highly motivated and had a rough time walking the line between his men and the wishes of Fred Shepherd, the Deputy Chief. He was a nice guy, with a nice family, but he was running himself into the ground trying to please everybody, and not necessarily succeeding.

Craig locked his desk as Brad Duffield came sauntering into the room. He wore the usual perpetual scowl on his face that for some reason seemed to suit his fifty-two years. He knew his job and was friendly enough, but he had a reputation for being grouchy. He had an even smile that crinkled his eyes, but even then he looked like a tough street cop, and as such he seemed a little unapproachable to some of the other men.

Craig knew Duffield didn't like Hugh Wong that much, mostly because Wong was younger and had less experience, and Duffield didn't like fence sitters telling him what to do. Craig watched Duffield as he threw off his windbreaker and looked in his direction.

"Hey, the jails complaining that you never gave them the location of your last bust, the jerk's screaming his head off. He wants a fix."

"Good to see you too, Brad," Tom yawned. Turning to Craig, he jerked his head to the exit. "I'll look after it, you go ahead."

"Thanks, I'm out of here." Craig patted Tom on the shoulder as he passed and waved his goodbye to the room.

Leaving the five-story building, Craig paused to speak to a couple of uniformed members then jumped into his four-year-old white Mustang. Lowering the window as he accelerated into traffic, he was immediately engulfed in warm summer air that carried exhaust fumes, the smell of the ocean, and other vague odors of the city.

As the car moved easily and quietly towards the city boundary, Craig felt his stomach churn with the familiar pangs of hunger. Looking at his watch he realized he hadn't eaten for six hours. Hungry or not he absolutely hated eating alone, and didn't have the ambition to dream up anything that appealed to him.

Needing bread and milk, Craig eased off the road and let the car coast into an all-night food and gas bar, parking to the right of several cars. The odor of gasoline fumes mixed with the heavy grease smell of fried chicken turned him from the thought of take-home.

Locking the car, Craig automatically glanced around the lot. A group of males were whooping it up around a late model purple Firebird, several of the local girls hanging goggle-eyed around the owner. Craig recognized him as Kelly Kaufmann, known as Kelly the Kook on the street because of his unpredictable actions when using drugs. Craig knew that was most of the time, and he knew that with his mood swings he could be dangerous.

With Kaufmann was his friend Jules Vincent, a wannabe mobster who had no imagination and who was totally hooked on drugs. Craig knew he was useless without Kaufmann's supply to keep his habit going.

As he entered the store, Craig thought of the number of times he had put Kaufmann in jail. B&E's, drugs, stolen property, dangerous driving, robbery, Craig couldn't remember them all, but he did remember that Kaufmann always caused a commotion when arrested.

As he was getting his purchases, Craig dwelled on the thought that Kaufmann was keeping his nose pretty clean of late, which meant he was probably busy pushing his merchandise to established low-grade pushers, and keeping out of sight.

Paying the clerk, Craig walked out of the garishly lit store into the humid night air. Kaufmann was leaning on the left front fender of his Mustang. He was in his late twenties, had a poor complexion, and weighed no more than the bag of groceries Craig was carrying. His eyes glittered like the eyes of a snake; the pupils were dilated with no depth to them. He was totally tripped out.

"Well, lookee here. Look guys, it's my old friend, Fletcher," Kaufmann said as his face brightened.

Craig walked by him, unlocked the door and put the bag on the front seat. "Get off of my car, Kaufmann."

"Ohhh.... 'Get off of my car'" Kaufmann mimicked, raising both hands shoulder high and wiggling his fingers back and forth. "You still a porker, Fletcher? You got a face like one," Kaufmann snickered, then for no apparent reason broke into a total laughing fit.

Craig felt himself getting upset. He'd had it with this day and just wanted to get home. He also knew that to accomplish that he would have to deal with the drugged out lunatic in front of him.

He was about to turn to get into the car, but Kaufmann had stopped laughing and spoke to him in a louder voice, looking towards his buddies to find an audience and support. He seemed to find it, because he stepped up to Craig and put his pock-marked face about six inches away. His breath smelled like formaldehyde. Whatever high he was on, it was blossoming to full effect.

"I asked you somethin', Fletcher. Are you still a po-liceman? You don't look like no po-liceman. In fact, you look like a piece of crap."

Kaufmann broke into another giggle, his friends laughing and encouraging him to continue. He giggled, then made a mistake-- he reached up and patted Craig's cheek as he said, "Yeah, mother..."

Craig almost lost it, barely containing himself as he reached up and grabbed Kaufmann's right hand and the two fingers next to his thumb. Inverting the fingers, Craig reefed upwards while at the same time stepping backwards.

"Hey, let the fuck go! Let the fuck go, you stupid pig!"

Craig's face was set in granite, his quiet voice concealing his true feelings. "You're bothering me, Kook."

Kaufmann's friends, led by Jules Vincent, started forward with the intent of coming to the rescue of the man who was doing a dance on the parking lot.

Craig looked at Vincent and shook his head from side to side, not easing the pressure on the fingers. Vincent stopped, but started to yell and scream obscenities.

Moving ahead, Craig made Kaufmann walk backwards towards the building and away from the Mustang. The man was saying nothing, but moans were coming out of his throat in a steady cadence.

"I'm going to do you a favor and let your fingers go, Kook, but you had better stop screwin' around or I'll cause you some pain. Understand?"

Kaufmann shook his head up and down rapidly, and as his fingers were released he cried out in renewed pain as the fingers relaxed and tried to regain their original shape. He bent over to examine his hand and Craig grabbed both of his ears and lifted with all of his strength, the anger still within him. He hooked a finger of each hand behind the addict's ears and into the pressure points. The pain was instantaneous and Kaufmann began to blubber and scream.

Craig let go, and as the man fell to the ground moaning, he offered some further advice. "You're not too smart, Kook. Don't try that again. Now get your friends and go home."

Backing out of the parking lot, Craig was in anything but a good mood. He was angry at himself for letting the scum upset him, and at the same time angry with himself for not pounding the hell out of him. He was left feeling very frustrated, and for the first time in over two years wished he had a cigarette. *"Or maybe it isn't a cigarette,"* Craig thought as he lowered the windows again, *"maybe I need a stiff drink."*

Pulling his private cellular out of the glove box and quickly punching the buttons with his thumb, he watched the white lines flip under the car as he waited for either Steve or Jackie Munroe to answer the phone. Both had been friends for a long time. Jennifer and Lorraine had moved in with the Munroes in North Vancouver during the summer school break.

As he pulled out and tromped the gas peddle to pass a slow moving transport truck, Jackie answered the phone on the third ring. "Hi, Jackie, it's Craig. How's it going?"

"Craig. Glad you called but you just missed Jennifer. She took Lorraine to do a little shopping and to see an early movie over at the mall."

"How are they, Jackie? Are they okay?"

Craig glanced down at the speedometer and realized he was quite a bit over the speed limit and eased off as he heard the reply.

"Look, they're both fine. They put on a good face, but they aren't happy. Jenn misses you and her home, and all Lorraine talks about is her daddy; it's daddy this and daddy that. I'm sorry you missed talking to her because it's what you both need. To talk."

"All right Jackie, thanks for helping us out. Tell them I called. If she wants to call I'll be at home."

"No problem."

"Tell Lorraine I love her."

"Just Lorraine?"

"No, Jackie, not just Lorraine. Tell Jenn I miss her."

Jackie gave a little laugh, "You men! I'll tell her but make sure you get that wife of yours back home."

Craig put the cellular back on the seat and directed the car into the now congested traffic. It was a slow grind, and to ease his tension and take his mind off of it all he reached up and pushed a C.D. into the slot. The sounds of Sinatra filled the car.

Finally hitting the open highway, the tires humming on the still hot pavement, Craig felt relaxed enough to turn his mind to his job and marriage, and wondered where it all started to come apart.

Work wasn't all that bad. Walt Telford, Art Campbell, young Sid Grabowsky, and even Brad Duffield were good guys to work with. He even got along with Hugh Wong. Hugh had to be pushed along in a gentle way once in a while, but Wong did have his hands full with the Deputy Chief.

"Shepherd! Now there was another one," Craig thought. Deputy Chief Fred Shepherd, fifty-three years old and on the Department for God knows how long, hated Craig's guts.

Craig could picture Shepherd in his mind as he drove. Five feet eleven, about two hundred and twenty pounds, gray hair and twisted eyebrows that gave him a mean appearance.

He had hated Craig ever since Craig started an investigation involving a city official: Councilor Gordon Parrento. Huge amounts of stolen property were being moved from the city, and Craig had tracked it to a warehouse that was owned by, who else, Councilor Parrento.

Digging deeper, Craig found that Parrento not only had dealings with known underworld connections, he had a few friends within the Department. One of them being Deputy Chief Fred Shepherd.

As he drove, Craig remembered being ordered off of the case by Inspector Wong. Of course Wong was just the messenger, and really didn't have a clue as to what was going on behind the scenes, but it hadn't sat well with Craig, and in fact made him more determined to nail Parrento.

It had not been easy. Other cases had been thrown at him, and the pressure to account for his time and whereabouts had increased. Craig got a break, however, from a little guy whom he had saved from a stretch of five years in the penitentiary. He gave Craig most of what he needed to know on the fencing of stolen property, payoffs and kickbacks, and who was involved. One of the names was Parrento's. Obtaining a warrant, he had hit the warehouse and grabbed all he could for evidence. He had Parrento nailed tight.

When Craig went to the Prosecutor, the shit hit the fan. The meeting between the Chief, the Prosecutor, Craig, Wong, and Shepherd was one that Craig would not soon forget. Shepherd had been furious and wanted Craig charged with disobeying orders, falsifying evidence, and anything else he could think of. He wanted the whole thing suppressed, but the Chief ordered it to proceed. Later in the Chief's office, Craig remembered with a chuckle, the Chief had given him a cross between a tongue lashing and a pat on the back.

The end result was a lot of publicity, the resignation of Parrento, and to Craig's disappointment, the staying of the charges. The end result was also the nonstop stalking-- the waiting game that Shepherd played with Craig, like a predator, waiting for him to make a mistake.

As Craig wheeled through the town of Ridge Meadows and turned North towards the backside of Golden Ears Park, he knew that Shepherd never ever forgot. In fact he knew that Shepherd had kept him in the Major Crimes Section to wait for that mistake. Waiting and waiting and waiting for that one mistake.

Rocky Creek Road was, for some people, a dead-end place to live. Not so for Craig and Jennifer. Neighbors lined the road at five-acre intervals, some hidden by tall timber, others open to the sun and covered in lush green lawns. Horses, a few goats and chickens, and even geese could be found at the edge of the road. At night, the symphony from crickets and frogs lulled them to sleep through the open window.

It was a paradise fast disappearing, and he and Jennifer had been fortunate to buy it years back when the prices were low and no one was in a hurry to live in the area.

Grabbing the mail from the mailbox at the end of the driveway, Craig pushed the garage opener and drove the car towards the low rancher and parked inside the garage. As the garage door lowered, he realized that he had again expected to see Jennifer's dark green Grand Cherokee parked on her side of the garage. His spirits dropping, Craig entered the house.

The rancher had a full basement with level entry from a sloping backyard that ended at a stream. A couple of trees allowed for shade at the front and back of the house.

Jennifer had done a great job of decorating the house in soft grays and greens, leaving his den and the downstairs game room for him to do. Her photographs were all around the house. She was a good photographer and her work was often displayed throughout art houses. It all made him feel even more dejected.

Opening the back door, Craig was about to whistle when two large paws planted against his chest threw him back. "Rusty, old boy," Craig laughed. The Irish setter followed him into the kitchen and after taking off his suit jacket, he gave the dog some affection and fed him.

Craig made a Caesar, the clam juice saturated with vodka, lime, hot sauce, and Worcester, and sat down in a foul mood in front of the T.V. and the local news. It made him feel even worse and after flicking through the channels, he made himself another drink.

The phone jolted him from sleep and the cramped position he had fallen into while watching television. Looking at his watch he saw that it was eight-twenty. Craig tried to get up but his left leg had fallen asleep and, swearing, he hopped to the phone thinking it might be Jennifer.

"Hello."

"Craig, it's Hugh Wong. You had better get down to headquarters."

Rubbing the circulation back into his thigh, Craig stood up straight and stared at the wall as he answered. "What the hell for? Jesus, I'm beat."

"Look, I'm trying to do you a favor. There's a complaint against you and I'm trying to nip it in the bud and handle it informally before it gets out of hand."

"What kind of complaint? Who by?" Craig wanted to know.

Wong, who spoke with no accent, continued. "You know a guy by the name of Kaufmann?"

"That asshole! What about him?"

"He's filed a complaint against you, Craig. In fact it's going to be tough to try and handle at the local level."

"Look, don't bullshit me, Hugh. Who's handling the complaint?" Craig was beginning to get angry because he knew Wong had a way of skirting around the issues.

Wong coughed, "Well, you know I'm supposed to handle all complaints initially, and that's what I'm doing. But this came straight from Shepherd."

"What the hell is Shepherd involved in this for? What's going on?"

"Look," Wong continued, "Don't give me a hard time. Just come in and let's see if we can get this ironed out."

"Hugh, you still haven't told me what the complaint is about. What is it that I am supposed to have done?"

"He says you assaulted him, Craig."

Craig wasn't worried about that type of complaint. Pushing the shit-rat away from his car was no big deal.

"In fact," Wong said in Craig's ear, "He says he has witnesses. Man, I don't know what happened out there, Craig, but he's got a black eye, a broken nose, and his left arm is busted."

Craig was flabbergasted, laughing involuntarily, then-- "You've got to be kidding!"

"No, Craig, I'm not kidding. Shepherd is probably preparing a case against you to send to the prosecutor right now, with criminal charges."

Looking down at the carpet, Craig let out a sigh and said into the phone, "Okay. Thanks, Hugh. I'll be in as soon as possible."

Stripping the clothes off of his six-foot-two-inch frame, he looked in the mirror before getting into the shower. He was shocked to see that he looked as old as he felt.

The dashboard clock said 10:34 when he cut the motor to the Mustang in the lot of the police station. Several men stopped him as he entered the building, each one with something to say. As the door closed, he heard: "Hey Craig, don't take any crap."

Craig never ceased to marvel at how fast news traveled on the vine, especially when it was confidential or involved another police member.

Getting off at the Detective level, Craig looked around the room. Walt Telford was at his desk. "How's it going, Walt?"

"Oh, hi, Craig. Not bad, except Shepherds been in and out of here half a dozen times. He is just simply glowing, and when he's glowing that means somebody is in deeeep shit."

"Yeah, and that somebody is me."

"Yeah, I heard. Kaufmann's a junkie; he can't even remember his name half the time, never mind anything else. Don't sweat it."

Pulling out a chair and looking over at Walt, Craig answered. "Normally I wouldn't. What's come down the line?"

"Just the usual. You had a run-in with Kaufmann; he says you beat the snot out of him, and he made a complaint."

"How did Shepherd get involved so fast at this time of night?"

Walt looked up and smiled. "Well, you know how it is around here-- when things look too hot to handle and you don't want to be caught sideways, get rid of it."

"Who took the complaint?"

"As far as I know, the Watch Commander. He then phoned Wong because of the seriousness of the assault, and then Wong hightailed it down here. You know of course that with something like this the Chief will even know by now, never mind Shepherd."

"Yeah, I know, but something isn't right here," Craig said, thinking out loud. "Besides, I didn't do it."

Walt got up and pointed to the hallway, "Tell that to Wong. Here he comes."

Wong came bustling in, motioning for Craig to follow him to his office. Once inside, Wong turned to Craig and smiled. "Glad you got here so fast, Craig. Have a seat."

Craig sat down and waited for Hugh Wong to say something. When Wong seemed reluctant, Craig spoke up. "Spit it out, Hugh. What's going on?"

"I did what I could, Craig, but Shepherd got to the Chief and the Chief has ordered you suspended for 30 days. Effective immediately."

"What the hell is going on, Hugh," Craig said quietly, as he felt himself losing control of the situation.

"I've already told you, you've had a complaint of assault causing bodily harm made against you. You could be arrested and that's what Shepherd was pushing for. He wants you locked up right now, but fortunately the Chief said no. I'm sorry, Craig, this is one bummer. I'll need your sidearm, badge, and a list of any files you're working on."

"I can't believe how this system works," Craig fumed. "Any other citizen at least gets to be asked what the hell happened before he's charged. Not us," Craig said, getting up. "What a crock!"

Craig put his badge and police I.D. onto Wong's desk, along with his open 40 cal. Beretta with the clip removed. "I'll have the files on your desk in a few minutes. You can report to Shepherd that I'm out of his hair for 30 days."

"Come on, Craig," Wong said in an exasperated tone. "This isn't my doing. If it were up to Shepherd, you'd be in a cell by now. Just get out of here until someone contacts you. Get yourself some legal advice or something."

Craig left the office and went to his desk and filing cabinet to retrieve his latest files for Wong. He picked the pile up off of his desk when Tom walked in.

"Jeez, what the hell's going on, Craig? I heard and hurried right down."

Craig moved toward the elevator pulling Tom along with him. "Not here, Thomas. You wanted to take me for supper, well now's your chance. I'm starving."

"Good! First thing intelligent you've said all day. I already ate, but I can eat Chinese."

Craig smiled, turning towards Gifford as they walked towards the elevator. "Good, I need somebody to cheer me up. I'll meet you at Chung Ling's. I've got to drop these files off."

Craig put the files on Wong's desk just as Wong entered his office. "Craig, Shepherd wants to see you upstairs."

Craig was surprised. Officers usually distanced themselves from proceedings until they were over with. "What's he want?"

"How the hell should I know? I'm just a bloody messenger boy around here! It's up to you; don't go if you don't want to. Just so you've been told."

Curious, Craig knew he couldn't walk out. He had to try to learn what Shepherd was up to. He started for the elevator.

"Well? Are you going up or not?" Wong asked.

"Yeah, I'm going up. I wouldn't miss this for the world."

Stepping out into the executive wing, Craig walked passed several artificial trees and plants and walked up to the secretary behind the desk.

She smiled and said, "Hi, Craig."

"I'm here to see God. He's expecting me, I think."

Covering her laugh between closed hands, she nodded. "You might say that, but tread lightly, Craig."

"Working a little overtime, Lillian?"

"Yes, and all because of you, gorgeous."

Craig opened the door and walked in. Shepherd was sitting in a high-backed chair with the back to the door. He was on the telephone and looking out over the city as Craig approached the large walnut desk.

He stood there, a little desk lamp the only illumination in the darkened office, and waited for Shepherd to turn around. When he didn't, Craig let out a small cough, watching with some satisfaction as Shepherd sat quickly upright and spun around.

"I'll call you back," he said, hanging up the phone.

Shepherd looked up at Craig, his eyes boring into Craig's, daring him to be the first to break contact in some childish little game.

Craig smiled and said, "What, not even going to offer me a chair?"

"You won't be here long enough to need a chair, Fletcher. In fact if I have my way, you'll never sit in any chair in this building again. You're a disgrace to the uniform. A...."

"What is it you wanted to see me about?"

18

"I want to make sure you fully understand that you are suspended and that you are not to enter this building under any circumstances. Is that clear?"

"I think you just wanted me up here as an ego builder," Craig smiled. "To give yourself some satisfaction to tuck yourself into bed with."

"You remember who you're talking to, Fletcher." Shepherd stood up slowly, took a deep breath, and leaned on his desk with two closed fists. When he spoke, he spoke in a low menacing tone. "A long time ago you made a choice. You made a wrong choice and fucked me around. You fucked some very important people around and embarrassed this city..."

"No, I arrested and charged a punk *pretending* to be an upstanding citizen," Craig said, just as softly.

"Well now you're the one who's going to be fucked, Fletcher," Shepherd continued as if Craig hadn't said anything. "When I'm through with you, you can kiss your job, your pension, your whole fucking career goodbye."

Feeling his dislike overwhelm him, Craig leaned across the desk towards Shepherd. "You're worse than any of them out on the street, Shepherd. At least they're out in the open as to what they are doing. You manipulate, and slip and slide around people like some snake. What you need to do is step outside like a man. Just to clear the air, you know?"

"You'll have no future, no references, nothing," Shepherd continued in heat.

Craig turned around and walked to the door, deciding to leave before he did anything that would make things worse. He slammed the door and waved to Lillian as he passed.

As he pushed the elevator button, he heard Lillian say, "Don't let him get to you. I'm here day after day, you were only in there for a few minutes."

Craig thanked her with a smile and a wink. The elevator door closed, and he was able to hear his heart thumping loud and fast in his ears; his anger was sitting there with no where to go. He knew he really needed a drink and a chance to wind down.

As he stepped into the warm night air, multiple flashes of light and a single strong strobe destroyed his vision.

"Detective Fletcher? I'm Carrie Carpenter from Mobile City News," she blurted, thrusting a microphone at Craig.

"Hold it!" Craig interrupted. "Turn those cameras off and tell me what this is all about."

Carpenter looked at Craig, and then turned to her cameraman. "Okay, Chuck, shut it down for a minute."

Craig looked around and saw two camera crews, several reporters from the local papers, and one radio hound who covered the police beat.

One camera was still running, but it was pointed at a woman commentator whom he recognized as Georgina Farnsworth. "*A real bitch,*" Craig thought, "*and not to be trusted.*"

Carpenter began. "We received a tip that you were involved in a complaint of assault on a young man. I'd like your side of it."

Craig laughed. "Carrie, I don't make a habit of airing my side of it, as you put it, to people in T.V. land. I know you're going to run something anyway, so I'll give you a brief statement only."

Carpenter turned and signaled. The lights came back on, framing Craig against the backdrop of the police building. "Detective Fletcher, is it true that you are being investigated for aggravated assault on a young man earlier this evening?"

"I'll give you a brief statement and that's all," Craig replied, looking directly at the camera. "I have just heard about this myself and I'm really in no position to talk to anyone about it."

"Have you been arrested, Detective Fletcher?"

Craig turned to see that the Farnsworth woman had directed the question to him. Her camera was also focused directly onto his face.

"No, I have not been arrested."

"But you have been suspended, isn't that correct?"

Holding back any sign of surprise, Craig nodded in the affirmative. "That's normal departmental procedure, you know that. Your sources are faster than mine since I only learned of this five minutes ago."

"My sources indicate that the young man involved in this assault received crushing injuries to his face and body, and..."

"Like I said, your sources are faster than mine. I'm not prepared to discuss this complaint in public. It will be handled through the regular channels. As *you* would know Miss Farnsworth, most of these complaints are blown way out of proportion. Thank you for your interest."

Craig turned and walked away, the glare of the lights following him to his car, and continuing until he pulled out of the lot. "*I handled that badly,*" he thought, pulling into the evening traffic. "*They'll slice me up on that one.*"

● ● ●

Chinatown was surprisingly busy. Couples were out strolling the sidewalks in the late evening air looking at all the weird and different Chinese delicacies hanging in the windows. The traffic, although light, was in no hurry, and it gave Craig a chance to cool down inside.

The air was starting to cool slightly with a breeze coming in off of the ocean, when Craig squeezed the car between a telephone pole and an old truck in the alley at the rear of the restaurant. The smell of food hit him like a punch in the stomach. Walking through the busy kitchen, Craig waved to the cooks and pushed his way through the curtain that hung limply between the kitchen and restaurant.

Looking around, he saw that the few customers who were finishing up were being attended to by Ling's granddaughter, who was smiling and laughing with each table of customers she visited. It wasn't a big place, and if you really looked it was a bit on the ratty side. But the food, that's what kept everyone lined up at the doors.

Tom and Chung Ling were sitting in the corner and Craig made his way to the usual booth close to the cash register. Craig had been coming and sitting in this booth for years, with old Ling always jumping in and out of the booth in a flash to look after his customers. "Hey you two, leave any food for me?"

Ling had a big smile on his face. "Ah, so you finally decided to come and see me. It has been almost a month now."

"And I've missed you, you ding-a-ling."

Tom and Ling laughed, Ling coming back with, "You watch your manners, and have some respect for your elders. I am much wiser and smarter than you, and have much to teach you still."

"Mr. Ling, I will never stop learning from you."

"Ah, finally you are learning to be humble," Ling said with a twinkle in his eye. "And also full of bullshit."

Ling was about five-foot-five. Approximately seventy years old, he was very slim and wore his glasses mostly on the end of his nose. He spoke English with hardly a trace of an accent, but liked to play the ancient Chinese philosopher or the Hollywood version of a kung-fu priest.

"I'll go and get Craig his drink," Ling said, bouncing up with the agility of a younger man.

As Ling walked away, Tom asked, "Well, are you going to keep me in the dark? What happened with Shepherd?"

"How the hell do you know I was in with Shepherd?"

"Very simple, and it's very modern. It's called the telephone. I phoned to see what was taking you so damn long. Wong told me."

Craig's white rum and Seven-Up was placed in front of him by Sue Ling. Looking up at her, he couldn't believe how beautiful she was. Her eighteen-year-old eyes sparkled with love of life.

"How do you stay so beautiful, Sue?"

Laughing, she bent over and kissed his forehead. "Every woman is beautiful to you, Uncle Craig."

"Yes, but you are exceptionally beautiful, and you are," Craig tasted his drink, "very talented as well."

Sue shook her head. "You're impossible, but I love you anyway."

When she had left, Tom continued. "So what happened up there? Did you lose your cool?"

Craig took a long swallow of his drink, feeling the liquor hit his empty stomach. "Not really. Just told him the truth. Told him he should be a man and step outside so I could kick the shit out of him."

"Oh wonderful, just wonderful!" Tom said smashing his hand against his own forehead. "You shouldn't have gone in there by yourself! You know the rules on C.Y.A. for Christ sake."

"This isn't a matter of covering your ass, Tom. I'd need a garbage can lid. I already know what he's up to, I just have to find a way to expose him."

Chung Ling came out of the kitchen with plates of steaming hot food and started to place them on the table. "We are all going to sit down like old times. It has been a long time and this is my treat."

Both Craig and Tom started to argue with Chung Ling, refusing to let him pay for the meal, but they were out shouted.

"It seems to me," Ling said, sitting down, "I remember you two coming in here not too long ago and grabbing me and taking me to a hockey game, and for supper at that fancy place." Chung Ling paused and looked from one man to the other. "Mrs. Ling would like this, it is like old times almost. I miss her so."

Craig placed a hand on Ling's shoulder and squeezed. "Yes, old friend, I miss her too."

"Let's eat." Tom said.

They all dug in, with nobody saying anything for a few moments as the aroma and spices assaulted them. Tom finally broke the silence with, "You're lucky, Chung Ling. All this good food everyday and all the cheap labor the grandkids provide."

Ling almost choked on a piece of shrimp. "Cheap? Cheap? They are robbing me blind! Grandpa I need this, grandpa I need that; smiling all the time. They are so beautiful they hurt my eyes. I tell you I barely make ends meet."

Craig listened to the banter between his two friends, feeling guilty that Jennifer wasn't sitting beside him and enjoying the evening.

"How is Jennifer?" Ling asked.

"What the hell, are you some kind of psychic? I was just thinking of her."

Ling laughed, "I know. Ancient Chinese saying-- it is written all over your face."

"Written it may be," Craig said pushing his plate away and looking at his watch, "but I have to get home. It's late." Craig got up, put on his leather jacket, and grabbed his cellular. He dropped twenty dollars onto the table. Tom saw it and did the same.

"What's the money for?" Ling questioned.

"For, Sue; she did a great job."

"Forty dollars? *I* did all the work! What are you trying to do?"

"Get her out of this place and into a rich neighborhood," Craig said, wrapping his arm around Ling's head. "You take care of yourself. I'll see you soon."

Outside in the night air as Craig and Tom said goodnight, Tom promised to phone Craig from work with any information that came his way.

Rusty was barking when Craig walked into the house, so he let him in for company. Checking the answering machine he was surprised to hear Lorraine's voice.

"Hi Daddy, it's just me. Mom told me you called. We were at a movie. I wished you had called again. Dad, ...can we *do* something soon? We could go to Stanley Park or the Science Center or something. Call me, Daddy, and let me know. I love you." Click.

Craig laid his head back onto the pillow, thinking that he was losing it all. Maybe Shepherd is right; maybe I am going to end up with nothing.

···CHAPTER TWO

Jesse Harris moved his six-foot-five scarecrow frame slightly out from under the covers, putting off that inevitable time when his feet would have to hit the floor.

Opening one eye, he looked at the clock, hating it. Somehow he just couldn't see going to the lab this Friday morning and was very much tempted to phone in sick.

Sighing, with a huge effort he jumped from the bed and ran for the ensuite. Turning on the shower to fully hot, he got out his shaving gear and started to shave, only shutting the shower off when the mirror started to mist over. The air in the room was hot and moist.

Slamming a cupboard door closed, he knew he could make all the noise he wanted this morning because Bev hadn't stayed the night. Finished shaving, Jesse plunged under the hot water, his thoughts still dwelling on Bev Carlson. *"Why doesn't she just move in with me here in North Bend?"* he thought. *"We get along well, and I* know *she wants to,"* Jesse convinced himself. He also knew she was waiting for the magic question that he was having trouble with. Women!

Walking downstairs, Jesse grabbed his newspaper off of the front step as he headed for the car. The air was crisp and clean, with the sun warming up the ground and causing small patches of steam to rise and disappear almost immediately.

Wiping the condensation off of the driver's mirror he backed the new Lincoln Towncar out of the driveway and drove through the quiet streets of North Bend. Connecting to I-90, he drove west to his turnoff, then towards Maple Valley, southeast of Seattle.

Jesse slowed at the gate, flashed his I.D. to the guard, and a few moments later eased the big car into his parking slot. He smiled at his good fortune for the thousandth time, at not having to worry about meters or daily parking bills. He had been parking in the same spot for nine years.

Jesse looked at the building as he approached; it still looked the same as the day he had arrived. It was a one-story building with rough concrete blocks painted dark gray, the windows providing a sparkling mirrored contrast. Low maintenance shrubs and trees had grown over the years to provide a pleasing setting. There was no identification on the building itself, but a low sign on the grass in front of a large maple tree proudly and tastefully stated '*Inter-America*' in highly polished foot-high brass letters.

Jesse made his way up the sunlit walk at the side of the building, the trees overhead filled with the chirps and warbles of birds, and pushed his card into the slot in the door. He was rewarded with the usual buzz and pulled the door open.

The card only allowed him into a small cubicle. The white wall facing the doorway had a wall mounted sign that ordered one and all: 'ABSOLUTELY NO SMOKING.'

There was a small trash can, and another sign on a reinforced door stating: *Display Your I.D. On Outer Garments At All Times*, and an encoder mounted flush in the wall.

Jesse stepped up, placed his right hand flat onto a pulsing green piece of glass, waited until the light stopped, then, following instructions on a screen, looked directly into a small mirror as his eyes were scanned. He was rewarded with a, 'Proceed' on the screen. The door clicked open and a small camera swivel slightly from the upper corner of the cubicle.

Five visible cameras recorded all movement as Jesse moved forward, but human eyes kept watch from behind the mirror at the end of the hallway.

Jesse entered room 87, his own domain, and closed the door. Throwing his paper onto the counter, he looked around at the various shelves of manuals, the computers, the test tubes, and several expensive microscopes. An inner courtyard allowed natural light without having to worry about privacy. It was a very efficient lab.

Jesse made a fresh pot of coffee, and while it was brewing he turned on the terminals and hit the main lights.

Walking over to the floor safe mounted in a concrete block in the corner of the lab, Jesse spun the combination until he heard the thunk, and opened the lid upwards and to the side. He was reaching in to get the days codes, when he noticed a small canister lying on its side. Looking closer, he counted three canisters; he was sure there had been four.

He was always the last one to close the safe. Picking it up, Jesse looked at the container and felt troubled for more than the first time. Little things had been happening over a period of time to disturb him, things he couldn't explain.

Placing the canister back into the safe, Jesse tossed the codebook onto the counter and picked up the daily log. The entry under inventory control read 'three cans.' Looking closer, he thought he could detect the outlines of a correction, but it was hard to tell. Troubled, he walked over to his locker to get his white lab smock while deep in thought.

Putting on the garment, he was about to turn away when he noticed an envelope sticking out of the pocket of Hank Corey's rain coat that he had left hanging on the open door of his own locker. Seeing what looked like part of a newspaper clipping jutting out, Jesse took a closer look. Pulling out the envelope, he saw a hand-written message in pencil on the outside.

I was told to pass this on to you, so you would know how
vital your contribution has been. Shred as usual!

Curious, Jesse pulled one of the news clippings from the envelope. As he started to read, the hair at the back of his neck started to raise, a feeling of dread engulfing him. He wasn't even sure why he was full of apprehension, but he could feel his skin tighten and a knot gathered in his stomach as the adrenaline start to flow.

Jesse carried the envelope quickly into his own office, the coffee forgotten. He found himself leaning over the article and trying to fathom what it was he was actually looking at.

PHILADELPHIA

A bizarre armed robbery trial took place in this city today, one that at least made this reporter sit up and take notice. The State of Pennsylvania was treated to a rare case of honesty in the case of one Barney Hilton.

Charged in the May robbery of a local convenience store, Hilton has maintained his innocence since his arrest. Today, however, under direct questioning from his lawyer, and while giving evidence, he not only admitted to the offense but also named an accomplice who no one even knew about.

His lawyer, appearing dumbfounded, tried to save the day by continuing to question Hilton, asking if it was true that he was held in custody for a long period of time without access to legal counsel. Hilton's answer made even the Judge sit up straight. 'I was treated good, better 'n usual in fact. I was offered th' phone as soon as I stepped in the door. That's when I phoned you.'

A check of Hilton's background shows that he is a person with a long history of arrests, coupled with a strong hate for the police and authority.

Against the objections of his lawyer, Hilton pleaded guilty to his third major conviction.

Postponing sentencing until next week, Judge Morgan commented, 'I never thought I would see the day-- somebody actually telling the truth.'

Jesse felt his heart begin to pound as a fresh surge of adrenalin shot into his system, as he thought about what he was reading. *"No, that's not true; it's what I think I'm reading!"* Jesse thought. *"I'm being paranoid!"*

With slightly unsteady hands, Jesse turned and sorted the clippings he had taken from the envelope. His eyes were riveted on one in particular as he leaned over his desk.

HOUSTON, TX
POLICE MAKE HUGE DRUG BUST

Police swooped down on a huge drug operation Monday and arrested six people. Although pleased with the operation, a police spokesman has revealed that police were baffled because of the source of their information.

Apparently one of the arrested males had been charged on a non-related matter earlier on, and suddenly provided police with details of the drug operation. As a police officer at the scene stated, 'It was really bizarre! The guy told us everything we asked him.' The unidentified male is under police protection prior to...

Jesse quickly looked at the other clipping, dropping a few into his lap, then onto the floor in his rush. "Christ!" he said aloud to himself.

Jesse remembered being fascinated by the story. He remembered the story and the headlines because it dominated the news for days. He also remembered that there were a lot of questions as to how officials were able to gather so much information, and how they would not divulge any sources or methods. The case was still before the courts.

NEW YORK CITY
17 ARRESTED IN DETROIT UNDERWORLD BLITZ

I.R.S. AND F.B.I. Agents swooped into the West Palm Beach home of suspected Detroit Cosa Nostra boss Jim Wesley Tiosco, 66, and arrested him and four of his captains.

Indictments ranging from extortion, racketeering, illegal gaming, counterfeiting, and robbery with violence were but a few named in the federal sweep.

At press time, federal agents were reported to be making major strikes in Boston, New Orleans, Chicago, Philadelphia, Cleveland, Newark, and New York.

Officials have indicated that organized crime has been severely wounded, with the whole of the Mafia hierarchy suffering a fatal blow. The 17 Detroit indictments included the capture of 'capos' Angelo Antinelli, 74, Tony Civadano, 70, and Anthony Boruzzi, 62, who are supposedly linked to Middle East connections, and a counterfeit cartel involving a so-called "super note."

Some believe that the counterfeit 100-dollar "super note" denomination may have caused an estimated 260 million dollar loss to American business.

Defense lawyers for Jim Wesley Tiosco were screaming foul as their client was led away, demanding access to all government evidence and sources. I.R.S. and F.B.I. federal agents, however, are not divulging their sources or informants.

There is some speculation that the evidence gathered would have taken more than a year to put together, but a high inside source has indicated that this was not the case. With the evidence

29

so explicit, somebody will be asking who is working on the inside of the Tiosco family.

Jesse walked quickly to the other room and poured a coffee, taking a sip as he walked back. A clipping caught his eye as it lay against the desk leg where it had fluttered to the floor.

BALTIMORE, MARYLAND
U.S. SENATOR SHOCKS CONVENTION
U.S. Senator Lawrence Green shocked a large convention crowd today when he admitted to receiving kickbacks from a large federally funded highway projects within the State.

Green, who was fielding a few questions prior to leaving the convention floor, was asked a simple question as to when contracts would be awarded, and he stunned everyone present, stating-- "It's already taken care of. The contracts have been awarded."

Pandemonium erupted, with a reporter asking Green who had received the contract, and why so suddenly. Senator Green apparently answered, "It's not sudden, the contract has been known from the start."

Green was whisked from the convention center, seemingly unperturbed by what he had said. Political ramifications will be horrendous and the President has ordered the F.B.I. to intervene.

Why Senator Green would make statements that could certainly ruin his caree, is beyond everyone in the media as well as his own political party.

Jesse picked up another, although he knew he was really just trying to convince himself that he was not dealing with a massive security leak from his lab. Looking at his watch, Jesse read the clipping.

LAS VEGAS, NV
Federal agents from the Drug Enforcement Agency seized a reported 2 million dollars in cold cash from a private hanger last night.

Although investigators are not disclosing why they seized the money, it has been learned that there may be a connection to a male by the name of Eddie Arrichi, who had been detained in custody.

Speculation has it that the money was destined for brokerage houses, where large purchases in securities were to take place. Sold at a later date, the clean money could not be traced.

Why the suspect divulged the whereabouts of the money is a mystery. Arrichi has since been released from custody. He has not been seen since.

The last article did not look like too much on the surface, and the fact of the matter was that if he were to show any of articles to anyone, none of them would seem that important. If you were just reading the paper you would just pass them off as another nutty day in the land of weirdoes.

They did, however, explain the little things that had been happening over the past months. Containers found in different locations, small discrepancies on written notes and samples, and of course the time that Hank Corey reported that a whole sample had apparently spilled. If he was reading what he thought he was reading in the papers, then samples had to have left the lab- - but who had taken them? And why?

Dumping the clippings back into the desk, Jesse's mind was racing. He had to find out what was going on to put his mind at ease. Looking at his watch, he saw that his assistant, Hank Corey, was due in at any minute.

If, and he had to think seriously about this, IF there was a leak, and IF some of the actual samples had left the lab, only one person could be responsible.

Walking over to the computer, Jesse sat down and punched in the elaborate security code, finally emerging into his working file.

'*PRECISE'.* The name popped up like never before. Funny how a little slant of awareness made you look at things differently.

Looking again, Jesse began to go through the whole file. He was looking for any sign of tampering, any little thing that would indicate that the inventory didn't balance with the actual samples on hand. After half an hour he hadn't found anything out of the ordinary.

"Morning, Jess. Boy am I bagged. Sorry I'm late. I got in late last night."

Jesse turned as Hank Corey threw his jacket onto a hook, and nodded in his direction.

"Coffee on?"

"Yeah, Hank, coffee's on. Help yourself."

Looking at Corey, Jesse tried to see him in a different light, but there really wasn't anything different about him. He was about five-foot-nine, combed his brown hair straight back, most of the time with his hands, had brown eyes, and was on the stout side. He also was pleasant most of the time and didn't bring his private life into the office. He had been with Jesse about thirty-six months.

Coming back with his coffee, Corey took a sip and said, "Jess, I'm going to run down to supplies for half an hour or so. We're low on inventory and I want to go over what we need. Okay?"

"By all means, go ahead," Jesse said as he exited from the 'PRECISE' file and headed for his desk.

As Hank Corey left the lab, Jesse began to read over the objectives set out for him by the Secretary of Defense. Working under contract for the Department of Defense was nothing unusual, because without the big bucks coming in from the government, Jesse knew that a lot of research would either stop, or slowly become an up-hill battle.

Picking up the original directive, it took him back to the time when he first got interested in the project.

> OBJECTIVE: *Research, and develop a psychoactive drug to assist the medical profession in narcoanalysis of psychiatric disorders. To provide a method by which the medical profession can induce patients to freely unload the subconscious troubled mind with passive receptiveness. To provide a vehicle upon which the exact truth of a distressed patient can be revealed, due to Post Traumatic Stress Disorder or P.T.S.D.*

Jesse had accomplished that. Nonstop research, long hours, and funds that flowed like water out of a tap had provided Jesse with very rewarding results.

The end result was a drug, code name: 'PRECISE'. So named by Jesse because it would compel a person to tell the precise truth in any circumstances in which the person was asked a question by his or her physician. Thus, a person is able to deal with the problems facing them because the truth, or root of the problem, is found sooner.

Besides saving millions of dollars in fees, Jesse felt that it would ease a lot of suffering. One of the reasons Jesse was gung-ho on the 'PRECISE' project was the fact that there were so many service vets who needed to unload after serving time in a theater of war.

The big boys in the Pentagon were always after assurances that 'PRECISE' was on time and was going to work-- and how does it work anyhow? So far he had managed to keep them all at a distance, telling them they could have regular bureaucratic reports, or have results. He didn't have time for both.

The simple explanation was that the brain contains a Reticular Formation Network and a Reticular Activating System. This keeps the human body awake and alert, receiving one hundred million messages per second with only a few hundred actually being received. Ten billion nerve cells send and receive messages at the incredible rate of fifteen to thirty feet per second.

'PRECISE' controlled the electro-chemical transmissions in the brain neurons, assuring a safe over stimulated activity in the neuro transmitters. Jesse had discovered just the right combination of proteins to manipulate the synapse, or network, between brain cells.

'PRECISE' had been developed to zero in on the electro-chemical transmissions, to stimulate, change, and disrupt proteins and a molecule called AMP, so that memory traces were released. Verbal and sensory information was manipulated and the person entered into a persuasive state. Not easily accomplished, Jesse thought, but memory was a biological process and gave up memory traces easier than he, or any of his peers, thought possible.

'PRECISE' allowed physical relaxation with mental concentration. A state of deep, though wakeful, relaxation occurred, with no short-term memory of having taken the drug or what was said during that period. A person was mentally and physically incapable of preventing what was in his mind from being released. Not only that, but a person did it in a normal manner and in a relaxed and frank way.

It worked! The trouble was it worked too well, and that was the stage Jesse was at now in his research. He had to know exactly why a subject couldn't remember telling the truth. So far he figured it had to do with the manipulation of proteins, and the fact that the mind couldn't gather information while it was being forced to expel it while under the influence of 'PRECISE'.

All research showed that motor functions, sensory capacities, intellectual abilities, and the ability to analyze, *appeared* to carry on as normal in all outward signs. In fact, all tests carried out showed that the test subjects appeared as normal as anyone else when they were being interviewed. They would even take commands and direction. The only difference was that they could not stop telling the precise truth.

Long and exhaustive follow-up studies showed that many of the volunteers had corrected their corroding rhythms, and were able to sleep and function in a much-improved state. The drug began to wear off within two to three hours, and traces lingered up to twenty-four hours. It was within this time frame that any patient would have to be safe-guarded against outside influences.

Jesse put down his notes and picked up a few newspaper clippings from the open drawer of his desk. He just *knew* something wasn't right! He also knew that if this was the case, then the Department of Defense wasn't interested in just medical applications.

There was only one way he was going to find out, and that was to confront Hank Corey. "If I do that though," Jesse whispered aloud without realizing it, "He'll just hightail it, or deny it if he is part of any conspiracy."

A very dim light suddenly exploded into an idea that he realized was there all along. He had the tools right at hand, with very little chance of being found out. 'PRECISE', once administered, wouldn't allow Hank Corey to remember if he had been questioned.

This was not only against all moral codes buried inside of Jesse, it was against the law. Having weighed the consequences of doing nothing-- he really didn't have any other choice. This was a very dangerous drug in the wrong hands. He needed to know!

Jesse got up from his chair, stiff with tension and anxiety and walked without conscious thought to the locked safe. He stood looking down at the tumblers, aware of the ever-present security camera. Bending his knees, he lowered himself slowly and began to spin the tumblers.

Reaching inside he pulled one very small aerosol can out of the safe. Straightening up, he looked at the small container and thought, not for the first time, that there were going to be a lot of surprised people in the medical field, as well as many researchers, when they found out how 'PRECISE' was administered and worked. It really was simple to administer.

An aerosol gas administered the drug in an extremely high concentrated form. There was no smell, and no visible sign of anything emerging from the can. Converted from liquid to gas, the drug emerged into the atmosphere in an invisible state.

A small dose inhaled into the lungs of a person was quickly absorbed into the bloodstream and thus to the brain. Jesse felt this was one of the best methods of administering a drug he had seen. It worked quickly! Plus, it was safe and effective.

"I'm back," Hank yelled across the room. "I'll put this stuff away, and finish up entering those results, huh?"

Jesse looked at Hank and nodded. "Sure, get started. I'll be with you in a moment."

Walking to the door, Jesse quietly locked it and turned on the security light. Outside in the hallway, a small yellow bulb flashed on and off above the door and a sign lit up displaying, 'NO ENTRY'. No one was allowed in, and all telephone calls were cut off.

Pulling the blind down on the window next to the door, Jesse walked to where Hank Corey was standing with his back to him. "Hank, I want to talk to you a moment. Come back to my office a moment will you?"

Hank put down the sheaf of papers he was holding and followed Jesse. "What's up?"

"Have a seat Hank," Jesse smiled, indicating his own leather chair. "I've a few things I'd like to discuss."

While Hank turned to lower himself into the deep chair, Jesse nonchalantly raised the aerosol can and shot a one second burst of 'PRECISE' in the direction of Hank's face, quickly crossing his arms and hiding the can in his left armpit.

Sitting back in the chair, Hank let out a sigh, then took a deep breath just as an envelope of what seemed like fresh air surrounded his head. He looked to see if there was a window open, then forgot about it as Jesse addressed him.

"How do you feel about our progress so far, Hank, are you happy about it?"

Hank put both feet out in front of him and crossed his ankles, then folded his hands across his stomach, and looked up at Jesse as he answered. "We've made great strides. It won't be long before we're through the testing stage and we can put it to use."

"You're right," Jesse answered, a frown on his face as he looked at the sweep hand on his watch. "I just want your input as to the speed in which we are proceeding."

"I'm happy. We are moving along with the testing phase just fine."

"All of the test results are already back, Hank. Don't you think the test phase is over?"

"No, there are still a few results to come in."

Jesse looked at his watch again. Something wasn't working properly. Maybe Hank *isn't* involved, he thought. Maybe I'm a paranoid, out to lunch, dumb shit.

"What do you see as the best use of 'PRECISE', Hank?" Jesse asked, trying desperately to think of questions to ask.

Hank looked at Jesse, a slight smile on his lips. He was very relaxed and confident as he answered. "Why the same as it always has been, for the Defense Department."

"You mean for medical use under a DOD contract, don't you, Hank?"

"I mean," Hank replied while looking directly into Jesse's eyes, "The Defense Department, the Justice Department, and any other department that the Pentagon wishes to give this drug to."

Jesse felt his pulse quickening. "You said there were still a few test results to come in yet?"

"It's almost done now. The tests are almost complete within the Justice Department and the courts. The Pentagon has requested more samples for their project..."

Jesse just stood there; dumbfounded. He didn't even know what to say for a moment. Here was Hank sitting there as calm as hell, telling him the things he had suspected, but he really didn't believe could be happening.

Jesse felt short of breath, but forced himself to calm down and concentrate on what Hank Corey was saying.

"... the C.I.A. involvement."

The C.I.A.!" Jesse sputtered. "What are *they* doing with 'PRECISE'?"

"They are running a short test on all of their own operatives. A security check."

"Whoa, go back. You said something about the Pentagon wanting *more* samples."

Looking at Jesse without the least bit of apprehension, Corey said, "More samples, yes. The Pentagon wants more samples. For their overseas project, I heard, but that could be miss-information."

"Christ!" Jesse exclaimed, wiping his sweating forehead. "Where did they get the samples?"

"From me. That's part of my job."

Jesse moved closer now, no longer afraid of what he would hear, but deathly afraid that he might miss hearing what was being said.

"How did you get the samples, Hank? I mean there are only so many, and none are missing."

36

"I was the one who directed that portion of the experiment. You told me to make sure of the exact measurement in each can. I just made more of the cans, and marked down what you were to receive. Some were recorded differently on the inventory logs. The rest were delivered to my coordinator and security advisor."

"Your... " Jesse exploded. "I'm *your* fucking boss!"

"You are in charge of the lab," Hank Corey said with the same calm look on his face, "and the research project. I take directions from you in regards to the development of 'PRECISE'. My boss is Major Strickler, when it comes to security and the distribution of 'PRECISE'."

"*I need a drink,*" Jesse thought. "Who is Major Stickeler?" Jesse asked with a forced calmness.

"Strickler," Corey corrected. "S-T-R-I-C-K-L-E-R. Major Nathan Strickler, Special Operations assigned to this project. In this case, Biochemical Research Advanced Testing, or BRAT. He is responsible for the security of 'PRECISE'."

Jesse went to a small corner fridge and took out a bottle of beer from the bottom rear shelf that had been there for ages. Alcohol was strictly prohibited in the building, but "*whoever called this piss - beer?*" he thought. Jesse took a large grateful swig and walked back to Corey. He looked at Corey for a good twenty seconds, trying to figure out what he still didn't know. Christ - everything! "Hank, who are you?"

"I am Henry Douglas Corey."

Remembering that he was dealing with exact truth here, Jesse rephrased the question. "If your boss is this Strickler, what company do you work for Hank? What is your function?"

Still looking as normal as ever, Hank Corey calmly continued in a steady low voice. "I work for the Pentagon. I am also attached to BRAT. I am a civilian with a very high security clearance, and have been seconded to this section. I have full knowledge of the use in which 'PRECISE' is going to be used, so that I can foresee any problems in the development. My function is also to assist you in any way that I can, then pass it on to my liaison-- Grant."

"Grant?" Jesse asked. "Who the hell is Grant? When did he enter the picture?"

"Captain Mark Grant. Special Forces attached to Major Strickler. I deal through him to Strickler. He is an asshole. He is a very dangerous asshole and I don't like him. I have to go to the bathroom."

Jesse ignored Hank's remark in order to think of what he should do. What *could* he do! They were going to take his project and turn it into a nightmare, with people running all over the place telling everybody else everybody else's secrets and everybody saying what was exactly on their minds. Enemies being made, careers ruined, marriages down the tubes-- a form a mind control!

Looking up, he was surprised to see Corey sitting calmly in the chair.

"What's the next step in Strickler's plan, Hank?"

"There may be a shut down of this lab within a month and everybody and everything moved to the east coast for production."

Feeling his world begin to tilt, Jesse asked, "What about me? Am I to go too? I know everything there is to know about 'PRECISE'."

"You are not required. Reproduction will be easy. You will be moved to a different location. You will apply your knowledge on patient experiments, to give you the impression that 'PRECISE' is being used in the medical field."

"And if I don't?" Jesse said in a tense voice. "If I complain to Washington?"

"Then you will be dead," Hank Corey said with a pleasant smile on his lips.

Jesse went pale, mostly from the very calm way in which it was uttered. "The whole world will know of 'PRECISE', Hank, especially if it's used for military purposes."

Corey did not respond to the statement.

"Did you hear me, Hank? Do you believe the whole world will learn of 'PRECISE?' "

"Yes, but not for a long time. There is no memory of being drugged."

"Where will you go, Hank?"

"I am supposed to go to oversee the proper application of the drug. Then-- I have no knowledge."

"Aren't you afraid? I mean aren't you afraid of what they'll use 'PRECISE' for? Think about it, Hank!"

"I have been assured that this is like any other weapon developed for the defense of the country. I'm not afraid. I am pleased about it's development."

Jesse looked at his watch. He had to make a decision. He had to act! But do what? If he did nothing he wouldn't be able to live with himself. Every single person in the country, as well as every other country on earth, would be at the mercy of a few select people in the U.S. Government. It could mean total control!

Jesse came to a decision. "Hank, I want you to sit there and go over all the things in your mind that you have done without my knowledge. Okay?"

Corey nodded. "All right."

Jesse moved rapidly to the other end of the lab. Looking down as he went, he realized he still held the aerosol can in his hand. "*The samples,*" he thought, and headed for the safe.

Taking his white lab coat off he quickly bent to the safe and lifted out the other aerosol cans, and three small vials of liquid. Next came the computer disks with all the compressed data.

The three vials went into a small transit container, cushioned on all sides by foam. He then removed some Velcro fasteners that he used to secure some instruments, and wrapped the three cans together. The cans were only two and a half inches high, and an inch and a half in diameter. Placing his briefcase onto the counter next to the disks and samples, he headed to the computer terminal.

His hands were shaking as he looked down at the keyboard. A small drop of sweat ran down his forehead into his eyebrow, and then skidded sideways down his nose. He never noticed; his breathing was becoming shallow as he realized what he was actually going to attempt.

Quickly gaining access, the program he wanted came onto the screen. It contained the formula and mathematical equations for 'PRECISE'.

Jesse highlighted the whole file and hit delete.

"*WARNING!!*"

PROPERTY OF THE UNITED STATES GOVERNMENT!!"

"*ACCESS... UNAUTHORIZED... SUBMIT ACCESS CODE.*"

"*Damn, damn, damn,*" Jesse screamed in his head. He had never, ever, attempted to delete any large portion of the file before, and now he wasn't even sure how many, if any security terminals had just lit up, or if he had set any alarms off.

Typing in the word 'PRECISE', nothing happened. The computer seemed to ignore it. Moving the cursor to the next position he typed in his personal code - "*PROBITY*".

Not even knowing why he was given that particular handle, he nonetheless had accepted it and had got on with his job. Jesse glanced at the screen and felt a chill.

"UNAUTHORIZED CODE"

"Mommy, mommy, mommy," Jesse whispered aloud. "Get me out of this shit." The computer came alive again,

"ACCESS NEW CODE."

"New code? What new code?" Jesse asked himself. "The damn codes are... oh yeah."

Rummaging through the drawer, he couldn't find what he was looking for. He then ran to the safe, then to the counter where he had thrown the small blue handbook that had DEPARTMENT OF DEFENSE typed across the front. Inside the cover on the first page, the warning was large: TOP SECRET. DO NOT OPEN BEYOND THIS PAGE UNLESS... .

Jesse opened the book to the page he wanted - DELETING DATA - and ran his finger down a list of codes for his terminal for this particular day of the month. He swore. He couldn't find any. He had to get back to the terminal within two minutes or it would lock itself out.

Checking the next page he found it, "There!" he said aloud, and ran back to the terminal and typed in "*Integrity.*"

Suddenly the computer allowed him in. Slowly, Jesse again reached forward and highlighted the whole 'PRECISE' file.

Pushing DELETE ALL, he was immediately rewarded with:

"ARE YOU SURE YOU WANT TO DELETE?"

Jesse typed in "Yes" and the screen produced a horizontal bar. It took a full minute for the bar to work its way across to completion. Then, it was gone. Every single thing was gone. Oh sure, it was still on some mainframe somewhere, but it was deeply hidden and compressed under numerous safeguards. This would slow them down.

Sitting back, Jesse pondered what he had done, knowing there was still time to put it back. He shut the computer off and hurried back to Hank Corey.

"Have you thought about what I said, Hank?" Jesse croaked in a restrictive voice. A voice of pent up fear.

"Yes, I have. Strickler and Grant work out of Ft. Lewis on a temporary basis. They have access to anything they want. If they need to they can override any local authority, civilian or military. They have authority from a very high command."

"Who is that person in high command?"

Hank looked at Jesse and said, "I don't know."

Looking around the lab for the last time, Jesse grabbed a few items and turned to Corey. "I want you to stay here for the rest of the day. You are to then lock up and go home."

"Yes, sir."

Jesse didn't know if giving Hank instructions would work, but he moved quickly towards the door, stopping to pick up the disks and samples. He placed them all into his briefcase then rushed to the door and raised the blind, and turned off the yellow light, which re-engaged the phones and turned off the No Entry sign. Jesse took one last look at Hank Corey. He was still sitting in the chair.

Walking down the corridor was far different from his morning walk in. He was sure everyone must know what he had done. It had to be obvious what was in the briefcase.

A hand grabbed Jesse's elbow. "Jess."

Jesse's stomach rebelled as a shot of fear surrounded his chest. Turning, he saw a man he recognized from the front office.

"You owe me five bucks for that pool you entered. The games tomorrow." Jesse had a hard time talking normally. "Oh! Sure, sure thing. I'll get it to you after lunch. I'm in a bit of a rush right now."

"Don't forget man. No payee, no getum."

Jesse hurried to the door, so relieved he felt sick. It was raining so hard drops were bouncing six inches back into the air. Activating the remote keyless entry helped, but Jesse was still soaking wet when he sat behind the wheel.

It felt warm and comfortable, like a cocoon. Starting the wipers, he watched as some seedpods, the ones that fluttered to the ground like helicopters, were swept aside, replaced by the steady pounding of the huge drops.

Driving slowly onto the highway, Jesse sat in a daze, reality starting to hit home. He was out. He was on his own. "What the hell do I do now?" He did the only thing he knew, he drove towards home. He reasoned that he must have lots of time to plan something. Well, not lots of time, but at least the rest of the day or maybe even until Monday morning.

The wipers were barely keeping the windshield clear. The speed of the wipers seemed to send a message that beat within his head. "I've burned my bridges! I've burned my bridges! I've burned my bridges!"

"I've burned my goddamn bridges!" Jesse screamed aloud. "I must be crazy!"

Starting to feel the effects of what he had actually done, Jesse couldn't describe how he felt, mostly because he couldn't remember feeling this way before. There was this *thing,* sitting right in the middle of his chest, like a giant lump that was growing bigger by the minute.

"I think I'm going to puke," Jesse said, lowering the driver's window about three inches. Somehow it felt better to talk out loud.

It struck Jesse with awe. *"I'm a criminal!"*

"Jesus, I've got to calm down and make a decision." Jesse thought, *"Remember what Dad always said, if something is bothering you, make a decision and you'll lighten the load."* Jesse laughed almost hysterically. "Decide! Decide what? I won't even have my house this time tomorrow. This is crazy!"

Jesse pulled over to the side of the highway. His nerves were too bad to concentrate on two things at once. "Concentrate man," Jesse whispered desperately to himself. He drifted into thinking how happy he was with his life. He liked his girl, his home and friends, and the security of a well-paid job that let him do what he wanted. He kept thinking of things the way they used to be. Used to be, up to a short while ago.

He didn't know how long he sat at the side of the road lost in thought. Looking at his watch he was surprised to see that it wasn't really that long at all. It wasn't even noon yet.

"Let's see, I left Hank about three quarters of an hour ago. 'PRECISE' will just about be reaching the halfway time of its cycle. I could still go back; could still put the samples back and replace everything as it was," Jesse thought.

"Yeah-- right!" Then, "Bull shit!"

Starting the car, Jesse pulled onto the roadway and headed towards home. Hitting the defroster, he decided that he really had very little time to grab everything he needed, and to move the hell out of the area until he could talk to someone.

"If only Craig were here. ...Craig!..." Craig?" Jesse said to himself. "He's a cop-- he can at least offer me some advice."

Keeping his eye open for a phone booth, he finally saw one at the side of a gas station and pulled in and stopped. Using his calling card, he dialed Craig's number at home. The phone rang and rang, with an answering machine finally kicking in.

"Damn it."

Jesse opened his wallet and took out a piece of paper with Craig Fletcher's cellular number on it. Punching in the numbers, he got an answer on the second ring.

"Hello?"

"Craig, it's Jesse."

"Jesse! You asshole, you haven't phoned me in one hell of a long time."

Jesse took a deep breath, feeling better just hearing his friend's gruff voice on the line. He leaned against the inside of the booth, "Buddy, I don't want you to think I only call when I need some advice, but I'm in deep shit. I kind of need some..."

Craig's voice cut in over the line. "What's wrong, Jess?"

"I, uh, I,... think I'm going to be arrested very soon. No, I know I'm going to be arrested very soon. I did a crazy thing, Craig."

"You didn't kill someone did you?"

"No, no, Craig, it's in relation to my job. Look—do you have some days off or something? Can I meet you? If you could come down I'll pay your expenses because I can't talk over the phone."

There was silence on the line for a few seconds and Jesse thought he had lost contact. "Craig, you still there?"

"Yeah, I'm here. I was just thinking if there were any last minute things to prevent me from coming down, and you know what? I can't think of a single one."

Jesse felt a surge of relief flow through his whole body. He didn't know why, but with Craig helping he felt he would be able to take some sort of decisive action.

"Craig, how soon can you get down here? It's, it's really important, you know?"

"When do you want me there, Jess?"

"Yesterday, friend. Yesterday."

"Okay," Craig laughed over the line, "I'll leave here in about half an hour. I'll be at your place in..."

"No!" Jesse cut in. "Not my place! Meet me-- meet me... "

"Christ," Jesse thought, *"meet me where?"*

"Craig, do you remember that motel North of Seattle that we stayed at with the girls on the way back from Reno? I'll meet you there."

"No problem, Jess. I should be there about three-thirty or four. Have a drink ready for me. See you buddy."

The line went dead, but Jesse was starting to feel alive for the first time since leaving Inter-America. He had a direction and purpose now. He started the car and headed home.

He knew he would have to phone Bev. How was he going to explain this to Miss Beverly Carlson? This was going to turn her world upside-down too.

Jesse got that fear feeling again. This wasn't just going to be him alone. He hadn't been thinking. It would be Bev and anyone else he was associated

43

with. She was in real danger! As he gunned the car, the only thing he wondered was how in the name of hell was he going to explain all of this to her.

Running in the front door, Jesse grabbed everything he could think of from clothes to personal papers. Running into his den he unplugged his computer and carried it to the trunk of the car. Even though it didn't have any classified information on it, it did contain his random ideas and homework from over a long period of time.

Finally he phoned Bev. She wasn't home. He left a message and the only thing he had the courage to say was he had to leave town on business for a few days and he would call her later in the day. He asked her to please stay at her own place so he would know where to reach her. The last thing he said before he hung up was, "I love you." He headed for Seattle.

• • •

The phone rang in the lab, and Hank Corey answered it. "Hello?"

"You alone, Hank? This is your ol' buddy."

Hank Corey very quietly replied, "Captain Grant. I am alone."

Grant's voice came back, irritated. "I don't care if you're alone or not, I've told you before not to call me by name over the phone. You idiot!" There was a pause, and then Grant continued in a reasonable tone. "Now, they're calling for some more samples. Can you supply any right now?"

"No. I am sitting down."

"Are you trying to stretch my patience, Hank? If you are I'll assure you I don't have much. By the way, where's Jesse Harris?"

"He is not here."

"What's that supposed to mean? Did he leave the room? Did he leave the building, or did he leave the fucking country? What?"

"I do not remember."

"Corey, are you okay? What's going on there?" Grant asked suspiciously.

"I do not know," Hank answered truthfully.

"Listen to me, Hank," Grant said urgently over the phone, "You are not to go anywhere, or do anything until I get there. Understand? Stay in that room until we arrive. That's an order."

Corey wasn't even aware that someone was in the room with him until he heard a chair scraping over the floor. Turning the chair around, Strickler straddled it, leaning his arms across the top before he spoke. "Well, Hank, we have a lot to talk about."

Strickler's thin smile was set below a small nose, close set piercing blue eyes, and surrounded by old acne scars. He was 46 years old, slim with short cropped blonde hair with gray running through it, and even sitting, he held himself erect. Anything remotely pleasant about him was erased by the meanness of his mouth and the coldness of his eyes.

He looked at Hank Corey like he was a lab specimen. "What went on here today, Hank?"

Hank, watching the two men, said, "I do not know."

Grant looked over at Strickler and spoke. "Just like I thought, he's had the stuff shot into him. He's not going to be able to tell us diddly shit,"

"Good thing we used the chopper," Strickler offered. "This looks like a major security breach."

"Yeah, well, whatever we decide to do, we better do it quick," Grant said from the corner of the room. "The safe is open, and empty."

Turning back to Corey, Strickler continued in a soft, friendly voice. "Hank, Hank, I want you to start at the beginning of your conversation with Harris, and I want you to repeat it all."

Hank looked at Strickler, appearing deep in thought, but saying nothing.

Grant spoke again, irritating Strickler further. "Look, I'm telling you, he can't remember anything. We had better get onto Washington with this."

Strickler wheeled towards Grant, his face mottled and flushed with anger. "Fuck Washington! We can get a lid on this fast! Get me Ft. Lewis; we need some manpower."

Heading towards the door, Grant said, "Why do I get the feeling I'm about to be transferred to Alaska?"

Turning back to Corey, Strickler smiled his cobra smile and said, "Okay Hank, you just sit nice and quiet while I have a look around."

Walking into Jesse's office, Strickler took his time looking for anything that was out of place. He slid open the top drawer to the desk. His eyes fell upon a messy pile of newspaper clippings.

···CHAPTER THREE

Craig cradled the phone, worried and puzzled about Jesse's call. It just wasn't like Jesse to unload onto anybody like that. He was a highly independent and proud person who didn't like to rely on anyone else. Something definitely wasn't right.

Picking up the cellular again, Craig moved to the curb lane and slowed as he punched in his number.

"Vancouver Police," a female voice declared.

"Put me through to Jennifer Craig in Communications, please."

Craig looked at the dashboard clock, waiting for the call to go through. If he was to keep his word, he had a lot of things to do in a short period of time.

"Communications, Jennifer speaking."

Craig smiled into the rear end of a bus as he answered. "Hi, it's me. How's it going?"

"Craig! Geez, I've been hearing all sorts of things since I got to work. What's... where are you calling from?" Jennifer said in a breathless sounding voice.

"I'm calling from the car."

"I'll call you back, this phone's being recorded," she stated, and hung up.

Craig got away from the stinking fumes of the bus and pulled onto a quiet residential side street and pulled to the curb, wondering what juicy grapevine news his wife had been hearing.

The phone warbled in his hand. "I'm still here."

"I haven't got long, Craig, we're busier'n hell and it's not even a full moon yet. What's going on, for God's sake? I get to work and everybody tells me you've been suspended for beating the hell out of some kid."

"Calm down, Jenn,..."

"Tom called me during my coffee break and explained a bit of it, but I'm worried, Craig."

"Com'on, you know the routine. First Shepherd suspends you to make it look serious enough, then they try to set you up to cover their own ass while they appear to be going to bat for you."

Jennifer cut Craig off, hostility in her voice. "Look! You're dealing with Shepherd. You know he's an asshole, and you know he's after your butt. It doesn't take much of a brain to know that it doesn't matter if you're innocent or not, the point is he's after you and *that's* what you're fighting."

"He can try, Jenn, he can try. Besides, that's not why I called. I've got to go out of town."

"Out of town! Come on, Craig, I can't handle this. I've got to talk to you. We need to talk about us! Everything seems to be falling apart."

Craig waited until she stopped talking, and then said quietly, "It's Jesse. He called and said he was in trouble. He wants me to drive down to help him out."

"What kind of trouble? You have enough trouble of your own right here, for Pete's sake!

Craig started the car and eased out onto the street again, driving slowly in the direction of home.

"I really don't know what the problem is, but it sounded serious. Whatever it is, I'm going. You know I'm going, and you know you want me to go. Don't you?"

"*No-- I don't!* What I want is for you to say you want me home and for you to be there when I get there. Christ, you're all over the fucking newspapers, Craig!"

Craig could tell that Jennifer was about to cry. He had to explain that he wanted two things at the same time. He wanted her, and he wanted to help Jesse. He had an idea. "Jenn, do something for me, will you? Would you come home right now? We'll go down to Seattle together and see Jesse."

"I can't do that! I told you we're swamped in here!"

"Okay then, how about this. You drive down and meet me right after you get off. I'm meeting Jess at that motel we stayed at when we came back from Reno."

There was some hesitation on the line, then Jennifer spoke. "How long will you be down there?"

"Just long enough to help, Jess, then we can do the town. Look, I tell you what, when this mess is over with Shepherd, I'll even ask for a transfer. I'm beginning to realize I'm sick of this shit myself."

Jennifer didn't answer.

"I want to be with you, hon."

Jennifer was crying now. She couldn't answer right away, and she was having a hard time keeping control. Taking a deep breath, she let out a small shudder. "Yes, all right. I'll start down as soon as I get off. You've made me very happy and I know it's hard for you to leave the Detective Section."

"Not really," Craig answered, turning onto the open highway towards home. "I'm just beginning to see what's important. You're more important-and, and I love you, Jenn."

There was silence on the line, neither spoke for a few seconds. Finally Jennifer spoke quietly into the phone.

"You tell that Jesse Harris to have a drink ready for me."

Craig laughed. "He already has his orders. Call me from your cellular when you're getting close, otherwise I'll worry."

"Okay, I've got to run, Craig, before I'm in deep cuh-cuh."

Craig hung up, the smile gradually disappearing from his face. He really didn't need this trip to handle Jesse's problems right now. But then, when is the right time?

Craig walked into the big empty house. It didn't take him long to gather the few things he required. Letting Rusty in through the back door, he quickly fed him, then got on the phone to his neighbor, Eldon Stark.

"Hullo?"

"Eldon, it's Craig, next door."

"Hi. What's up?" Eldon answered in his unhurried fashion.

"I just wanted you to know that I'm leaving for a couple of days. Jennifer's going to be home then she's going to meet me."

"Glad to hear that, by God! I was getting sick to death of smelling you cook the same thing over and over. Now don't you go worry'n about a thing, it'll be just fine with you two."

Craig could hear Eldon Stark talking to his wife on the other end of the line, breaking the news that Jennifer was coming home. The two women always got along. "Eldon, I've got to run. I've fed Rusty, and you don't have to...."

"You run along, Craig, everything will be fine, just fine. I'll look after him."

Craig left a note that the dog was looked after, then headed out the door.

The line-up at customs was unusually small, considering the summer traffic and the coming weekend. Sitting in the line-up, he took the opportunity to scan the morning newspaper. He was on the third page when the article caught his eye.

COP BEATS YOUTH

"Christ, what a slanted rag," he thought as he continued to read.

> *Criminal charges may be pending against a long-time member of the Vancouver Police Departmet. Detective Sergeant Craig Fletcher is the subject of a complaint alleging that he severely beat a young man while in a fit of rage outside of a local convenience store last night. The victim, identified as Kelly Kaufmann,states the beating caused massive bruising, facial lacerations, and a broken arm and nose. Witnesses to the incident say that Detective Fletcher was out of control at the scene. An internal investigation....*

Craig threw the paper onto the seat in a fit of disgust and anger. He was so angry, he didn't notice the large gap in the line ahead of him until horns started to blare behind him.

He cleared Customs in another five minutes and was soon moving at highway speed along I-5, leaving the Southern limits of Bellingham a half-hour later.

Leaving the car windows open, Craig let the warm air rush through as he drove between the mountains south of Bellingham. He thought of Jesse. Something wasn't right at all. The guy had a fantastic job. He'd told Craig many times that he loved every minute of it. What the hell did he do?

Of all the times that he and Jesse tore up the city, neither one of them had ever done anything illegal. Unless you count disturbing the peace, drinking in public, fighting, and having a good time as breaking the law.

For no reason, his thoughts switched to Shepherd. Even the wide expanse of the roadway with little traffic couldn't alter his mood. He had phoned his lawyer earlier in the day, and Lou Maynard had told him to "Let things happen, Craig, then we'll deal with it."

Craig had tried to tell him that in police circles, case-hardened senior administrators, who usually suspected your guilt, had already predetermined the case or else you would not be involved.

Maynard had replied that he was very familiar with Shepherd and his kind, and to wait it out. Craig wasn't sure if he felt any better about that or not, but knew he had better concentrate on one problem at a time, or he wouldn't be able to handle any of it.

Craig saw the familiar motor-hotel sign in the distance. Taking the exit, he waited his turn at the traffic light, and then backtracked one block to the entrance. A pickup truck was just pulling away as he pulled up under the canopy. About to get out, he noticed a familiar figure ambling across the parking lot with a plastic bucket in his hand.

Jesse looked the same, except he had a deep frown on his face. He was totally lost in thought as Craig called to him. "Is that bucket for ice, or is that your glass?"

Jesse looked up, startled. "Craig!" Jesse's face changed to the accustomed one that Craig had always known. "Damn it's good to see you," he said as he came over and gave Craig a manly hug. "Pull over to number one-eleven and I'll be right back."

Craig got out of the car into the humid air, eyeing what looked like dark heavy rain clouds in the distance. Reaching back inside the car, Craig pressed the buttons, and the whirling sound of the windows going up greeted Jesse as he returned.

"Com'on. I got booze. Vodka for the Caesar's, plus white rum and seven for later. Right?"

"Right," Craig said, following the lanky frame into the room. "Is this going to be a drunk, or are you just going to soften me up before you spring this awful news on me?"

"Probably a little of both if you really want to know," Jesse said, putting the ice onto the cheap bureau top. "Let's get the drinks going first though, I can't stand talking on an empty stomach."

Looking around the room, Craig took in the small table with two chairs, the suitcase stand, and the bureau with the T.V. on the end. Everything was done up in brown and a variation of brown. "Nice room, Jess."

"Funn-ny. My taste has improved, you know." Jesse moved to the table and put two Caesar's onto the surface. "We actually stayed here and had a good time with the girls. Remember?"

"Yeah, I do. I remember lots of good times we've had." Craig took a swallow of his drink and nodded his approval. "Nice and spicy. Now, quit stalling and tell me what the problem is before I bust a gut." Craig watched Jesse, waiting for him to collect his thoughts.

Jesse took a swallow of his drink, and seemed to lose some of his color. It was obvious he didn't know where or how to start. It was also obvious that Jesse was scared. Craig had seen enough scared people in his life to know all of the signs.

"You've never had trouble talking to me before, Jess," Craig said quietly, avoiding Jesse's eyes. "Whatever it is, you know you can talk to me."

"Yeah... well," Jesse hesitated again. "To be truthful, I don't want you to think... well, I don't want to hurt our friendship."

Craig looked at Jesse and tried to keep it light. "The only thing that will stop this friendship is you keeping me in suspense much longer."

Craig made a nervous smile and took another quick swallow of his drink. Then, like a burst dam, he started to talk. "I've been working on a secret project for the U.S. Government. It's supposed to be for medical research, but... "

"Hold it right there, Jess. If it's secret, are you supposed to be telling me any of this?"

Jesse laughed, a tiny hysterical kind of laugh that ended on a high note. He drained half of his glass and looked back at Craig. "No, you shouldn't know any of this stuff. It's top secret, an 'eyes-only' type project, and very dangerous. In fact ,I'm out of my mind bringing you down here. I'm being very selfish, because it could put you in danger."

"I've been there before, Jess, and I know by looking at you that you need somebody to help think out your problem. Now, go ahead."

Jesse took a deep breath and settled back in the chair. Looking directly at Craig, all the years of trust tumbled into place. Besides, he knew he was in dire need of help.

"I found out that the government is going to use what I have been working on as a weapon, a deadly weapon against society. So I, I uh, sort of took it."

Craig sat still, not offering any criticism or encouragement. He knew Jesse had to get it out of his system.

"I also wiped the computer clean. Man, I took the computer disks, plus the samples. I left them nothing. I got out of there in such a hurry I didn't even have a chance to think. I took it! I can't even believe I'm fucking saying it!" Jesse stopped, the hand coming to his mouth was shaking badly. He waited for Craig to speak, looking for some sign of condemnation or cracking of their friendship.

Craig smiled. "Go on, Jess, I'm not judging you. Tell me the whole thing so I can help."

And Jesse Harris did. He started with the type of project, and the years of frustration that had finally born fruit. He told Craig of his earlier suspicions that he himself thought were childish and improbable until his discovery earlier in the day. Then he mentioned Hank Corey, the conversation, and the theft of 'PRECISE.'

Much later, Craig asked, "You expect me to believe all this shit, don't you? This is one of your big funnies isn't it?"

Jesse looked at Craig and just shook his head minutely from side to side.

"I was hoping you were going to say, 'Gotcha, boy did I have you believing this or what!' But you're not going to say that, are you?"

"I wish I could, Craig."

"Seems to me the government is doing everyone a favor. From my standpoint, as a cop I mean, this has got to be the greatest thing since..."

"Craig! This is for medicine, not mind control of the population!"

"Jess, look at me. There is no such thing as this drug you're talking about. They've been talking about truth serums forever."

"No, it's real, Craig-- 'PRECISE' works."

Shaking his head, Craig got up and pored a large white rum and emptied half a can of 7-Up onto the ice. He turned and, taking a swallow, felt the liquid make its way into his stomach as he returned to the table. "But how did you stumble onto what they were doing behind your back? I mean, just from newspaper articles? Come on!"

"Things were happening within the lab, things that I didn't have any answers for. Little things over a period of time like inventory totals, and canisters in the wrong place. This morning when I found the envelope with the message on the outside, I... well what was I supposed to think when I read all of the clippings?"

"And it was all confirmed when you talked to this guy, Corby?" Craig asked.

"Corey. Hank Corey. I really surprised myself there. Mild mannered Jesse Harris, daringly uses his assistant as a guinea pig by spraying him unexpectedly in the face."

Craig shook his head. "I still have a hard time believing that this stuff works the way you say it does. I mean, it's fantasy stuff."

"Look, have you ever heard of a project called MK Ultra?"

"Can't say that I have," Craig answered.

"Remember a newspaper story about a woman who underwent brainwashing by a doctor in Montreal? It was funded by the CIA, of all people. Then later, the Canadian Government kicked in some money through their health system. It was all done in the name of research to promote better health and a cure for mental disorders. The C.I.A. did about seventy-five people, between the nineteen fifties and nineteen sixty-five. Remember?"

"Vaguely,"

"Craig, whole memories were wiped out. They were called depatterned persons. Memories were gone, including those of their husbands, wives, marriages, children, plus years of learning. I mean these people had to be toilet-trained, man. They were released not able to recognize anyone or anything to do with their lives. They used up two to three years of people's lives in those experiments, and it's taken thirty years for them to recover."

"What's that got to do with this stuff you're working on now?" Craig asked.

"Those experiments were in the late fifties or early sixties, Craig! Do you know how far we've come in another fifty years? I'll tell you. It's staggering! All that information gathered over fifty years on the human body. All that information gathered on the human brain and how it works. D.N.A., mapping genetic codes-- computers helped more than a lot, and again, it's all to better the health of mankind. Trouble is, I didn't know what the CIA or the U.S. military were up to."

Jesse was quiet a few moments, then continued. "I don't blame you for being skeptical; if this were to become public, the scientific community would question my work. I'll try and explain, in layman's terms, what takes place. You may or may not understand what I am talking about, but Craig, believe me it does work."

"This 'PRECISE" is a very dangerous drug in the wrong hands. That's why I took it, I guess. Remember," Jesse said moving to the bed and lying down with his back against the headboard, "we're not necessarily talking about memory here. It's not what they remember, but the *truth* of what they *stored* in their mind. There is a difference. Someone could promise to tell the truth, and then couldn't deliver due to conscious faulty input/output, or they could promise to tell the truth, and then simply lie."

"With 'PRECISE', they tell the truth straight from the source without any interference from other uncontrolled or controlled signals. It sounds complicated, I know, but 'PRECISE' cuts back on distortion, contamination, and alteration of the brain wave feedback."

"Some tape recorder," Craig offered.

"The brain doesn't work like a tape recorder; the brain stores information all over the place. The trick is to gather that information without interference. I can get the unadulterated truth from a person's mind, and then I can find out what they actually think and feel about any given subject-- not necessarily the way they consciously want to remember it, or consciously want to tell others about their thoughts."

Craig put down his glass. "All this is making me hungry, and to tell the *truth*, no pun intended. I'm starving. Are we ordering in or eating out?"

Jesse jumped up. "Let's get the hell out of here. I'm in the mood for a huge steak."

Craig drove to a well-known hotel a little further north on I-5 and they both sipped on a glass of wine while their identical meals were being prepared.

"Lets grab the salad bar, Jess, then I've got something to tell you."

Five minutes later, both men were at the table and were a quarter of the way into their salads when Jesse asked, "What did you want to tell me?"

Craig looked around the dining room; the room had few customers and privacy wasn't a problem. "I'm off work for thirty days or so," he answered.

"What does that mean? Are you on a holiday?"

Craig looked at his friend and smiled before he answered. "Yeah, a holiday; a paid holiday. Actually, I've been suspended because someone made a complaint about me."

"Oh man!" Jesse said, putting his fork down and leaning back. "I feel the shits. You've got problems and here I am just adding to them."

Looking directly at Jesse, Craig leveled his fork and waved it back and forth. "No, you're not. I'm not exactly having the time of my life here, but hey, they say a change is as good as a rest. Don't sweat it; it'll turn out okay."

"What happened?"

Craig filled him in until their meal arrived, leaving out nothing. He even mentioned the problems between Jennifer and him.

They ate quietly, sipping the wine, lost in their own thoughts for a while. Jesse broke the spell. "I'm only halfway through and I'm stuffed. I can't believe it! I was starving."

"No Jess, that's the ol' rats in the stomach. It's caused by nerves, fear, anxiety-- whatever. Sometimes they make you think you're hungry, so you eat to get rid of the feeling. Hell, one year I thought I would gain fifty pounds, I ate so much to get rid of the rats."

"You? You never get upset about anything!"

"Not now. I've learned what's important and what isn't. Well almost. Jennifer says that's my problem-- I'm not putting the important things first. Geez, I forgot to tell you! She's driving down after her shift. She wanted to see you and it was an excuse to spend some time together and start off fresh."

Craig looked at Jesse a moment, weighing what Jesse had told him. "That was before I knew how important your problem was. Maybe I should phone her and cancel out."

"No, don't do that, Craig. I just needed a sounding board until I could figure out my next move."

The coffee arrived along with two Grand Marniers, and after a few moments, Craig asked the sixty-four thousand dollar question. "Well, what *are* you going to do, Jess? Have any ideas?"

"Shit, I never had any ideas when I took the stuff. I may have a glimmer of an idea that might work. I may need your help though," Jesse murmured while he blew on his coffee.

"I'm listening."

"I know you are. Can you hold the samples and the disks until tomorrow? I have to make a quick trip back to the lab to get another item."

Craig shook his head in the negative. "You never, and I mean never, return to the scene of the crime, Jess. You'll be arrested as soon as you poke your nose anywhere near that building."

"No, I think there's still time. Corey will have gone home and he won't remember a thing. I forgot about my notebook on my desk."

"Jesse, you don't have a clue as to what took place when you left. You said yourself you weren't sure what, if anything, happened when you downloaded all that data from the file."

"That's just it. I didn't download it. I erased it. Man, this is unreal. I'm talking about espionage."

"Like I said," Craig noted. "Stupid."

"Stupid or not, I have to make a quick in and out. Anyway, to get back to the point, what I thought I might do is to take everything to a professor friend of mine in Chicago. She's at the State University."

"She?"

"Her name's Dorothy Eldridge. Dr. Dorothy Eldridge. She has a rep for very exact and very, very good work in medical research. I don't know what she's researching right now, but she can probably be trusted to do the right thing." Jesse gulped the rest of his drink and got up, throwing some bills onto the table. "Let's go, we'll talk in the car."

Outside, the humidity hung like a heavy cloak with no sign of air movement at all, and the interior of the Lincoln was no improvement, with the air smelling like some forgotten sealed tomb.

"Okay, Jess. When we get back to the room, you give me all your goodies and I'm heading for my parents' place over by Ocean Shores. You can reach me there."

Jesse turned sideways in his seat, his face lighting up with enthusiasm without being aware that it showed. "I forgot about that place. Yeah, that might work. It gives me a little time. I'll call you at their number..."

Craig cut him off. "We'll figure the rest out later. I've got to wait for Jennifer, then I have a couple or so hours of driving ahead of me after that."

"Here," Jesse said, extending his hand when they were inside the motel room. "This is the address of Professor Eldridge, and her phone number in case something happens to me. The samples and disks are all in this briefcase."

"Jess, you shouldn't go near that lab."

"I'll be okay. Okay?"

Jesse walked out to his car, followed by Craig. He stood awkwardly for a moment, and then turned to Craig. "Look, this makes you part of the crime. Do you understand, Craig? You of all people should know that."

"Yes. Yes I do, Jess, but if it's like you say, and the stuff is that dangerous, then I'll take your word. Besides, I'll only have it a short while until you get back."

Jesse looked at Craig for a long moment before getting into the Lincoln, then finally offered his hand to Craig. "Guard that stuff real close, Craig. I'll call you in the morning."

"No problem. Just make sure you do call. I won't know what the hell to do with this stuff."

Jesse smiled, and as he started to drive away he said, "Just don't try brushing your teeth with it."

Craig watched the car disappear around the corner, a bad feeling sitting in his lower stomach. Now that he was alone with this so-called 'PRECISE' thing, he wasn't sure if it was a feeling of dread for Jesse, or a feeling of dread for himself. As he settled down to wait for Jennifer, he knew one thing for sure. He was playing for higher stakes than he ever had in his life.

• • •

The sky was black and low. The wind came up in sudden gusts, swirling paper and other debris into mini whirlwinds along the edge of the freeway where all the dirt and dust had collected. The car buffeted from side to side from heavy blasts from Mother Nature and semi-trailers rocketing by. Large drops the size of quarters smashed into the windshield as Craig turned onto highway 405 to bypass Seattle.

Jennifer followed close behind in the Cherokee, her wipers working furiously. Craig had waited two hours for her, and hadn't let her get into any long conversation, but promised her a full explanation after they got to his parents' place. She wasn't happy about that, but seemed glad to be back doing things with him.

Looking at the briefcase on the seat beside him, it was hard to believe that everything that Jesse had said was true. It sent a slight shiver down his neck when he thought of what Jess had actually done. *"Man oh man, Jess, you're asking a lot this time,"* Craig thought. *"This is Uncle Sam and the United States Marines all rolled up into one."*

His parents' place sat right on the Pacific Ocean on a bit of a rise. The both of them used to love coming here to spend a weekend with his parents. They never seemed to have time anymore. The place was empty now; his parents were at their home in British Columbia.

At this time of the afternoon the town of Ocean Shores looked deserted, and except for one delivery van he didn't see anyone during the ten minute drive out to south point. At least the sky was clearing.

Dragging himself out of the car, Craig read the familiar and corny sign hanging crookedly on a heavy chain between two posts: *Ron & Donna's Hideaway.* As he stretched and took a deep breath of salt air, he took in the gray weathered siding and the chains connected at knee height to other posts around the perimeter.

He well remembered running back from the beach one night and hitting one of the chains at full tilt. It was only his training that had prevented him from breaking every bone in his body.

He looked over at the spot where he had laid in agony while looking up at a stupid concrete seagull on top of a post. His dad had painted the chains white at his insistence, with Craig jokingly talking about calling a lawyer. He still had a scar from that damn chain.

Jennifer, carrying her suitcase, joined him as he started for the rear of the house. Craig reached under a log by the infernal seagull, feeling around for the key that was always there.

"It's been a while, hon. Looks like your parents are keeping the place up."

Craig nodded. "Yeah, not bad, not bad at all."

The whole of the ocean side of the structure was glass, and when they entered, the slanted rays of the sun lit up the family room and part of the kitchen.

It still had the same cozy atmosphere. The kitchen was straight ahead, and was designed to be practical and efficient. A main floor bathroom and master bedroom peeked at Craig as he put the groceries onto the counter. They would sleep in the guest bedroom.

Opening a couple of beers, Craig plopped into an old beaten leather chair that had been in the family for as far back as he could remember. A black, but highly polished wood stove brought back numerous memories of the times he and Jennifer had sat around in the warmth, and on other occasions had made love with the sound of the heavy breakers thundering against the long stretch of beach.

"Okay, Craig, you've had time to relax a bit. Now, what's going on?"

Craig looked over at Jennifer and took a moment to adjust his thinking. "When I asked you down here, Jenn, I had no idea how serious it was. Jesse is in very serious trouble."

"What kind of trouble? Law kind of trouble?"

"It's all tied in with where he works. He's working on, or was working on, a government project. In fact, it's a top-secret government project. And, well… "

Craig told her all about what Jesse had been working on, and how Jesse thought the government was stealing samples and using them to control people. He went on to tell her how Jesse had taken everything from the lab to stop them, and then had called him for help.

Jennifer sat there the whole time saying nothing, and when he stopped talking she still sat there. Finally she looked up at Craig.

"Unfuckingbelievable!"

Craig smiled. "Isn't it though?"

"What if he gets caught with all those things on him, Craig? He'll go to jail for the rest of his life."

Craig looked up, startled for a moment, then he turned red in the face with what he had to say."Uh, I wasn't finished telling you everything. Uh, I, uh...well, Jesse asked me to hold onto the things he took until he gets back tomorrow."

Jennifer went white as her hand flew to her mouth. "What are you saying, Craig? Say you didn't do that. My God, you're a police officer. How the hell could you let yourself get involved in this? How could you make such a decision, for God's sake! Our whole future is at stake here!"

"Look, all I was doing was helping Jess out. He needed help immediately and I couldn't turn him down."

"He never gave you much time to even *think* about it!" Jennifer said in anger.

"Right now, I'm just worried about him getting caught," Craig countered.

"Do you believe what he says? How can a spray make you do all that? I mean, to tell the absolute truth about anything and not remember doing it."

Craig took a sip of beer, then got up and walked to the window. "He explained it to me, and I can't even begin to try and tell you. He was scared shitless about this getting into the wrong hands, I'll tell you that much."

"When is he to call?"

"Soon, I hope," Craig answered, turning towards her. "I haven't had time to think this out, but what should I do with the briefcase if he gets caught?"

"How the hell should I know? You're asking me! I do know this though, you had better get your priorities straight, and get them straight fast. You have to do something about that, ...that package you're carrying around. Good God, they could burst in here right now and I'd never see you again."

"Easy, Jenn."

"Easy my ass," Jennifer said around tears. "You get this stuff back to Jesse as soon as possible. You have to try and get hold of him."

"I don't have any way right now. I have to wait for him to call."

"Some great weekend you've arranged, Craig."

"I'm sorry, Jenn. I really didn't know how serious it was, and if you had seen Jess you wouldn't be in such a hurry to jump all over me. He thinks he's doing the right thing."

"And you, do you think you are doing the right thing?" Jennifer challenged.

Craig sighed, then sank down beside her on the couch. "I don't have a clue. I do know I can't leave Jesse hanging there without some help. If anything, I might be able to stop him from doing something stupid."

"He's already done *that*!" Jennifer shot back, sitting up straight and away from Craig. "And so have you!"

Craig didn't reply, knowing that Jennifer was absolutely right. "Jesse talked about taking the briefcase to Chicago, to a professor. What I didn't tell you is that I am planning to try and get Jess onto safer ground until he can get it back to the proper authorities."

"Safer ground where?"

"Canada. At least there he can have time to think about where to return it."

"Well, at least you're thinking about returning it," Jennifer said, reaching for a tissue. "But you won't be the one to take it across the border, Craig. I won't allow it! You'll be called a spy!"

"I didn't enter into any conspiracy with Jess you know. I..."

"Oh yes you did! The moment you agreed to take those samples from him. Since September 11th, the Americans would charge you with espionage for sure. Did you think of that?"

"I was just trying to help, Jess, and to remove some of his worry," Craig muttered, lamely.

"Well, you have certainly done that. Now *we* have it."

"Jenn, I want you to go back home first thing in the morning. I'll stay here and..."

"I'm not going anywhere! It's obvious you're the one that needs counseling. I'd go stark raving mad if I went home. No thanks!" Jennifer got up and started down the hall.

"Where are you going?"

"I'm going for a shower. I want to at least be clean before they come and arrest us."

Craig settled into the chair by the window. It was going to be a long night.

• • •

Jesse was emotionally drained as well as being physically tired. He was alert, however, as he slowed, then coasted the last hundred yards to the entrance of Inter-America. Some loose gravel crunched under the wheels as he pulled even with the gatehouse.

"Evening, Mr. Harris. Working late again?"

Jesse nodded while signing the log, and said, "You know the rules, Burt, the higher you go, the more people you have to please."

61

Jesse put the car in gear and drove away as Burt chuckled and called, "Ain't that the truth."

"Everything must be fine if ol' Burt isn't giving me any suspicious stares," Jesse thought. *"Four minutes. That's all I need. Four minutes, in and out. Forever!"*

Parking the car in his usual spot, Jesse got out into a warm wind that was stirring the leaves in a gentle motion, and glanced over to Hank Corey's parking spot. It was empty. In fact, the whole lot was deserted except for two cars.

Jesse had gone through the security measures so many times they had become automatic, but tonight he was nervous while going through the procedure. Everything looked normal; the long halls were half-lit to conserve energy, and only a few labs had any working lights on at all.

The lab was in darkness. There was usually a night-light left on for members of the security detail, and for the cameras to scan the interior.

Trying the door, Jesse found it locked. Corey had not only locked the door, he had shut everything off. Turning to his right after entering the lab, Jesse reached for the light switch and turned it on.

He was immediately locked in a powerful neck lock. The side of his neck was starting to hurt, and despite his height he couldn't break the grip. In a manner of seconds his vision started to blur, and Jesse felt himself being swallowed by total blackness.

"All right, all right! Don't kill the asshole!" Strickler said.

Looking at him from a kneeling position, Grant nodded and stood up. "That's exactly what I should do to this prick."

Grant dragged Jesse to a hard-backed chair, heaved him onto the seat, then handcuffed him with his hands behind him.

Ten seconds later, Jesse came to, not knowing where he was during the time it took to focus his eyes. He couldn't understand who was trying to talk to him. Then he came fully alert.

"Do you hear me, asshole?"

Jesse looked towards the voice. It came from a guy wearing frameless glasses. He had a full head of cropped gray hair, and was wearing a leather bomber jacket over an open-necked shirt. Despite the jacket, Jesse could see he was built like a gorilla, all chest and arms.

Jesse turned to his right and saw a second man leaning against a counter. This one was blonde, had scars on his face from old acne eruptions, and had a nasty look about him.

Jesse figured the nasty looking one must be in charge and asked, "Who are you people?"

Moving away from the counter, Strickler spoke quietly as he stopped in front of Jesse. "We ask the questions, not you. But so you know who you are dealing with, we are with the Pentagon, Mr. Harris. Now, let's get to the matter of the theft of United States property."

Jesse went to wipe his face, but realized his hands were cuffed. He started to sweat involuntarily, not knowing what to do or what to say. "Look,-- I, I want a lawyer. I'm entitled to a law..."

"You're entitled to a grave, you asshole," Grant said, grabbing Jesse by the hair and pulling it hard to the left.

"That's enough, Mark," Strickler said to Mark Grant. "We have a different method, thanks to our friend here," and sprayed Jesse full in the face with a blast of what felt like air.

"Where the hell did you get that!" Jesse yelled.

"From your assistant. Didn't he tell you?" Strickler asked as he looked at his watch.

Jesse looked around frantically, but gradually his face became calm, losing the animal look of fear and unfamiliarity. Something clicked into place in his brain and he just sat there, waiting. He watched as the blonde man pulled up a stool and sat down in front of him.

"Where are the 'PRECISE' samples, Harris?"

"They are with Craig," Jesse stated.

The lines around Strickler's eyes smoothed out, and his eyes became hard. He leaned ahead menacingly, and asked, "Who is Craig?"

"He is my friend. My hands are hurting me." Jesse moved his arms around uncomfortably.

"Take his cuffs off, Mark."

As Mark Grant moved to the rear to remove the cuffs, Strickler continued. "What is Craig's full name and where does he live?"

Jesse thought for a second and said, "Craig Ronald Fletcher. He lives at 7825 Rocky Creek Road, in Ridge Meadows."

"Where's Ridge Meadows?"

"Canada."

"Oh, shit!" Mark Grant exploded. "If it's out of the country..."

"Can it, Mark," Strickler said, raising his hand for silence without taking his eyes off of Jesse. "What does Craig do for a living, Jesse?"

"He is a police officer in Vancouver, British Columbia."

Both men looked at each other in disbelief. They seemed at a loss as to explain this set-up. "What the hell... why is a guy like that involved in this for?" Grant asked.

Jesse answered. "Because I asked him to help me with the canisters and the disc."

"Disc! What disc?" Strickler asked anxiously.

"The computer discs."

"What is on the discs, Harris?"

"I took all of the back-up discs, then erased the computer of all information."

Strickler felt the blood drain from his face. He got up off of the stool and walked to the counter, leaning on it while he regained his composer. Turning, he walked back and sat again in front of Jesse. "What are you going to do with the samples and the discs that you took, Harris?"

"I don't know."

"Why did you come back here, Harris? What did you want in this lab?" Strickler was looking around while he asked, trying to see if there was anything of importance lying around.

"My notebook. It is on my desk."

Strickler nodded to Grant and continued with Jesse.

"Where is Craig Fletcher now?"

Jesse looked at Strickler and truthfully stated, "I do not know."

"Come on, Jesse, think. He must have told you where he was going."

Jesse did not answer the statement.

Strickler was becoming very impatient, but knew full well how important these moments were, before everything was lost. "Did he tell you where he was going, Jesse?"

"Yes."

"Where did he say he was going to go?"

"He said he was going to his parents' place on the coast."

Strickler felt his pulse quicken. "What coast? In Washington or British Columbia or Oregon? Where?"

"In Washington."

Strickler was doing a slow burn. This was taking far too long. "You're making me work very hard, Harris. Tell me everything you know about where Craig Fletcher is going."

"He said he was going to his parents' place at Ocean Shores. I don't know the address."

"Fine. Now how are you to get in touch with him? Are you to meet him or phone him?"

"Yes," was all Jesse said.

"Jesus Christ! I suppose that means both. What is the phone number you are to call him at?"

Jesse had a slight frown on his face, "I don't know his parents' telephone number. He has a cellular number."

"If he has a cellular," Grant said, returning with a small notebook in his hand, "that's not good. He could be on the move."

"Don't you think I know that? Let's just keep at this."

Turning back to Jesse, Strickler asked brusquely, "How will you get this cellular number Harris?"

"By looking in my wallet," Jesse said, looking blank-faced at Strickler.

Turning to Grant, Strickler pointed to Jesse and sighed, "This is getting tedious. Get his wallet, will you? I'm afraid that if I don't ask for the exact information, I may miss something."

Mark Grant dug into the left rear pocket of Jesse's pants, pulling the wallet free with a tug. He began to search the wallet as Strickler continued.

"Now, tell me all you know about Fletcher's personal life. I want to know about his family; his job, what he drives, who his boss is and anything that you can think of. Got that?"

And Jesse did. He started with their friendship, and then told the two men about Craig's wife, Jennifer, and where they lived. Jesse stated what Craig did within the police department and the problems with Shepherd. He talked of Craig Fletcher's suspension from the job and the reason for it. When he was finished, there was very little that Strickler and Grant didn't know about Craig Fletcher.

"Harris," Strickler quietly explained, "you took government property. Who is paying you for this?"

"Nobody is paying me. I took everything so there would be nothing left."

"Obviously," Strickler acknowledged, "but why?"

"Because the government is going to use theformula as a weapon, and not a tool to combat mental illness."

"Okay, Harris," Strickler said, looking at his watch and getting up off of the stool, "that's the easy part, now let's get down to business."

Much later, Nathan Strickler sat back and sighed. "Time's running out on the drug, Mark," Strickler said, pointing to a phone. "Call off all the other surveillance teams we had set up. Nobody's going to be showing up and there's no sense wasting all that manpower."

When it was all over, Jesse Harris was led out to a waiting car, and then to a helicopter. Very shortly thereafter he was deposited in a heavily guarded room at Ft. Lewis. He fell into a deep sleep.

Strickler looked over at Grant. "We have until tomorrow to get 'PRECISE' back. I want to hit Ocean Shores early in the morning by land and air. If we don't get this stuff back, we, my friend, are dog meat."

"We'll get it. How about I get onto the wire to San Francisco and talk to Richard Bishop. Maybe he and Marion can come up with something on this Fletcher guy."

"Like what?"

"You know how he is with those computers of his. He seems to be able to pilfer information from any source."

"Fine. You do that."

Grant got up and headed for the door.

"Oh, and one more thing," Strickler said. "Tell Marion Thackery I expect her to set up a command relay. I want instant communication."

When Grant had left, Strickler thought of Miller. A slight twinge of anxiety hit him just above the stomach area. Miller was in charge of advanced research projects, but it was made clear from the moment that the project was a known success, 'PRECISE' was Miller's number one priority.

Miller reported directly to the Assistant Secretary of Defense, and Strickler knew that from there it was only one or two steps to the President of the United States.

Picking up the telephone, Strickler hesitated a moment then punched nine, an area code, then the information operator. When prompted by a recording, he answered, "Vancouver Police."

The operator came onto the line, stated there were several numbers, and asked which he wanted. Strickler didn't really know, so he took a guess. "Try the Duty Sergeant's office."

A number was given to him electronically and after dialing it, Strickler was rewarded with a male voice answering, "Vancouver Police."

"I would like to speak to Deputy Chief Shepherd please."

"I'm sorry, sir, he is not on duty, can I take a message?"

"This is Major Strickler of Army Intelligence. I'm calling long distance from the Pentagon in Washington, D.C.. Can I have his home phone number please?"

"I'm sorry sir, we are not allowed to give out home phone numbers. If you care to leave your number, I'll have him call you if it is an emergency."

"Let me speak to your Supervisor please."

There was a click on the line, followed by some music, followed by a gruff "Sgt.'s Office, Johnson speaking."

Strickler went through the whole routine again, and got nowhere. "Look, is there anyway at all I can get hold of this man, Shepherd-- it's a matter of national security to us down here."

"Yeah? Well it's a matter of local security to us up here. We *don't* give out phone numbers, especially Shepherd's. Look, give me your phone number, tell me what it's about, and I'll see what I can do for you."

Strickler nodded in the negative, then realized he was on the phone and couldn't be seen. "I can't tell you what it's about, but it involves a Vancouver Police Member."

"A police member? Who?"

Strickler waited a heartbeat or two, then plunged ahead. "A guy named Craig Fletcher. A Sergeant, I believe."

"Give me your number and I'll have Shepherd call you immediately."

"Great. Its area code two oh six..."

"Two oh six?" the voice interrupted, "That's Washington State. I thought you were calling from Washington, D.C.?"

"Oh," Strickler laughed. "No, no. I am from the Pentagon, but I'm at Ft. Lewis, just south of Seattle."

"Oh, I know where it is, all right," Johnson replied, "Just make sure you give me the correct phone number."

A short while later the phone rang, and Strickler quickly grabbed the receiver. "Major Strickler speaking."

"Yes, this is Deputy Chief Shepherd of the Vancouver Police, you were calling me?"

"Ah, thank you for returning my call. I wanted to talk to you about a person we both seem to be having a little difficulty with."

"And who might that be, Major?"

"Detective Sergeant Craig Fletcher."

"Between you and me Major, I'm almost afraid to ask. You have me hooked, however, so reel me in, Major and tell why in hell the United States Armed Forces would be interested in Fletcher."

Strickler smiled to himself before answering Shepherd. "Let me fill you in on a few details, and then possibly we could help each other out a little bit. Okay?"

···CHAPTER FOUR

Jesse woke up with a jolt. He actually felt his body lift into the air. Turning his head carefully he looked around the room. He didn't recognize anything. The floor was some kind of highly polished brown linoleum. The walls were green halfway up before hitting a border of some description then turning white.

There were several wires suspended from the ceiling, ending in glass globes. The lights were turned off. He could see a faint sky outside of a window; it appeared to be the start of dawn.

Sitting up, Jesse groaned and rubbed his neck. It hurt like hell. *"I must have slept wrong,"* he thought. "Where the hell am I?" Rubbing his face, he tried to remember how he had gotten onto the bed. Nothing. Not a thing. In fact the last thing he remembered was going to the lab.

"The lab! Why the hell did I go to the lab?" Several moments went by before the answer came to him without warning. *"The notebook".* Then again, *" 'PRECISE'! Craig! - holy shit!"*

Taking the rest of the room in, he saw that there were three other beds in addition to the one he was on. The other three had rolled up mattresses, exposing the springs, and beside each bed there was a small night desk, lamp, and cupboard. There was a door in the center of the wall.

Getting up cautiously, Jesse walked slowly towards the door and saw that it was slightly ajar. He was about to open it when he heard two men talking.

"We better wake him up, Major, and get him to a cell. We have ground to cover."

Looking through the crack at the back of the door, Jesse saw a gray haired man with very short hair. He quickly moved away, his heart pounding. *"I've seen him before."* He tried to think, but nothing came to mind.

He heard the other man answering, "I don't know if that's the right way to go. He told us everything we wanted to know while under 'PRECISE', and he won't remember a thing."

Jesse couldn't believe what he was hearing. His mind was a blank. *"What did I tell them? Craig! He had to think of Craig! He had to protect Craig!"*

"No, I think we can safely return him to the lab, that way if this guy Fletcher tries to get in touch, we can manipulate the outcome. I don't want to count on the guy still being at the Ocean Shores place."

"Then how do you explain him being here this morning? He's going to want to know, Nathan," Grant said in an almost sarcastic tone.

"I don't know yet, and what's more, right now I don't give a shit. Let's just get him out of here."

Grant continued as if Strickler hadn't even spoken. "Look, why don't we have two guys make like medics, and simply drop him off. They can say they got a call from security and he was found on the floor. It looked like he had a seizure or something. He looked confused, so they brought him here."

Strickler looked at Grant, one eyebrow raised. "Not bad. Sometimes you simply amaze me, Mark. Okay, get two guys and drop him off at the lab. Give one of them that notebook also. He can throw it on the desk for him to find."

Grant got up to leave, but Strickler held him back, his hand on Grant's elbow. "Don't fuck up, Mark. He had better be under constant surveillance at all times."

"Don't worry, I'll lay it on thick."

"You do that, then get back here. I've got to finalize the logistics and set a fire under someone's ass. The men and choppers should be ready to roll."

Jesse quietly returned to the bed and eased himself onto his side facing away from the door. A few moments later the door swung open lighting up the room, then it was closed quietly. His heart was pounding so hard he thought it would break inside his chest. He knew he had to get his anxiety level down if he was to think rationally.

To have learned that he had been given the drug at the lab was more than a stroke of luck. He never would know what had actually taken place, but it didn't matter now; he had told them everything they wanted to know. He had to let them think he knew nothing about any of it. At least he was in a better position to help Craig, but how?

The door opened without warning. Jesse stopped breathing, forcing his eyelids to remain still, but his heart was pounding again. A cheerful male voice spoke to him, just before he felt a hand on his shoulder.

"Mr. Harris. Get up please. You have time for a shave and shower before breakfast."

Jesse feigned waking up. Acting befuddled, he said, "Where am I? Who are you?"

"It's okay, sir," the guy in the army fatigues said. "You were brought in here last night after some sort of seizure. You've been checked out at the Base Hospital though, and everything's just fine."

"Where is here?" Jesse asked dutifully.

"Ft. Lewis, sir. You were brought here for security reasons because of your job classification. Now if you will hurry, you will have time for breakfast before we have someone drive you back to your lab. I understand they have a car lined up for you."

It was still early in the morning by the time he entered the lab with two men in tow. It was standard procedure, they had said. To make sure there had been no breaches in security and there was no threat to him, they had told him.

Jesse watched, looking for some slip-up on their part, but no matter where he went or what he did, one of them was always in eye contact with him. He would have a very difficult time calling Craig at this rate.

Jesse looked at his watch. It was almost eight! Craig must be going ape shit about now! He *had* to do something, but what? He needed to be alone for a few moments. Twenty minutes later he got his opportunity.

Ignoring the no smoking sign, one of the men lit a cigarette in the lab. Jesse watched out of the corner of his eye, waiting. The highly sensitive smoke detector went off with a suddenness that shocked even Jesse, who had been poised and ready to spring into action.

Amid the piercing chirp of the detector, Jesse added to the confusion by quickly reaching over and pulling the emergency fire alarm on the wall just behind the coat rack. The fire alarm was deafening and resounded throughout the whole of the structure.

Uniformed guards descended upon the lab from all directions, having been alerted by the smoke detector and the manual fire alarm. Doors automatically shut and sealed off various parts of the building, closing he long hallways down into short stretches of claustrophobic tubes.

Any threat to a lab was treated very seriously, especially one that contained highly secret government work. It took no time at all before the two men were overwhelmed with questions and accusations and were surrounded by very angry security personnel.

Jesse slipped out of the lab and moved rapidly down the hallway, disappearing behind one, then two fire doors. Removing his white smock, he quickly dumped it in the garbage container in the inner security chamber at the entrance and ran for his car. He was passing the front of the lab, the car aimed at the front gate, when the two men ran from the main entrance. One started to head towards the gate, while the other ran towards a car parked a short distance away.

The entrance and exit gates were open. It was another security measure due to the fire alarm. This allowed incoming fire apparatus to respond, and allowed personnel to leave the parking lot unimpaired.

The man tried desperately to reach the exit gate before Jesse. It didn't matter, because Jesse roared out of the incoming entrance and skidded into a right turn and onto the highway. Putting his foot down hard on the gas pedal, his knee began to shake up and down violently from pumped up adrenaline. Jesse had never experienced this kind of reaction from his body before. His body seemed to be acting totally opposite from his wishes.

The car seemed like it was hardly moving, but in fact, the machine was reaching a tremendous speed, and when Jesse looked in the mirror, the car that had pulled out onto the highway was nothing but a pinprick in his vision.

He had no idea where he was going, and no plan. He was on highway 18 with the nose of the car pointed towards home-- the one place he couldn't go. The other car was only a minute or so behind him.

Jesse swung west onto I-90 and with traffic now on all sides, he had to slow down. At every opportunity however, he pushed the car and his driving abilities to the limit by surging into every available road space.

As he approached the I-90 and the 405 connectors, he felt a little more confident. He was just one more ant amongst a whole nest of ants. He doubted they could locate him after so many turnoff opportunities. The trouble was, there was no way of looking back to try and spot a following vehicle.

He found a phone booth on the corner of an old run down gas station lot. One of those no stations that offered cheap fuel, had filthy washrooms, and had an attendant who couldn't give directions on how to get across the street.

Parking the car beside the open door, Jesse fished inside his wallet for

Craig's cellular number. Amazingly, none of the contents had been touched, or if they had, they were put back. Looking at the passing traffic and feeling very vulnerable, Jesse punched in the telephone number.

The phone was picked up on the second ring. "Hello?"

"Craig, it's Jesse."

"About bloody time you called. I've been worried sick about you."

"Listen to me, Craig," Jesse interrupted, "you have to get out of there. They picked me up last night when I went to the lab... "

"I told you not to go back there!" Craig butted in. "Where are you, in jail?"

"Will you please *shut-up?* I got away from them by a very big stroke of luck. Not only that, but I found out they used the drug on me at the lab. That means they know everything, Craig. They know about you, the samples, the discs, your job, your wife, your dog, and even the color of your toilet paper. They certainly know you're at Ocean Shores, Craig."

"How do you know they used it on you? I thought you said you would have no recollection of it being used."

"Because," Jesse explained with impatience, "I overheard them talking; I wouldn't know a thing otherwise. They wanted to turn me loose so I would lead them to you if they couldn't find you. You have to get out of there now. There could be a S.W.A.T. team or whatever you call it outside right now for God's sake!"

There was silence on the line.

"Are you there, Craig?"

"Yes, but don't worry, Jess, we've left Ocean Shores already; I was just too nervous sitting there. Let's meet."

Jesse came back, "Look, ...don't under any circumstances head for Canada. They'll have all the approaches to the border covered."

"Wonderful," Craig sighed. "What are you going to do?" The line was silent for a few moments, and Craig could hear the sound of traffic through the earpiece.

Jesse said, "I'm going to ditch my car, I guess. Then rent another one. They won't have had time to start thinking about that yet. Then? I'm not sure."

"You're on a roll. You're ahead of them and you need time to break this open. Hole up someplace for a day or two, then call me. If you would only break down and buy a cellular, Jess."

Jesse was about to answer when Craig continued. "Look, go north, out of the area. I'm going the opposite way."

"What, ...south?" Jesse asked.

"Yes, then probably east to some remote spot where we can make a meet. Okay?"

"Yes," Jesse said, "And Craig, watch out for helicopters, they... "

There was a loud blare of a car horn over the phone, then Craig could hear Jesse's voice a long way back from the telephone.

"Jesus!" Jesse said. There was a loud bang, and then the line went dead.

"Was that Jesse?"

Craig sat looking at the cell phone, and then turned to Jennifer who was standing by the driver's open window. "Yes, and it doesn't look good. Get back to your car and we'll keep going."

It hadn't take Craig long to gather up the few things from his parents place and throw them into the vehicles. He had made his parents place look as unused as possible and had locked the door and put the key back in it's hiding place.

He had not wanted to stay there and couldn't explain why to Jennifer. They were only half way to Hoquiam when Jesse called, and Craig had pulled over to the side of the roadway.

On the outskirts of Hoquiam Craig watched as three vehicles approached him. They were all bumper-to-bumper and moving very fast. Jennifer was still following like they had a tow bar between them and Craig stepped on the gas briefly and widened the gap to three vehicle lengths.

The vehicles shot by in rapid succession, the familiar sound of turbulent air colliding at high speed. All Craig got was a brief picture of two men per car. The vehicles, a mixture of Chevrolets and Fords, stood out like they had flags attached to them. That was enough confirmation for him. Looking in his mirror, he saw the vehicles disappear around a bend in the road.

Going into Hoquiam, the highway split and became a one-way highway, and Jennifer and Craig lost sight of any on-coming vehicles. Craig couldn't see anything approaching from the rear, but he was becoming very nervous. The area was perfect for roadblocks.

At Aberdeen, Craig entered a gas station, fueled up both vehicles, paid with the last of his Canadian money, and swung onto highway 101 South. This far inland the traffic was lighter and visibility was greatly improved, allowing him to boost his speed well above the limit.

High walls of twisted storm-blown evergreens shot by on either side of the roadway, and as the Mustang rounded a curve, his forward vision improved. He found himself facing an oncoming Washington State Patrol car. He immediately tapped the brakes and as he glanced down, he saw he was doing seventy-five miles an hour.

He felt a quickening of his pulse, and had a desire to stomp on the brakes, but he resisted it as the patrol car entered his rear view mirror. Craig increased his speed as the police car disappeared around the bend. He had difficulty seeing past the Cherokee, but a mile further on, the patrol car still had not reappeared in the side mirror. Slowing the car down to five miles above the limit, Craig decided he had enough time and distance for the moment.

Back in Ocean Shores, the quiet beach community was shattered by the deep beat of an approaching helicopter as it came in low over the water. It hovered precisely, allowing the pilot to line up his guns on the little chain link fence and the tired old concrete seagull.

At the same moment, six heavily armed men in flack vests descended on the front and rear of the small home, wasting no time on niceties. Within seconds, the house was entered and searched; the men came out shaking their heads a few minutes later.

As the chopper left, the men began the task of sifting through all the items in the seaside home. The large crowd gathering on the beach and on the roadway was going to be more than a nuisance.

The trip down the coast was not pleasant for Craig or Jennifer. The fog had rolled in and the sun still wasn't hot enough to burn it off. Visibility was down to twenty-five feet at times, and it began to look like it was going to be an all day thing.

Following ponderously slow traffic, Craig knew he and Jennifer were losing time and covering a small amount of distance. It was mid-afternoon when he was able to increase speed and get the hell away from a large transport. They moved eastward towards Interstate-5.

Accelerating onto 'Oregon 84,' Craig found himself swiftly leaving most of the population behind. He was now in the Columbia Gorge. It had been a while since he had been in this part of the country. It was a world of majestic beauty. Washington State and the Columbia River were on his left, and the high cliffs and plateaus of Oregon on his right.

Banners were strung across the street, welcoming people to the wind surfing capital as Craig and Jennifer entered Cascade Locks. A hamburger stand at the side of the highway beckoned, and Craig knew that Jennifer desperately needed a pit stop.

Craig stopped the car and walked back to Jennifer. "Hungry?"

"I'd kill for a cup of coffee and a dozen aspirins."

"You need something to eat. You go and freshen up and I'll get us something."

As he crossed the street, a large paddleboat could be seen coming down the river. It was loaded with tourists hanging onto the rails. A loud steam whistle blew as Craig walked up to the outdoor counter. A man was flipping onions as Craig leaned on the counter.

"Nice town you have here."

"Yeah, it'll do, I guess. No hell in the winter, though. I hafta move back to the city or it'd be starvation time."

"Speaking of which," Craig smiled, "I'll have two of your biggest and best burgers to go. Fries on one, and a small salad with the other."

"There all the same, friend. They're big, the best, and they all gotta go."

While walking over to a small park with the food, the whistle on the paddleboat announced its arrival at, of all places, the park he was sitting in. He sat at a picnic table with the long shadow of the sun warming his skin.

"Isn't that simply gorgeous?"

Craig turned and looked at Jennifer. "Nice spot," he answered. "Kind of makes everything surreal."

Jennifer sat down and picked up her food. "What do you mean?"

"Here we are sitting and eating hamburgers like a couple of tourists, surrounded by some of the most peaceful country around, and I feel like it's all a dream. It's like it's phony, or artificial."

Jennifer pointed to the people walking down a ramp from the paddlewheel. "Right now, I wouldn't mind trading places with them."

They ate their food with an unspoken mutual agreement then walked back towards the vehicles, finishing the last of the coffee as they did. Craig heard the cellular ringing through the open window as he approached.

Running the last few feet, he flung open the door and picked up the phone. "Too damn late," he said aloud.

"Whoever it is, they'll phone back, hon. Let's get going, I don't like it here anymore."

Craig hugged her and smiled. "If anyone calls I'll let you know."

• • •

The sign said, 'Welcome To The Dallas', and as they drove into the middle of town, Craig realized he had had enough for the day. He hadn't really covered that much distance, but God knew when the next place would pop up. He didn't care to be out in the open for too long of a stretch either. As he parked the car and got out, the Oregon cliffs were on fire with a deep golden glow, leaving the river and the town in mirrored splendor. *"We take so much for granted."* he thought, feeling slightly sorry for himself.

The motel wasn't anything fancy, but Craig asked for a rear unit so the vehicles would be out of sight. Putting his credit card back into his wallet, he pushed on the screen door and beckoned Jennifer to follow.

Jennifer was in the shower and Craig was in the middle of sorting some clothes when his cellular warbled again.

"Hello?"

"Is this Craig Fletcher?" a male voice queried.

"Yes. Who's this?"

"I'm a friend of Jesse's, and he asked me to call you."

Jennifer poked her head out from the shower, her eyes burning from the soap running off of her forehead.

"Is that Jesse?" she asked.

"What about Jesse? Hold on a moment."

Craig put the phone down and quickly shook his head no, throwing Jennifer a towel.

"I'm back. What's going on?"

The voice, which sounded like that of an older man, replied. "Jesse gave me a parcel and asked me to get it to you. He said it's important, and that you would know what it was all about."

Finding this strange, Craig asked, "Look, who are you? Jesse can call me himself if he wants."

"Look, that's all I know. Jesse just asked me to call you because he wasn't in a position to do so. He said to tell you it's a slipped disc. Whatever the hell that means."

Craig was feeling uncomfortable about this, but a slipped disc must mean Jesse had another computer disc to unload.

"He really wanted me to get this to you, Mr. Fletcher."

"Okay, okay," Craig said, sitting down on the bed. "I've got your message Mr.... ?"

"Archie Evans. I'm a friend of Jesse's."

"Okay, Archie, where's Jesse now?"

Evans' voice said, "I really don't know, but he asked me to give you the parcel. He thought you might be close to Olympia. Where are you now, Mr. Fletcher?"

Craig was thinking furiously. Something stank. "Where did you see Jesse?"

"Mr. Fletcher?" the guy said, "Where are you now?"

Warning bells were going off at maximum rate. He quickly replied, "I'm in my car right now and I can't make a meet. If you see him, tell him I'll call him in the morning. G'bye."

"Wait Mr... "

Craig hung up. "Stupid, stupid, stupid," Craig said aloud.

"What is it, Hon?"

I don't know, some guy wanting to meet me. Says he has something from Jesse. Maybe I'm just paranoid, but it stank to high heaven." Getting up off of the bed, Craig looked at Jennifer standing wrapped in a bath towel.

"Whoever it is, they obviously think we are still in Washington. Wanted to see me in Olympia."

"He had your phone number," Jennifer offered.

"Yeah, and what else?"

Craig went and had his shower, wondering where the hell Jesse really was. He hoped he wasn't back in the Government's hands. He didn't like this at all.

The aroma of cooking food hit them as they entered the small restaurant. Sitting at a booth at the window Craig looked around at the small group of people eating their meal. One table in particular caught his attention. Two grandparents and a boy and his younger sister seemed to be having a good time.

"I've got that feeling again."

Jennifer, who had been watching Craig closely, asked, "What? What's wrong?"

"Oh, you know. That nothing seems in place. I look at normal people, and I feel like I've been thrown into a vacuum or a nightmare within the last twenty-four hours."

"I know," Jennifer said. "I'm getting a really deep down scared feeling."

Jennifer wiped a loose piece of hair out of her eyes and looked out the window and away from Craig as she spoke. "I... I know it's serious, and it's a decision you had to make on the spur of the moment, but... I wish you hadn't made it. I'm not condemning you, but I guess we wouldn't be sitting here with the hunted feeling we have if you hadn't jumped into it. In fact we wouldn't be sitting here at all."

"I'm not going to lie to you, Jenn," Craig said around a sip of coffee. "It was a stupid decision. A macho decision that I'm caught up in. I just need to think of a way to get out of it without hurting Jess."

Jennifer reached over and rubbed the top of his hand, smiling her reassurance. "We will."

"That's what I like about you, Jenn."

"What? What did I say?"

"You said 'we.' "

The waitress approached the table, and Craig ordered a sandwich.

Jennifer looked at him, and then nodded to the waitress. "The same, thank you."

As she left with the order Jennifer turned to her husband. "You usually have a good appetite."

"I'm just not hungry."

The food arrived and Craig and Jennifer ate without enthusiasm, washing the food down with coffee.

"I have just the thing to relieve anxiety," Jennifer said with raised eyebrows. "If your interested in hearing the remedy, that is."

Craig smiled and leaned forward. "I think I can guess, and it sounds like the best thing I've heard for a long time."

"Pardon me, sir."

Craig looked up at the waitress, noticing her for the first time.

"Can I interest you in some pie?"

Craig and Jennifer looked at each other and burst into laughter, the waitress smiling, but not knowing why.

"Just the bill please," he said, and left a tip on the credit card.

Craig double-checked the Mustang and the Jeep Cherokee to see if they were secure, then strolled to the end of the parking lot. Nothing appeared out of place. He knew it would appear as normal as hell anyway, until they struck.

The room was in darkness as Craig dropped the briefcase onto the floor. Turning from locking the door, Craig was about to call to Jennifer when he felt incredibly soft lips mesh with his.

He closed his eyes and wrapped his arms around her slender body, pulling her close as her lips did fantastic things.

"Let's forget about everything for now. Okay?" she whispered.

"Okay," Craig answered softly against her lips, feeling himself becoming aroused. "First one to the bed gets to be on top."

Laughing, they broke apart and raced across the short distance, Jennifer skidding across the bedspread ahead of Craig.

"You win," Craig smiled into the darkness.

"I know, and don't think for a moment that I don't know you held back."

Craig found her lips. It had been a long time and his desire grew as he tasted the sweetness of her mouth. Her tongue, thrust deeply into his mouth, suddenly disappeared as Jennifer leaped from the bed.

Craig heard the rustle of her clothing. He quickly followed suit, laying back on the bed as Jennifer approached in the darkness. Her whole body covered his in one smooth motion. She was incredibly smooth, and her firm slim body molded to his along the entire length.

While their lips found each other again, he ran his hands over her firm buttocks, pulling her closer and against him. Feeling an instant need, he whispered, "God you feel so damn good."

"We haven't done anything yet," Jennifer said, breathlessly.

"Then I'm done for. I'll never be able to last."

Jennifer chuckled. "You'll last. You always last, and last."

Craig felt her reaching for him, and he was more than ready. He let her take over completely, letting her maneuver and guide him as she wanted.

Craig was instantly engulfed in a feeling of warmth and well-being. But as Jennifer started to rotate her hips, and move up and down the length of him, that feeling of warmth and well-being changed to an urgent demand. Without warning, Craig reached a climax. He felt instantly disappointed. He felt cheated and satisfied at the same time. He wanted more of her.

"I knew you'd do that to me," he said huskily. "It's been too long."

"It doesn't look like that to me," Jennifer said into his ear, and Craig was surprised to find that he still had an erection. Rolling Jennifer onto her back with the two of them still locked together, Craig now sensed her urgency.

It was a time lost. The world didn't exist, except for the time and space reserved for the two of them. All that was pent up, was released. All that was squandered, was regained. Sleep came easy, and time passed without any problems at all.

• • •

Morning came early, and Craig felt a bounce in his step he hadn't felt in a long time. He actually felt pretty good as he looked out over the Columbia River as the early sun was striking the Washington hills.

Craig kissed Jennifer and gave her behind a smack. "Up and at 'em, kid.

We've got to move."

After a quick breakfast they walked towards the vehicles under a light crystal blue sky, smudged with high wispy white clouds that moved slowly in the crisp morning air.

Getting into the car, Craig thought that at least the drive would give him time to think. Looking into the mirror, he saw that Jennifer was just about ready and was busy arranging some unknown article.

Pulling out of the lot, Craig spotted a do-it-yourself car wash about a hundred feet down the road on the opposite side. Looking at the Mustang, and especially Jennifer's Jeep, he decided on a quick wash. Not so much because they were dirty, but because he understood the thinking of most beat cops: if it looked scrungy and out of place, check it. Craig didn't want to be checked.

At the rear of the wash, Craig was surprised to see both stalls in use. An older man was lovingly soaping down his 'fifty-six Ford Fairlane. Smiling at the man and waving, he admired the pink, black, and white colors of a bygone era. The other stall had a young man who was quickly spraying out the box of his pick-up. It didn't look like he was going to be too long.

Craig got out of his car and strolled back to Jennifer.

"Why are we stopping here?" she asked.

"Clean vehicles fit in better than dirty ones. I'm going to take a look around while we're waiting."

Craig walked around the lot, taking in the uniqueness of the town. There were so few of them left, with many of the small towns having lost their own personalities. They all wanted to jump on the franchise bandwagon, and they all ended up being clones.

Two gray Fords, a black Chevy, and a Chrysler New Yorker caught Craig's attention as they all pulled to the side of the highway just west of the motel. One man got out and walked back to each vehicle, then a short time later he got back into the lead car.

Craig watched as they all accelerated at once and entered the motel lot in a cloud of dust. A few moments later there were men with flack vests and shotguns taking cover behind buildings and vehicles, and a couple of marked cruisers pulled up to the front of the entrance and stopped.

Craig's good mood evaporated in an instant. His body was trying to respond to what his brain was trying to tell him, with little success. When it finally registered that he shouldn't be standing there like a spectator, he ran, stopping Jennifer as she was about to enter the self-wash. "Follow me, and do it slowly."

Craig clicked the door of the Mustang quietly shut. The gravel crunched as he eased towards the wash bay then drove through and onto the highway. He accelerated smoothly in an eastward direction with Jennifer following close behind.

He was amazed that his heart was banging within his chest. He had faced danger more times than he could count and his heart had never reacted like this. Then it hit him, he had never been hunted before.

Jennifer was gesticulating in his mirror like mad, wanting to know what the hell was going on. He waved, hoping to tell her it was all right.

Driving east passed the dam he began to climb and was able to look back on the city. There was nothing behind him but a couple of semi-trailers and a fifth wheel recreational vehicle. Craig increased his speed, glad of the light morning traffic.

He hadn't realized it, but his grip on the steering wheel was death-like. He gradually eased it off, sat back, and let out his breath. This was bad. When you react instead of plan, you get trapped.

"Where in Christ did they come from!" Craig thought. He tried to think of what he had done that would lead them to him in the Columbia Gorge, but there was nothing. He hadn't decided to stop until the last minute. *"They must have gotten a tip or something. I haven't even heard a news broadcast."*

The sign said "YAKIMA WASHINGTON - NEXT LEFT." He didn't even have to think about it as he re-crossed the bridge back into Washington State, passing the oasis of Maryhill State Park as he climbed into a backdrop of beauty and peace that made a mockery of how he felt. He wished Jennifer could ride with him.

Climbing out of the gorge onto the plateau, he found himself on highway 97, an uneven stretch of narrow blacktop that dwindled towards the horizon. He pushed the car as fast as the highway would allow, passing a sign that told him the town of Toppenish was some 60 miles ahead. The open plains stretched in all directions. He felt so... so visible and vulnerable. He knew there were only so many roads the police needed to cover.

The drive to Toppenish was uneventful, and it wasn't long before they turned onto highway 82 for the trip to Yakima. The freeway was busy with heavy traffic heading in both directions. Once through Yakima it was all up hill, but the big power plant under the hood had no trouble climbing over the Yakima Ridge.

Looking out to the side Craig saw a high rugged desert with scrub brush and tumbleweed. A dirt road meandered between the hills. A sign warned: *Private Road - Yakima Test Area.*

Looking down into the flat lands of Kittitas County, Craig turned his thoughts to Jennifer. She was in real danger being with him, and he had to be more assertive in getting her to return home. It had been pure foolishness on his part to let her tag a long.

He had to get her back across the border. He felt bad about separating because Jenny didn't really have any family of her own. All she had was him and Lorraine and the relatives on his side of the family.

She had been orphaned when she was a baby, with no other known relatives to look after her. She was eventually adopted and took the name of Montgomery and had, she said, a great childhood. The Montgomerys had been killed in a car crash three years before Craig met her.

He always felt the need to look after her. All he had to do was close his eyes and he could hear her voice and see her standing in front of him. Since he had first laid eyes on her, there had never ever been anyone else for him but Jennifer. He looked in the mirror and felt better seeing her image.

He stopped at a gas station in Ellensburg. He could tell by Jennifer's expression as she got out of the Jeep and into the hot wind that she was not too happy about being left in the dark.

Craig filled the car with gas then pulled to the parking area. He hand signaled Jennifer as she was gassing up to meet him in the restaurant. She nodded and he entered and found a booth overlooking the highway. A few minutes later Jennifer slipped into the booth.

"I ordered two beers. All right?"

"Fine. Now will you tell me what the hell is going on? You've got me worried half to death. What was that all about, back at that car wash?"

"We got out of that motel with only minutes to spare." Craig looked at Jennifer's puzzled expression. "Several cars pulled up to the motel when we were at the car wash Then somebody's emergency response team hit the driveway. I mean, they new *exactly* where they were going."

"Who were they?"

The beer was placed in front of them, and they were asked for their order. Jennifer, becoming impatient, ordered two Patti melts and turned back to Craig. "Well, who were they?"

"I'm not sure. I'd say it was a mixture of locals and some higher agency."

"My God, this is an Abbott and Costello movie," Jennifer said. "I mean this just doesn't happen in real life. It... "

"I've been trying to figure out how they found us. I can't, unless they had a tip. During the night someone may have spotted the cars."

Placing her beer back down, Jennifer asked, "Did you give your own name

BARRY LEE DAVIES

or address at the motel when you registered?"

"Well, I had to use my credit card, and it makes it difficult to use two names at the same time, Jenn."

"You've been on the job long enough to know that the first thing you *do*, is check all local motels and hotels along given routes. How many times have you told me that's how you nab some of these guys?"

"Yeah, well they knew what they were doing, I'll tell you that much."

Craig paused, took a large swallow of his beer, and looked at Jennifer. "I just wish I had an idea what was happening with Jess."

• • •

While the tires on Craig's and Jennifer's vehicles hummed eastward on the hot pavement, Richard Bishop sat back from his keyboard in San Francisco with a smile of satisfaction. "Call ol' Strychnine Miss Thackery, and tell him I have an update for him."

"You're going to get caught calling Strychnine, strychnine, one of these days," Marion said, and they both laughed together as only two close friends can. "Okay," Marion smiled, "What have you got on this Fletcher guy? And it better be good. Nothing pleases Strickler that often."

"Oh, it's good. Right now he's in Ellensburg."

"How'd you find that out?" Marion Thackery asked, sitting on the edge of his desk.

"It's magic. In this case however, it's just a matter of tapping into various things such as his bank cards, gas cards, when he uses his cellular..."

"Yeah, I can see it would be simple," Marion offered in a sarcastic way.

"Well, I have a little help from a friend called *Echelon* and the National Security Agency. It sort of provides me with some little inroads."

"*Echelon*. Never heard of it," Marion stated.

"Not many have," Bishop said, turning serious. "Uncle Sam is very serious about protecting *and* gathering raw information and data. Other countries are always trying to hit on us, not to mention Joe-schmo in his bedroom."

"All right, when you get it all together let me know and I'll open a direct line to Strickler and his pet ape, Grant. I don't want to pass everything in bits and pieces. The less I talk to him the better."

As she was leaving the room Bishop asked, "What package? Right now all

I have is a new location for him to follow up on."

"Fine, but it'll be a while. I'm still trying to set up this command relay."

"It's your ass," Bishop said turning back to his monitor. "And not bad, either," he muttered.

"I heard that, Richard," Marion said from the other room.

He was a big likable guy with a six-foot-four-inch, two hundred and twenty-five pound frame. He wasn't the type you looked at and thought of as a computer hack. He looked like he should be roping cows, or cutting the tops off of trees two hundred feet off of the ground. But he wasn't.

Born thirty-one years ago in North Dakota, he did his regular stint in the local schools, and then moved to New York State for his university education. Over a period of time he fell in love with computers and found a job with the federal government. The fact was, the government found him, in the name of the National Security Agency, and had held onto him at Ft. Meade.

His expertise landed him at Ft. Huachuca, Arizona and the USAIC, the United States Army Intelligence and Security Center. A few years later he found himself involved in the *Echelon Project* and was moved to the San Francisco area. He took on many projects as required. Right now, orders were to avoid everything else and fill all requests of Major Strickler.

The fact was, he could track down anything, anywhere, as well as intercept any communication whatsoever. He didn't know what his digging was used for, or why people were being tracked, but he didn't care. What mattered to him was the chase.

He had access to airlines, credit cards, banks, some very surprising corporations, and government agencies that thought they were ultra secure. He was able to get into most places, get what he wanted, and leave without a trace.

Sometimes, but not often, he shuffled complicated strings of computer code and he was into a world of information that would boggle the imagination of the average citizen. Thank God he was honest, because he had the ability to move vast amounts of money around the globe.

The tracking of one or two individuals was infinitely easier. All he had to do was sit back, like a spider, and wait for them to shake the web. It didn't matter that the web was the size of Washington State.

• • •

They moved east on Interstate 90 at a fast clip. Crossing the Columbia

River again at Vantage, they began the long climb to flat, open farm country. Approaching the town of George, Washington, Craig thought it would be thriving. He passed it in a blink.

He couldn't just keep driving eastward! He needed to talk to Jesse. Spokane was getting near to his limit and he was soon going to turn north.

Traffic was fairly brisk on the outskirts of Spokane, and Craig soon realized that the city seemed to always be below him and was passing him by. Signaling, and easing over to the pull-off ramp, he kept an eye on Jennifer as he exited at the next ramp.

Driving the main artery, Craig scanned all the available motels for a combination of comfort, security, and easy access. He wanted to feel secure and out of sight, but he didn't want a dump.

A few minutes later he found what he wanted. Scouting the area and the layout of the local roads, he was satisfied that he wasn't boxed in, and went back to register.

"What's with all the driving around?" Jennifer asked as she got out to stand next to Craig.

"Just a precaution. If we have to leave, I want more than one direction open to us." Craig looked up and down the motel parking lot. "This okay with you?"

"Yeah, I guess, but it's a little early isn't it? We could keep going to the border."

"Jesse told me to keep away from the border for the time being, but I want to be off of the road and out of sight."

Jennifer dug into her purse. "Here, take this. It's the last that I have. There's no sense in charging anything."

Craig took the Canadian bills, gave her a quick kiss on the lips, and walked to the motel office. The friendly manager accepted the Canadian money, apologizing for discounting the dollar. A few moments later, Craig and Jennifer found themselves in a bright, clean, and very modern room.

He had registered under a different name this time, and had even altered his license plate. He hoped that Mr. Alderwood wouldn't be under too close a scrutiny.

Craig walked to a corner deli and picked up some food and a couple of bottles of wine. They both needed to relax and get rid of some stress. When he returned, Jennifer was wearing new faded jeans, a dark maroon top, and just the right touches of gold jewelry. Her blue eyes sparkled when she looked up at him, her dark hair framing a welcoming smile.

Craig placed the parcels on the table and put his arms around her. "I don't know how you do it. I put you through hell, you drive all day in dust and heat and traffic, and you still look absolutely gorgeous."

"Sweet talk will get you everywhere, if you're careful," Jennifer smiled.

"Look, I brought some yummies, and some wine. Then you and me are going out for supper."

"Are you trying to cheer me up, or yourself?" Jennifer smiled, sitting down at the table to see what Craig had purchased.

Picking up a bottle of red wine, Craig answered. "A little of both." Showing the bottle of wine to Jennifer, he asked, "So, you happen to have a cork screw?"

Jennifer and Craig looked at each other, then laughed at the same time. It felt good to laugh.

• • •

They drove at a leisurely pace, taking in the sights and sounds of a different city, and decided supper could wait for a while. Craig pulled into one of the city parks, and they walked along the Spokane River for a while. Craig steered her towards a park bench.

"You keep a lot inside, don't you, Craig?" Jennifer asked. "I mean, you must be worried."

Craig leaned back and watched the river moving past before answering, aware that Jennifer expected an honest answer. He looked over at her. "Of course I'm worried. I'm worried about Jesse and I'm worried about us, and I'm worried about what I'm involved with here. Christ, I'm even worried about Shepherd, if you want to know."

"Well, I can ease your mind on one item, Craig. You can stop worrying about us. I love you and we're back together again. Okay?"

Craig picked up her hand from her lap and squeezed it, looking into her eyes before he spoke. "Yes, but it's because I love you that, well... you're going to have to go home, Jenn."

She turned sideways on the bench, instantly alert to something she didn't like.

"Now wait a moment while I explain," Craig continued. "I can't have you on my conscience if we get arrested. I don't want you to be any part of this. If something happens, you could be the only outside help I would have."

"I'm staying with you," Jennifer said, her lips set in a determined fashion.

"Well, we can talk about it later."

"No, we'll talk about it now. We are very close to the Canadian border and I want the two of us to leave here and go home."

"Tell you what, let's see if we hear from Jess. It might even be better to go further east before trying to cross over. The further east we are, the less the pressure will be on the border points. Let's go for supper. We can talk some more while we eat."

• • •

"God, that was good. Thank heavens I didn't have to eat another hamburger."

Craig laughed. "Yes, it was good."

On the way back to the motel, Jennifer leaned against him in a comfortable way. He was about to put his arm around her when she broke the silence. "You know, it doesn't make sense. What did you do to lead them to you? Can you think of anything?"

Pulling away on a green light, Craig scratched his head absently, then brought his hand back down to the steering wheel with a whomp. "Nothing. Not a damn thing! They came down on that motel in The Dalles like they knew exactly what they were looking for. They knew we were there, and they bloody well *expected* us to be there when they made their move."

"Craig, we have to get back into Canada. Do you understand what I'm saying, Craig? The border is your best protection until you can make a decision."

"Let's wait and see if Jesse calls." Locking the car, he opened the trunk and took out the briefcase, quickly crossing to the motel door. "I'm going to take a quick walk around. Take this inside and lock the door; *don't* go to sleep."

"Don't worry lover boy, I'll be awake."

Craig kept to the shadows and skirted the main entrance. He walked around the block, taking in anything that appeared to be suspicious. A dog barked at him as he walked too close to a fence, causing him to jump and curse his own nerves. Twenty minutes later he was back at the room, and let himself in with his key.

After entering, he closed the door, and was about to turn on a light when Jennifer spoke. "Don't turn it on. Everything all right?"

"Looks okay," Craig said as he took off his shirt and sat on the edge of the bed.

He felt Jennifer move on the bed, and a few moments later her arms wrapped around his shoulders from behind. "You okay?" she whispered.

"Okay," he said, turning around and giving her a kiss on the lips.

Getting into bed a few moments later, he reached over and his hand fell on her satin covered breast. He ran his hand down to her waist and pulled her close.

"Mmm, nice," he breathed.

"It's called a T.R.M.," Jennifer said.

"What is a T.R.M.?"

"That's short for tension reliever machine."

"Some machine. Get me the mold so I can make more."

Jennifer grabbed him by his ears and lifted him to face her. "You don't need anymore than what you already have, you greedy little boy."

"Okay. Let's see, where do you start this thing. Here? Or here? Or maybe..."

"Ohhh, I think you've found the main switch."

"Good, now lets see how well this machine of yours works."

• • •

Jennifer had to shake Craig several times to pull him out of his deep sleep. "Come on, Craig, get out of bed."

Craig stirred, looked up, and reached for her. "Come here a moment."

"Not on your life. Remember what you said about the last motel we stopped in? Let's get out of here."

"You're right," Craig said, instantly awake, and heading for the shower. "We'll check out of here, then take both cars and get some breakfast."

• • •

Sitting by the window, they both accepted another cup of coffee as their breakfast dishes were cleared away.

Jennifer pointed out the window. "Look, a police cruiser over by your car."

Turning and looking over his shoulder, Craig saw the police car parked slightly to the rear of the Mustang on the opposite side of the street about a half a block away. A uniform police officer was standing at the rear of the car talking on a portable radio.

"Jenn, we've got big trouble. I should have listened to Jesse. I dropped the samples in the trunk instead of keeping the briefcase with me," Craig said, looking into her concerned eyes.

"Damn! He warned me."

"Once he checks, you can bet you're not going to get your car back," she said, looking up, then down the street.

They both sat there, waiting to see what would happen. The marked police unit had backed off, parked further to the rear of the Mustang, and against the curb near a large truck.

"He's waiting for something," Craig said.

"Yeah, us. If we go near that car we'll be arrested for sure."

"No, Jenn, he's waiting for something else. He would have had back-up by now if that's all it was."

An unmarked car slowly glided to a stop next to the marked police car. The uniformed officer could be seen pointing towards the Mustang. The unmarked car backed up and the patrol car left, the vehicle with the two men sliding into the vacant spot.

"Jenn," Craig sighed, "I think I just lost everything-- my clothes, the car, and Jesse's samples. They've got 'PRECISE'."

•••CHAPTER FIVE

Lieutenant General Randolph Miller left the officer's dining room at the Pentagon in a foul mood and headed back to his office in answer to a page. He had been looking forward to a leisurely lunch followed by a round of golf, but he knew he could probably kiss that idea goodbye. He simply didn't get a page unless it was important.

Miller was director of Defense Advanced Research Projects,(DARP), which included Biochemical Advanced Research Testing (BRAT), officed in Arlington, Virginia. He also had office space in the Pentagon.

The corridors were practically deserted due to the weekend routine, and although Miller was almost used to the structure, he couldn't get over the fact that someone had the gall to build an office building with six million, five hundred, and forty thousand square feet of office space-- and not an elevator to be seen anywhere.

Sitting down to his desk, slightly out of breath because of his five-foot-ten, one hundred ninety pound frame, he re-lit the cigar he had been enjoying when his pager had gone off. Punching the glowing light, he growled, "Miller here, Sir."

"Yes sir, General Miller, this is Major Strickler, Sir."

"Ah," Miller said somewhat relieved. "This better be good. In fact, it better be bloody important to have interrupted what I was doing." Miller could detect the pause before Strickler answered, and knew he wasn't going to like what was coming.

"I'm sorry, sir. There has been a major development in connection with our program… Ah, General, could I ask if your phone is secure?"

Miller reached over and activated a switch, leaned back and puffed on his cigar, dropping ash down the front of his immaculate uniform. "All right, get on with it, Major."

"Yes, sir. It's to do with 'PRECISE.' We've had a serious security breach at the lab in Maple Falls."

Miller sat forward, the blood draining from his face, dreading hearing how much of a security breach had taken place. This was *his* ass on the line here. "Go ahead," he said in a strained voice.

"It can't get much worse, Sir. The whole thing is gone. The…"

Miller burst out, "What do you mean, Miller, by the whole thing is gone?" Miller could hear Strickler take a deep breath before answering the question.

"On Friday…"

"Friday!" Miller exploded. "Something happened on Friday and you're just getting around to telling me now?"

"Please, General, I have a lot of information to pass on to you."

"Okay Major, you just go ahead and spell it out. Spell it out nice and clear." Miller flipped a switch and started the tape recorder.

"On Friday, Grant made a routine call to our agent in place, Hank Corey, and when he did, Corey was giving him some strange answers. We paid a visit and found out that he had been given the experimental drug. He had told Jesse Harris, the person in charge of the lab project, about the military application and the field testing for the Justice Department."

There was no interruption, just silence on the line, so Strickler continued. "When we arrived, Corey was alone and Harris was gone. Along with the samples, discs, and… I'm afraid all of the information on 'PRECISE.' "

"Oh my God!" Miller whispered to himself. He heard Strickler continue on the other end of the line.

"He wiped his computer clean, sir. The back-up information is still on the mainframe of course, but it's obvious he tried to take everything, and he carried top secret information out of the lab."

Miller sat there, stunned. His mind refused to absorb the colossal blow, not only to the program, but also to his personal position. He began to feel personal ruin, and his thoughts were starting to drift. His career could be over. Strickler said something that brought him back to the conversation

"…have Harris in custody again soon."

"What was that, Major? I missed that."

"I said we should have Harris in custody again soon, Sir."

Miller was not hearing right. "*I must be in a dream!*" Miller thought.

"What *are* you talking about, Strickler? What do you mean, *back* in custody?"

Strickler sighed over the phone, hesitated, and then reluctantly began to recount the events. "Sir, we arrested him on Friday. We had a stakeout and we were lucky to grab him. Before taking him to Ft. Lewis, I shot him full of 'PRECISE'. He told us he gave everything to a guy by the name of Fletcher for safe keeping."

"Fletcher? Who's this Fletcher?"

"He's a Canadian cop. Harris called him to help out after he took the stuff. Anyway, sir, after we learned all we could, I ordered him taken back to the lab, under close surveillance, so he would lead us to this Fletcher."

"If I'm not going completely out of my mind, Major Strickler, what you are about to say is that you fucked up! Tell me it isn't so."

"He was under guard at the lab. During a fire alarm, in the confusion, he left the lab in a hurry in his car. We have a full alert out for him now."

Thinking clearer now, Miller asked, "Where is this Fletcher person now? What have you learned?"

"Sir," Strickler could be heard rattling some pages. "Harris filled us in on personal stuff. The rest I got from his boss in Vancouver. A guy named Shepherd. There is no love lost there, sir. He bent over backwards for me. He said Fletcher is charged with various departmental charges, and is facing dismissal."

"So, now we're dealing with a rogue cop. Wonderful. That means he's been trained to some degree and probably has plenty of street smarts. This is not good, Strickler," Miller commented quietly. "What else have you dug up?"

"We almost nabbed him at a motel in Oregon."

"Oregon!" Miller thundered towards the speakerphone. "This does not look like containment to me at all. Next you'll be telling me he's in Texas."

"He has a cellular, General, and we're able to track his movements every time he uses the phone. In fact... Could you hold for a moment please? I have some Intel coming in."

Miller sat and fumed. He was still having trouble adapting to the abrupt turn of events. He had gone from a delightful lunch to a full-fledged nightmare.

"*How am I going to pass this up the chain?*" Miller thought. "*The minute*

I say anything, I'm finished".

There was a task force set into place for this kind of problem, but there weren't supposed to *be* any problems. There were just too many irons in the fire right now. The C.I.A., Justice, The State Department, and the National Security Agency were all counting on him to deliver. My God! It was incomprehensible. How was he going to explain this?

He yelled in frustration, "Where the hell are you, Strickler?"

The phone rattled in his ear and Strickler's voice filled Miller's head. "Sir?"

"Oh, I'm still here, Major."

"Yes, sir. I just received word that Fletcher's vehicle is under surveillance in Spokane. The local police spotted it and called the F.B.I. They're waiting for us to show up."

"Your boy does get around, doesn't he, Major. He's also closer to Canada. You think of that?" Before Strickler could reply, Miller continued. "You get your ass over there, or up there, or whatever direction it is, and get our goods back. And keep the goddamn F.B.I. out of it. Clear?"

"Of course, sir."

"Another thing," Miller said, flipping the switch and turning off the tape. "I don't give a fiddler's fuck about this, Fletcher. I want that package back with or without his co-operation. Do we understand what I'm saying here, Strickler? This is a national security matter and if extreme measures are required, use them. Are we on the same wavelength?"

"You bet, sir."

"Oh, and Major, I'm ordering up a full electronic scan on the *Echelon Network*. Any son of a bitch even breathes the word 'PRECISE' in this country, and I'll have more fucking marines in his backyard than you can bivouac.

Miller briefly thought of the massive communications at his fingertips, and the global electronic surveillance system neatly placed between Saddle Mountain and the Rattlesnake Hills just outside of Yakima, Washington.

Project P415 was the National Security Agencies ultra secret operation, and the Army's Yakima Firing Center with over two hundred and sixty thousand acres was just one of a series of centers geared to retrieve just about every signal on earth. Other countries such as Canada, England, and New Zealand were also involved in the intelligence gathering.

With key words entered into computers Cowboy, as Yakima was known, could hear or receive every telex, cellular phone, e-mail, fax, or microwave transmission, in the Western half of North America and the Pacific. The easiest pickings were individuals, such as Craig Fletcher.

"Sir? Is there anything else?" Strickler said over the speakerphone.

"Yes, I'm going to send you back some of the drug. Just in case you need it in the field."

"Yes, sir," Strickler stated. "What about Hank Corey, our man at the lab?"

"I'll ship him out; get rid of him. He'll be sent to some remote area with a promotion. You remind this Corey fellow that he will live a long life, as long as he remembers to keep his mouth shut."

"I'll do that, Sir," Strickler promised.

Miller sat back, sighed, and brought the conversation to a close. "Now get your ass moving, Major, and don't be shy about keeping me informed. I am *not* a happy soldier." Miller, reaching for another telephone, couldn't control an inner feeling of dread.

• • •

Jesse, the subject of everyone's attention, was in Burlington, Washington, holed up in claptrap of a motel used by migrant fruit pickers. He hadn't been able to sleep, and he felt like hell.

His clothes were rumpled and he had been afraid to take them off to sleep. He had even skipped his shower because it made him feel vulnerable. He had the feeling that someone was going to burst into the room at any moment.

He asked himself for the hundredth time, "W*here the hell is Craig?"* He had been trying to reach him non-stop with no luck. The last time he had talked to Craig, he had called from the telephone booth.

He remembered catching the black car out of the corner of his eye. Two men were looking at him as they passed slowly on the other side of the median. He was about to say something else to Craig, when the driver of the black car gunned the engine and turned left, trying to bounce the car over the center concrete curbing.

Gray and white smoke billowed up from the tires as the vehicle got hung up on its undercarriage. The air vibrated with the sound of horns and squealing brakes.

Jesse remembered yelling something as he dropped the phone and ran for his car, the sound of metal crashing into metal, and tires spinning on pavement as he slammed the door.

The driver was rocking the car back and forth, shifting from drive to reverse in an effort to break free of the barrier. The passenger, holding onto the dashboard, had a large black pistol in his hand.

Jesse floored the Lincoln across the remainder of the parking lot, bouncing off a paper box and entering the road by flying off of the curb. Looking into his mirror he saw the car gain access to his side of the highway. Jesse was no pro, and he knew it. As long as he stayed in their line of sight he was doomed.

At the first opportunity he turned right, then made an immediate turn into a back lane behind a group of businesses heading back in the direction he had started from. Taking a chance after reaching the end of the lane, Jesse turned right and reentered the highway. As he passed the street for the second time, he saw no sign of the black car. He knew they wouldn't be fooled for long.

Increasing speed, Jesse blended into traffic until he reached Bellevue, then crossed Lake Washington on highway 520 until he hit Interstate-5. The car was his giveaway. He had to find a place to hide it.

Jesse angled over to highway 99 just North of Lake Union. He was starting to relax a bit when the radio came to life with a bulletin. All I-5 traffic had been reduced to two lanes north bound, and State and local police sealed all exits for vehicle checks. What Jesse had heard next almost made him run into the rear of the car in front.

> *"Federal, State, and local police, are at this moment, searching for an escaped fugitive by the name of Jesse Harris, sought by federal authorities for espionage. Harris was last seen driving a late model white Lincoln Towncar. He is described as being 40 years of age and six foot, five inches tall.*
>
> *Harris is wanted for espionage and theft of government property. Police advise the public not to approach Harris, as this individual is armed and dangerous. Contact your local F.B.I. office or your local police immediately. Stay tuned to this station for breaking developments. We now return to regular programming."*

Jesse felt alone and hopeless. There was no direction or person to turn to. *"There isn't anyone!"* Jesse thought. He headed North on 99, not knowing his next step and wondering if he should try to reach Craig again.

A mini-storage complex was passing by on the left, the word *VACANCY* was scrawled across a small billboard. Jesse slowed, an idea emerging like the early morning sun over a dark mountain.

Fifteen minutes later he had rented himself a full garage, bought a padlock, and walked away from the Lincoln. It was safe, and out of sight. The guy hadn't looked twice at him. Hadn't asked any questions other than his name and address, and was glad to accept two months cash, in advance.

After getting directions, a ten-minute walk from the mini-storage complex took him to the car rental agency. He had no choice, the only thing available was a small red Taurus. He completed the paperwork and climbed inside. He was surprised that he had the leg room he needed.

He was tired, hungry, and felt like he needed a shower. All his decisions were being made on the spur of the moment, and it caused tension. There was no planning. But then, maybe that was what kept him from getting caught.

The sign announced '*MUKILTEO FERRY,*' and again on an impulse, Jesse turned west. He felt the tension starting to ease as he got further away from the main flow of traffic. The ferry was loading the last row of cars as he pulled up to the booth. "Can I make this sailing?" he asked the woman.

"Pull into row one," was all he received in reply.

Jesse pulled the red Taurus ahead, and was surprised when he was waved towards the ferry. The sound of clang, clack, reached his ears as the vehicle passed from the dock to the ferry. He was waved to the left, and was squeezed between a motor home and a van full of dogs. Five minutes later, the ferry left for Whidbey Island.

The island was like another world. Tall trees flicked by as he drove casually north on the road from the ferry. The sun played tricks on the windshield at it was filtered through the trees above the car, and Jesse began to feel sleepy.

He could see the ocean to the left with a few ships visible on the horizon, and he got an unexpected yearning. He wished he could be free and traveling somewhere new and different. Suddenly he realized that he hadn't actually had a real holiday in four years. "*Unbelievable,*" he thought. "*All that time trying to build something, only to turn around and destroy it.*"

No, that wasn't true. He wasn't going to destroy all he had worked to accomplish. There was good in what he had made, but there was also the corrupt. Somehow, he had to put an end to that corruption.

He drove northward, frustration turning to depression. He was down on himself for bringing everything he loved to an end. He was down on himself for involving a very good friend, a friend who would do anything just for the asking.

Passing through Coupeville, the surrounding countryside turned into rolling hills and winding curves, with high trees using the ocean as a backdrop. Again, it was a place out of time and synch with his dilemma.

Jesse topped up the tank in the navy town of Oak Harbor and decided to buy a map of Washington. He was walking back towards the door when he casually looked towards a newspaper dispenser. The front page displayed a full color photo of a man. Jesse took another three steps before he realized it was a picture of him.

Jesse looked around nervously, and quickly put the required coins into the slot. Back in the car, he drove off of the lot and drove a mile further north before pulling off of the road to glance quickly at the article.

There was nothing different to enlighten him. It was a repeat of what he already knew, and the article didn't mention where the authorities were focusing their search. It didn't mention Craig, which was good. He knew he would feel better if he could only talk to him. He vowed to do that at the next phone booth.

● ● ●

He had located the motel room in Burlington, staying in the room as much as he could until the sight of the walls drove him crazy with anxiety. Finding a phone booth beside a quiet store, he dialed Bev's number. It was picked up within half a ring.

"Hello," she said, with an almost urgent plea in her voice.

"It's me, Bev."

"Oh, Jess! Where are you? What's going on? They're saying all sorts of things on the news about you."

Jesse tried to speak calmly. "I know, Bev, I know. I'll tell you everything I can, but not over the telephone. I... "

"I've been going crazy," Bev said in a rush. "I feel like I don't know you. You haven't told me a thing about this. What's happening?"

"This wasn't planned, Bev."

"You know you can trust me to do anything for you, Jess, just don't let anything happen to you," she said, starting to cry.

"Look, I do trust you. I just don't want you hurt. I can't stay on this phone too long so would you do something for me? Pack your bags. I want you to go to Canada."

"I don't know anyone in Canada, for crying out loud!" Bev said in a hysterical voice.

"Yes you do, Bev. You know Craig, and Jennifer, and you like them a lot. I want you to go to Craig's place and stay there until I call."

"How long will you be?" Bev asked.

"I don't know. I do know I'll have a lot off of my mind knowing you're in a safe place. Please Bev, don't argue. Just do it."

There was a bit of a pause, and then she said, "All right, I'll leave in the morning. I have their address and phone number written down. Is there anything you need, Jess?"

"I need for you to be out of there. Please don't wait until morning. Pack-up and go now."

"Be careful, Jess. I love you. You know that don't you?"

"Yes, yes I do, and I love you. Please promise you will leave right away."

"Yes, okay. Jesse, what is *going on*? The television said there is a large manhunt taking place. They said..."

"Bev, it's too much to tell right now. Please leave like I asked."

"All right," Bev said, her world falling apart.

"Good. I have to go. I love you," he said quietly, and lowered the handset onto the cradle.

That had been yesterday, and he was no further ahead. He hadn't contacted Craig, and he hadn't slept until the first rays of dawn. Then he had overslept.

He had taken a quick shower and headed for a phone booth. The heat was starting to build, the road taking on a glassy appearance in the distance as he entered the phone booth. Craig punched in the numbers to Craig's cellular.

"The cellular customer... "

He hung up and stood there feeling his blood pressure rising. There weren't many options left open to him until he got through. Picking up the handset again, he dialed Craig's home number. The phone rang three times; a male answered it.

"Hello?"

"Ah...is Jennifer or Craig there please?"

"No, they're not. You got a message?"

"I'm a friend of Jennifer and Craig, and, ah, can you tell me who I'm talking to please?"

"Me? I'm just a neighbor. Looking after the dog and the plants. Just happened to be here when you called. Names Stark. Eldon Stark."

"Mr. Stark, I'm trying to find Craig. Do you know where I can reach him?"

"Well... no I don't.

"Has he telephoned you? Have you heard from either of them, Mr. Stark? It's really important."

"No, no I haven't. You want me to tell them you called?"

"No. No thanks, Mr. Stark."

"Call me Eldon. Try again, maybe they'll phone and I'll tell them you called."

"Thanks. Bye Eldon."

"Good..."

Jesse almost forgot, but spoke just before Eldon Stark hung-up. "Oh Eldon, I almost forgot. My girl will be arriving to visit Jennifer. She doesn't know that Jennifer is gone. Could you keep an eye out for her and let her into the house?"

Stark answered quickly. "Oh, I don't think I can do that. I'm responsible for this place, and I just can't let anybody into..."

"Eldon," Jesse said. "Honestly, we are not strangers. I'll tell you anything you want to know about Jennifer and Craig. You won't get into trouble."

"Well... I'll see when this girl gets here. I like to look people in the eye. What's her name?"

"Bev. Her name's Bev, and you'll fall in love with her as soon as you see her."

Stark laughed. "Oh I will, will I? Well, I guess I better be careful." Then, "Oh, I'll see what can be done, don't worry about it."

Jesse thanked him and rung off. He stood there with the phone in his hand, not knowing what to do next. He couldn't even drive in any particular direction.

Jesse walked to a nearby cafe and grabbing a paper, he buried himself in a corner booth. Scanning the headlines Jesse looked for new developments, but it was *U.S. Today* and he couldn't find anything concerning him.

Ordering his breakfast, he turned back to the paper, sipping his coffee.

PRESIDENT TO ADDRESS THE NATION.

The White House announced that the President will address the nation on Wednesday at 3.00 p.m. Washington time.

Foreign relief programs, such as those provided to Russia, are expected to be the key issues advanced by the President, but a reliable source from within the Administration indicates that the President may deal with the problem of crime.

The announcement that the President wanted more airtime came as a surprise to network executives, as the President spoke on national airwaves only two months ago.

Jesse scanned the rest of the paper but found nothing in relation to him or Craig or Inter-America. Leaving the cafe, Jesse walked out into brilliant sunlight and headed to the phone booth. Swirling dust from passing vehicles lingered in the windless air, and he had the beginning of a headache from the bright sun and the glare.

He ended up in what wasn't really a booth, but one of the half-baked extrusions that stick out from the wall and do nothing to keep out the weather or traffic noise. Jesse put in the coins and pressed each button firmly, as if he could force the call to go through.

It rang, and again, then-- "Hello," a female voice answered.

"Jennifer! Is that you? It's Jesse." Feeling a great weight lifting off of his shoulders, he said, "What's left of my poor nerve-wracked brain, anyway."

"Jesse! Where... wait. Wait, I'll put Craig on."

Craig came onto the phone, thundering into his ear.

"Where the hell have you been, friend? I've been worried sick waiting for you to call!"

Jesse smiled in exasperation. "That makes two of us. I haven't *exactly* been on a holiday. Don't you *ever* answer your phone?"

"It's been on, Jess. Maybe I've been in a bad area when you called. I've been worried sick since you dropped the phone on me."

"Two guys came at me in a car. One of them had a big mother of a gun... I was lucky."

Craig spoke into his ear. "I don't like this, Jess. This is getting rough, and you're not geared for this game. Are you in a safe spot?"

"Yeah, right now I'm..."

"Don't tell me over the phone, Jess, I'm getting paranoid about everything I do."

"Yeah?" Jesse guffawed. "Well I'm glad I can share some paranoia with somebody. More like agony." Jesse paused, almost feeling euphoric now that he was talking to Craig. "I want to meet with you right away. I want the package back and the two of you to get back to Canada."

"Easier said than done." Craig sounded pessimistic over the miles. "At this moment, ol' buddy, they are sitting on my car, and I.... ah, got a little careless."

Jesse didn't want to hear any bad news. "They're watching your car? Craig, get away from there!"

"We can't. I left the samples in the trunk."

"Ah shit, Craig, I asked you to keep them with you. Without them I won't have a leg to stand on."

Jesse was immediately contrite, aware that he had put them through hell. "I'm sorry, Craig, I have no right to come down on you. I guess the samples are as good as gone."

"Not yet, I think they're waiting for us to show up. They could even be working blind. Told to look for the car, not knowing why."

Jesse leaned against the small cubicle, scratching his unruly hair in the rising heat. "What are you going to do? What's... ?"

"You let me worry about that. You're not here and can't help. Let's concentrate on where we should meet up."

"All right, Craig, but I don't want you or Jenn taking any chances. Understand?"

"We'll be careful," Craig stated. "If I can get the samples back, Jess, I will. I think the police are biding their time until someone else shows up."

"Okay! Where should we meet? I got to do something or I'll go nuts."

"I can tell you where I am, Jess, because they already know. I'm in Spokane. Look, head east. Let's plan to meet in, ah... hold on, I've got to think about this."

Jesse waited while Craig went over things in his mind, contented to let him take over.

"Jesse, meet us in Montana, somewhere around Havre, okay? Then you can decide what you want to do with your package."

Jesse groaned. "Ah man, that's just it, I don't *have* a plan; none at all. It's crazy...."

"It's not crazy," Craig announced. "It's normal. The drive to Montana will give you a chance to formulate one. Think of your contacts over the years. Think of the honest people you know. You can't finalize a plan until we have a chance to sit down and talk rationally anyway. Come on, Jess, buck up!"

"Okay, I'm on my way. Havre it is."

"Jess, I said the Havre area. There's a big difference. Keep your eyes and ears open and call me when you're within a reasonable distance. Listen, Jess, I have to go, Jennifer's spotted something."

"What? What's going on?" Jesse asked.

"Can't talk, gotta go. Call me!"

Jesse heard the click, and hung up. He felt sick with worry. The tension was coming back. He put his head against the plexi-glass, the coolness spreading across his forehead in welcome relief. There was a click of a car door. Standing erect, Jesse turned and looked into the mirrored sunglasses of a Washington State Trooper. *"I never even heard the car pull up for Christ's sake!"* Jesse thought.

Jesse looked left, then right, in desperation, looking for a means of escape. He knew he was acting weird. Guilty was more like it. He should say *something!*

"You got a problem buddy?" the uniform asked.

"Ah,... Ah, not really officer. I, ah, just got some bad news and I was just standing here thinking about it, is all."

"You look a little green around the gills. You want me to take you down to Admitting?"

"No," Jesse said a little too quickly. "I'm fine. I... I just need to go home that's all. Thanks anyway." Jesse turned to leave and the police officer placed his hand on Jesse's shoulder.

"Just a minute."

Jesse turned and looked at himself in the mirrored sunglasses, unable to gauge what was coming next. He quickly saw his chance for Havre, Montana disappearing. The officer was speaking, and he hadn't heard everything he had said.

"....The news"

"Sorry? I didn't hear you." Jesse was sweating. *"He saw me on the news. He knows!"*

"I said," the mirrored sunglasses repeated, "are you sure you're okay? I'm sorry about the news. You know? You said you got some bad news. By the looks of it, it's sure as hell shook you up, fella."

"I'm okay," Jesse stammered. "Thanks for your concern."

He started walking away, not sure he was going to make it, knowing if the cop called to him again, he would run like he had never run in his life.

• • •

The sign read: *East - Washington 20.* Jesse was trying to calculate how long it would take him to get to Montana, when something caught his eye in the rear-view mirror. Four flashing strobes on the top of a police car were rapidly filling his mirror. Growing with each second.

Jesse licked his lips and his hands started to sweat on the steering wheel. He was on the outskirts of Burlington, with nowhere to hide.

Seeing a gas station, he quickly pulled off of the road and up to the pumps as the cruiser flew by, a siren shrieking ahead of it. Looking over at the building, he saw a sign in the window. '*CLOSED.*' The place was boarded up.

His hands were trembling on the steering wheel of the idling car. How long was this going to continue? His nerves were shot and he jumped at everything! He thought for sure that cop was coming for him.

Pulling back onto the highway, he found himself behind an old stinking diesel bus, the fumes belching out to the rear every time the driver shifted gears or stepped on the gas pedal. Passing was impossible for miles because of limited visibility.

Finally getting the chance, Jesse pulled out and charged ahead. Rounding a bend, the car dipped into a bit of Mother Earth's cleavage then rose, coming straight over a rise at sixty-five miles an hour towards the flashing lights of a police unit.

The police vehicle was parked across the road, blocking east bound traffic, and half of the west bound lane as well. The only way to get by was a tight squeeze onto the shoulder of the road. Four vehicles were in front of Jesse. Some guy in a red-checkered shirt was waving the lead vehicle, a farm truck, through the tight squeeze.

Jesse couldn't see the police officer anywhere, but he now had a better view of what was happening. The rear of a pick-up truck was jutting out from the right ditch, the driver's door hanging open at an odd angle. The roadway and ditch gouged out where the door had come in contact with the ground when the truck left the road.

There was something else, but the car in front obstructed his view. Pulling ahead, he saw why the road was blocked. A cop in uniform, his back to Jesse, was bent over a man lying on the roadway.

The checkered shirt was waving at, Jesse, glaring and yelling, "C'mon, jerk! Drive the friggin car."

Easing ahead, Jesse came along side the cop just as he stood up and turned around. He found himself looking into the hard-mirrored sunglasses of the same man he had talked to earlier. The sunglasses were looking straight back.

As he eased the car ahead and passed the accident, Jesse looked into the rearview mirror. The cop was still standing there, staring at Jesse's departing car.

"He doesn't have anything! He didn't even get my name!" Jesse told himself with little conviction.

Jesse kept looking into the mirror, and what bothered him the most, as the cop dwindled in size, was that the cop never stopped staring at Jesse's car. He stared until he disappeared from view.

• • •

Just outside of San Francisco, Richard Bishop moved back from the array of equipment and yelled towards the other room, "Hey, Marion, c'mere a minute."

Marion came into the room, her hips moving beneath the slippery material of her dress. Richard watched appreciatively as she moved. He liked what he saw, but she was more like a sister. Besides, he wasn't fond of red hair.

She moved over next to him and put her arm across his shoulders while she leaned down towards the computer screen. "Okay, what wonderful thing do you have that's so exciting?"

"Now that's a leading question. You do have a way with words."

"Okay, okay, I get the message. What have you got for me?"

"Now there you go again," Bishop accused, jokingly.

Marion straightened up and looked at him. "What is it with you today? You're in some kind of real mood."

"Nothing really. I guess I'm glad for the overtime, plus I don't have to cut the grass and entertain Judy's mother."

"Richard!" Marion said, punching him on the shoulder. "That's awful!"

"I'm only kidding. I have a barbecue all set up for later."

"Yeah, right. Now what is it you want to tell me? I have my own work, you know."

"This *is* your work, honeybunch. Now look," Bishop said, pointing to the screen. "This is our friend, Jesse Harris. His driver's license, his U.S. green card, his Canadian Social Insurance Number, Visa card, two gas cards, government security clearance, and even his telephone calling card."

"So?" Marion Thackery said, placing her hands on her hips. "You called me in here for that?"

"No, I didn't call you in here for *that!*" Bishop mimicked. "The guy's been using his cards. He rented a car in Seattle, bought some gas in a place called Oak Harbor, and made a call to Canada using his calling card from another town called Burlington."

"How come you didn't tell me this sooner?" Marion wanted to know.

"Because I was told to concentrate on Fletcher. This guy has been talking to his buddy in the Spokane area on Fletcher's cellular. They're going to meet up."

"Now how the hell do you know that, Richard? You had better be right on this."

"I know, because I listened to the conversation. Every time he uses that phone, it's like he's calling Uncle Sam. It's not really a phone, Marion; it broadcasts a signal, just like a radio, through the air.

"Anyone can lock onto the radio band with a small-scale scanner, or you can go big with the computerized technology like I have at my beck and call. He's in a strong cell area right now, and stationary."

Marion Thackery stood there, waiting for him to continue.

"Well? Are you going to get hold of Strickler or not?" Bishop asked.

"Humph!" she said, walking away. "Put it in writing so I can relay it to him."

Watching the twin cheeks of her butt move in rhythm as she walked away, he said, "Then don't go away-- here it is, already to fax."

Coming back to the desk, she said, "Verrry funny." She took the sheet of paper and leaning over, planted a kiss on his forehead, leaving a large outline of lipstick for all to see.

After she had left the room, Bishop decided it was enough, and thought of the barbecue, the beer, and the sunshine. He walked out with a smile on his face, and the imprint of Marion's mouth on his forehead.

Marion sat at her desk and began to set up the fax that Bishop had given her, along with her own, for transmission. Her mind drifted to Strickler. She thought of all of the times that he was mean and rude to her. "The hell with you, Buster, I'm going to lunch." She threw the prepared fax onto the desk and left the office.

She would never know that by not sending that fax, Jesse Harris was able to move unimpeded through the narrow mountain corridor of Highway 20.

···CHAPTER SIX

Jennifer was tugging urgently at Craig's sleeve, telling him to get off of the phone with Jesse. He could see that she was looking towards the stakeout car, but when he looked, all he could see was a bunch of kids from a nursery school or day care center walking down the sidewalk. Turning back to his wife, he shrugged. "What? What do you see?"

Jumping out of the booth, Jennifer grabbed her purse and nodded towards the car. "I've got an idea. When you get the chance, get to the car. I'll see you three or four blocks east of here."

Craig went pale. "What do you mean, you have an idea? You're not going anywhere, lady!"

All eyes in the restaurant were turned towards Craig as Jennifer stomped out through the door. Looking around, he realized he looked foolish, and walked to the doorway and watched Jennifer move in a business like manner away from the restaurant.

He was about to follow her, but checked himself. As long as she wasn't in danger, he would wait and see what she was up to. She was walking briskly, stopping occasionally to look briefly in store windows. She looked like an office worker hurrying back to work.

Jennifer walked passed the stakeout car on the far side of the street, cutting diagonally across the street and ending up at the rear of about twenty kids who were approaching the car from the back.

Two adults were leading the tots, all of them holding a bright yellow rope as they clomped, then jumped from one sidewalk crack to another. She moved in amongst the last of the children listening to them talking about going for ice cream. She smiled despite the cold feeling in the pit of her stomach.

Waiting until they were halfway past the stakeout car, Jennifer suddenly lunged towards the car door and started screaming, "Help... Police!" Perverts, perverts!"

Jennifer opened the door on the startled plain-clothes officer and started to swing her purse. He couldn't get out, and he didn't have a clue what was happening.

"Lady, lady, hold it. What the Christ are you doing?"

Jennifer was still swinging, and yelling so loud she could be heard at the end of the quiet block. "Child molesters! Child Molesters! Help! Call the police! They're after the kids, they're after the kids!"

The two adult women ran up as the kids started screaming and crying. The two women joined in, grabbing the hair and clothes of the passenger of the car. It had happened so fast the driver sat as a spectator, not thinking to get out of the car. Then Jennifer screamed as if she had been hit and fell down.

One of the women yelled, "He hit her, he hit her. Did you see that, Rose?" Both women started to scream, the children running in circles, tripping over the rope and ending up on the sidewalk.

They came in a hurry. They came from three stories up where construction was in its last stages, and they came fast. They ran their own business, and they were used to long hours, working weekends, and working hard. They had kids.

"Steve, Carlos, get that other fucker!" one of the hard-hats yelled.

The driver got out of the car, and managed to say, "Stupid bitch," just as a fist smashed into his mouth. He hit the ground hard, his vision filled with a large sweaty chest leaning over him. "Hold it," he whispered, "I'm a pol.. .."

"You're a fuckin' pervert, is what *you* are," the man said, and smashed the cop in the mouth again.

Breaking free of the women, the passenger ran around the vehicle and drew his service revolver. "All right, break it up. Stand back!"

Steve and Carlos were fighting mad, and they didn't like a man who attacked women on the street. Carlos backhanded the cop in the face, while Steve yanked the gun out of his hand.

"Stop. We're police!" the passenger yelled. "We're police officers for Christ's sake!"

"And I'm Captain Marvel, you son-of-a-bitch," Carlos bellowed, and drove his fist into a soft stomach.

Jennifer was no longer part of the scene. She was running as hard as she could towards Craig and the Mustang. Unable to yell because she was out of breath, she banged on the roof as Craig started to pull away.

She jumped into the car, taking a moment to get her breath as Craig gunned the engine and went in the opposite direction. "That was wild, utterly wild. Man, these people don't need any neighborhood watch. It's a wonder if there's any crime here."

Sirens could be heard in the distance, and Craig pulled into a lane-way to get off of the road. The car bounded forward, dust filling the air like the exhaust from a jet fighter. "I have to get onto a residential street and slip away quietly. They'll be setting up quadrants and I don't know the streets at all in this city."

Jennifer, shivering despite the heat, looked at Craig and told him, "They'll know the car's gone by now."

"Jenn, I don't believe you! Do you have any idea what you did?"

"It kind of scares me now that it's over," she laughed nervously. "But I saw these kids and this crazy idea came into my head and I just knew it would work. I knew you only needed a few minutes to get to the car and... "

"Jenn, you are one terrific woman, just don't ever do anything like that again. You gave me a cardiac arrest."

They both rode in silence for a few minutes while Craig tried to figure the street layout and the way around any police net.

"Craig, we forgot my Jeep. We have to go back and get my Jeep."

Craig, swinging onto a main business road, looked over at her a shook his head in the negative. "Forget the Jeep. We're heading out of town."

"I will *not*, as you put it, *forget my Jeep,*" Jennifer said sternly with an instant flush on her face. "That is mine! I will not leave it."

Craig drove on for a few hundred feet further, looking at the stubborn set of her mouth and jaw, her face red with emotion. Sirens were approaching from what seemed like several directions, and Craig pulled to the curb with other traffic as a cruiser entered the intersection and roared off towards Jennifer's riot.

"Those two cops are going to be really pissed off at me," Jennifer said, turning back from watching the receding police car.

"I think you're right, Jenn," Craig said, ignoring her remark. "I'm the one who has to ditch the car. They don't know yours, but they sure as hell know mine."

Craig drove directly to the motel lot, and Jennifer jumped out and ran to her own vehicle. She gave the thumbs up signal, and Craig pulled out into traffic. He headed east, Jennifer riding his bumper until traffic started to thin out.

How was he going to ditch the car? They were heading into an industrial area with no sign of any car dealers anywhere. He had to do something before hitting Interstate-90 again.

A rusty old sign, swinging on an iron pole, caught his attention as he passed a driveway. It read: *'AUTO WRECKING.'* Craig slowed rapidly, signaling to Jennifer that he was going to turn and entered the far side of the U-shaped gravel driveway.

A flat roofed building, covered with ancient metal advertising signs and looking at least fifty years old, sat between two meshed gates. Rusted corrugated iron fencing held up the gates. Craig got out of the car, the dust catching up and surrounding him in the shimmering heat.

Two German Shepherds hit the gate at the same time, running from side to side, snapping their jaws and showing large white teeth. Making enough noise to bring anyone out of the building.

Jennifer pulled up and Craig said, "Energetic buggers. Stay in the Jeep and I'll see if anyone's around."

Just to the right of the door, a sign read, *'Closed.'* Craig was about to leave when he noticed movement inside. Walking over to the door, he knocked.

"It's open," a gravely voice said.

Walking in, Craig was met by the aroma of grease, oil, and dirt. It smelled like the dirt floor of the garage at his dad's house when he was a kid. The walls were covered in wheel covers and the shelves had numerous radios and spare parts.

A man, a pipe in his mouth and wearing grease covered coveralls and a cap with no peak, stood there looking at Craig.

"Hi," Craig said. "Glad you're open. The sign said closed."

"What're you after?"

"I don't really need anything, but I..."

"Well, we're not much for window shoppin'."

Craig laughed, liking the man instantly. "No, what I meant was I.... well, to tell the truth," Craig said, trying to look embarrassed, "I'm a little short on cash. I was wondering if you would be interested in buying my car."

Looking out the window, the man asked, "What's wrong with it? Looks almost new. Can't go giv'n you no big bucks for no Mustang."

"I told you, I'm kind of desperate. The car is only four years old, and you should be able to sell it for a good profit. I need some cash."

"As you can see, I'm in the parts business. Don't get much call for a whole car that runs. Is it stolen or somethin'?"

"No, of course not. I have all the papers. I just need the cash."

"As you can also see, I'm no drive-up bank teller. You're goin' to take a big loss on that car, you know."

"I know."

"How much you lookin' to sell it for?"

"I really don't know, but I think five thousand would make you one hell of a profit."

"Five thousand dollars is a lot of money. I don't have that just lay'n about, you know."

"Oh, well I appreciate your time," Craig smiled, and started for the door.

"Now just hold on a second there," the man said, coming from behind the counter and wiping his hands on an already filthy rag. "I might, *might* mind you, be able to scrape together twenty-five hundred. But that's all. Otherwise, won't be able to help you none."

"Twenty-five hundred!" Craig exclaimed. "I want to sell it, not give it away. I want to sell it because I need the money. The key word here is money."

"Well just hold your horses a moment. I'll be right back."

The guy walked off into another room and Craig went back outside to talk to Jennifer. "I may be able to sell the car to this guy."

"How much will he give you?"

"I don't know, probably whatever he has. I can't be choosy right now."

"Maybe it would be better to park it and pick it up some other time," Jennifer offered.

"I don't know; I'll go see what he has."

"I'm sorry, Craig."

"Don't be, Mr. Jesse Harris owes me a car." Craig went back inside and waited a few moments until the man returned.

"Okay, this is all I got, and it's the God's truth. I got two thousand, nine hundred, and thirty-seven dollars. You're not gettin' a penny more, because there ain't no more."

Craig sighed, knowing he had to take it because he had to get rid of the car or risk arrest. "You have a deal. I'll get my personal stuff out of it if you will be kind enough to take the plates off and throw them in my wife's Jeep."

"Suit yourself. Here's the cash. I'll make a receipt up for you to sign and you can sign the transfer papers too."

When the transaction was complete, Craig loaded his suitcase and articles from the trunk into the Grand Cherokee.

"I'll drive, okay?" Craig said as he pulled away, both of them waving to the guy in the coveralls. He had a happy smile on his face as he wiped the car fender with the greasy rag. Craig found route 90, and it wasn't long before a sign announced their entry into Idaho. They hadn't seen a police car the whole way.

• • •

Through whirling dust that was kicked, then sucked up by the rotating blades, Strickler and Grant made a dash towards the waiting police vehicle. Once out of the backwash, the blowing heat hit them like a sledgehammer.

"Holy shit!" Grant yelled. "It's a fucking blast furnace here."

"Then let's get to the car. Let's hope it has air."

They both removed their jackets as they cut across the field, walking through a ditch and up onto the road. Two men waited for them, one in the uniform of a Spokane Police officer and the other in casual slacks and a short sleeve shirt. He had a sidearm strapped to his belt.

"Gentlemen, I'm Major Strickler and this is Captain Grant. We're working on direct orders from the Pentagon. I presume you have been briefed."

The one in the short-sleeved shirt came away from the car and shook hands. His grip was firm. At five-foot-eleven, slim, and balding, it was hard to judge his age. "I'm Special Agent Payne. Friends call me Dennis. This is officer Carlton."

"Thanks for your assistance, Dennis," Strickler stated.

Grant, who had not come forward to offer his hand to either of the two men, received a critical look from the uniformed cop. Grant noticed it and asked, "Problem?"

Carlton, leaning against the car, shook his head from side to side. "No, none at all, friend."

"Let's get in out of the heat," Strickler ordered. He had seen the interaction between Grant and the cop, and wanted to put a stop to any further nonsense. He knew Grant had a very vicious and nasty streak inside of him.

Payne opened the rear door and Strickler slid into the back seat beside him as Grant entered the front passenger seat.

"Okay, let's get down to business. What have you got for us? I'm running low on patience and sleep and I want the target in my custody as soon as possible."

Looking a little embarrassed, the agent murmured, "He gave us the slip."

Strickler just looked at the agent.

"We had his vehicle under surveillance, but before we could get teams in position..."

"I... don't... fucking.. .believe... it!" Grant said from the front seat. "You guys had... "

"Never mind!" Strickler cut in. "Let's hear the damn report. The sooner I can move on this the better chance I have of nabbing him. How long ago?"

Looking at his watch, the man answered, "About an hour ago. At least that's when I was notified."

The buildings passed by at a fast rate, the heat rising off of shopping center parking lots, the parked vehicles wavering in a distorted dance.

"This guy either has very good luck or he knows what he's doing. Please fill me in on the details," Strickler said, wiping the dust from his face with a handkerchief.

"We think he had an accomplice. A... "

"Jesse Harris!" Grant said from the front seat. "They've joined up already."

"I don't know who this Harris guy is, but we think it was a woman," Payne stated. "Whoever she is, she distracted two detectives who were watching the car, even managing to have the shit kicked out of them by some drywallers."

Payne filled Strickler and Grant in on how the disturbance had taken place, and the disappearance of the car. They were rolling to a stop at the scene when Payne added, "I've got agents combing the area and asking questions. It shouldn't be long before I find out where they were staying for the night."

"Good," Strickler said, getting out into the heat, "And while your at it..."

"Is there a Mr. Strickler or Grant here?" a man asked, pushing his way past a throng of uniformed and plain-clothed police.

"Over here," Grant acknowledged.

"I've got a message for you in the van, sir. You're to call a California number. If you follow me, you can use our equipment."

Turning to Strickler, Grant said, "Must be Bishop or Thackery. Want me to take it?"

"Yeah, go ahead, I've got to figure out our next step."

Grant walked the half-block to a waiting white van. As he approached the mirrored windows, the side door slid back, revealing a black female in tight blue jeans and a thin T-shirt, her nipples erect from the cold interior.

She smiled and waved him into the white van.

"You can use that phone over there," she smiled as she handed him a fax message. "I'll wait outside until you're finished."

As the door slid shut, Grant glanced at the fax and saw it was from Marion Thackery.

As the phone was ringing, Grant looked out the side window at the woman. She was smoking a cigarette, and perspiration was running down her neck and into the deep V in the front of her T-shirt. Looking at her hard nipples, Grant was starting to feel the beginning of an erection. The phone was abruptly picked up at the other end, jerking his mind back from the sweat-soaked cloth a few feet away.

"Hello," a female voice answered, not announcing any agency or service.

"It's Grant. What have you got?"

"I was going to fax you all of the information, but I didn't know who would be accepting it."

"That's fine," Grant said, not sounding the least bit pleasant.

"Jesse Harris, the other one you are looking for, is headed your way. Bishop says he's rented a vehicle, of which I will give you the description in a moment, and is leaving from the Burlington, Washington area."

"How did Bishop find that out?" Grant asked, looking out the window at the woman again.

"I really don't know, except he listened in on a cellular conversation and learned that they were making a meet."

"Go on."

"This guy Harris will have limited routes through the mountains to get to this man, Fletcher."

"Good. What highways have been outlined as possible?"

"Just a moment."

As he sat there in the cool 68 degrees, a rustle of paper could be heard over the telephone. He sat patiently for another few moments, watching the black woman with her hands on her hips, her breasts pulled taunt against the now fully damp T-shirt.

"Okay," Marion Thackery continued, "he will most likely have used highway 20."

"Okay, put out a state-wide request for assistance to all law enforcement agencies. Use the same shit as a narrative. Now, what kind of car are we looking for?"

"It's a red Ford Taurus, rented from an agency North of Seattle."

Grant jotted down the description along with the license number, and was about to ask the time frame, when Marion Thackery spoke first.

"Oh, another thing, they are not going to meet in Spokane. You should know in case you don't grab Harris. They made arrangements to meet in the Havre, Montana area."

"Shit!" Grant snarled. "Why the hell Montana? Did Bishop say?"

"No, just that they were working east."

"Okay, get on with that alert. Be in the office early in the A.M., and keep yourself available for any call."

"No kidding! I though I was supposed to have a day off," she said sarcastically.

"Just get your tail moving. You know how to do that don't you?"

Just before the phone clicked Grant heard, "Smart ass!"

Grant smiled and punched in another number from a notebook that he pulled from his shirt pocket.

"Hello."

"Is this Mr. Shepherd?"

"Yes. Who is this?"

"Captain Mark Grant. We talked to you a while back."

"Oh yes, Captain Grant, I've been waiting to hear from you. I hope you have my man in custody."

"No, not yet. Tell me Mr. Shepherd, does Fletcher's wife have the day off today? We had some woman help him escape today, and I suspect it could be her."

"You've got to be kidding! I don't know. Jesus! If you'll hold on a moment I'll find out on the other phone."

"Sure, take your time." Grant heard him put the phone down. A radio or T.V. was playing within the house.

Within three minutes, Shepherd was back on the phone. "You still there?"

"Yes I am, Mr. Shepherd," Grant replied.

"Jennifer Fletcher booked a week holiday at the spur of the moment. I tried her home number but some other woman answered and offered to take a message. I couldn't get any information as to her whereabouts."

"Do you know what she drives, Fred?" Grant asked, using Shepherd's first name intentionally.

"No, I don't. Leave a number where you can be reached and I'll get back to you."

"That would be great." Grant gave him a number and hung up.

Stepping out of the van was like stepping into hell. The heat was suffocating. The woman, obviously relieved that he was finished, walked towards Grant with a white, even smile brightening her face.

"Thanks for the use of the van."

"You're most welcome."

"You know, you are one hell of a good looking woman," Grant said, looking at her protruding nipples.

"Thanks, but put your tongue back in your mouth. I already have all the man I can handle."

Grant's face darkened, not liking the put down.

"I always wanted some dark meat," he said, deliberately trying to insult her. "Too bad I don't have more time."

"You could have a whole year Mr., and it wouldn't do you any good at all."

Turning, Grant walked away and muttered, "Bitch."

The woman, smiling at her small triumph, said even louder, "Prick."

It took Grant five minutes to locate Strickler. He was in an air-conditioned restaurant, sitting in a corner booth with the two other men. Grant filled him in on what he had learned.

"Then we're wasting our time here. Fletcher and his wife are heading east already. The trick is finding which route."

"No," Grant said. "The trick is finding out what they are driving. She had her own vehicle, and they could be in that instead of the Mustang."

"Maybe they have both of them," the F.B.I. man offered.

"Let's get something to eat, then get moving on this. You have any maps handy?" Strickler asked the uniformed police officer. The man nodded yes, and hurried out of the restaurant.

Grant turned to Strickler and said quietly, "Just a reminder, Miller wants to be kept up-to-date."

Sighing with resignation, Strickler walked to the public phone and punched in a number using his calling card. "This is five-five-five-, triple two one," a female voice answered.

"General Miller, please. Major Strickler calling."

"Stand by," was all Strickler heard.

Miller's voice was easily recognizable as he came on the line. "Got some good news for me have you, Nathan?"

Measuring his words, and dreading the conversation, Strickler took a slow breath and forged ahead. "Yes and no, General. We have some good Intel on where Fletcher's heading, and..."

"What do you mean, where Fletcher's heading? I thought you had him boxed in at Spokane."

"*I* didn't have him boxed in at Spokane, sir, the locals did. I was heading to Spokane when he outfoxed them and took off. It seems his wife has arrived on the scene and they are headed to Montana."

"I'm going to tell you right now, Major, that if I didn't need you on the scene right now, I'd court martial you and have you fired for being one big screw-up," Miller said in a normal tone. "Surely I don't have to tell you that you and I are being monitored very carefully. This theft is placing the nation in a very high-risk situation. This is an emergency situation we have here. Now, you have two choices. Pull this off and fly to the heights with me, or get fucking buried. It's that simple."

"I don't work well under threats General, never did. I..."

"Oh," Miller said in mock sincerity, "I'm sorry if I have offended you, Nathan. You mustn't take this personally. This is a do or die business you're in, and I'm sure you're going to do just fine. Just wonderfully."

"Yes, Sir..."

"Now, listen to me Nathan, enough pussyfooting around. I want Fletcher and Harris nailed. Cut them off from all support, and make it difficult for them to do anything. Close down the bank accounts and credit cards. Put out anything and everything on these people. I want bells and whistles blowing if they even get a parking ticket. Understand?"

"Excuse me, sir, but that may not be a good idea." Strickler turned and saw the uniformed officer return with some maps. "If we cut him off altogether, we'll be cutting off our own leads. We won't know where he is then. The telephone and the credit cards are what are leading us to him. He's as good as caught if he keeps using them."

Miller was quiet on the other end of the phone for what seemed a long time, finally speaking firmly to Strickler. "Okay. Carry on your way, but I caution you, you are not only to keep me informed on a six hour basis or less, you have to have this thing wrapped up within forty-eight hours. Got that, Major? Two days."

The doing it *your way* was not lost on Strickler. "Yes, Sir."

"Don't let me down." Miller hung up without saying goodbye.

"Goodbye to you too," Strickler said, slamming the receiver into the holder. Back at the booth, Strickler sat down again, his mood darkening.

Payne turned and spoke. "We found Fletcher's Mustang. He sold it to an auto wrecker on the edge of the city, and the new owner had it parked in front with a for sale sign on it."

Strickler perked up. "How'd you find it?"

"Seems like your man Fletcher was in a hurry. Only took the back plate off. The old guy who bought it parked it nose out, and there for all to see was the Canadian plate. It's been towed in for forensics to go over."

"I've got a call into Fred Shepherd in Vancouver," Grant said. "He said he'd phone me back on what Fletcher's wife drives. That should at least put us back to square one."

"No need," Payne smiled. "I was about to mention that your suspects drove away in a Jeep Cherokee. Grand Cherokee I think it is, and it's dark green."

Turning back to Grant, Strickler nodded towards the phone. "Get back to Shepherd anyway. Tell him it's important that we have the license plate number."

As Grant walked away, Strickler turned to Agent Payne. "Tell me, Dennis, you've been working this area for a while, what's your guess as to their route?"

"I'd say they'd be after two things: speed and distance. That means I-90, cut over to Helena, then north to Havre."

"I'm inclined to agree with you, which means we may have an opportunity here," Strickler said, pulling the map onto the table.

• • •

Craig was pushing the Jeep steadily Eastward through Idaho. There had been nothing but routine traffic for miles. "You know Jenn, I've been thinking maybe I should quit the force and get us out of that west coast rat-race. The traffic and pollution and the commuting and expense-- look at this country, this is where people should live!"

"Well I *guess* so!" Jennifer laughed. "It's national forest. We have national parks in Canada, do you think they'd let us move in and build a house?"

"That's not what I mean. I'm just beginning to admit to myself that all I have is a job, the same as thousands of other people, and there's other things besides work."

Jennifer leaned over and gave him a kiss on the cheek. "That's what I've been trying to tell you for quite a while now. I think we have to have a balance between our jobs and raising a family, though. You know, take..."

And now for the news.

A massive manhunt that started in the State of Washington has now escalated. Local and federal authorities are expanding their dragnet into Idaho and Northwestern Montana, as they hunt for a researcher by the name of, Jesse Harris. Police are also searching for two Canadian companions by the name of Craig and Jennifer Fletcher, who are reported to be in possession of top-secret federal documents, stolen by Jesse Harris from Inter-America Pharmaceuticals.

Harris' whereabouts are unknown, but police are now concentrating their search in the Idaho and Montana area for the two suspected Canadian accomplices. Police ask that you be on the watch for a dark green Jeep Cherokee with Canadian license plates.

Notify your local police or the nearest F.B.I. office. Do not attempt to apprehend the suspects, as both are considered armed and dangerous.

"That's us!" Jennifer whispered, turning wide eyed towards Craig. "They're talking about us! Shit, they're talking about *us*!" Jennifer repeated.

"Jenn, I need you to keep calm. We don't know what's happening. We're out in the middle of nowhere."

"Yeah, and all of a sudden I feel like the only person on the road. I feel like I'm sticking out like a sore thumb. How many Jeeps with Canadian plates do you think there *are*?"

"They must have found the Mustang if they know about the Jeep," Craig uttered aloud.

"All I want is to get off of the road. They could be over the next hill, or following us," Jennifer said, turning around in her seat.

"I've been watching. Not a soul in sight, Jenn."

Craig increased the speed to make her feel better, and in truth he admitted, himself as well.

"Don't worry, I'll find us a hole to swallow us up for the night."

Jennifer looked over at her husband and the apprehension showed on her face. Looking back at her, Craig felt a trickle of fear also. He was afraid of losing her. He was afraid of something separating them. He was playing with her life, the person he loved the most in the universe.

Looking at her quietly sitting beside him, as the filtered sun performed tricks on her young face, he again had the feeling of being stalked. He couldn't shake it. Craig increased his speed as if to escape his feelings. The trouble was, he didn't know if he was rushing from, or rushing towards danger.

He was starting to admit to himself that he was afraid, deathly afraid for the first time in his life. He couldn't handle losing Jennifer. It was his turn to shudder as he realized that if it came right down to the crunch, he might not be able to protect her.

•••CHAPTER SEVEN

Lt. General Randolph Miller turned from the telephone and sat in thought for a moment, looking inward. He didn't see his study, lined with two walls of books and a large stone fireplace, nor did he see numerous photographs of presidents, politicians, and entertainment celebrities, all of which were autographed: 'To Randy.'

His guest, who was sitting at the far end of the room on a comfortable lounge which was arranged around a very large coffee table in front of the fireplace, might as well not have been there for the moment.

The only light in the room came from Miller's desk, and that placed his guest in a Cimmerian atmosphere that really wasn't on the sinister side, but rather actually cozy.

Miller came back to the present, becoming aware of his guest and grateful for the few moments he had been allowed without interruptions. Getting up, he walked to the stone fireplace, its cavernous mouth cold and black. He was reaching for a light switch when his visitor waved him off.

"Don't turn that on, on my account. I prefer to sit here and nurse my drink just the way it is. Too many lights give me a damn headache."

"As you wish," Miller said, indicating his guest's glass. "Let me freshen that up for you. I'm going to need one myself."

Handing Miller the glass, the man nodded towards the phone, "Not bad news about our program, I hope?"

Walking towards a wet bar set between the shelves of books, Miller thought of his answer very carefully as he began to make the drinks.

"My man in the field indicates that he's having a few problems. I fully expect he can overcome any obstacles."

"Randy, don't bullshit me. This is too important to play head games here."

Miller walked back with the drinks, the ice cubes tinkling against the glasses.

Accepting the drink from Miller, the guest said, "Let's hear the problem before it builds into something we can't handle. You know, of course, that we just simply can't allow any problems at this stage."

Miller didn't waiver from the man's direct gaze, and waited patiently to speak. "I'm well aware of my responsibilities here, sir, and although there is a problem, we're on top of it."

"I'm glad to hear that," his guest replied. "Good drink, by the way."

Miller nodded in acknowledgment, raising his glass in a mock toast.

"So, Randy, what's the problem?"

Taking a deep but quiet breath, Miller took a swallow of his drink and looked at the powerful person sitting across from him. With just a nod of his head, Miller knew the other man could accomplish things that he didn't want to think about.

Miller spoke with as much confidence as he could. "We have had a theft of the drug, 'PRECISE'. We are currently one step behind the person. A man by the name of Fletcher is carrying it, and we have good leads on Harris, the one responsible for this whole mess in the first place."

"But," the voice across from him cut in.

"But," Miller quietly continued, "we... I have a problem with some of the up and coming programs that have been slated. When this Harris took the samples, he left us in a bind. What samples we did have we used freely within the Justice Department phase. We didn't expect any shortages at that point.

"You had better be prepared for '*Operation Trust,*' I'll tell you that, Randy! There..."

Miller stopped the other man from continuing, raising his hand slightly. "I fully expect to get everything back, along with the bastards involved. As I was about to say, I see no problem with our main objective, '*Operation Trust*;'-- but the ones to follow? The samples are just not there. I did send one sample to an agent. If he apprehends Harris, some of it may have to be used in the field."

"I don't care how you do it, Randy-- you know that. It was put into your hands because, as you put it, you can't do your job if you are restricted or checked every step of the way. You said that your job was to get results. Remember?"

When there was no reply, the man continued quickly. "Anyway, I didn't come here to discuss your problems. I came to iron out the final steps on *'Operation Trust.'* Then if there's time, to go over some of the other programs."

"Very well, sir. I'll get the file out," Miller responded, moving to the safe to retrieve the necessary papers. He was glad to get off of the subject of the missing 'PRECISE.' Returning to the coffee table, his guest looked at him and Miller wondered what was coming next.

"You know, Randy, I've been thinking of why we originally started this project. You and the rest of us were in full agreement that this country needs to get back to the basics, like family, morality, education, work, and good honest government. I don't mean to come down hard on you, but you know how important this is. The testing stage is just about complete at Justice, and look how it cut through the crap in those few small tests alone. I don't mind telling you I'm excited about this. The cost of prosecuting these bastards has plummeted."

His guest paused to take a drink, and Miller did not speak. "By the time we're finished, every court in this nation will have an appointed federal officer who's function will be to, ah, stabilize the court environment and to assist the courts in fact finding. You and I know that this fact finding only means one thing, finding the truth. *Without* a whole lot of lawyers clouding the issues."

"Yes, sir," Miller said, dutifully.

"This country has fallen into a most decadent system, one that could not have been imagined by the fathers of these United States. Truth means nothing, just the system. Victims mean nothing, just the system. This country used to pull together for a common purpose. We were growing together. Not now!"

Miller's guest scowled and put his glass on the table. "Randy, I tell you the time has come to put this truth thing to work everywhere. No more backlogs in our judicial system, no more corrupt corporations ripping off government, no more wondering if some celebrity really is guilty, and by God we'll stop organized crime in its tracks. Put all these fucking lawyers to work doing honest work for a change, instead of screwing up the country. No more fat fees, with guilty people walking free because of some stupid loophole, and

123

think about it, no more innocent people being held in jail either. I tell you, the time is right and I want you in this with me, Randy. You'll be proud of what you have done for this country."

Miller looked at his visitor and had to admit he agreed with him. "It's a tall order. I want it as much as you. You know, of course, that there will be very strong opposition to this."

"Anything worthwhile that has taken place on this planet has been set in motion by men such as yourself. Big thinking men! Men who helped set up this country. The Constitution was put there for the protection of the people, and you and I know it isn't doing that. It's protecting the wrong people, the clever manipulators."

Miller's guest handed him his empty glass, and as Miller refilled it, the man continued. "This program is well within the Constitution as far as the Committee is concerned. It always comes down to interpretation, of course, but the Committee, with help from certain agencies, thinks we will be able to sell this to the American people. It will be very gradual process, and one in which the legal profession will certainly have an interest. Not necessarily a *say*, but an interest."

Miller handed the drink to his casually dressed guest, and sat back to listen further.

"Think about this. In the courts, for example, all we are determining here is the truth. That's what courts are for anyway. What we will introduce will just be the modern way of getting to the truth, that's all. We won't interfere with the jury system, and if a man does or doesn't want to take the stand, fine. All we will do is ask him how he pleads. Guilty or not guilty."

"Yes, sir, I know all this," Miller smiled. "I'm just as eager to see it in full swing. Please believe me when I say I'm doing everything I can to get this thing back on keel. It will be okay!"

"Good. Then let's turn our attention to *'Operation Trust.'*"

Miller smiled again, feeling a lot more at ease. "How's your drink?"

"Fine. You know I really appreciate your hospitality and letting me use your house for these meetings."

"No problem. I'm quite excited about what we're doing. I just wish we didn't have this... this complication."

"That's what makes life interesting, isn't it? Winning, but with just the chance of losing."

Miller found the folder for *'Operation Trust.'* "I'm not in a position to know anything but my part of the operation. I know the intent is to sell the

American people on the use of 'PRECISE,' but I don't know the actual specifics beyond my need as a supplier."

"Maybe you're right. It's time I let you in on a bit more, something to wet your whistle and help get your butt moving. *'Operation Trust,'* " the other man said, "as you know, involves educating the public, and supplying the Executive Wing with needed supplies. The President is going to address the nation on Wednesday. He has been given a prepared speech, which he has approved, but prior to the broadcast, he will be administered the drug 'PRECISE,' and will be given a different speech and told to read it."

"That won't work, sir!" Miller said, sitting up straighter. "'PRECISE' is about remembering the truth. The President's mind can only tell the truth about past events or it won't work. You can't make him read something, or do something against his wishes."

"Oh, but that's the beauty of it. He does agree and believe in what's written in the speech. There have been numerous off-the-record and candid conversations with the President and he privately agrees that the best thing for the country would be drastic change. Tapes have been made of his thoughts, and they have been incorporated into the speech. He agrees, as do most of the law-abiding people in this country, that the pendulum has to swing the other way. Remember: truth, justice, and the American way."

"I don't mind telling you, this is rough shit to swallow. Maybe I would feel better if I knew the logistics of the operation. I'm a military man and I would feel better knowing the planning behind this thing with the President."

"You have no need to know. You can be sure of one thing though, professional people who are *very* close to the President will handle it. Simplicity is the key. It will be a very simple operation," the visitor said from the dark shadows of the deep cushioned couch.

"Okay, I'm not prying. I've been in this business long enough to know to mind my own business. But there are very, very, dedicated people in place to protect the President from any harm, and they will shoot the hell out of anyone who tries."

"Who's going to harm him? We're all for him. He has the same ideas we do and we are not overthrowing the government. We are just, what... giving him the courage to speak out? People will applaud him as the greatest President in the history of the United States."

"Yes, sir. You said you wanted to go over some of the procedures dealing with this operation," Miller said, flipping over the first few pages of the Top Secret document.

"Yeah, it's getting late. The first thing is the sample aerosol container of 'PRECISE.' I need it so it can be put into place."

"That's no problem," Miller offered, feeling good that he could provide something. "You'll have it when you leave. There is also a field manual on how to use it, and what to expect in the way of results."

"What about contamination? We don't want a bunch of people running around shooting off their mouths and saying everything that comes to mind."

"The method recommended is to spray when the person is not looking. The person spraying is to turn and walk away for a distance of four to five feet while the drug is inhaled. It apparently deteriorates rapidly in the air."

"Okay, I'll have to go over this thoroughly." The man looked directly at Miller again. "You do know I'm giving you a breather here, don't you?"

"I do appreciate that. How long do I have?"

"Let's just say you have the same forty-eight hours you gave Nathan Strickler, plus another forty-eight to get organized before serious plans can be laid."

"I didn't realize you knew Major Strickler," Miller said raising his eyebrows.

"You'd be surprised at what I know, General, you'd be surprised. Now, I have to be on my way," he said, getting up. He walked directly to Miller's desk and pushed a recessed button, popping open a recessed compartment. Reaching in, he removed a cassette and put it in his pocket. "Handy, don't you think? I have one of these in my desk too. I don't like being taped, General. Remember that! Now, the sample if you please."

Miller, flushed with embarrassment, extracted the prized sample from the safe and returned. He handed it over to his visitor.

"Remember, Randy, no more mistakes." The man turned and walked out of the room, and a second later the front door opened and closed.

Miller watched out of the window as the car pulled out of his half-circle drive. The sweat was trickling down his spine, and a little knot of fear seemed to be sitting just in the center of his chest.

Miller picked up a heavy ashtray and hurled it with all his might at the row of books. "Strickler, you son-of-a-bitch!"

● ● ●

Richard Bishop's computer screen lit up with incoming information as Marion walked into the room. "Well, looks like my little mole is starting to pay off. Let's see what we have."

Credit Verification...
Card 555.300.212.90001/ 09/11
Morey's Garage
Hungry Horse / Montana
Purchase: $24.00....

Marion, looking over Bishop's shoulder laughed. "Where the hell is Hungry Horse? It sounds like it's out of some movie."

"I really don't know. Pull over that map and we'll have a look."

Finding the map, Marion took a few moments to sort through the pages of the Northwestern States until she located Montana. She brought it back to the desk and spread it out for Bishop to see.

"It's got to be in the Northwest somewhere, I would think. Let's see...Kicking Horse Reserve... Horseshoe Park..."

"They sure like horses up there," Marion said.

"Let's see-- Whitefish... Great Bear Wilderness... Going-To-The-Sun Highway. Man, the names. Hear it is, it's on highway 2. Hungry Horse and the Hungry Horse Dam."

"Why didn't they just feed the damn thing?" Marion asked.

Bishop looked at Marion and smiled, giving her a printout. "Go pass this on to Strickler. He may be in a position to nab this guy even though he's further north than they realize."

"You know, I don't know why I'm even here. You can do all this shit right from your own desk."

"Because, little lady, when it gets hot and heavy, I don't have time to be dealing with Strickler or his heavy."

"I hope this guy's up a mountain. Then Strickler can freeze his balls off trying to find him," Marion said leaving the room.

Richard sat there, trying to formulate an idea that was playing at the outer fringes of his mind. Sitting forward, he began to work his way into Fletcher's life. He didn't really have the authorization, but maybe he could slow him down a bit. Besides, he could always remove what he put on, or visa versa, he reasoned.

Ten minutes later, a computer terminal in Toronto, Canada, made a slight alteration and Richard Bishop sat back and waited for the results.

"I expect to hear from Mark Grant any minute," Marion said, sticking her head into the room. "Anything else to add?"

"Not yet. I've got my line out, now I'm waiting for the fish."

• • •

Jennifer was driving. Craig had needed to ease his aching shoulders, plus he needed to look at the map and get a lay of the terrain now that they were in Montana. Halfway through Idaho, they had switched drivers and had headed northeast and away from Interstate-90.

"Don't say it," Craig said from behind the map.

Looking startled, Jennifer gave a little laugh and asked, "Don't say what? I didn't say anything."

"You were about to say that 93 takes us north, or something similar."

Reaching over, she took Craig's hand and smiled. "It doesn't matter; we'll head north after we meet Jesse."

"Ummm. Maybe I should come over there and stick my tongue in your ear."

"You just stay right where you are unless you want an accident on your hands."

"Yeah, right. I can see it now. Accident on highway two; couple rushed to hospital to try and remove tongue from woman's ear."

Jennifer laughed along with Craig. "Yeah. Woman baffles doctors by refusing operation."

Laughing together, Craig and Jennifer managed to cover a few miles, forgetting everything but being together.

• • •

A sign caught Jennifer's attention: '*HUNGRY AS A HORSE? STOP IN HUNGRY HORSE. FINE DINING ONLY FIVE MINUTES AHEAD.*'

"What do you think, Hon? I'm about ready to quit. I really am."

Squeezing her hand he nodded. "No sense going any further today. I guess it'll give Jesse a chance to catch up."

Six minutes later, Jennifer brought the vehicle around a bend in the road and entered Hungry Horse. The wide highway didn't do much to hide the fact that it appeared just about deserted at this time of day. A few tourists were coming out of a large general store that specialized in local T-shirts and souvenirs, and some cars surrounded the local cafe.

Craig took in the hills on all sides, noting that the tree line started quite a distance back from the road. "Kind of peaceful."

"I was just about to say the same thing. What's first, food or a place to sleep?"

"The first thing is fuel. I want this thing gassed up and ready to go at all times."

Jennifer nodded, pointing through the windshield. "There's one up ahead on the left."

As they drew nearer Craig smiled and looked over at Jennifer. "Talk about your old time gas station. I didn't think they had any real gas stations left."

She stopped at the pumps, reading aloud from the sign above the door. "Morey's Garage. He sells our brand too."

"Do me a favor, will you? Gas up. I have to visit the can," Craig said, opening the door.

A voice at the window said, "Howdy. What can I do fer you folks?"

Turning, Jennifer looked at what must be the owner. He was dressed in fairly clean mechanic's overalls, and was rubbing a clean gray cloth over his hands. Looking at him, she was reminded of some characterization of a warlock. His eyebrows twisted upwards at both ends, gray in the center, but ending as black as tar at the tips.

As he came closer, Jennifer answered, "You must be Morey. A genuine mechanic in a genuine garage."

"Yep. Not too many of us around anymore, I guess. Somethin' like shoemakers. Don't seem to see many of them around anymore either. Fill 'er up?"

"Yes, please. And check the oil and the brake fluid and stuff," Jennifer said as she released the hood.

"Kind of hard to check stuff, but I get yer message."

Smiling, Jennifer liked the older man. He seemed to fit into the town and it's surroundings. "Tell me, is there a place we can spend the night? We would like to get off of the road."

Morey's voice came from under the hood. "Oh, we won't send yah away. Go up the road a spell, just like yah was doin', and the place will be on the right. Tell 'em I sent yah around and they'll feed yah proper too."

Jennifer followed him into the small office. Green painted walls, covered long ago with large calendars and advertisements, seemed to compliment the cluttered desk and countertop.

"That'll be twenty-four dollars. Cash or credit card?"

"I don't have quite enough cash. Put it on my card please," Jennifer said, handing him the card.

Completing the transaction, Morey handed the card back. "Oil's okay. So's the brake fluid, and so's the stuff."

Laughing, Jennifer thanked him and walked outside to find Craig back in the Jeep.

As she opened the door, Craig said, "It's an old fashioned garage all right, you should see the black sink in the washroom."

"Maybe so, but he's a real nice person. We just go up the road a little further and there's a place we can spend the night."

"How far?"

"Up the road a spell," Jennifer drawled.

They rode in silence for the few moments it took them to reach a small family run cafe and motel. Checking in, the woman asked, "You folk's be wanting supper later?"

"Yes. I'll pay for the room now," Craig answered.

"You can do that, or you can pay for everything later. I'm running behind time here."

"That's a lot of trust," Craig offered. "People could drive off and not pay."

"You goin' to do that?"

"Well no, but..."

"Well, there you go then. I don't have a thing to worry about."

Back in their room, Jennifer started to haul items out of the suitcase.

"Not too much, Jenn. If we have to leave in a hurry, I don't want to leave essential things behind."

"I just want to lay out a change of clothes," she explained. "Man, it's good to be able to walk around. Plus I'm ready for a good meal."

Walking back to the cafe, the late afternoon sun beating down on the open parking lot, Jennifer stopped then turned to Craig. "We should phone Lorraine, she'll be worried about us."

Craig, carrying the briefcase in one hand, started patting his pockets. "You go ahead and call, I forgot the cellular in the Jeep. I want it close in case Jesse calls."

130

Craig walked back towards the room, looking at the Jeep parked away from the building and behind some trees. He retrieved the phone, and was walking back from the Jeep when a car pulled into the lot. It was the local sheriff's department.

Craig changed direction slightly as he walked towards the cafe, watching the car as it moved slowly down the row of vehicles towards him. The driver was looking at the license plates as he did so.

The vehicle came abreast of Craig and he smiled at the driver in a friendly manner. The man smiled and gave a short wave of his hand, then returned his gaze to the vehicle tags, writing down license plates as he went. He was getting closer to the Jeep and the British Columbia license plates.

Craig heard the radio come to life in the patrol car. "Base to Chuck. You out there, Chuck?"

Picking up the microphone, he became instantly annoyed at the dispatcher, stopping the police car while he talked. "Now where else *would* I be?

The whining reply came back over the speaker. "Chuck, you promised to relieve me for supper. We're short handed and you're ten minutes late already and I'm getting starved."

Snapping the button down, Chuck commented, "The whole damn country could go to hell in a bucket, and all you worry about is your belly. I'm comin' in, just sit tight."

Putting the car in reverse, he slowly backed out to the edge of the roadway, put it in drive and roared off in a cloud of dust.

The dust was still hanging in the air when Craig opened the outer door to the cafe and saw Jennifer on the pay phone mounted on the wall between the outer and inner doors. "I don't know sweetheart, I'll let you talk to your daddy in a minute. Now you make sure you're in the house by nine o'clock, okay?"

Jennifer paused, listening to the reply, as Craig leaned against the door jam. "I know," she continued, "but we'll hammer it out in a few days. Good news too! We'll all be together again sweetheart." Jennifer listened for a moment then interrupted Lorraine on the other end. "Okay, okay, I'll let you talk to your father."

Taking the phone from Jennifer, Craig spoke into the mouthpiece. "Hi, beautiful. I miss you."

"I miss you too, daddy. When are you and mom coming home?"

"In a couple of days I hope. We'll see. I... don't want to promise anything specific, because we are really busy helping Uncle Jess. It should be soon though."

"Daddy, did you know that Uncle Jess's girlfriend is staying at our house?"

Laughing, Craig answered her question. "No I didn't, but that's no problem. Say, if you want, you can move home and stay there if she wants you."

"That's what I wanted to ask you. Good, cause she wants some company and doesn't like being by herself."

"Okay then that's settled. Has Bev heard from Uncle Jess?"

"No, Daddy."

"Okay, have Bev take you home and into your own room. Oh, and get Rusty from Mr. Stark next door and look after him."

"Thank you, Daddy. Say goodbye to Mom."

He hung up and opened the door to the cafe. Long shadows were playing across the room as the sun hit the nearby hills. In the distance the clouds seemed to be thickening and turning dark.

"Looks like rain coming." It was the woman who had greeted them earlier. She looked better in the warm light than she had earlier in the harsh sunlight of the office.

"A little rain wouldn't hurt," Craig smiled. "Tell me, I was just talking to the Deputy Sheriff outside. Seems like a nice guy. How many are there in this town?"

"Well, they don't just do Hungry Horse of course, but around here there's Steve and Dan, then there's Chuck and Cal. They all come in for breakfast when they work the day shift. They ain't too bad a bunch. Don't get into our hair and all. If you know what I mean."

"What time do you open for breakfast?" Jennifer wanted to know.

"You be here at six and you'll have the freshest coffee you ever tasted."

The woman walked away after they each ordered a beer, and Craig relaxed against the back of the booth. "We'll be here for the six o'clock breakfast, Jenn. I don't want to be eating with a bunch of inquisitive cops."

Turning down an offer of dessert and more coffee, they both got up from the table.

"Great meal," Jennifer said. "Don't forget our wake-up call please."

"Not to worry. You folks have a good rest. You'll find it real quiet around here. I'll put everything on your morning tab."

They both slept soundly, neither of them aware of the world around them until the phone jarred them awake at four fifty-five. The wake-up call was not welcome, but Jennifer managed to say thank you before sinking back onto the bed.

She would have stayed there but knew that Craig would never make the first move. It was just before six when they finished packing what they had taken out of the Jeep, and walked into the cafe for breakfast. Thirty minutes later, they were finished and ready for the road.

As the woman cleared some of the dishes from the table, Craig remarked, "Nice place, and good food. Thanks for making the stay pleasant."

"Heck, I get a kick out of it too, you know. Just tell your friends to stop in and see us. Tell them Maggie looked after you."

"I'll go get the car, Jenn, while she's figuring out how much we owe."

Jennifer waited patiently for a few moments while the woman tallied the bill.

"Grand total including breakfast, is $110.80. Coffee's on me," Maggie announced.

"Thanks. There's no sense in waiting for my husband to come in, I'll pay for it now. Reaching into her purse, Jennifer opened her wallet. "Oh I forgot; I didn't even have enough to pay for the gas yesterday. Here's my card."

Running it through the old fashion imprinter, the transaction was quickly completed. She handed Jennifer a copy. "You people come back real quick now."

Jennifer smiled her thanks and left the cafe, opening the door to the Cherokee as it pulled to a stop.

"What about the bill?" Craig asked.

"I paid for it. Didn't have any cash but thought you wanted to get going, so I used my Visa."

"Jenn, I don't want you using..."

Three cruisers from the Sheriff's Department pulled into the lot, and stopped with their noses pointed at the cafe. The men got out and entered the building, looking for their early morning coffee.

"I didn't want a record of us being here. I wanted to pay cash."

"Oh, I'm sorry," Jennifer said testily. "Let me have some money for my purse, then. I won't use the card anymore."

"No matter, let's get going. I'm eager to meet up with Jesse today." Pulling out onto the empty highway, he pointed the vehicle eastward, noting great black clouds to the south. "Looks like one mother of a thunderstorm coming this way."

"We shouldn't be long getting to Havre, should we?" Jennifer wanted to know.

"Nothing to stop us now."

Back inside the cafe the deputies were leaning over their first cup of coffee, the steam enveloping their faces in a pleasant aroma.

"Well, I'll be!" Maggie exclaimed, hanging up the telephone. "Those people just didn't look the type at all!"

"What's the problem, Mag?" one of the men asked.

"You know that Jeep type car that left here when you guys was comin' in? Well, they took me for breakfast, supper, and a night's stay for cryin' out loud. Used a stolen credit card," she said, wiping hair off of her forehead. "Who would have thought?"

"Hell, they're not far gone, we'll see if we can catch 'em."

"Aw, I'm covered for the one hundred and ten bucks. Don't worry none about it."

"Bull! There using a stolen card, we want them."

"Well, they were Canadians. They're either headin' for West Glacier, or over to Columbia Falls for the border," she added.

As the police cars roared out of the parking lot in search of their quarry, Maggie leaned on the counter. "Now who would'a thought. Such nice people too."

About twelve hundred miles away, Richard Bishop said, "Bingo."

•••CHAPTER EIGHT

Nathan Strickler and Mark Grant sat at their terminals in the helicopter, totally exhausted. The information relayed from Marion Thackery about Jesse Harris had started a massive effort to box Harris between the towns of Rockport and Twisp.

Harris was supposed to have left Burlington on highway 20, and Grant and Strickler knew there was virtually nowhere to go between Rockport and Twisp, except the North Cascade Park. The search had produced absolutely nothing. Grant couldn't understand it; they had moved very fast, and every eastbound vehicle had been checked.

Grant was pissed off because Jesse Harris was his responsibility. Strickler was concentrating on Fletcher, because that's where 'PRECISE' and the data was supposed to be.

The chopper was bucking and rocking in extreme turbulence as they moved at maximum speed, and Grant was beginning to feel slightly nauseated. He looked over at Strickler, who was talking to the Montana State Police.

Strickler was very agitated. "I don't give a Goddamn what it will do, I'm working under the authority of the White House, mister, and there will be *no* bullshit. I want the area west of St. Regis on I-90 bottlenecked. We're working with an extremely dangerous situation here. There's a killer heading your way with top-secret government material, and he has got to be stopped."

Strickler listened for fifteen seconds before speaking again. "Fine, I... no, no, no! I don't want any police roadblocks or anything that's going to scare anyone off. Make it look like an accident." Strickler listened, frustration showing in the lines of his face. "Jesus, do I have to spell everything out? I said an accident! Use your fucking imagination. I want spotters well in advance of the accident scene checking for the suspect vehicle, and I want airtight containment when he moves into the net. It shouldn't be so damned hard to find a Jeep Cherokee with Canadian plates on a bloody freeway. Also, I want things ready to be put in place at Great Falls."

Again Strickler was forced to listen, the noise of the chopper not making it easy. "I am well aware of the cost and the manpower. You will be fully reimbursed by Washington. How long will it take you to set up the accident?"

A smile spread over Strickler's face and he sat back in his chair for the first time. "Very good. You will be remembered for your co-operation when this is all over. I'll be landing at the scene probably just after you set up. I remind you that this man is dangerous and he is carrying top-secret material. I do not want him removed from the area until I arrive. ...No, no, the material is not dangerous to your people, now will you please get on with it? Thank you. Goodbye."

Breaking the connection, he reached for the weak, cold coffee that was vibrating in the cup at his left elbow. Taking a swallow, his face took on an expression of disgust.

"I don't know about you, Nath, but I could do with something a lot stronger than coffee," Grant half yelled, taking the intercom set away from his face. "We've been on the go now for I don't know how many hours."

Strickler nodded in silence and Grant got up and walked stiffly towards the rear of the cabin, returning with a shimmering bottle of amber liquid. "Genuine Canadian Whiskey," he said, arching his eyebrows in question.

"Hell, yes," Strickler nodded, offering an empty coffee cup to Grant. "It'll help relieve the pain in my backside."

Pouring a generous amount in the cup, Grant said, "Nothing on Jesse Harris, yet." Sitting back he took a sip of his own drink, noting the worried look on Strickler's face. "You know, of course, that we're flying around like a fly in a horse turd, don't you? This guy can be anywhere."

"He could be anywhere, but he's not. He's down there," Strickler said, pointing with his thumb towards the floor of the chopper.

The intercom came to life and buzzed in their ears, the pilot's voice clear and calm. "Please fasten your seatbelts, gentlemen, we're running into thunderstorm activity on a wide front."

The UH-60 Black Hawk came in low and fast from the west. The freeway was lit up with slow moving vehicles for miles. Rising with gut wrenching suddenness, the Black Hawk shifted sideways over the low lying hills, dropping in heavy side winds towards a field by highway marker number 53. Slashing rain and wind caused swaying and yawing as the pilot tried to center on the circle of road flares.

Looking out the portals, they saw men in yellow slickers holding their hats and turning away from the blast caused by the downdraft. Grant and Strickler silently wished they were somewhere else.

Both men had expropriated armed forces squall jackets against the storm's deluge, and as they left the warmth of the helicopter the rain slashed across their face like thousands of miniature blades, wiping away all traces of tiredness. Grant followed Strickler towards the highway and firm ground, as millions of raindrops were turned into red, then blue flying colors caused by the police strobes.

A man in uniform met them at the side of the highway, motioning for them to follow as he hollered above the storm and traffic noise, "Follow me to the command post."

They followed obediently, their shoes water logged and their pants already clinging to their legs like painted on material.

"In here please, gentlemen," the patrolman said, opening the door to a long step-van, and holding it tightly against the wind. Two men were sitting at a desk in the humid air, communication gear in front of them, along with topographical maps and two steaming cups of coffee.

"Got anymore of that?"

"Sure, grab yourself a couple of mugs and help yourself. Space is limited in here. Once you get that wet gear off, we might even have a sandwich for you two."

"Thanks. I'm Nathan Strickler, Major, Special Operations out of the Pentagon. This is Captain Grant."

"Glad you two got here. My name's Matt Boulton, and this here's Ray Fraser. Get yourself seated when you get your coffee, and I'll fill you in on what we've done."

The rain was pounding in a rage, rocketed by the wind and thrown with a vengeance against the vehicle, rocking it on its heavy springs.

"We really do appreciate all your help, Matt. I know your men are taking a pounding out there, and they must be thoroughly pissed knowing it's not for real. However, I can't stress enough how important this is."

"We know what's going down," Fraser said speaking for the first time. "So don't think we don't take it seriously. No son-of-a-bitch is going to rip this country off if we can help it."

Smiling in agreement, Strickler followed Grant's example and took off the wet jacket and sat down. The warmth enveloped his body as he sipped the coffee.

"What we got here, Major," Boulton said, pointing over his shoulder, "is one mother of an accident— a tipped tanker with a poisonous and corrosive substance that can't be touched for hours because of the rain. Any exposure to water would be disastrous. Least that's what the media have been told. Sound good enough for you?"

"Perfect."

Lightning fractured the atmosphere in earsplitting harshness, followed immediately by reverberating thunder that rolled off into the distance.

"Jesus!" Boulton said, clearly startled. "Scares the hell out of you. Never did like this lightning and thunder crap."

Strickler nodded in sympathy, waiting for the other man to continue.

"Anyway, where was I? Yeah, all approaching vehicles have to go through a series of checks to make sure the occupants are aware of the danger. This gives us an opportunity to scan the vehicles and the occupants. Once they zigzag through our check lanes, some go to the left and some to the right. The ones to the right get a good going over. If your car comes this way, I guarantee you, he won't be going anywhere."

Grant nodded his approval. "You've done a fantastic job."

Boulton flushed slightly, nodding his thanks. "Appreciate what you're saying, but it's nothing special."

"It's special in this weather."

"Any communication needs you fellas have, we can probably handle right from this command center," Boulton continued. "Doesn't matter to where or to whom, you should have a good connection."

"I'll keep that in mind, Matt, but I may need to be in private."

"We understand. How long before your boy hits this area, you think?"

Looking outside at the sky artificially darkened by the thunderstorm and the mountains, Strickler looked at the long line of traffic being pelted by the rain and lit up by flashing lightning. "He could be out there right now, just waiting to inch ahead a few more feet. Or he could be an hour down the road.

It's not a certain thing, just a very good bet. You men know what it's like searching for these types of people."

"Yes we do, Major, but if I could make a suggestion?"

"Certainly."

Jerking his thumb over his shoulder he said, "Get rid of the chopper. It's Army, and it stands out like a wart on the end of your nose."

"That's our only transportation, Matt. It gets us around in a hurry."

Boulton smiled. "How many army gun ships you ever see at a traffic accident? No matter how you analyze it, your boy could panic and take to the hills."

"He may have a point," Grant said to Strickler. "We can send the chopper to the nearest base for fueling and a check-up, and get it back fast enough. I don't know about you, Nath, but I'm getting bagged. This storm looks like it's around for a while and the pilot must be fatigued also."

"You're right. I'll go tell them," Strickler said, starting to rise.

Boulton placed his hand on Strickler's shoulder, forcing Strickler to stay put. "No need, my men can look after that. They can land at Missoula and I'll have a car waiting to take them to a motel. You can get in touch with them at anytime through us. That's if they can still fly in that stuff out there."

"With the navigation they have on board, they should be just fine, Matt. Thanks."

They sat in silence, studying the map and watching the slow-moving traffic in the failing light. Five minutes later the whine of the rotors built up into a steady beat. The helicopter took off, leaving only the sound of the slashing rain as it hit in waves.

Strickler got up, wanting to pace the floor but finding it impossible. "We haven't heard from Bishop. Maybe he can't get in touch with us."

"Could be," Grant agreed. "Want me to try and contact him?"

"Yeah. We could be beating our heads against the wall here for nothing."

The phone rang three times before it was picked up. "Bishop! Is that you?"

"This is Richard Bishop. Who's calling? You sound full of static."

"This is Captain Grant. I'm in the middle of a thunderstorm. Anything to report?"

"We've been being trying to get hold of you. We haven't been able to get you at all on regular channels."

"We're a little off the beaten path right now. What have you got for us?"

"Well as far as Fletcher is concerned, we had a... can I ask where you are presently situated, sir?"

"We're in, Montana, West of Missoula. Maybe a hundred or so miles on highway 90."

"Hold it on a minute, I'll be right back."

Grant waited, listening as the rain engulfed the whole of the vehicle, glad that he was under cover.

Bishop came back on the line, rattling the telephone handset uncomfortably in Grant's ear. "From what I can gather you are about one hundred and fifty miles away as the crow flies from your man."

"When was that?" Grant asked, apprehensively.

"About hour and a half a go. The only thing I have is a gas purchase using a credit card in a place called Hungry Horse, Montana. He probably gassed up and kept going, with a head start of well over an hour."

Grant turned to the men beside him, "Check for a place called Hungry Horse. They had a gas purchase there an hour and a half a go."

"Don't need no map for that," Boulton said. "It's north of here. Look, I'll show you."

"Oh no," Strickler moaned. "We're too far south of the bastard. And the time! Jesus, the time!"

Turning back to the phone, Grant asked, "Anything else?"

"No," Bishop stated, "but I have a few ideas. If you stay in touch you may be able to turn this around. You never know."

"We'll be in touch." Grant hung up and turned to Strickler. "Well, we tried."

"Look, we can call the chopper back and be up there in no time."

"Not in this weather. And not through those mountains," Grant shot back. "Major, you are tired!"

Looking at Grant, then the other men, Strickler realized that he was at a zero functioning level. "You're right. Matt, break it down. Get your men the hell out of here and get your traffic moving."

Picking up a microphone, Matt Boulton barked a couple of orders and turned back to Strickler and Grant. "You two had better catch the first car out of here. It can have you in a motel in no time and you'll be fresh in the morning to call up your pilot."

"That would be greatly appreciated," Strickler said, and got up to put on his jacket. Rubbing the haze off of the window, he could see a crane moving into position at the overturned truck. The rain had not ceased one iota. Ten minutes later, they were in the back of a state police car, heading east towards more rain and darkness.

• • •

Morning showed itself on a gray dreary horizon. Grant reluctantly pulled himself out of bed, went to the bathroom, and carried out the usual morning ablutions, then shook Strickler awake. "You ready for another one of those days?"

"Don't fucking talk to me. It's too early."

"Fine, I'll be in the coffee shop checking on things."

The air was wet, the kind of wet that coats your face without there actually being any rain. Walking to the coffee shop, Grant took deep breaths of air, coming awake with each step. A long truck went by as he approached the doorway, the tires hissing on the wet pavement and spray following it like a swarm of locusts. Finding a booth with a newspaper still on the table, Grant settled in and waited for service.

"What'll it be?"

Looking up, Grant found the tired eyes of an older man with a white cap and a dirty apron tied around his middle. "Just coffee for now. I'll order when my friend arrives."

"Suit yourself. Don't 'spect too much service 'til the waitress gets here though. She's late again."

The man came back and poured his coffee, and Grant asked, "What time does the desk open? I may have some messages."

"Oh, 'nother half hour should do it."

Strickler came in a short time later and sat down across from Grant. "How's the coffee?"

"Passable. We had better order. The bird is supposed to be here in half an hour."

Running his hand through his hair, Strickler nodded and said, "We'll make it." Taking a map from his pocket, he placed it onto the tabletop. "I circled the place that they gassed up at. We don't know if they are still there or gone. Imagine being so tired you don't have somebody check the place out during the night."

"Don't blame yourself, I was too tired to think clearly too. You can only keep on the hunt so long without resting." Grant looked at Strickler and pointed to the map. "Looks like they had quite a choice of directions to take."

"Yeah, but they're supposed to be going to Havre, remember?"

141

"What say we close everything down somewhere between Shelby and Havre? We can easily jump ahead of them."

Strickler thought for a moment, and then looked over at Grant. "Might work. Let's order."

They finished the breakfast of eggs and hash browns, and were sipping their second cup of coffee. "It's seven ten, where's the...."

"Right there on the horizon," Grant pointed. "Coming straight at you."

"Right, let's go. "Strickler was suddenly full of energy as he bounded up to go to the door.

"Wait, I've got to check on messages." Grant ran into the small lobby and pounded on the bell.

A woman, obviously not ready for the day, came through the door. "A little early ain't it?"

"Room 28. Any messages?"

The woman started to shuffle the unorganized pile of papers on the desk, finally taking one in her other hand and passing it to Grant. "That's all there is," she said, shuffling out of the room.

The paper simply had Bishop's phone number on it. After he had punched it through on an outside wall phone, Bishop answered groggily.

"What have you got, I'm in a hurry," Grant said with no introduction.

"Christ, these hours are going to kill me. Hold on while I grab the printouts."

Grant waited longer than he wanted, the sound of the helicopter growing louder and louder.

"Oooo-kay. Might as well tell you right off, I tried something that wasn't authorized. Thought it might slow your target down."

There was a pause on the line as if Bishop expected Grant to say something. He remained quiet.

Bishop began again. "What I did was, I put their Visa in the stolen category. This morning they used it to pay a bill."

Now Grant did interrupt. "Where? How long ago!"

"That's the good part. They used it at, let's see, at 0642 hours, your time. That's roughly a half hour ago. Left a message and told the woman to give it to you pronto. Thought you would have called before now."

Grant swore, then realized it wouldn't have mattered without the aircraft. "Good work. What was the location?"

"That Hungry Horse town. They didn't move after gassing up last night. Stayed at a motel."

The helicopter was making a hell of a racket and he had trouble hearing. Water vapor was flying everywhere and people were coming outside to see what was happening.

"Okay," Grant yelled, "I want you to get through to the local police in that area and learn what you can. Reach us in the chopper."

Jumping into the helicopter, Grant buckled in while the crewmember secured the door. "Get this bird up and moving northeast on the double. Tell the pilot his destination is Hungry Horse for now. I'll fill you in on the way."

The helicopter rose and turned to the northeast, sending both Grant's and Strickler's breakfast to the bottom of their stomach.

Quickly filling Strickler in on what he had just learned, they went over their options on a map in front of them.

"I may just get this smartass yet," Strickler said with eagerness. "Mark, get on the horn and contact the state police. See what they can do for us on U.S. 2 towards the east."

"Right."

Grant turned to a console and punched a single number on the board. The speed dial was almost instantaneous. After identifying himself, he was asked to wait a moment.

"I have an urgent message for a Major Strickler, please stay on the line."

Holding his hand over the headset microphone, Grant turned to Strickler. "They have an urgent for you. I'm waiting on line if you want to join in."

Patching himself into the circuit, Strickler waited patiently also. The MDT came to life and Strickler motioned to Grant. "See what that is, will you?"

Grant sat in front of the terminal; the message port flashed and rang. Hitting the message line, his screen filled with an instantaneous message from the sender.

A voice spoke into Strickler's ear: "This is Matt Boulton, is Major Strickler on the line?"

"Yes, I'm here, Matt. What's happening?"

"On your vehicle, I left word that the moment it was queried on the computer, I was to be notified. Just got a call from dispatch. Your friend is the object of a local hunt by Deputy Sheriff's in the Hungry Horse area. Apparently they're hunting northeast of that area."

"Did they have them in sight, do you know?"

"I kind of get the idea that they do not have them in sight."

Strickler thought furiously, trying to put all the facts in order. "You got

143

anything in that area to help us out? They will be heading to Havre and should be on highway two."

"To tell the truth, Major, I'm still at home. I'll get on it right away though and get back to you."

"Fine. Thanks. I'll wait to hear from you... oh, are you able to get the radio frequency for the Sheriff's Department? We can probably patch in without any problem."

"Like I said, I'll see what I can do and I'll be in touch."

Clicking off, Strickler turned to Grant. "You won't believe this, they..."

Finishing it for Strickler, Grant said, "They're chasing Fletcher out of Hungry Horse. Just got it on the mobile data terminal. By the way, the reason the police are chasing them is because Bishop put his credit card on the computer as stolen."

"He didn't have authorization to do that," Strickler stated, tight lipped.

"He was playing it by ear."

"Okay, I give him his due. Not much we can do at the moment until we hear from the police. They may have him in custody for all we know."

"Sure," Grant sneered, "We're not dealing with Joe Klutz, by the look of it."

"Pessimistic bastard," Strickler replied. "Give the pilot a new heading. Tell him... Cut Bank. Best I can do for now."

Looking out the window at the ever-changing landscape, Strickler felt the pangs of frustration already beginning. The horizon tilted as the large helicopter banked further to the east, the vibrations intensifying.

Grant disengaged the intercom and turned to Strickler as the chopper leveled off. "Be about an hour I think. They.... " A light began to flash on Grant's counsel and he put his earphones on. "Captain Grant speaking."

"This is the Montana State Police for Major Strickler or Captain Grant."

"Yes, this is Captain Grant. Go ahead."

"One moment please, Captain."

The line seemed to go dead, and it was becoming frustrating to have to wait every time you needed information. Looking over at Strickler, he saw that he was listening in on the same line.

"This is Matt Boulton speaking."

"Go ahead Matt, what have you got for us?"

"If that Jeep keeps going in an easterly direction, it's heading into some pretty rough country. Good roads, but high country. No side roads to scoot off on. Get my meaning?"

"I get your meaning, but we're still about an hour out and heading towards Cut Bank. Should we divert to," Stickler looked at the map, "what, East Glacier or Browning?"

Boulton sighed into the phone. "That's up to you, gentlemen. I've got cars converging on the area as fast as I can, but you must remember it's a remote area and we don't require a lot of manpower in that location. The parks people look after lots of things up there."

"Okay, Matt, we're going to head for Cut Bank and give them a little rope. Your boys know their job, and who knows, maybe they'll nab them. I just want to be in a position of waiting and not chasing."

"Suit yourself," Boulton answered. "I know you're limited."

The landing in the Cut Bank area was uneventful. There was a stiff cross wind in the very hot, dry air, and the long parched brown grass laid over in alternating waves of gold and yellow as they dropped into the landing zone.

Strickler turned to the crew of the chopper. "Okay, same drill as last time. I want you out of sight. So find a place to hide this thing and be prepared to land back here in short order."

Two and a half hours passed, the wind and dust blowing constantly in the shimmering heat. The pollen was starting to get to Strickler, and his eyes were getting red around the edges.

"I don't get it," Grant fumed. "Where the fuck are they?"

Strickler wiped his running nose and blinked his watery eyes against the sun. Looking over at Grant, he shook his head with disgust. "I'm starting to get in an ugly mood over this hot shot. I *know* he is..."

"Excuse me, sir," an approaching officer was holding a piece of paper. "This just came in. Seems your vehicle got by us somehow."

Strickler snatched the paper without even thanking the man, the wind whipping it back and forth so that he was unable to read it. Turning his back to the wind, Strickler slowly read the fax printout.

ATTN: Maj. STRICKLER / Capt. GRANT...RE: Subject FLETCHER...Phone signal data received in area of Shelby, Montana. Unable to determine if FLETCHER is east of Shelby, or north/south of that point.
M. Thackery for R. Bishop....

"Son-of-a-*BITCH!*" Strickler yelled. "That's east of us. He's already gone by Cut Bank!"

"Yes sir," the officer said. "I have a message from headquarters also. All of U.S.-2 will be locked down between Shelby and Havre by the time you read this."

"How the hell is he doing this?" Strickler said pacing back and forth in the heat. "Get me the chopper, and get it now!" Strickler yelled at Grant.

They were in the air and heading east within twenty-five minutes. Grant, having kept quiet to this point, spoke up. "Look, this Fletcher guy never went by us on that damn road unless he changed vehicles again; you know it and I know it. Either that, or he's going across country in that damn Jeep."

Looking at the map, Strickler then sat back as the countryside flew by beneath the window. "At least we're a little closer this time. Real close."

• • •

Having left Hungry Horse behind, Craig moved rapidly north and east on U.S. 2 until he reached West Glacier. He turned off of the highway into Waterton-Glacier International Peace Park.

"What are you doing?" Jennifer asked, a little astounded.

"I don't know. I just don't want to follow a pattern. Maybe by getting into an area off of the beaten path, we can gain some time."

"If you ask me, we're losing time. It's a straight drive to Havre."

"Yeah, too straight. Just bear with me for a while."

They passed Lake McDonald, clean and clear in the rapidly changing terrain. The road narrowed as they drove deeper into the Park.

"Jesus, look at that!" Jennifer said, pointing upwards at a forty-five degree angle towards a mountain in front of them. "There are cars up there!"

Craig looked up, seeing small toy-like vehicles moving across the side of the mountain as they ascended or descended what looked like a sheer rock face. "Looks like we have a climb on our hands."

"You call that a climb? That's suicide!"

"It won't be a bad as it seems, Jenn."

"No, of course not."

A sign read:
GOING-TO-THE-SUN-HIGHWAY
OPEN.

The elevation shifted as they drove deeper into the park and into thick forest. A narrow mountain road soon became a shear drop-off as they climbed above the tree line. A small stone wall separated them from a drop of thousands of feet.

The air was crisp and clear as they watched the ant-like movements of vehicles far below, hugging the mountainside as they headed for the roof of the Continental Divide.

"How do you feel now?" Craig asked.

"I'm astounded. Not only at the beauty, but that man actually built this road. I'm glad they did though. It makes me realize how small we all really are."

"Let's hope we get so small nobody recognizes us up here. The only way is up."

Craig and Jennifer looked to their right and watched cars cross an arched stone bridge built against and into the side of a cliff not more than fifty feet away. A few moments later as they crossed the bridge, both of them watched in awe as the splendor unwound before them.

Craig didn't stop at Logan Pass, the summit, and the top of the Continental Divide, even though the Information Center beckoned.

"Well, what did we accomplish?" Jennifer said, turning sideways to look at Craig.

Craig drove on for a moment, thinking quietly to himself, then turned to his wife. "Get the map. I want to stay off of main roads."

Looking at the map, Jennifer pointed as Craig drove. "Your going to have to go south on 89 to connect with highway 2 again, but if you want to stay off of main roads I think we should keep going south, to East Glacier, then head over to Shelby. There will be lots of roads according to the map."

● ● ●

Jennifer was behind the wheel traveling south and east of Cut Bank, when the cellular startled them both. "I hope that's Jesse," Jennifer said.

"Hello?" Craig said against the wind.

"Thank God! You are impossible to get hold of."

"Hi, Jess," Craig smiled and nodded to Jennifer.

"Where are you guys?"

"Uh, I don't really want to say right now, but we are close to our agreed meeting point."

"Well, I'm not that close. Look, I want to meet somewhere else, okay."

"Like where?" Craig asked.

"Canada. I mean it. It makes more sense, Craig, they'll just keep on hunting us."

"Hold on a minute while we pull over." Craig motioned to Jennifer to pull to the shoulder of the deserted road and pulled the map towards him. "Jesse wants to meet somewhere in Canada instead of Havre."

"I wished he had called sooner," she said as she put the vehicle in neutral.

"Jess, think you can meet us in Pincher Creek?"

"I could if I knew where it was."

"Alberta, Jess. West of Lethbridge on highway 3. It's small enough to make a stop over."

"You're fading out, Craig, we meet in Pincher Creek, right? Can you hear me?"

Jesse's voice was barely audible as Craig answered, "Yes, that's right."

Craig didn't receive a reply and pressed the disconnect button. "Well, at least I know he's okay. Now, Jenn, we head for Canada."

• • •

Traffic was fairly heavy on the freeway north of Shelby and Jennifer looked over at Craig and touched his arm. "You look tired. Want me to drive for a while?"

Shaking his head no, his hair whipping around in the wind, he looked at her with a smile. "No, you drove all the back roads."

The cellular warbled, causing them to look at one another. It rang again. "This is getting to be worse than home," Jennifer said.

"I'm almost afraid to answer in case it's good news," Craig said as he activated the cellular. "Yes?"

"Craig Fletcher?"

"Yes. Who is this?"

"Ah. I hope you can help me."

Craig was looking for an opportunity to pass, but was stuck behind an older man wearing a ridiculous hat, and driving what looked like the first car he ever owned. A truck moving painfully slow in the fast lane had him boxed in.

"We've never actually met," the voice continued, "but I talked to you once before; name's Evans. Archie Evans. I'm worried as hell about Jesse. He's just disappeared and... "

Craig interrupted the man on the phone. "How did you get this number?"

"I kept it from last time. Have you heard from Jesse?"

"Just a moment." Craig covered the mouthpiece by pressing it against his leg and turned to Jennifer. "This guy's phoned me before. Says he's a friend of Jesse's."

Jennifer thought for a moment, and then said, "Ask him where he's calling from, then wherever he says he is, say you'll meet him in an hour. See what happens."

Putting the phone back to his ear, Craig said, "Mr. Evans?"

"Yes, I'm here."

"Where are you calling from?"

"Kent, just South of Seattle."

"Good, give me your address and I'll stop by and see you. I'm only an hour away and I want to talk to you about Jesse."

"Hold on," the voice said, a harshness entering the tone.

"The guy's stalling or something," Craig said to Jennifer. "I'm going to hang up on him."

"Mr. Fletcher, can I call you back?"

Finally finding an opening in traffic, Craig pushed the accelerator half-way to the floor and passed the sleepy old man at the wheel. Looking in the mirror as he pulled back into the slow lane, he saw the old man and his hat receding rapidly. Craig spoke into the phone. "You do that, Mr. Evans."

Craig hung up and turned to Jennifer. "You know, the last time I talked to this Archie guy, I almost got caught at the motel."

"Did we use the phone in the motel?"

"I can't remember. If I did, I guess they could trace it back, but the only guy I talked to was this Evans guy on the cellu... Holy shit!"

"What? What is it?" Jennifer said, anxiously.

"The cellular! They've been on my ass every time I've used it. Jesus, what sneaky bastards."

"You can't be sure of that, Craig. Can you?"

"Can we be sure of anything?" Craig answered, watching the road surface flip under the hood. "Jenn, do you remember the Attorney General who screwed up his career because someone was able to tape his cellular phone conversations, and caught him making the wrong remarks at the wrong time?"

"Sure, in Victoria a couple of years ago."

"Well, you can be sure they just didn't stumble onto him and record him that one time. He was locked onto by a scanner and someone was waiting for some dirt."

"But that didn't tell the guys who did it where the Attorney General was at the time, did it?" Jennifer asked.

"No, because I think he was always in the same area. We are moving, and every time you move you move into a new area that is controlled by what they call a cell. So every time you use the cellu..."

"They know what cell area you are calling from," Jennifer finished for Craig.

"That's right. Some cells are small and some are quite large I guess, but I read somewhere that you're location can be pinpointed down to five hundred yards. I'm not sure how good they are, but the United States Government won't be dicking around with a little scanner. I know they do very well with technology in their drug enforcement."

Craig pushed down further on the gas peddle without realizing it. "If that's the case, Jenn, we had better make that border as soon as possible. It may be too late already if they have it sealed."

Craig looked for every opening, using skills he had learned over the years in pursuit driving, a touch of the gas pedal, a nudge of the brake pedal with his left foot as he slipped sideways, and sudden acceleration as he roared into an open spot.

The sign read:
PORT of COUTTS
CANADA CUSTOMS
Five Miles

Jennifer was watching the highway to the rear, her forehead knit in lines of concentration and dread. "Nothing yet. I think we'll be all right. Only five more miles and, wait I want to put my sunglasses on." Fumbling around on the dash, she finally found the Polaroids.

"Any trouble we encounter may not come from behind, Jenn," Craig said. "They could be waiting for us. In fact, I would be surprised if they aren't."

Jennifer wasn't watching the road, however, she was searching the sky to the rear.

"What do you see?"

"I thought I saw a..., yeah there it is; a helicopter. It's coming awfully fast, Craig, and straight down the highway." Turning to Craig, her skin was tight around her eyes and she was growing pale. "Hurry! We're so close. Hurry!"

"You just get yourself back into that seat belt and cinch it up good and tight," Craig said, as he pulled into the fast lane again and wound the Jeep up as fast as it could go.

It was all a race against time. All the people in the chopper had to do was radio ahead and block the border point. Turning on his lights, Craig continually flashed his high beams at the traffic ahead of him in the fast lane. It worked; they got out of his path.

"Craig!" Jennifer screamed against the wind. "It's right behind us. It's monstrous!"

The chopper slid alongside the driver's side of the Jeep, the whomp, whomp, whomp, pounding against Craig's ears as the camouflaged Black Hawk raced up the center median. The menacing looking machine registered on Craig's brain again as he took another quick look, but he had to concentrate on the traffic because of the speed he was going.

"They're sliding a door open," Jennifer yelled, as she leaned behind Craig's seat to look over and up.

Taking a quick look, Craig saw two men in the open hatch, their hair and clothes being blasted by the turbulent air. One had gray white hair close cropped to his head. He was looking directly at Craig with hard piercing eyes.

Moving his head back and forth, Craig got flashes of traffic flying by at an extreme rate, then the helicopter, more open road, the two men in the open hatch, a slow truck in the fast lane. *The truck!* His mind screamed an alarm and Craig brought his right arm down on the wheel, and then back again. The Jeep jumped from the fast lane to the slow lane, moving directly in front of a car. The sound of a fading horn dimly registered on his brain as the Jeep continued to move ahead.

Craig couldn't make the Jeep go any faster. The chopper was floating beside him with ease, rising and falling with the terrain. The noise was deafening and the whirling blades seemed to be reaching out to him, beckoning as if he was something to be devoured.

"Craiiig! They've got a gun!" Jennifer screamed, digging her fingernails into his shoulder with all her strength.

Looking over, Craig saw the gray haired man kneeling in the open hatch wrap a sling around his right elbow. The sling was attached to a rifle with a large scope.

"We're almost there, Jenn. Hold on!" Craig hit the brakes hard. The Jeep dropped to the rear drastically as the helicopter continued forward at high speed. Now they could both see the powerful helicopter easily as they continued to drop back. The man in the hatch fired, the powerful recoil visible against his shoulder.

Instantly, a great tearing slice appeared in the hood in front of Jennifer, the ricochet continuing into the high bank at the edge of the road to Craig's right. As the guy swiveled to realign, Craig hit the gas pedal hard, throwing the man's sighting off. Jennifer was screaming in the seat to his right.

Craig slid the Jeep to the right, and moved behind a large transport, riding the paved shoulder between the truck and the ditch.

In the helicopter, Strickler screamed at Grant in unrestrained rage. "Shoot the bastard! What the fuck are you waiting for?"

Looking back over his shoulder at Strickler, Grant gave him a scornful look. "I'm waiting for a fucking target," he yelled against the wind and noise of huge blades turning so close to the ground. "He went behind that truck."

"Fuck him!" Strickler yelled. "We'll cut him off at the border."

Looking out and forward, Grant saw a small line of traffic approaching to his left. He realized that they had hit the border in record time. "You had better hurry up then," he said pointing down. "We have arrived."

Strickler switched on the intercom and yelled into the microphone to the pilot, "Land at the border, land at the border. Cut the son-of-a-bitch off." Looking out the open hatch, Strickler was in time to see the Jeep darting out from behind the truck and enter a small line leading to the port of entry. He was about to tell Grant to fire on the stationary vehicle when the chopper swerved to the right, taking the roadway from view. "Get this fucking thing down," Strickler yelled in frustration, pounding the bulkhead with his fist.

The big machine turned once again, the doorway now facing north as the ground rapidly leaped towards Grant and Strickler.

Grant pointed to the line of cars in front of him as the helicopter dropped towards the pavement into no man's land between the two countries. "He's in lane three, and he's next to go through customs."

"Down, down, down. Hurry *up* for Christ's sake!" Strickler yelled as he undid his safety harness and prepared to jump out the open hatch.

Jennifer and Craig got the green signal to move into the customs port as the helicopter hit the ground.

"It's okay, Jenn, we're in Canada now." Craig pulled ahead to the waiting customs officer.

Jennifer punched Craig on his shoulder. "The helicopter's landed. They're jumping out!"

"Both Canadian citizens?" the customs officer queried, looking towards the United States and the whirling blades of the landed helicopter.

Craig answered yes, and the man asked, "How long were you away?"

"Just for the weekend. No purchases." Looking to the rear, Craig smiled at the customs man. "Americans! They sure like to do things big."

Laughing, the man leaned back in his seat and looked towards the helicopter, unable to see the running men because of the barriers and cameras. "Oh well, if you got it, use it, I guess." He waved for Craig to proceed. "Way you go then."

"Thanks," Craig said and eased out of the port then accelerated rapidly. In his mirror, he could see the two men run up to the custom's booth.

"Stop that vehicle!" Strickler yelled to the customs officer, his face red with anger and exertion. "Stop that vehicle," he panted, the adrenaline level falling within his body.

The customs man looked at Strickler and Grant, hiding his instant irritation. He had an instant dislike for Strickler. It wasn't necessarily what Strickler had said, it was the chemistry between the two men. He looked at Strickler and just didn't like him. "Nice of you to drop in," he said with a trace of sarcasm. "Now, who are you, and how may I help you?"

Strickler watched the Jeep disappear down the highway, growing smaller and smaller as the customs man just sat there doing nothing. If looks could kill, the customs officer would have been a very dead man.

···CHAPTER NINE

onday afternoon was not going so well for Louis Barclay. At two o'clock he was ushered into the holding room just off of the courtroom. He rubbed his wrists as the handcuffs were removed, and asked for a cigarette as he sat in the indicated chair.

Barclay was a man of fifty who chose to wear a heavy mustache and one of those cute pony tails that stuck out a couple of inches at the back of his severely pulled back hair. A single earring in his left ear completed his macho image. Barclay wasn't a big man physically, but his bearing and menacing demeanor made him appear quite a lot larger than he was. The other man in the room with him thought he looked like just another asshole.

He took nervous puffs from the cigarette, his dark brown eyes refusing to reveal his tension. Ash fell on his expensive slate-blue suit as he took in the color of the walls in the windowless concrete room. He smirked, and turned his attention to the other man in the room. "Pink? Gimme a break; this is a room for fuckin' faggots."

Laughing, the C.E.O. acknowledged the joke and looked at the walls. "Yeah, well, it's supposed to soothe you, take away your anger. At least that's what I'm told."

"Oh, I'm soothed. I feel really soothed since I came in here," Barclay said, pissed off that someone was trying to manipulate him.

"Good. Look, I'm your Court Environmental Officer. My name's Vic. It's my job to make you comfortable and to make sure you understand court procedures prior to your appearance."

"How fucking nice," Barclay said, dryly.

"No, this can be serious stuff here, Barclay, you're facing life in prison for importing and trafficking in dangerous drugs. I've got to make sure you get a fair shake."

"Bullshit! That's what I'm paying that grease ball lawyer of mine for."

"Help yourself to some coffee," the C.E.O. said, pointing to a corner table.

Getting up, Barclay walked the few feet to the table. "Uncle Sam must be getting soft in the head. What, no cookies?"

As he reached for the coffee pot, the C.E.O. placed a small oxygen mask over his nose and mouth to protect himself, and pushed a small recessed button under his desk, sending a brief but invisible blast of 'PRECISE' into Barclay's face. The only way that the C.E.O. knew he had released the drug was by a small red light high up in the wall that flicked on for two seconds.

The C.E.O. waited to see if there was any reaction, and when there wasn't, he asked Barclay, "Feel nervous about going into court today, Louis?"

Louis stood in front of the coffee pot for a moment, then turned around and nodded. "Yes."

The C.E.O. looked at a list of questions that would normally antagonize most people and chose one from the list. "What's your sexual preference Louis? Men or women?"

"Wimen. I like pussy."

"You ever have sex with a man?"

"I tried a couple ah guys when times was tough, when I was in the joint, but I like wimen."

"Do you have any secrets, Louis?"

"Yeah, I got lots of secrets."

"What's your biggest secret, Louis?"

Without any hesitation, Louis Barclay looked at the C.E.O. and answered in a straight and quiet manner. "I can't get it up too much any more. I think it must be the coke or something."

Vic, satisfied, reached over and pushed a button by the door. "You'll be going into court now, Louis. You'll be asked to make a plea. Your lawyer will be waiting for you."

Barclay was sitting beside his lawyer a few minutes later when the court was brought into session. "All rise! United States District Court is now in session, Judge William Oliver Thomas presiding."

William Oliver Thomas climbed the short rise to his domain, looked out over the court, and sat down.

"Be seated!" the voice rang out. "The United States versus Louis Jack Barclay."

Leaning forward, Judge Thomas asked, "I trust that you both are ready to proceed?"

The prosecution and the defense were on their feet at the same time, both clamoring for attention.

"Good. Please read the Sworn Information."

The court clerk rose and turned to face Barclay, and looked at him. "Please stand."

Louis Barclay got to his feet, along with his lawyer, and turned to face the court clerk. His face was a neutral mask.

"Count one: Louis Jack Barclay, you are charged that on the 3rd day of August,"

Barclay stared straight at the court clerk, seeming to take in every word.

"... City of Miami, State of Florida, without lawful excuse did possess and illegally import a nonprescription drug, namely cocaine, for the purpose of trafficking..."

Barclay's lawyer leaned over and whispered to him, advising him what to say when the reading had ceased.

" Count two: Louis Jack Barclay..."

Barclay's lawyer looked at him, expecting a confirmation of his advice, but none came.

"...And did enter the United States illegally for a purpose prejudicial to the United States of America... Louis Barclay, how do you plea to count one, guilty or not guilty?"

With his hand on his client's shoulder in a fatherly fashion, the lawyer turned to Barclay with a smile on his face as Barclay stated loud and clear, "Guilty."

In a state of confusion amidst the loud courtroom buzz of conversation, the lawyer tried to confront his client and the court at the same time. "Louis?... Your Honor?... Your Honor, ... I think my client is confused here. I need a moment, your Honor."

"By all means, take a moment. I don't want any confusion here."

Leaning close to Barclay's ear, the lawyer whispered fiercely, "What the fuck are you doing, Louis? You almost blew it for Christ's sake! Now I know you're nervous, but think before you speak for God's sake!"

"Okay," Barclay answered calmly.

"I beg the court's forgiveness, but could you have count one read again, so my client can enter a plea?"

The judge nodded, and the exasperated clerk read count one over again, knowing full well Barclay had understood every word.

"How do you plea, guilty or not guilty?"

Barclay answered in a steady, calm voice. "Guilty."

The lawyer just stood there looking dumbfounded. He looked to see if Barclay was on drugs or something, but could not detect anything. "What are you *doing?*" He whispered in anger. "Your making me look like an asshole! I can *beat* this case."

Barclay didn't say anything, and his lawyer turned to the court. "I must respectfully ask for a continuance at this time. My client doesn't appear well."

Turning to Louis Barclay, the judge said. "Are you not well, Mr. Barclay?"

"I'm fine, your Honor," Barclay answered.

The judge turned and stared at the lawyer, not saying anything, waiting for the lawyer to continue.

"I respectfully request a short recess to talk to my client."

"Denied! How do you plea, guilty or not guilty?"

The lawyer jumped in immediately, "He pleads not guilty, your Honor."

"Now just hold on here. In my court I want an answer from the accused so that I understand fully what the individual wants. The record must show what the accused's plea is. He has already pled guilty twice, so let's not confuse the issue here."

The judge looked from Barclay back to his lawyer. "I don't want anyone putting words in other people's mouths. Is that understood?"

"Yes, your Honor."

"I want a complete reading of the indictment again. No misunderstandings about what is happening here."

Again, the long drawn out indictment was read by the droning voice of the court clerk followed by, "How do you plea, guilty or not guilty?"

The whole court sat in suspended animation. The prosecutor, who hadn't uttered a word since the proceedings had started, sat with a smile on his face as others waited for Barclay's answer.

"Guilty."

Moaning, his lawyer sat down, shaking his head from side to side as reporters ran for the door, and police officers and DEA officials smiled and began to talk about their good fortune.

"Quiet in the court!" Thomas bellowed. There was immediate silence, the only noise coming from the outside hallway as the door silently closed on its hinges.

Turning to look at Barclay, Judge Thomas spoke quietly. "This court has no alternative but to accept your guilty plea, Mr. Barclay. Do you understand the consequences of not following the advice of your lawyer?"

"Yes."

"I must say... this is a refreshing turn of events. I have heard both sides, and it is the decision of this court that as a result of your attitude and the fact that you take full responsibility for your actions in this matter, that penalty will be greatly reduced in hopes of restructuring your life. You are hereby sentenced to thirty years on each of the charges, the sentence to run concurrently. Court is adjourned."

The reports started to arrive at the Department of Justice just as fast as they cleared the local courts. A few more discreet calls were made from that point on scrambled phones. One found it's way to General Randolph Miller as he was making his way out of the office.

"General Miller, a call for you on the white phone."

"Shit, what now," he said to no one, as he walked back into his office. "General Miller speaking, sir."

"Good to hear you, Randy. Thought you might like to know how things went today across the country."

"I'd be delighted to know, sir. I trust it is as we expected."

"It went absolutely perfect, Randy. In fact we had a twist in the scenario that I didn't expect so soon."

Miller sat down, not knowing what to expect. "A twist, sir?"

"Yes. A male in California was administered the prescribed dose, then entered the court and made a plea of not guilty."

"What!" Miller said, astonished. "Are we sure he was given the correct dose?"

"Absolutely. We have to accept the fact that he's not guilty, I guess. That's what this whole exercise is all about. Remember? Weed out the innocent from the guilty without all the bullshit."

"Yes, I know, I just never thought about a not guilty plea."

"All the cases were strong, and it was felt they were all guilty. That's why they were chosen. Anyway, we probably saved a pile of money and saved one guy from jail. The only thing is, we have one pissed off prosecutor. Apparently he's taking a lot of local heat because he dropped the charges."

"Well they're all getting paid well, and they're big boys," Miller offered.

"That they are, that they are. I've got to go now, ... oh, by the way, times getting short. How are you making out with Strickler and our samples?"

I knew it! Miller thought. "Sir, you won't believe it, my man is right on the ass of Fletcher and his wife. Last report I got he was trying to head them off at the Canadian Border in Montana."

"And what if they get across, General? What contingency plans do you have in place?"

"One, I don't think they will get out of the country, and two, if they do I have some resources in Ottawa that have started the ball rolling. Anyway, border or no border, Strickler and his watchdog will be on Fletcher's ass and we *will* get our merchandise back."

"Remember the classification, Randy. We definitely cannot afford an international incident, and we have to keep 'PRECISE' away from the media at all costs."

"Yes, I know, sir."

"Randy? What is today?"

"Today? I don't know what you mean, sir. It's Monday... Oh, yes sir. It's Monday."

"Tomorrow is Tuesday, Randy, and time is getting short. Don't forget to watch the President on T.V. the day after tomorrow. You'll be proud of him." The man hung up, leaving Miller with an empty feeling.

A phone burred softly at his left hand. This time it was the beige one and he had an idea where it was coming from since it was routed through the com-center. "General Miller."

"Yes sir, it's Major Strickler reporting."

"I was just thinking about you, Major. Have you made an apprehension or a seizure of the goods?"

"What I have, sir, is a sighting, and a brief chase to the Canadian Border of this Fletcher and his wife. There was a brief containment at the border, but before we could get the chopper down, customs officials let them through to the Canadian side. I couldn't follow in the chopper with the military markings."

Miller sat there saying nothing. He felt a little empty inside. He couldn't even get angry with Strickler. He wanted so much for this thing to end, so he could go home and think about the ordinary things in life.

"Sir? Are you there, sir?"

"Yes, Nathan, I'm here. I'm going to put the push in for their capture in Canada. I'll have to go through the State Department. That will be the official part. You however will take your friend, Captain Grant, and with every means at your disposal stop them and obtain the samples before our friends north of the border beat us to it. You do that, Nathan, and you will be well taken care of, regardless of the fact that this got away from you in the first place. Got that?"

"Yes, thank you, sir. I'm dropping the helicopter and going in by car with Captain Grant. I have an idea where they are headed."

"Then you had better get going, Nathan, and remember this is American business. Top secret American business that is not to fall into the hands of our Canadian friends."

"Yes sir. I..."

"While I have you on the line, what about this Jesse Harris? Where is he?"

"I don't know exactly, sir. All I know is he is very close. We have a make on the car he's driving and the fact that he is supposed to meet up with Fletcher."

"How did you get onto this information?"

"A couple of ways, Sir. First through our computer hookup with the *Echelon Network*, and secondly we had a report back from the picture we circulated on Harris. A Washington State Patrol officer remembers dealing with him in the Burlington area. Says he last saw him heading east from that location while he was dealing with an injury accident. He said Harris was all spun out."

"This guy, Harris," Miller said. "He may not be in Canada yet. I want him."

"So do I, sir. I have other people working on it with the help of the Montana authorities and quite a few plainclothes MPs out of the air force base at Great Falls."

"Good, Major. I will repeat my earlier message. Keep the F.B.I. out of this as much as possible. This is our problem."

Miller hung up and walked out of his office to his secretary's desk. "Anything comes through from Major Strickler or Captain Grant is to be treated as priority one. Make sure the night people know this. I'm to be called no matter where I am or what time it is."

Without waiting for an answer, Miller walked out into the hallway, his step quickening as he thought, *"Time for a double. No, time for a damn triple."*

• • •

Jesse Harris could feel his excitement building at the prospect of seeing Craig again. Hooking up with Craig would mean an end to a lot of anxiety. He felt less alone. He started to feel, unrealistically, that things would work out.

Craig had said that they were to meet in the area of Pincher Creek. That suited him, because now he could head north on highway 89 instead of going to Cut Bank. He could switch to highway 17 and cross the Canadian Border at a remote area south of the Pincher Creek area.

Jesse thought back over his trip from the coast. There had been a lot of police and military vehicles heading rapidly in a westerly direction, but he hadn't hit any roadblocks for some reason.

Making a hasty decision, he had cut off the east / west route he had been on for a long time, and had driven down to Spokane. Once there, he had traded the Ford Taurus off for another rental, this time a large Chevrolet. The different car gave him renewed confidence, and maybe that's why when leaving Spokane, he picked up a fairly well-dressed guy on the on ramp. The guy had held a sign that said '*O-HI-O*', on a piece of cardboard. He was tired of traveling alone, and he needed the company. Besides, they would be looking for one guy, not two.

"Thanks," the man had said, jumping in and closing the door.

"No problem," Jesse said, picking up speed to enter the freeway. "I'm not going all the way to Ohio, though."

Laughing, the man put his sign on the floor by his feet. "Every bit helps, believe me." Reaching over he offered Jesse his hand. "Name's Ernie."

Taking the hand, Jesse looked at the guy closely for the first time. He was in his thirties, clean, and dressed neatly.

"Hi Ernie, names Harry." Looking at him again, he spoke his thoughts aloud. "You don't look like the hitch-hiking type."

"I'm not really," Ernie answered. "But I have no choice this time. I have a job waiting with my uncle's firm in Akron, and I've been out of work too long to pass it up."

"Why didn't you ask him for the fare home?"

"No way. I feel bad enough having to work in the family circle as it is. How far you going anyway, Harry?"

"Just to Montana. Not quite sure yet."

"You sell stuff, or what?" Ernie wanted to know.

"Uh, yeah. I look after a fairly big area, so I have to move around."

"Cool. Anyway I'm grateful for the ride."

The ride with Ernie had been uneventful. They had enjoyed each other's company and the miles had melted away with the conversation. To Jesse, however, the big thing was having two people in the car instead of one. He hadn't heard a thing on the radio since arriving in Montana. He hoped they were still turning Washington State up-side-down looking for him.

Jesse had to let Ernie off west of Missoula, on the off ramp to highway 135 so he could head back up to U.S. 2. Ernie waved goodbye, and dwindled in the mirror as Jesse swung onto 135. Now that he was alone, he felt a little vulnerable. He hated to admit that he had enjoyed the security of someone being with him.

Now he was heading north, and to Canada. He eased the Chevy up another notch, noting that in another fifty miles or so he should cross into Alberta. He would try and contact Craig then.

The roadblock sprung out of nowhere, four miles north of the town of Babb. It came at him without warning, and was situated in a small depression in the landscape.

He braked, noting about ten vehicles inching ahead towards the waiting police vehicles that were criss-crossed on the highway. He was able to see down the line towards a cop who was very carefully checking the occupants against a photograph he held in his hand. Another man was standing to the side with a shotgun pointed in the direction of the roadblock.

Finding himself approaching the head of the line at an alarming rate, he didn't have a clue what to do. Looking left and right, he saw that there was nowhere to turn. It was a good roadblock location.

A large truck pulled up behind him, staying two car lengths to the rear. Jesse, needing to stall for time, did the first thing that came into his mind and pulled the hood release. He got out of the car and lifted the hood, waving the trucker around. The trucker hesitated, looking like he was going to get out and give Jesse a hand.

Jesse waved his hand back and forth signaling the man to stay in his rig, and waved frantically for him to pass. A cop was looking in his direction, and had taken a few steps towards him when the sound of the large engine magnified, and the truck started to move. The cop stopped, waiting for the tractor-trailer to pull into the waiting line.

The truck stopped about forty feet in front of Jesse, the sound of the air brakes hissing back at him. He was about to lower the hood when another car took the truck's old spot behind him. Jesse waved him on too, then slammed the hood down and got behind the wheel.

Backing up, Jesse tried to keep the big truck between him and the roadblock. Looking for a spot to turn the large Chevy around, he did not see the approaching driver in his mirror. A blast from the other vehicle's horn made him jump; as it swept by a young driver gave him the finger.

Finding an old track at the side of the road, Jesse backed into what used to be an entrance to a field. He then quietly accelerated and pointed the car south. Looking into the rearview mirror, he saw a police officer moving rapidly towards a police vehicle. If it hadn't been for the guy blowing his horn, he might have slid over the horizon unnoticed.

Jesse looked into the rearview mirror and saw the tiny speck and distant flash of double blue, double red, strobes. Jesse accelerated with his foot to the floorboards. The lights were growing larger in his mirror. "Shit!" Jesse said aloud, and tried to put the gas pedal further into the floor. A few seconds later he looked down and was surprised to see his speed was ninety-five miles an hour. The police vehicle had disappeared from view.

The Chev entered the town of Babb at twice the speed limit, Jesse's attention riveted forward for signs of any danger. He passed through the town without stopping, increasing his speed even further. A few miles further on down the road an old sign at the edge of the road caught his attention. He could barely make out the numbers: *464*.

He braked hard and swung the car into a left-handed skid, almost loosing control as he hit the gas pedal to urge the car eastward. He had no idea where he was or where he was going, all he knew was he couldn't afford to be checked by the police. A sign came into view and rapidly drew near, disappearing to the rear in a blur, Jesse barely able to comprehend what it had displayed.

BLACKFEET

INDIAN RESERVATION

The road abruptly turned south. There wasn't a building or a single living thing visible. No cars, nothing. A sign read *BROWNING - 12 miles.* "Christ, I'm going right back where I started from."

Jesse was beginning to feel trapped. He was thirsty, hungry, and needed to use the bathroom. He had been in such a hurry to get to Alberta, he had decided not to eat or stop.

"I just hope they haven't any roadblocks out here", Jesse thought. Then he remembered that police have radios for a reason.

Slamming on the brakes, the car slid to the side of the road, the back wheel hitting the dead grass and weeds at the side of the road. Jesse rummaged through the glove box for his map, finding nothing but the registration, insurance, and rental agreement. It took a few seconds of looking around before he saw a corner of the folded map between the passenger seat and the door.

Getting out of the air-conditioned car, Jesse felt the heat assault him with each gust of wind. The country was desolate and hostile to the eye. Quickly he walked to the other side of the car and retrieved the map that had jammed around the seat belt. Looking along the deserted stretch of road for any sign of approaching traffic, all he saw was blowing dust.

The air inside the car was a welcome relief as Jesse scanned the map. A road, he saw, would take him east, and then north, if he turned before he got back to U.S.-2. He had no choice. Jesse threw the map, still open, onto the other seat and pulled back onto the road.

Thirty-five minutes later, the car was close to State Highway 213. From there, the border was only a few miles distant.

Great clouds of dust billowed up from the dirt road. It was dry and hot, the dark brown grass lying inert in the burning sun. It was a lonely stretch of highway.

• • •

Jesse was the second car in line to enter Canada at the Del Bonita border crossing. Strangely, he hadn't seen any show of force or interest on the U.S. side at all. He pulled up when the light turned green.

"Citizenship?" the customs man asked.

"Canadian."

"Where's home?"

"I live and work in Washington State for the time being, just outside of Seattle," Jesse answered, feeling a little nervous.

"I guess that accounts for the American license plates. How long are you planning to stay?"

"Hopefully it will be permanent. New job offer." Jesse smiled nervously.

"What's the value of the goods you're bringing in with you?"

"None, nothing. Personal items."

"You have firearms in the vehicle, or alcohol?"

"No. No to both."

"Okay, now what about the vehicle? It's American. You say you're staying in Canada, then your going to have to pay duty."

"No, it's a rental. Forgot to mention it's a rental. Want to see the papers?"

The customs officer looked at Jesse, then waved for him to proceed. "Way you go."

Jesse pulled away from the Border Inspection Station, gathering speed slowly. He *hated* crossing the border; they always made you feel like a criminal.

"Fuck! I am a criminal," Jesse thought, then laughed nervously, not recognizing his own voice.

• • •

In Cardston, Alberta, he once again tried Craig's cellular. He looked around at the near deserted streets as he waited for the call to go through. It rang once, and then twice, then a voice was speaking into his left ear. It was a couple of seconds before he realized the phone had been answered.

"Hello? Hello?"

"Hi, Jennifer. It's Jesse, is everything okay?"

Her deep throaty voice came back in his ear. "We're okay, Jess."

"Where are you guys?"

"We're... hold on a minute, Jess."

Jesse could hear Jennifer talking to Craig in the background, obviously asking where they were. She came back on the line. "We are about twenty-five miles from Pincher Creek. Where are you?"

"I'm in Cardston. I'll see you guys very shortly. How will I find you?"

"Look for a..., look for a library. We'll be watching for your car."

"I'm driving a rental now, Jenn, it's a dark green Chevrolet Caprice. See you soon."

He heard Jennifer hang up, then replaced the receiver and got into the car. Watching his mirror, Jesse made several turns around Cardston before heading west, and out of town. There was no way he wanted to be followed at this point.

Unfortunately, Jesse wasn't a trained observer. He didn't see the black sedan as it pulled out of the parking stall a block and a half to the rear and kept pace with him as he left town for the open highway.

···CHAPTER TEN

Craig was the first to see Jesse as he coasted slowly to curb at the library. He watched as he got out and looked up and down the street, his hair blowing in all directions from the strong south wind. A great whirlwind of dust and paper blew by, causing Jesse to turn his face away from Craig.

Starting the motor, Craig pulled out from the side of the closed gas station. Jesse turned, saw the two of them, and started to wave. "Look at that bean pole, you'd think he was happy to see us."

As they got out of the car, Jesse was grinning from ear to ear. Jennifer and Craig walked up to him and stopped a few feet away. They all stood there, saying nothing.

Jesse started to talk, "You don't know how glad... "

At the same time Craig was saying, "Where have you been, buddy... "

Jennifer was laughing, and stepped forward to give him a hug. "We have been worried to death about you."

Craig reached out and shook Jesse's hand. "That was the *longest* weekend I've ever had in my life!"

"You have no idea how much I want to sit down and have a drink like a normal human being!" Jesse cried in feigned anguish. "Any problem with the samples, Craig?"

"Everything's cool, Jess."

167

They were through their second drink inside of ten minutes of sitting down. The Greek restaurant provided just the right atmosphere for them to unwind, with soft background music, a quiet corner, and low light. They hadn't ordered; all three of them were content to just sit.

Jesse looked at his two friends sitting across from him. Swirling the ice cubes in his glass, he said, "You two have had a rough go of it the last couple of days, haven't you?"

Craig looked at Jennifer, then back at Jesse before he answered. Quietly, he said, "There have been moments. Nothing we didn't handle. We were lucky a few times."

"Yeah, well let me tell you," Jennifer butted in, "I was damned scared approaching the border. I thought we were going to get killed for sure."

"Now never *mind* that, Jenn, we don't need to go over that." Craig placed his arm around her. He didn't want Jennifer talking about it and becoming anymore upset than she already was.

"No!" Jesse objected, "I want to hear everything that's gone on. It's not just out of curiosity; I have to know what's been happening so I know what decisions to make about the lab samples and data. I need to know to what extreme they've gone to get it back. And I need to relieve you of those items tonight."

Wiping off a drop of water that had fallen from the bottom of the glass onto her blouse Jennifer asked, "Just what do you plan to do, Jess?"

"There's been a lot to think about. I originally wanted to just unload the samples onto someone, but it would just be placing someone else in danger. Now, ...I don't know."

"You have to think, ol' buddy," Craig said. "Remember, they have wrung you dry of every bit of information you had before you got away. If you try to send, deliver, or otherwise contact any person you had in your mind, they will hone in on you like some sort of cruise missile."

"You mentioned the border. Tell me what happened. And what happened in Spokane?

Craig and Jennifer filled him in on everything they could for the next twenty minutes, along with their suspicions about the cellular phone and the government's ability to track them.

"Then I don't like this," Jesse said. "Like you say, we spoke over the phone after we crossed the border."

"We've driven quite a distance since then. We are only in danger if they were actually able to listen to our conversation. If they did, then they know we are here."

"Can they do that?"

"Probably," Craig said bluntly. "With some difficulty I think, but I don't doubt that the U.S. Government has the ability."

Jennifer gave Craig a dirty look. "Thanks a hell of a lot! I was planning to have a good sleep tonight. Now I have to watch the window every time a car goes by." She looked at the two men and didn't receive an answer. "I'm starving. Can we order before they close?"

As they ate, they almost forgot their underlying fear. Craig knew that their safety was just an illusion. He couldn't afford to relax his guard just because of a line drawn on a map.

"Well, where do we go from here?" Jennifer asked.

"Very simple," Jesse answered. "You two go home and give me my stuff back. As of now."

"Oh? And just what are you going to do with it?" Craig wanted to know.

"I haven't decided yet. I have a few ideas, but I don't want to involve you two any further. God knows you've done enough, and you will have a lot to answer for when you get home."

Jennifer looked at Craig before speaking. "I don't think so. That is precisely why we can't just drop out. We *are* involved, Jess, and we can't just let you wander off. We are going to figure out something together. I was furious at you for getting Craig involved in this, and I know how terribly frightened you must have been once you committed yourself. I hesitated because I was scared. I'm still scared, but I'm not hesitating now. You need us."

With a tear brimming at the corner of his right eye, and emotions in danger of erupting, Jesse nodded his thanks. "You have a right to be angry, Jenn, because I *have* committed a serious crime and people *are* after me. They are after you and Craig now too, because of me. I didn't know what else to do."

Jennifer leaned over and kissed Jesse briefly on the lips, then pushed him away roughly, "By the way, you have a hell of a nerve keeping Bev from us for so long, then putting her up at our house when we're not home."

"Bev! Jeez, I've got to call her. She'll be worried sick." Turning to Craig he said, " I didn't think you would mind, but I knew she would be hauled in and questioned."

Craig held up his hand to silence Jesse. "We got a full report and everything is fine, but you're right, you'd better call her."

Jesse sighed, "I feel a lot more at ease being on this side of the border."

"So do we," Jennifer smiled.

Craig didn't say anything. He knew that the people who wanted

'PRECISE' weren't about to be worried about any border.

"I think I only have a couple of choices. One, turn 'PRECISE' over to the Canadian Government..."

Craig looked at Jesse, surprised. "I don't know if that's an option. What do you think the Americans are planning if such an event takes place? They'll end up with it all back in their hands, and this will all have been for nothing. Besides, we are all in danger of being arrested, no matter what side of the border we are on. You cannot take stolen government documents and jump into Canada without facing the consequences. The pressure on the Canadian government to co-operate will be immense."

"Why?" Jesse asked. "It happened in the U.S., not here."

"It's against the law to bring property into Canada that has been obtained illegally in another country. Simple as that."

"Wonderful! There goes my sleep for sure," Jennifer said.

"What's the other thing you were going to suggest?" Craig asked Jesse.

"Going public somehow. You guys must know some news people who would like a good story."

Craig laughed. "Hell, they've had lot's of good stories out of me over the years, but I don't know if they would believe *this*. It may be dangerous."

"There may be some sort of damage control if everyone knows about it." Jesse offered.

"I may have the man for such a story. He's a talk show host. Can't stand the bastard myself, but who knows, he may be able to get it out. It would be an incredible story for him. We would have to do it over the phone and on the move," Craig said, thinking out loud more than anything. "Who knows, they may not even touch this thing, never mind broadcast it. They may want to verify it first, and when they do, they could be prevented from airing it."

"If it can be done, it might take the heat off of us a bit," Jesse concluded.

"There is a third option," Jennifer chimed in.

Both men turned and looked at Jennifer, not knowing what she had on her mind and eager to hear. She didn't keep them in suspense. "If this stuff is so potentially bad, why not simply destroy the samples and discs? Forever."

"Don't worry, Jenn, I've thought about doing just that, but it really wouldn't work. It would defeat the purpose of taking 'PRECISE'. Nobody would know about it and I wouldn't have anything to back up any claims. Remember, even though I have the data in the briefcase as proof, they can still probably reproduce 'PRECISE'. For all I know, they still have all the data. They just don't want me running around with it."

"Go make your call to Bev," Craig said. "Tell her we're on the way. I think your news release is the best way to go, not only for our protection, but to obtain the results you want with this stuff."

"Wait for me!" Jennifer said, as Jesse threw some bills on the table. "I want to talk to Lorraine. She will still be up, knowing her."

The two of them went in search of a pay phone, and Craig slipped outside. Several cars were parked at the curb, with an occasional car or truck moving on the highway, but no one could be seen walking around. A lone dog crossed the road, stopping in the center to lift his nose to the wind. Seeming to find nothing of interest, he continued off into the darkness.

They rented two small rooms and Craig thought he would have a hard time falling asleep, but the last thing he heard as his head settled into the pillow was the sound of the wind buffeting the building.

Walking into Craig and Jennifer's room at six a.m., Jesse still looked tired. "I want to dump the rental as soon as possible. We have a lot to talk about."

They left the car parked outside the rental agency and hit the open highway without breakfast. It was early afternoon by the time the three of them entered the downtown streets of Nelson, British Columbia.

● ● ●

Jennifer opened the door and climbed in, turning around in her seat to pass the coffee to the men. "Coffee and ready-made sandwiches. That's the best I can do for now."

Heading east out of Nelson, they gradually moved north, passing Valhalla Provincial Park and the Slocan Lake area. Jesse tried to catch up on his sleep, but there just wasn't enough room, and his mind kept wandering. A continuous ten-foot wide rush of burbling mountain water sparkled as it moved alongside the roadway. "Nice."

"I thought you were supposed to be sleeping," Jennifer said, turning in her seat.

"Yeah, I tried, but nothing happens. God knows I didn't get any last night. ...I was just sitting here thinking– did you guys know that scientists have found that the suprachlasmatic nuclei has a different function than earlier thought? It..."

Craig and Jennifer looked at each other in wide-eyed astonishment, and then burst out laughing, only able to get themselves under control after several attempts.

"Sorry, Jess," Jennifer snickered, "but honestly, you *are* funny. What the hell is a superplastic nuclear?"

"It has to do with the biological clock. It was thought that it promoted daily rhythms, but actually it keeps you awake and stops you from falling asleep at the wrong time. The suprachasmatic nuclei is two tear shaped areas of the brain that..."

"We get the picture Jess, now if you could just figure out what the world will end up doing with that stuff you took from your lab, that will be a real discovery." Craig said.

"It was supposed to be to help people, but that remains to be seen. Nothing criminal will be done with it if I have anything to say about it."

The creek wandered away from the road, and campers and trailers could be seen in the turn offs. Fishermen were standing casting their lines, while the women could be seen in the shade of the big trees. "Look at those lucky devils," Craig scoffed. "Do you have any idea what we are missing?"

"Yeah," Jennifer winced. "Smelly fish."

Pulling onto the ferry to cross Arrow Lake, Craig couldn't help but notice the sharp contrast between water, sky, and the surrounding hills. The countryside had turned from lush green forest and mountain streams to rolling hills covered with sagebrush and large boulders. The small ferry provided them a chance to stretch their legs and gave Craig an opportunity to scan the other passengers during the short trip across the lake.

The sun beat down with a vengeance as they came away from the lake, the breeze falling behind as they entered Needles. Jennifer found a strong station with music and left it there.

> *This is the top of the hour news, the latest news on the hour, every hour.*
>
> *There is still no word from authorities on the report that an American forces helicopter was seen firing upon a northbound vehicle as it raced along highway 15, just South of Sweetgrass, Montana.*
>
> *Witnesses indicate that the helicopter actually landed on the Canadian side at Coutts, Alberta. Persons from the helicopter demanded the apprehension of the people in the same vehicle that the heavily armed army helicopter had been firing upon.*

As the unknown vehicle had already legally entered Canada by the time the helicopter landed, Customs officials say they had neither authority nor evidence to assist the Americans.

No further comment is being offered by Canada Customs, however, sources in Washington State indicate the chase is tied in with a massive manhunt. Two Canadians, Jesse Harris, an employee of a pharmaceutical company in that State, and Craig Fletcher, a Vancouver police officer, are being sought.

The U.S. manhunt, tied in with the border incident, is fast approaching international dimensions, but the American Government is offering little information. It is known however, that the Americans are desperate to locate Harris, as he may be involved in missing or stolen classified documents.

Craig Fletcher, the Vancouver police officer, is somehow tied in with Harris, but the Vancouver Police Department is offering no information on the apparent connection at this time.

Turning to the international scene, U.S. President Reardon will address U.S. citizens tomorrow, on..."

Craig reached over and turned the radio off. "There is absolutely no doubt now, Jenn. We are now famous. Or is it infamous?" Looking over at Jennifer, he took her hand. "Going to be a little rough when we get home, sugar."

"We'll handle it," Jennifer answered. She turned in her seat, getting the seatbelt twisted around her arm, and looked at Jesse. "We all make our own decisions, Jess. Don't worry about the news story right now."

Jesse reached up and squeezed her hand. "Your a great gal, Jenn. I hope that monkey sitting beside you knows that."

"He's coming around. Slow, but coming around."

Looking out the rear window while still facing Jesse, she frowned slightly. The dotted lines of the highway were receding into the distance with a continual flash on the senses, but every once in a while a burst of light glinted off of a piece of metal or glass where the dots met the horizon.

Noticing the change in Jennifer's expression, Jesse turned around to look out the back window. "Something wrong?"

"I don't know. I get the feeling we're being followed. Other cars have a right to use the highway, but, I don't know, I've just got this feeling."

Craig looked into his mirror. "I've been checking every few minutes, and I haven't seen a soul back there. If there is anyone back there, they're doing a hell of a good job."

Leaning ahead, Jesse filled the gap between the two front seats, resting his head on his hand. "You're a crafty bugger, Fletcher, you still haven't given me back the samples and discs. I don't want you in possession of them anymore. I'm serious, if we are stopped, I want them with me."

"They're in the storage area behind you. We'll stop at Vernon and I'll give them to you then."

Sitting back, Jesse nodded to Craig in the mirror, "Let's make it sooner than later. Jennifer's giving me the shivers with all her premonitions."

Mile after mile rolled by, the country gradually changing from hot to hotter. Descending into the Okanagan Valley, a narrow picturesque road twisted through apple, peach, then pear orchards. Trees were heavily laden with fruit, with two-by-four lumber helping to hold up the branches of some of the trees.

The heat was oppressive. There wasn't a breath of a breeze except the occasional whiff of moist air from huge sprinklers that provided moisture to the orchards. Pickers wore everything from bandannas to wide brimmed hats to protect themselves from the heat.

Pulling to the side of the road, Craig stopped next to a group of men that were stacking wooden crates in preparation for filling and shipping. Stepping out of the car and walking to the edge of the orchard, he immediately began to sweat. The difference from the air conditioning made him feel giddy for a few moments. In a matter of a few moments, his shirt was clinging to his back.

Jennifer and Jesse watched as Craig talked to the men. Yellow butterflies moved listlessly about in the heat. The worker left Craig and returned with a paper bag full of apples. Craig paid him and returned to the driver's side." Sink your teeth into one of these beauties," Craig smiled, while starting the motor.

Craig pulled away from the side of the road, the wheels biting into the soft sand and dirt before grabbing the pavement. The dust hung in the hot dry air like fine powder as they pulled away. It was still there a few minutes later when the black sedan drove by.

• • •

Vernon had a nice downtown park, and Craig managed to find a shady spot as an older couple pulled out. Lowering the windows, a cool breeze filled the interior, bringing with it the scent of flowers. Jennifer got out and walked to a bench that faced a flowing stream. Huge old growth trees provided shade and comfort from the overhead sun.

Craig got the samples and discs out for Jesse and put them on the floor. "You sure about this?"

"Yes. I won't be long."

"Yeah, well you could tell us what you're up to."

Jesse got behind the wheel. "Nothing to worry about. I'll be back in no time and we'll grab something to eat."

Craig closed the driver's door and spoke through the open window. "Maybe we should stop in Kelowna tonight, then hit Vancouver early tomorrow. That way we'll be fresh and I'll have more time to make my contact."

"You guys decide. I'll see you later." Jesse drove off slowly, and entered the city traffic pattern.

Craig sat down on the bench next to Jennifer, a frown etched on his face. "What is it? Something's wrong."

"I don't know what it is... I guess I don't like Jesse taking off by himself. Or like you said, something isn't right. Things are too casual."

"Maybe it's leaving the States where we had all that pressure on us, to being here where there is none. Maybe that's what it is."

Getting off of the bench, Craig shook his head in the negative and started to look around the park and the surrounding area. "Nope. As soon as Jesse gets back we are out of here. I don't know what he's up to, but I hope it isn't anything foolish. As a matter of fact, I hope he hasn't taken off on us."

"Now why would he do that?" Jennifer said, looking at Craig with some surprise.

"Because he cares for us. Because he doesn't want us with him when he's arrested."

"Oh, Craig," Jennifer moaned.

"Come on, let's get some popcorn to feed the ducks. All we can do is wait."

They waited exactly one hour and twenty-three minutes before Jesse eased to a halt on the hot pavement. Leaving the cool of the trees, Craig hurried towards Jess, with Jennifer close behind. "Christ, he even washed the damn thing."

Craig came up even with Jesse and playfully reached up and ruffled his hair. "Here we are worried sick, and he's out washing the damn vehicle. All right, now tell us what you were up to."

Jesse climbed into the back seat again, waiting for the other two to get settled before answering.

"Look, there are certain things I don't want to tell you. Now don't go getting offended," Jesse quickly added, seeing the expression on Craig's face. "This is my responsibility, and I have to take certain safeguards. The less you know, the safer you are."

Craig turned and started the motor, speaking as he drove towards the park exit. "Jess, you're the expert, I'm just trying to help. I just hope you still have it."

"Yes, I have it. We'll figure out what to do with it when we talk to your reporter, or whatever he is. When do you think you'll call him?"

"As soon as we settle in for the night in Kelowna. I won't mention what it's about just yet, but I'll hint... "

Jennifer looked at Craig in disbelief. "You won't tell him what it's about? Craig, the whole fucking world's talking about you! Just mention who's calling and they'll be clamoring for your attention."

"What I meant to say was, I'll hint at an exclusive interview, but won't disclose when or what I want to say. He has to agree to our agenda."

Craig was surprised to get two rooms on the bottom floor of a motor inn and, paying cash, he was given the keys for rooms 112 and 125. Filling out the registration cards, he put down Christopher Fleming and Jake Harper. Outside, he threw a key to Jesse. "You're in number 112, Mr. Harper. If you want us, I registered under Fleming in 125."

Grabbing his overnighter, Jesse got out of the back seat. "Shit, you never know who you're traveling with anymore."

The room was surprisingly cool, done up in soft colors. "I should call Tom Gifford, Jenn. He'll be wondering what's happening, and he may even have some information."

"Let's eat first. If you call Tom at home, he may be able to say things he can't at the office."

Supper was a boring and tense affair. The three of them were too wound up to really enjoy the food, and Craig couldn't relax for constantly looking for something out of the ordinary.

"Let's find a phone," Craig said, reaching for the check.

Jesse whipped it out of his hand while standing. "Let's get something straight here, we are not on holiday, and I pay for all expenses, including your room."

Craig didn't argue; he knew Jesse was right. Outside, Craig stopped and turned to the other two. "You guys go and make the call, I'll make mine in a moment. I want to go and gas up before dark."

Craig walked towards the Jeep, keeping his head up and eyes busy. Everyone he saw seemed to be doing their own thing, but then, if there were professionals out there, he probably wouldn't be able to spot them anyway.

Coming up to the vehicle, he noticed that the passenger door was slightly ajar, with a few pieces of paper lying on the ground. Coming closer, he saw other papers strewn about. The interior had been ransacked.

Craig's heart rate doubled at the same time that he made note that there was no forced entry to the locked door. Turning, he did an immediate scan of the area, taking in everything and everybody. Four doors away, he could see that the door to their room was open.

Flattening himself against the wall, knowing it was already too late, he moved along the building until he could look through the doorway. The room was empty, but the contents of their suitcases had been scattered everywhere. It looked like a normal break-in, but Craig didn't like the timing and knew deep down it wasn't normal at all.

Backing out of the room, he started to head back to Jesse and Jennifer, then stopped and ran towards Jesse's room. Seeing the door open, he hit it at a run and burst into the center of the room. This unit wasn't as bad, even with the overturned bed, but there was no doubt now. This was no ordinary break-in.

Jesse was on the phone when Craig hurried up to them. "Break it off," he said looking around. "We've got major problems."

Jennifer looked questioningly at Craig as Jesse said a quick goodbye. "Someone hit the Cherokee and both our rooms while we were having supper."

A little sound escaped Jennifer's lips, her eyes darting everywhere. Jesse said nothing, but he looked stricken at the news.

"You leave anything in the room, Jess?"

Jesse shook his head. "Like I said before, I'm not letting this out of my sight."

"Who... who was it, Hon?" Jennifer asked with a shaky voice as they moved quickly to their rooms.

Craig grabbed her hand and tucked her arm between his elbow and body. "Look, we are all still together, so try and be calm. We are not as clever as we thought we were, and we have a very big problem now that they know exactly where we are. We still have what they want though, and they are not going to go away."

Jesse shrugged, waiting for directions. "Now what? We just gather our stuff and leave?"

"You're missing the point, Jess," Craig said, slowing down as they neared their rooms. "They didn't find what they wanted, and that indicates to me that they would have been satisfied to grab it and run. Now they can't, and that means they will have to come and take it."

"It must be Strickler and what's his name... Grant. They've found us," Jesse said in a strained voice turning towards his room. "Let's get out of here."

"But to where?" Jennifer said. "They know where we are headed."

It took five minutes to pack everything. Once they were on the road, the traffic was heavier all the way to the floating bridge crossing Okanagan Lake. It wasn't until they left West Bank that traffic returned to normal.

"There's nothing suspicious back there," Jesse said from the back seat. "My neck is getting damn sore in this position."

"They'll be back there, Jess, you just have to be good at spotting them."

"How can you tell, Craig?" Jesse asked. "I mean, there's traffic back there, but how do you pick them out?"

"You don't. Not if they're any good at what they do. You might as well relax, Jess, we'll worry when we get to Merritt."

Jennifer looked in her own side mirror, and also saw nothing. "Why don't we find an out-of-the-way place and hide for a while?"

"We will," Craig answered. "We can't keep going forever, and neither can they. I figure by the time we reach Merritt, we'll all be totally bushed."

Turning onto the connector, the long climb began towards Merritt. The freeway was a marvel of engineering, the four lanes offering superb driving conditions through the roughest terrain imaginable. Passing laboring tractor-trailer units and slow moving recreation vehicles, they could see mountain range after mountain range.

"I forgot what fresh air smelled like," Jesse said from the back seat. "I can see forever."

"Almost like being on another planet, isn't it?" Craig said into the mirror at Jesse's reflection, then looked back at the far away snow capped mountains, florescent white in the sunlight.

Getting a room in Merritt wasn't easy. Jesse came out of the motel and walked over to Craig and Jennifer. "All they have is one room. It's a queen bed, but they can put a cot in it for you two if you want."

"Man has a sense of humor," Jennifer chuckled.

It didn't take Craig long to fall asleep, however he didn't beat Jennifer or Jesse. He did his usual walk around, but try as he might, he couldn't spot anything out of the ordinary.

When Craig did fall into a deep sleep, his mind was free to wander in its universe. A door opened in his mind, and he found himself standing in a strange room with wooden floors and sparse furniture. He knew that he was in a different city and a long way from home, and he was confused and upset for some reason.

An older man entered the room, with Jennifer and Lorraine following close behind. He smiled at Craig, displaying crooked teeth in a full-lipped mouth, drool falling on a sweater that was filthy, and buttoned wrong.

"I have spoken to your wife and daughter," he slobbered. "After giving them 'PRECISE', they have truthfully informed me that they are tired of you and your problems. They will be going to a new life."

Craig knew that this didn't make sense, but nonetheless he broke out in a sweat, and fear knotted his stomach. He tried to speak but nothing came out. Looking at Jennifer, he now saw that she was holding suitcases in her hand. "We are leaving you," she said with a chuckle, the same chuckle that Craig had come to love. "We won't be back because we have a new husband and daddy to look after us."

Craig tried to speak, and couldn't. He was shouting in his mind, but they didn't hear him; the two of them just stood there and smiled. Now that he looked closer, he saw that Jennifer didn't speak either. Her words came to him without her lips moving. "When the phone rings, it will be my new husband. He will be with me always."

Just as Craig feared, the phone rang. It was on the floor in a barren corner, and it rang and rang and rang. It was bringing the end to his life, and neither Jennifer nor Lorraine was making a move to answer it. It was up to him. Jennifer said with her mischievous grin, "Aren't you going to answer it? You will like him a lot."

Craig felt himself getting very angry. Why should he answer it? He knew if he did he would have to kill the son-of-a-bitch.

"Craig, are you going to answer the phone?"

The phone rang once more then stopped. He tried to figure out why this was happening to him, but couldn't. It rang once more and this time Craig managed to shout out loud at the instrument. "Go away. You asshole!"

Someone was poking him in the ribs, and he came awake. Confused, he heard his cellular next to his ear.

Jennifer was saying something and it took a few minutes to sort out where he was. "The cellular, Craig, are you going to answer it?"

Reaching out, he fumbled in the dark and found the instrument. He couldn't get the dream out of his mind and thought for sure he was about to speak to the asshole that was ruining his life. "Lo."

"I kind of thought you would eventually answer, Fletcher."

Rubbing his eyes then looking at his wristwatch, he saw it was 4:28 a.m. by the soft glow from the dial face. He was coming awake and now seemed to recognize the voice. "Who is this?"

"We've talked before if you remember, but it's time to stop playing games. You have property belonging to the United States Government. We want it back."

"Who am I talking to?" The light in the room went on, and Craig shielded his eyes, seeing Jennifer and Jesse looking at him expectantly.

"The name is not important," the voice said. "What is important is what it will take to get that property back."

Craig had a hard time coming back to reality after the dream, but he sat up, trying to think before asking another question. "You're running a fix on me right this moment, aren't you?"

"Look friend, all we want is the goods. We are finished fooling around with you. From what I hear, you have a nice place there on Rocky Creek Road."

Craig, still a little angry from his dream, fell into that same mood easily. "What are you getting at, mister?"

The voice came back in the same low, calm, and threatening tone. "We understand you have a nice daughter too. What's her name again? Lorraine?"

The anger was replaced with anxiety, then a powerless feeling of anger again. "What are you saying?"

"What I'm saying, fuckhead, is that I don't give a sweet fuck for you, your wife, your daughter, your dog, or anything that you hold dear to your heart. If, and I say if, we don't get back what belongs to us, I am going to start to take out each and everything on the list that's important to you."

"You should never threaten a man when you want something from him," Craig said with a calm he didn't feel. He motioned for Jennifer and Craig to get up and get dressed. "I don't take threats lightly. I've dealt with them for years."

"Oh yes, the policeman strong and true, the public defender against all evil. What you want to ask yourself, Fletcher, is one question. Will you be able to defend your family? What happens if you make that one little mistake? Mmmm?"

Craig didn't answer; he knew it was pointless. He felt a growing tightness in his chest and a real fear that he knew would be revealed to the other man if he didn't take a moment to adjust.

"Now listen carefully, Fletcher. I want you to stay by that phone. I will phone you in one hour. If you don't answer, I'll leave you with nothing but fucking memories. Besides, you might want to hear about your daughter."

Craig gripped the cellular and pressed it against his ear, swinging his feet to the floor without conscious thought. "What are...?" The phone had gone dead.

Both Jennifer and Jesse were watching and waiting, not saying anything. Craig stood, reached for his clothes, and turned as he started to dress. "He laid it on pretty thick. He said if he doesn't get the stuff back right away, nasty things would start to happen."

"What..." Jennifer started to ask.

"I have to phone home, sweets. He made a threat about Lorraine. He's going to phone back in an hour."

Jennifer sat down, turning deathly pale as she thought the worse. "What's happened, Craig," she whispered. She spoke louder, fear coming to the surface. "What's happened? Have they got her?" She started to cry, her face hidden in her shaking hands.

"I'll phone right away, don't get excited yet. They could be just trying to scare the hell out of us."

Dialing his home number, Craig listened as the connection was made almost instantly. The phone gave a half a ring, and then settled into a steady ring with no answer. He was about to turn to Jennifer when he heard the phone being picked up.

A sleepy voice answered. "Hello?"

"Is that you, Bev? It's Craig."

"Oh, Craig. What time is it? Is everything all right?"

"It's going on to five o'clock, Bev. Look, I'm phoning about Lorraine, can I speak to her please?"

"She's not here, Craig, she went to spend the night at a friend's house."

"A friend? Who?" Craig asked, getting that cold chill at the base of his spine, feeling a clamp encircle his heart.

"Let's see—just a minute until I turn on a light and go into the other room."

Craig waited, silently furious with himself for not seeing the danger to his family.

"Craig? Here's the number she's staying at. I said I would pick her up in the morning. What's wrong?"

"It could be nothing, Bev, but the people that are out looking for us made a threat about Lorraine. I'm just checking to see if she's okay. I'll call you back and let you know. What's the number?"

Using a pencil from the motel desk drawer, Craig jotted the numbers down and found himself punching them in as soon as the line was clear. The phone was answered on the second ring.

"I'm sorry to bother you, but this is Craig Fletcher, Lorraine's dad. I understand she's staying at your place for the night."

"Oh, hello Mr. Fletcher," a female voice answered. "Yes, she was supposed to, but then we got a call that she had a change of plans. Hold it a moment please."

Craig listened as the woman talked to her husband, the fear rolling in his stomach.

"My husband said he thought it was you who phoned. Whoever called said they were taking her out for the evening instead. You mean she's not home?"

"No, she's not. I have to make some calls, but if you hear anything please call my home."

"Of course..."

Craig hung up and turned to Jennifer. "Lorraine isn't there either. Somebody called and canceled her overnight stay."

Jesse moved over towards Jennifer, and put his arm around her shoulder for comfort. "Bev, what does she say?"

"Everything appears normal as far as Bev's concerned. Let's get moving; I don't want company dropping in on us. Jess, you drive, non-stop all the way. I want to use the phone to call some very useful friends."

• • •

They were dressed and heading south on the Coquihalla Highway within fifteen minutes. It was no longer dark, and there wasn't a soul in their way. Jesse had the tires humming on the super highway through the high mountains, keeping the speed at a steady 85mph.

Craig was on the cellular trying to contact Tom, and getting no answer. He tried Art Campbell, then Brad Duffield with as much success.

"No luck?" Jesse asked.

"I'll just have to keep trying. They..."

The phone came to life in Craig's hand and made him jump, proving to him how scared, nervous, and worried he really was. "Craig Fletcher," he said in a brisk tone.

"Hi, Daddy."

"Lorraine!" Craig bolted upright in his seat, looking out the windshield as the fence posts flew by in a blur. "Where are you, Hon?"

"I'm okay, Daddy. I want you home."

"Where are you, Lorraine? Where have you been all night?" Craig turned and squeezed Jennifer's hand over the back of the seat.

"I'm home. I was goin' to Tracy's house, but a man stopped me and said he was a policeman and that he worked with you. He took me to the police station and another man asked me all sorts of questions. After a while he gave me somethin' to eat and I slept on his couch."

"Shepherd!" Craig said, taking the phone away from his mouth and covering it with his hand. "The bastard!" Then into the phone, "Where did he take you, honey?"

"You know, where you work."

"Yes, I know, but where in the building did he talk to you?"

"Oh, it was a nice office, and really big. He had some fish in the corner... he was sort of fat and had no hair in the middle. I can't remember his name."

Craig felt a desire to kill. He had never hated a man as much as he hated Shepherd.

"Is everything all right, Daddy? You aren't mad at me are you?"

"Sweetheart, I love you to death. You just stay with Bev until I get home."

"Okay. Oh, that man, the one with the fish? He asked about you and Mommy and where you were and when you would be home. He had awful breath. Yech!"

"He actually kept you there all night?"

"He gave me a hamburger and fries. He was nice after he quit askin' me questions."

Craig wiped his forehead, surprised at the sheen of perspiration that came away on the back of his hand. "Okay, I want you to say a quick hello to your mom, then I have to speak to Aunty Bev, so don't talk long."

Craig handed the phone over to Jennifer, then flopped back on the seat, the wave of fear gradually dissipating. He closed his eyes for a moment while the two of them were talking, then finally took the phone back off of Jennifer.

"Bev's on the line."

"Bev, it's Craig. I want you to do something for me. I want you both to pack an overnight bag and stay with a friend of mine. It won't be for long, we aren't that far away. His name is Tom Gifford and his wife is Jo-Ann. Look in the top drawer by the phone and you'll see his phone number and address. Call right away, okay?"

"Sure, Craig, but what's going on?"

"You have a lot to catch up on Bev, but not now, okay? Keep calling until you get him."

"Sure."

"When did Lorraine get home, Bev?"

"About half an hour after you called. She said a policeman brought her home but I was in the back of the house and didn't see her drive up."

"Okay Bev, thanks. We'll talk to you later."

• • •

Their anger continued unabated as they passed through the tollbooth and started the downward part of the journey to the coast. Jesse was passing vehicles at an incredible rate, and although Craig was concerned about brake burnout, he didn't say anything.

Jesse turned to Craig as he whipped past a slow moving truck. "You said Shepherd might not be working alone. Who would he be involved with?"

"Your friends in the United States will be in constant contact with him, and they'll be using him to get at us. That's what happened here, with Lorraine, a little behind-the-scene maneuvering to put the pressure on us. He can always say he was concerned about us and wanted to ensure her safety. No, it was a scare tactic all right, to remind us how vulnerable we are."

"It seems to have worked," Jennifer volunteered from the back seat. "I was so scared I could hardly breath."

The phone made several chirps, as they were passing through Hope, and entered the lush Fraser Valley.

"Yes."

"You do see how vulnerable you are, don't you Fletcher? It could have been very real, and it still can be."

Craig sat listening, not sure what he was supposed to say. He knew he would probably come face to face with these men soon. "Go on."

"Good. We want what belongs to us, friend, and today."

Craig was trying to think. Lorraine was okay for the time being, and...

"Oh, and one other thing Fletcher, this invitation is not extended to that traitorous slime that you have with you. Harris also has to return with the goods. In fact, he's part of the goods."

When Craig didn't respond, the voice continued. "Just remember, we want it today and," the man laughed into Craig's ear, "don't think that pissy-assed partner of yours is going to protect your daughter. I can blow him away at the same time."

Before Craig could respond, the phone went dead.

···CHAPTER ELEVEN

WASHINGTON, D.C.

President Howard Reardon finished reading over the speech that he had to give in a matter of hours, thinking that for the most part it was pretty good. Certain phrases dealing with law and order were not to his liking, however, and he had penciled in certain thoughts of his own, even though he knew he would be causing last minute chaos amongst the staff.

The new legislation was basically the same old pouring of millions of dollars into an already gluttonous system, but strong lobbyists were always in the way when any of his people came up with a new way to turn things around.

Reardon knew he was no different than most Americans in that he was sick to death of all the crime, all the violence, all the indifference, and all the suffering of all of the victims.

There was no way he could introduce hard legislation at this time, however. It would mean coming down hard on the gun issue, and the gun issue was connected to powerful special interest groups which he needed for the time being. You scratch mine and I'll scratch yours was the way it worked, and it took forever to accomplish anything. And let's face it, there was a lot of money to be made, and was being made, fighting crime.

He glanced briefly at his foreign aid package he had to try and sell to the American people. His foreign policies were taking a beating of late, and people just didn't seem to give a damn about other countries– not when times were rough at home. But hell, try explaining that if you didn't help these countries get on their feet, they couldn't buy American products in the future, or worse yet, someone else would move in and promise them the world, and then take over.

Reardon lifted his five-foot, ten-and-a-half-inch frame out of the chair he had been sitting in and walked over to his desk. He punched a button and spoke almost at once into the speakerphone. "Bill, would you come in and see me please?"

Bill Culbert entered the office, followed by a secret service agent who had been standing at the entrance to the office the whole time.

"Yes, Mr. President."

"I don't like this law and order portion of my speech. It's too damn wishy-washy. People want something with teeth in it."

Throwing the prepared speech down on the desk, he pointed to the pages. "We've got to give them more than just the promise of money. Those people out there aren't stupid, and the media will be all over me if I don't show some leadership here. Mull it over some more."

"Sir?" Bill Culbert blinked, stepping closer to the President, not noticing the secret service agent move away from the wall. "Your speech is only hours away, and you want me to think of something to give to the American people in that time frame? Sir, I respectfully suggest that this is a pretty tough speech. They want to hear you tell them that if people commit crimes, they'll be thrown in jail."

"Then damn well say so!" the President shot back. "Not," Reardon picked up his copy of the speech and started to read, "not... *America can rest assured that those acting outside the law of the land will feel the full weight of the justice system.* Now what does that mean? They know it's a crock, and so do I. Change it."

"Mr. President, your speech already outlines your accomplishments, and the public knows your position on security and protection."

"I am well aware of the facts, and so is the public. I just don't like what I am about to tell them. Give the speech back to Loretta, and have her beef it up."

Sighing quietly, Bill Culbert nodded and took the speech offered to him. He left the room, followed by the secret service agent, and returned to his office.

It was extra work and a total waste of time, because Culbert knew the

President would never deliver the speech he just handed him. The one that he *would* deliver would make him immortal. He was about to become a President that would stand far above George Washington and Abe Lincoln in the eyes of the American people and the history books. He would appear as a man of great courage and vision, and a man who was finally going to make America safe.

Sitting down at his desk, Culbert tried to think of something that would appease his boss, rather than send it back to the speechwriter. The phone hummed, and Culbert punched a button without picking up the receiver. "Bill Culbert, may I help you?"

It was a male voice, one that Culbert recognized. "Secure line please."

Culbert activated the scrambler, and brought the mouthpiece to his lips. "What's up? I'm up to my ass here on last minute changes to his speech."

"Not *the* speech I hope," the voice said in Culbert's ear.

"No," Culbert said, letting out his breath. "Christ, I'm tired. No, I have to come up with a tougher approach on the law and order package. He says it's to wishy-washy."

"Aha! Things couldn't be better. That confirms his thinking. He'll fall right in line with the speech, and maybe even agree with what he said after it comes back to haunt him. Anyway, that is not why I called. The shift change has been arranged on the Security Detail. Do you have that small room set up where you can..."

"It's all looked after. I'll get him there."

"I'm sure you will," the voice said on the other end. "We are down to the failsafe point."

Culbert finished the changes and put the only copy on the desk of the President. Reaching into his briefcase, he brought out the other copy of the speech. Flipping through the pages, he stopped to read certain passages as he had often done in the past. It was a new feeling of power for him, to be able to help place words and thoughts in a President's mind and mouth. This would be a speech that would go down in history.

He read a few lines, hardly able to wait for the time when the president actually said them in a few hours time.

> *As your President, I have a sworn duty to protect these United States and its citizens. As your President, I can no longer stand idly by while citizens suffer at the hands of organized crime, or at the hands of terrorists planning to destroy America.*

> *From this point on, you will see a carefully drafted plan of action come into being. This plan, fully established within the Constitution of the United States, will remove the fear from our streets and place criminals where they belong...*

Culbert flipped ahead, looking for juicier selections, his heart starting to beat faster despite the fact that he was trying to control his mounting excitement. He was part of this, and there was no turning back. He ran his fingers down the page as if feeling the words, and again realized that he had helped to form history.

> *This country is based on truth, justice, and the very foundation of 'In God We Trust.' No longer will our courts and our system be made a mockery of by the twisted words of those who wish to bend the law to their own advantage.*
>
> *If truth is the very foundation of these United States, sworn before Almighty God, then truth is what we will have. We cannot have justice without truth. We cannot have a whole system based on telling the truth before God if the truth is rarely brought to light. We cannot continue with the staggering cost in lives, property, and the administration of justice.*

Culbert decided to treat himself to one more morsel before putting it away. He knew he would watch the speech over and over again on tape, but it was the anticipation that grabbed him. Or was it the danger?

> *... Scientific instruments, such as the breathalyzer, are now common place in the battle against alcohol induced road carnage, and just as citizens are presently required by law to submit to breath tests, new methods are also required for greater protection against other forms of crime.*
>
> *Now, there's a new breakthrough in the fight against crime, a breakthrough that will protect the innocent against mistaken incarceration, and a breakthrough that will make the guilty accountable. Under strict Federal Guidelines, a new scientifically approved instrument...*

"I read over the speech, Bill," the President said, appearing suddenly behind Culbert. "It's much better. Thank you."

Culbert felt anesthetized, unable to answer as the blood drained from his face. The President's sudden arrival was sending out alarm signals as he sat holding the secret speech.

"Yes, sir. Thank you," he said in quiet panic, as the President walked out.

He sat looking at the pages of the speech, not seeing the words, but thinking how sometimes great things in life sometimes hang by the simple threads of chance. Culbert quietly placed the pages back in his briefcase and locked it. *"This had better work,"* he thought. *"Brilliant minds have thought of this plan, and they were doing it for the country. This is good for America,"* Culbert thought. *"Isn't it?"*

• • •

Captain Mark Grant disengaged his own cellular and placed it on the table. Nathan Strickler sat across from him in a kitchen booth of a rented thirty-two foot class-A motor home. Two empty cans of beer sat in front of them on the table.

Getting up, Grant opened the fridge and brought out two more beers. "Looks like our target is on the way home. Shouldn't be long now."

"This is where it gets tricky," Strickler stated. "So far we've had the help of that egotistical idiot, Shepherd. Now it has to be a strictly hit and run operation. No outside help, and we do whatever it takes to get the goods back. We can't afford to fuck around. We're now on Fletcher's home turf."

Taking a swallow of his beer, Grant belched quietly, setting the can back on the tabletop hard. "Jesus! I can't believe the time element here! We're right down to the wire. Yeah, we'll have to move in fast, delete the subjects if necessary, and get the hell back across the border."

Strickler looked at his watch and did a quick calculation in his mind. "I figure they'll be here within a couple of hours. Considering the time zones, we are not going to have it back before the General's deadline."

"Fuck, Miller... Sir. He'll be happier to get it a little later than not at all." Grant drained the can, looked out the window at an older couple walking their dog, and spoke without looking at Strickler. "You know? I can hardly wait to get my hands on our friend, Harris. He has to pay, and pay well, for what he's done."

"Only, and I mean only, if necessary. The priority is the retrieval of 'PRECISE.' If we get it back with little problem, we skip. Harris can be dealt with later."

"Not without Harris and his buddy. We can have it all and you know it. If they die during the retrieval... well, sue me. The Canadians will just have to piss up a rope."

Strickler looked at Grant for a long moment, silently agreeing with him. It was all or nothing. "Let's get this rig out of here then," he said, getting up and throwing the empty can in the sink. "We need a quick recon of the area and we don't have much time."

"Time enough for a few surprises that I have in mind. Time enough," Grant said, as the motor sprang to life, and then settled down to a soft purr.

• • •

Craig took over the driving at Hope, and the driving conditions had deteriorated like his mood. To his left, fog and haze hung halfway down the mountain, with the Fraser River hidden on his right by heavy slanting rain and ground mist. As a result, traffic had slowed and visibility had dropped due to the road grime thrown against the windshield.

"It's going to take another three hours at this rate," Craig fumed. "The radio said sunny, and look at it. They couldn't tell the weather if they controlled it themselves."

Jennifer reached over the top of the seat and started to knead Craig's stiffening shoulder muscles on each side of his neck. "Relax, Hon, it'll be all right."

From the right front passenger seat, Jesse picked up the cellular and handed it to Craig. "Why don't you try reaching Tom again?"

"Because I hate the damn thing. I swear I'm going to garbage it when I get through this; they've known our every move." Craig increased the windshield wiper speed, found an opening in traffic, and managed to pass a long line of dawdlers. "Maybe I could use a pay phone and..."

"Look at that!" Jennifer said, pointing to the southwest, then poked Craig. "Blue sky. See it's going to be nice, and it will probably be clear when we pass Chilliwack."

The Cherokee moved westward, the road turning from wet to a damp steamy reminder of the passing rain. The traffic got heavier on the other side of Chilliwack, and Craig decided to exit for coffee, an aspirin, and a pay phone.

Abbotsford's fifth exit provided the fuel, phone, and coffee all in one spot, and Craig pulled from the traffic light at the freeway exit, directly into the gas mart. Pulling to the pumps he shut the motor down. "I'll hit the phone if you get the coffee. Don't forget something for my headache."

"Make the call, I'll look after the gas."

Craig stuck his head in the half booth and dialed Tom's number, letting it ring three times before it was picked up.

"Hello."

"Tom, it's Craig."

"Well, my God. I don't need to tell you I've been just a tiny bit worried about you."

"I'm sorry, Tom, I've been really busy."

"Busy...Busy...That is an understatement if I ever heard one. Kee-rist, Craig, you're in every newscast from here to Mexico."

"What are they saying, locally?" Craig inquired.

"What aren't they saying? Let's see, mostly small stuff like espionage, conspiracy, grand theft..."

Craig cut him off in mid sentence. "I get the idea. You have Lorraine under wraps?"

"Listen, don't you even think about worrying about her. She doesn't move without me knowing about it."

Craig took a deep breath and told Tom about the phone call and the threat against Lorraine and him, if he got in the way.

"Oh, I'll be in their face all right," Tom answered. "They don't want to show up here."

"Look, Tom, make sure you're armed at all times. These people are playing for keeps and they don't care about the bodies they leave behind."

"You did say they were government, didn't you, Craig? I mean, com'on, they gotta answer to someone too, same as us."

"Not in the real world, Tom. They are going to get what they want or kill us doing it." Craig paused. "Look, don't call me on the cell phone, they're using it to trace my location. Not unless it's an emergency. And I'd feel better if you took Lorraine and Jo-Ann and Bev somewhere different for the night. After tomorrow morning it shouldn't matter."

"Why, what are you planning?" Tom asked, sounding apprehensive.

"I'm helping Jess go public on what he's done. Legal or not, it's something the public has to know about."

Tom didn't say anything for a few moments, and decided to change the subject. "The guys said to say hello if I just happened to talk to you."

Craig laughed, feeling warmth towards his partner. "No second thoughts about your partner, Tom? I mean with this espionage and everything?"

"I've been working with you for a long time buddy boy, and I admit I had to do a lot of thinking. Then I thought to myself, when in hell would you ever even *get* the chance to be involved in anything. Your life's too fucked up to be involved with anything else."

"I did become involved rather suddenly, Tom," Craig replied over the noise of a truck, "but nothing planned. Okay?"

"No sweat, although you do have a lot of people astounded around this town, Craig."

"Tom, find a place for the night, okay? Or at least get one of the guys in for the night."

"It's looked after, okay? You call me real soon. I mean that."

"You got it. I'll be in touch."

Craig hung up, feeling somewhat better. Looking around, he saw Jesse and his wife still in the building at the counter. Craig entered and walked up to Jennifer. "What's taking so long?"

"Trouble with the gas card. He says he can't get it to work."

"I told you, no cards. Here, pay cash."

"Jess already gave him the money, but he won't give me the card back."

Jesse poked Craig on the shoulder and pointed towards the parking lot. Turning, Craig saw two white patrol cars pull to a stop at the front door.

Two young officers entered the store. "Hi, Glen. Who gave you the plastic?"

The man behind the counter pointed to Jennifer and said, "She did, but they are all together." Then pointing to Craig, "He wanted to pay cash in a hurry and leave."

Turning, the police officer sized Craig up and down briefly without saying anything. After a few moments, he held out his hand.

"Identification please, all of you. I'm investigating the use of a stolen credit card, and you seem to have it."

"There is no stolen credit card, believe me," Craig smiled, trying to remain calm and reminding himself how these things went. "There's just been a balls up with the cards."

"That's good. Then you won't mind showing me all of your identification, will you?"

Craig looked at the officer standing in front of him, and knew by his stance and manner that he could handle just about any situation. His partner was off to the side, watching the exit, and nobody was about to leave. Flipping open his wallet to get his driver's license out revealed the empty space where his badge usually sat.

"What's this? You an ex-police member?" the cop wanted to know.

"No, not ex. I'm a Detective Sergeant with Vancouver. I don't have my I.D. on me right now. Look, the card isn't stolen, it's in my own name." Turning to the clerk behind the counter, he motioned for him to come over. "Show the officer the card, will you? It's okay, I'm not mad at you."

Sheepishly, the guy walked over and handed the card to the uniformed police officer, who started to compare signatures and names. "How long have you been with Vancouver?"

"Ages. Ages and ages, and right now it seems like forever."

The man smiled and returned Craig's I.D., all except the driver's license, which he handed back over his shoulder to his partner without taking his eyes off of Craig.

Pressing a button on the hand microphone attached to his shoulder epaulette, the other man began speaking to the police dispatcher.

"Your credit card seems to check out against the rest of your I.D., and it's probably a company screw-up like you say, but I'll just hold on to it, seeing as it's reported stolen. You understand how these things work. Right?"

Craig nodded, and put his wallet away. "Right, I'll call them about it. Thanks for your help."

Craig made to move towards the door but an outward palm stopped him. "It'll be a few moments, Fletcher. You're so famous, you're going to have to wait until we get an answer," he said, pointing to his partner. "Besides, he has your driver's license."

Jennifer moved up beside Craig and held his hand. "So," Craig smiled. "You watch the news, I see."

"Friend, there isn't a police officer in British Columbia who doesn't know your name. Whether it's true or not isn't up to me, it's what comes up on the system. Anything comes up, you're history."

Jennifer whispered in his ear. "We'll be home soon, sweets."

Squeezing her hand, Craig turned towards the other police officer as the radio came to life.

Abbotsford - Echo one.

"Echo one, go ahead," the man said, his eyes on Craig.

Echo One, On Fletcher, Craig Ronald, six-foot-two, two hundred and five pounds, green eyes, brown hair, - I have a hit.

The two police officers looked at Craig and moved slightly apart, both of them now with a clear line of fire.

"What the hell," Craig said, "There can't be anything on the system for me."

"Fine, let's just wait and see," the cop said patiently.

Abbotsford - Echo one. Use caution, possibly armed and dangerous. Wanted on an outstanding warrant out of Vancouver for assault causing bodily harm. Entered as of yesterday.

"You heard it, there's a warrant for your arrest. Place your hands on the counter and spread 'em."

Jennifer started to move towards the nearest officer, "Look, this is all a..."

"No, Jenn," Craig said, holding onto her arm. "Let's do this right, okay? They have a job to do, and the sooner I get to their H.Q., the sooner we are on the way."

"Good thinking," the other cop said. "I'm sure there's some explanation for all this, especially if you're an active Member. You are an active police member, aren't you?"

Looking down at the floor, then at the two men, Craig said, "Would you believe I've been suspended for thirty days?"

"This is getting interesting, Fletcher," the one closest to Craig said, motioning for him to lean against the counter.

Craig was thoroughly searched, glad that he didn't have one of his own guns on his person. Placed in handcuffs, he was led outside to the patrol car.

Stepping closer to Jennifer and Jesse, the other officer remarked, "There's nothing on you two for the moment." Looking at Jesse with suspicion, he continued, "Follow us in if you want, and we'll let you know what happens."

Within four minutes a large bay door lifted, which allowed the police vehicle inside, thus securing Craig from any escape. "Let's go, Fletcher. You want to use the phone it's just inside the door."

"Thanks, I know the procedure. I'll make a call when I know what's going on."

The cellblock was modern. Freshly painted concrete walls and clean floors met him as he entered. Halls, lined on both sides with cells, lead off in different directions. Walking up to a booking counter, Craig came face to face with a civilian guard. His handcuffs were removed.

"Empty your pockets," the guard said.

As his personal effects were being placed in a bag a door opened and a uniformed Sergeant entered the detention area. He was about six foot, sported a neat mustache, and had a bit of a paunch.

"Are you Craig Fletcher?"

"Yes, I am." Craig read the name Holliday on the Sergeant's nametag.

"From what I hear, you do get around. The officer says you're suspended. That right?"

"Yes, it's tied in with the warrant. It stems from a complaint that was supposed to have been investigated internally, not go criminal. I ran into a shit-rat, and I have a Deputy-Chief who doesn't like me too well."

"It looks like you are lacking friends in high places, Fletcher. Being a police member makes you fairly trustworthy to appear in court on such a minor charge. Someone trying to make it hard for you?"

The arresting officer leaned on the counter next to Craig. "I've got a few buddies in Vancouver. This D.C., it wouldn't be Shepherd, would it?"

Nodding yes, Craig continued. "He and I go back a long way. His main function in life is to make me miserable."

"Looks like he's doing a good job," the Sergeant noted.

"Yeah," the arresting officer laughed. "Doesn't pay to be on the wrong side of Shepherd. I heard he never forgives or forgets."

"How do you know Shepherd?" Craig wanted to know.

"Word travels. What I heard, he's a number one prick."

Looking at the Sergeant, Craig asked, "The warrant, has it been endorsed for my release?" Craig waited for the answer with some apprehension. If a Justice of the Peace countersigned the warrant, the Sergeant had the authority to release him for a later date in Vancouver Court. If it wasn't, Craig was stuck in jail for transportation into Shepherd's waiting arms.

Picking the computer printout up again, Holliday scanned the sheet. "Yeah, it's endorsed. Looks like someone doesn't care what your friend Shepherd wants. If I give you a court date and let you out, will you show up?"

"Of course I will," Craig nodded.

Twelve minutes later, Holliday reentered the cellblock. "Okay Fletcher, you're to appear in Vancouver court at 0900 hours, on a charge of assault, exactly five weeks from today's date unless the matter is cleared up in some other manner."

Signing the release form, Craig received his copy in return. "Thanks Sergeant Holliday, I'll look after it."

Craig was escorted to the front reception area, and the officer chuckled as he let him out the door. "Good luck with Shepherd."

Craig looked up and saw Jennifer sitting in a chair by a window. Jesse was reading some brochures in another corner. "Thank God. I thought you would have to stay in here for sure."

"Let's get out of here and get the hell home." A few minutes later they were back on the freeway.

In the police station, Sergeant Holliday sat back down at his desk and looked ruefully at the pile of complaint files sitting in front of him. He was about to dig into them when the phone rang. "Sergeant Holliday, Station Commander."

"Sergeant Holliday, good to talk to you. It's Deputy Chief Shepherd, Vancouver Police."

Holliday groaned inwardly, leaned back in his chair and wished he had the night off. "Yes sir, what can I do for you?"

"I've just received word that you have apprehended one of my officers on an outstanding warrant. Now, being as he's one of mine, I don't want him escorted by the Sheriff's Department."

"Well you won't have to worry about that," Holliday smiled into the phone, keeping his voice serious.

"Good. I'll have a Sergeant Johnson and one of his men drive up the valley to get him. They should be about an hour getting there."

"Ahhh,... Deputy, you don't understand, you don't have to send anyone out here."

"Nonsense Sergeant, you obviously don't know what Fletcher's done."

"The warrant says assault, sir, and that's what I dealt with."

"No, no, that's the minor part. Between you and me and half the world, you know perfectly well that he's been involved in some major activity. He's way over his head, and I'm co-operating with American authorities on this."

"Yes, so I heard," Holliday remarked, "but he was arrested on an assault warrant, and nothing else."

"Now don't go getting technical on me, Sergeant," the voice said in syrupy sweetness. "I'm just saying I'm glad he's off the street, and I'll be glad to have him in my custody."

"I think," Holliday cut in, "that you will find that the warrant was fully endorsed, sir, and that Fletcher will appear in court when he is supposed to."

"Damn right he will. He... what do you mean, when he's supposed to?"

"He was released on his own recognizance, to appear..."

"Whaat! You did what? What the hell to you mean, you released him! Do you realize what you've done? You've aided a major felon to escape. The whole United States fucking government is after his ass."

"Well, with all due respect, sir, Craig Fletcher is *not* in the United States. He was arrested on a Canadian Warrant, placed on the system by the Vancouver Police Department." Holiday continued, his temper starting to rise. Those who had ever witnessed it in the past knew it was slow to come, but ferocious to watch. "He was not arrested for murder, or treason, or plotting to assassinate the Pope."

"Don't you go getting cute with me, Sergeant, I'll have your job by tomorrow morning. If you worked in my Department, you'd be gone already. You had no authority to let Fletcher go. Now, I demand that you pick him up a.s.a.p, you understand?"

"Do you have any further warrants for Fletcher, sir?" Holliday asked, barely keeping his voice level.

"I can damn soon get them, Holliday. This is the biggest screw up..."

"If you have anything else to say, Deputy Chief Shepherd, I suggest you say them to my Chief of Police. I don't have to listen to your threats and babble. You're not my superior, and I don't work for you," Holliday got to his feet without realizing it, his voice now above normal. "And from what I've heard, the screw up, as you call it, is on the other end of the line. Now that's on tape, so if you want to use it, come and get it!"

"Oh, you have made a major mis..."

Holiday hung up, frustration and anger barely in control. Looking out of the door to his office, he could see the office staff and several police officers all in a fixed position, looking at him with disbelief.

He looked back at them, and then threw his hands in the air. "The asshole is an asshole! I even bet his police I.D. shows nothing but an asshole!"

Cooling down some, Holliday sat down and let out a stream of obscenities under his breath. He'd have a lot to answer for when he put in his report before going off shift. The release of Fletcher was legal and proper, but he knew that losing his cool would be his downfall.

Looking into the Dispatch Center, Holliday was met with a group of smiling faces shining back at him. Feeling foolish, he quietly closed the door to his office, only to have it opened a few moments later. "What is it, Steele?"

"You and I have been around the block, Sarg," the older street cop said, "and that little episode I just witnessed looks like a direct call to the Chief. Better you clue him in, so he knows what to expect, than you trying to defend yourself later."

"Yeah, I'm aware of my temper, Larry. Thanks, I'll give him a call then file the report. Why on my shift?"

"Shit happens," Steele said, closing the door.

"Yeah," Holliday answered, picking up the phone, "In this case it's major diarrhea."

• • •

Craig was rolling along in fairly steady traffic, glad to be out of the confines of the jail. The cellular interrupted everyone's quiet thoughts, causing them all to look at each other. "What do you think? Should I answer it?"

"This close to home," Jennifer remarked, giving him the phone, "who gives a damn. Besides, it would drive you crazy not knowing who it is."

"Yes," Craig said frostily into the instrument.

"Craig, this is Hugh Wong. I'm calling from my office. Shepherd has learned of your arrest and release, and he's seething. He's making calls all over the place trying to get you while you're on the move."

"I hope the hell he doesn't have a heart attack or anything, Hugh, because I won't be at the funeral."

"Look, I have a request from the Chief. He wants a one-on-one with you with no bullshit, and no Shepherd. The Mayor and the Police Board are on his ass something fierce ever since you started making the national news. Please, Craig, talk to the ol' man. You know he'll treat you right."

"Look, Hugh, I'll be in to see him personally as soon as I get a few things squared away around town. I won't be going near my house, so tell Shepherd not to bother staking it out; he'll be wasting his time. If I come near headquarters, I'll be in a cell before the Chief knows I'm in the building. I can't afford the time right now."

"Okay, then give me a time frame, or something to get back to him with. I need to tell him *something.*"

Craig looked into the rearview mirror and moved into the slow lane while thinking of a reply. "Let's see what tomorrow brings. Keep in touch. I'll do my best. You're right, Hugh, the Chief deserves to hear from me. Just one thing though, if Shepherds involved, I won't be cooperating."

"I'll do my best. You have no idea how wild he is. We don't even dare mention your name around here today."

"Thanks for calling, Hugh. Tell the Chief that I'll be in touch as soon as I can. Bye." Disconnecting, Craig filled the other two in on the conversation. "The Chief wants to talk to me one-on- one. He probably wants my resignation."

"Before you're found guilty or anything?" Jennifer asked.

"It's called C.Y.A. - cover your ass. If Craig Fletcher is gone, then the problem is gone and everything returns to normal. Besides, there's a little section called Discredible Conduct. It's a catchall. If anything is done to discredit the Department, you have to answer for it."

"Not to mention the fact that you are hanging around with a notorious criminal," Jesse said. "That's enough..."

Craig held up his hand to silence Jesse. "Look, I'm pretty sure we're being followed. No, don't turn around. I'm going to leave the freeway at the next interchange and see what happens. If he follows, maybe we can lose him in the back hills and curves between here and the river."

"What plates does it have? Can you see if it's Canadian or American?" Jesse asked.

"I can't tell, and I know what you're thinking, but it doesn't matter what the plates are."

Craig increased speed gently, watching as the other vehicle kept pace about two hundred yards to the rear. Approaching the exit, Craig moved to the fast lane and to the left of about ten vehicles, and increased his speed as he passed. The vehicle to the rear also moved to the left lane.

Just prior to the exit, Craig made his move. "Okay, hold on."

Craig slid from the fast lane to the slow lane, moving between two cars then right onto the exit. The sound of blaring horns and screeching brakes followed, as the other car tried to make the exit.

"Did he miss the turn off?" Craig asked Jesse.

Turning in his seat, Jesse saw the black car laying on the brakes, swerving then accelerating onto the exit ramp. "'Fraid not, he's still back there."

A sign whipped past:
HISTORIC FT. LANGLEY
SEVEN MILES.

"I know this road," Jennifer said, turning in her seat. "It's full of twists and turns, and hills and hidden driveways. If you get far enough ahead, you could lose him."

Craig nodded, but concentrated on his driving. He knew his abilities when it came to driving, but this wasn't a beefed-up cruiser and the center of gravity was too high for fast cornering. No matter how hard he tried to gain the advantage, the vehicle always showed up in his mirror on a straight away.

"He's managing to maintain his distance," Craig said to no one in particular. "I've got to try something on the next curve or hill, or we'll be at the river."

Craig passed a vehicle at the top of a hill on a left hand curve in the road. The sound of the horn came through the closed windows, and Craig could see the vehicle slowing to a stop. As a result, the black car was held in place momentarily to deal with the startled, angry driver.

Rolling farmland started to turn into flatter ground as they neared the river and Ft. Langley. Several small bridges flew under the wheels as they crossed a network of small creeks.

"I've got a choice. Head for the river and the ferry, or stay on this side and cut across the prairie."

"Head for the ferry." Jesse suggested. "Even if we have to wait, there should be quite a few people around."

The Grand Cherokee was well above the legal speed limit as it entered Ft. Langley. Houses, old growth trees, and then storefronts went by in a blur. The historic river town was busy with tourists, but fortunately, no traffic tie-ups held them back.

"He's a long way back, Craig," Jesse said.

Jennifer looked ahead through the windshield. "They usually have two ferries on the go to handle river crossings, one on each side, and passing in the middle. If we catch it right, we may get on."

"Not a good bet," Craig remarked, rapidly approaching the small terminal. "They will only be a few minutes behind, and you know what ferry line-ups are like."

They entered a narrow two-lane road, directed by a sign that indicated ferry traffic only. A truck was parked off to the side selling sockeye salmon, the prices marked on a crude sign at the edge of the road.

"There's traffic coming out from the ferry," Jesse pointed. "It must have just unloaded."

Nearing the loading area, Craig could see the tail end of a battered pick-up moving down the ramp towards the ferry. A traffic signal turned from green to red, and a traffic barrier started to lower as Craig swept by underneath and drove swiftly down the ramp towards the ferry.

"Hey!" a uniformed ferry worker bellowed, gaping at the Jeep as it charged passed his position. "Hold it! Stop!"

Jesse pointed back down the road leading to the ferry. "Here they come, and they are not wasting any time!"

The metal ramp was six inches off of the boats deck, and lifting, when Craig landed on the deck and came to a slightly sideways halt. An older woman watched the Jeep as it bounded onto the deck, her eyes wide in disbelief. A pig in the back of her pick-up began to squeal in outrage and fear, it's nose sticking out between the wooden crate.

The deck began to vibrate, the distance between the loading ramp and the deck lengthening with each second. "We've got trou-ble," Jennifer indicated with her finger, as two uniformed men approached them in a hurry.

"Better them," Craig said, looking as two men ran towards the ferry dock from a black car parked on the dock, "Then the two from that car."

"Let me talk to them," Jesse said, getting out and walking to meet them half-way.

Craig got out of the car and turned to look at the departing dock. The men were standing watching the ferry, their car door left open in their rush. One looked at his watch, said something to the other, and they hurried back to the waiting car. Jesse climbed back inside, a smile on his face.

"Well, I take it the police won't be waiting for us on the other side?" Jennifer asked.

"I'm a genius! It just came to me out of the blue! I told them the first thing that came to my mind. The only thing I could think of was this poor woman," Jesse said pointing to Jennifer, "who's sitting here with labor pains."

"Do I look pregnant to you?" she burst out. "Good thing they didn't come over to check," Jennifer admonished.

"We'll be okay. Nothing that a hundred bucks each didn't cure."

The bright sun hit the water, causing sparkles mixed with eye-hurting glare. Old growth trees grew along the bank, the deep green foliage contrasting with an old log boom tied close to shore a little further downstream. Scanning the oncoming shore, nothing seemed out of the ordinary.

Returning to the driver's side, Craig got in and settled behind the steering wheel, a moan escaping unwanted from his lips. "The closer I get to home the more tired I feel, and that's not good. We are going in exactly the direction we shouldn't be. Maybe it would be a good idea to camp out somewhere else until..."

"We... are going home!" Jennifer instructed, in a firm manner. "It's only for tonight; it'll all be public soon anyway."

The ferry docked, and Craig was the last one to drive off, waved off by a deck hand shaking his head. He headed west on the Lougheed Highway, turning north after a few miles onto back roads that lead into the mountains.

"Not a soul behind us that I can see. Course they don't need to, do they? Just come up and ring our front door bell, and Jennifer will serve tea."

"We are going home, Craig," Jennifer cut in, "and you're not funny."

"I'm not trying to be, and I think we should stay somewhere else tonight. Are you going to be the one to stay up all night and keep watch in the dark?"

Jennifer looked over at Craig, then at Jesse. "With two strong, virile men in the house? Not likely."

"This is serious stuff here, Jenn." The tension was obvious in Jesse's voice. "They won't hesitate to kill us if they have to."

"That's why I want to go home. I'll feel safer there than in a bloody box of a motel room with one door. We have alarms all over the place, we've got Rusty, we've got guns galore– you can call Tom, and... and... and we are just going home. Okay?"

Craig watched as high trees flowed by on each side of the road, moving shadows providing cover from the glare of the western sun. Looking at Jennifer, he could tell she really needed to be home, and she was probably right in one sense, it probably was safer than a motel room. "Okay, home it is."

Thirty-six minutes later, Craig pulled into the long driveway and stopped in front of the garage. Jennifer pushed the door opener, got out, and started to walk towards the locked interior door to the house. "Don't go in yet, Jenn. Jesse and I are going to do a walk around the outside first."

Every door and window appeared normal, and a few minutes later, Craig and Jesse joined Jennifer in the garage. "Okay, open it up and shut the alarm off, Jenn."

"Thank heaven for that. I'm bushed."

As the garage door returned to the down position, none of them noticed the motor home parked down the road at a neighbors. A motor home with two tourists who were lost, tired, and paid good money just for the right to park in the driveway for the night.

···CHAPTER TWELVE

President Reardon looked at himself in the mirror and was not happy with what he saw. He couldn't get used to the heavy make-up that was required. He looked like something out of a wax museum. Adjusting his tie, he noticed it matched beautifully with the dark suit and light gray shirt. He must remember to thank his valet. Turning, he smiled at his make-up lady. "Got me looking younger than ever, Mrs. Zimmer. You're a magician."

Mrs. Zimmer blushed, and then laughed with her President. "I have very little to do, to make you presentable, Mr. President."

Looking at the small entourage, Reardon nodded. "Not long now. Give me plenty of advance warning so I can have a few moments alone before air time."

Bill Culbert hurried over as an aid ran a lint brush over the President's shoulders. "You have twenty minutes, sir, how much leeway would you like?"

"Oh, four or five minutes should do it, and that's after they have finished all the farting around with lights and microphones. I just want a moment to glance at the speech and the changes."

"Yes, sir. I will have your speech ready for you when you sit down." Culbert hesitated, seeming to come to a decision. "There is one thing, sir, one of the technicians apparently has a very sick child on his hands, and the men in his crew wondered if you could stop by and offer a bit of private encouragement. They think it might boost his morale a bit."

Turning to Culbert, the President nodded in agreement. "Now, you know I wouldn't object to something like that. A little more advanced notice would have been nice, but that'll be okay."

"I'm sure he will be pleased, sir. It will only take a moment." Culbert excused himself and walked to a phone in the corner of the room, dialing an in-house number.

"Yes?"

"About five minutes. The President has agreed to see the technician." The line went dead.

Hanging up, Culbert returned to the center of the room and walked up to the Agent in charge. "We are ready to move. The President will make a brief stop in a private alcove to talk briefly with one of the media technicians. He apparently has a sick child, and the President wants to offer his best wishes."

"This isn't on the agenda," the Agent said, not liking last minute and unplanned events.

"Oh come now, he's only going to offer some support to the man."

The President entered the hallway for the short trip to the old and cramped pressroom. He was preceded and followed by the Secret Service, with Mrs. Zimmer, his speechwriter, and his press officer also in the group. Culbert walked slightly to the rear on the President's left side.

"What's wrong with the child, Bill? I don't want to be talking to the man and not have a clue as to the illness."

"Yes, Mr. President," Culbert paused. "Her name is April. She has advanced Leukemia. I'll introduce you to the man when we get there, Mr. President, however, may I suggest that if you spoke to him on a personal level, without all this staff, it might not embarrass him."

The President turned to Culbert as they continued the walk. "What do you have in mind?"

"Oh, nothing elaborate, Mr. President, I assure you. Just a few quiet words out from under everyone's gaze. I have a small room set aside."

"Fine, I don't have much time left, I see." Looking around, Reardon commented, "Seems we have more agents on The Detail than usual, Bill."

"There's one thing I've learned since coming here with you, sir, and that's not to question what the Protective Detail are doing at any given time. They are the most suspicious people I have ever come across. I've been afraid to scratch myself at times."

Reardon laughed, patting Culbert on the shoulder. "At least you can scratch. Presidents aren't allowed. Which puts me on the same level as a baseball player I guess."

"This is the room here, Mr. President," Culbert pointed.

"Okay," Reardon said, and started to enter.

"Excuse me, Mr. President, but this is an unscheduled occurrence," Agent Walter Thoronson said, stepping in front of Reardon. "I'll have to check the room, and the person who is inside."

"Oh, nonsense," Culbert blurted. "These people have been checked and double checked. We're inside The White House, for Pete's sake."

"Let them do their job, Bill. It'll only take a few moments, and we don't have a say in it anyway."

Thoronson, who really liked Reardon for his down-to-earth, and 'we're all in this together' approach, moved towards the doorway. "Thank you, Mr. President."

The door opened, and the agent re-emerged a few moments later. "All clear, Mr. President. Sorry for the delay."

Reardon walked into the room; Culbert moved into a far corner. A brief current of air moved across the President's face as he glanced up and saw a smiling man sitting with a headset wrapped around his neck.

"I wanted to stop by and say hello. I understand you are facing a day to day struggle on the home front."

"Mr. President, I would like to introduce Douglas Ridoch," Culbert said from the corner.

"I am very honored to meet you, Mr. President," Ridoch said, his face flustered, starting to get up.

Reardon raised his hand, placing it on the man's shoulder lightly. "Please, don't get up. We all have our jobs to do."

"Tell me, Mr. President, how do you feel about gun control and gun ownership?" Ridoch asked, looking closely at the President.

A puzzled look spread across Reardon's face just before he answered. "Why, personally, I feel every private handgun in this country should be in the hands of the U.S. Government. There's just no room in today's society for weapons that are designed for the sole purpose of killing other human beings. Rifles and shotguns should be allowed, of course, for legitimate hunters."

"What about the Constitution, Mr. President? It guarantees the right to bear arms."

Reardon watched as Ridoch removed his headset from around his neck, then he answered the question. "The Constitution was drafted at a time when citizens were needed at a moments notice for a call to arms, and as a part of a government militia they were allowed to bear those arms. It is a matter of interpretation, and a great many citizens feel that it was not intended to be interpreted as the right for all people to bear arms all of the time. The people are no longer members of a militia, protecting themselves against British troops. They are simply killing each other."

"What about," Ridoch continued, "the right to protect yourself against criminals, and the fact that guns don't kill, people do."

"All rhetoric, a play with words. Take the guns out of their hands, and all they can do is point their fingers. All handguns should be purchased by the government, or confiscated, with very severe penalties for those in the underworld who think they are above the laws of society."

"I have only one more question, Mr. President. Would you strive for a change in the justice system, even if it meant your Presidency, to protect the lives of Americans?"

"Yes," Reardon said calmly. "In some parts of the world, Americans are looked upon as barbarians. The fact that twenty thousand Americans are murdered per year can be revolting to the senses."

"Your speech tonight reflects your thinking, Mr. President, and will be a basis for a gradual, but a determined change for a better America." Standing, Ridoch shook Reardon's hand. "Good luck, Mr. President."

Upon entering the pressroom, The Detail fanned out, watching the camera crews and various technicians. No reporters were allowed for this broadcast, so it made their job easier.

A desk had been set up in front of royal blue curtains, with the American flag and the President's Standard standing out brilliantly as a backdrop. Reardon sat down at the desk, the 'Seal of the President of the United States' predominately displayed on the forward panel facing the cameras.

Culbert placed a small pile of papers in front of Reardon. "Here you are, Mr. President. It will only take a moment to hook you up, and then you will have a few moments to glance at the changes. The changes will be reflected on the TelePrompTer as well, sir."

"Thank you," the President said in a monotone voice, patting his suit pocket as he answered. "Bill, please go to my office quickly. My reading glasses are on my desk and I need them."

Culbert was annoyed, but didn't allow it to show on his face. "I'll send someone right away..."

"No, Bill, I want you to get them. Please hurry."

"Yes, Mr. President. I will be right back." Glancing at his watch, Culbert knew he would make it by airtime, but was a little annoyed at having to act as a messenger boy. He reminded himself that the President wasn't his usual diplomatic self, and was sure to offer his truthful opinions while under the influence of 'PRECISE.'

Reardon, left to himself, glanced at the speech as the microphone was attached to his lapel, with the lead wire concealed under his jacket. He was not interrupted, and from time to time he nodded in agreement at what he read.

"Two minutes, Mr. President," the director stated.

Reardon nodded, knowing that in a few minutes the seal of his office would be displayed on the screen for the whole world to see. Reardon was cognizant of the fact that the whole world literally was watching, and he wanted to make sure everything was correct. Patting his pockets again, he found his small reading glasses in his shirt pocket and put them on. They made him look paternal and friendly, the father figure of the country.

"Five, four, three, two, one... " The director nodded to Reardon as the camera light came on.

"Ladies and gentlemen, the President of the United States."

The camera slowly panned up from the Presidential Seal, finding the pleasant face of Reardon, waiting patiently. "Fellow citizens of the United States, thank you for taking time from your busy schedules and inviting me into your homes, offices, or wherever you may be in this vast country of ours.

"I have some sweeping changes to announce. Changes that will help make our country stronger, safer, and economically sound on the domestic front.

"First, I want to address the horrendous problem of law and order and the justice system. I want to address the federal court system, the cost of bringing a person to trial, and the staggering backlogs facing the system as a whole. To approach these problems, your Government must take a leadership role to ensure a cost effective, and equitable, system."

As Reardon began his speech, several men sat quietly in a small private den, nervously watching a television screen. They smiled and looked at each other knowingly as history unfolded in front of them.

● ● ●

209

Across the continent, Grant looked at Strickler as he sprawled in the driver's seat of the motor home, his feet lying across the motor cover. He hadn't moved in over half an hour, and hadn't said anything for the past fifteen minutes. Grant felt his anger rising, and it was all he could do not to get up and leave the motor coach. "For Christ's sake!" he muttered.

"What's the problem," Strickler said, stretching his body to a new position.

"The problem, if you want to know, is I'm in a rotten fucking mood! Here we sit, doing not a damn thing I might add, while over there, not further than you can spit, two ass wipes sit with the drug of the century."

"Why don't you take a nap," Strickler said with annoyance. "We've got the place covered and they sure as hell aren't going any place."

"Yeah? Well I'm for hitting the place and getting the fuck out of here. I've seen the place and I can pretty well guess the interior layout. Let's get it over with!"

Getting up, Strickler looked at Grant and shook his head. "That's not very professional, Mark. It will soon be dark. We'll go in then."

Grant looked at Strickler a moment, then relented. "Okay. But it's a mistake to wait until they go to bed. Everything is too quiet then." Grant shifted his own position and looked up at Strickler. "That's when the neighbors turn off the television and become nosy at every sound they hear. Hit them about a half hour after dark, and long before they hit the sack."

Strickler thought for a moment, leaning against the kitchen counter. "You're right, the longer we wait around the more we expose ourselves. We could actually be back across the border before midnight."

"Yeah, with Mr. Harris in tow," Grant said with anticipation.

"We'll see," Strickler responded. "By the way, so much for your promise to Fletcher."

"What promise?" Grant asked from his place at the kitchen booth.

"That he had until the end of the day to turn 'PRECISE' over. Remember?"

"Yeah, well, you're the one who changed the plans, so here we sit. If it was me, I'd have his little fluff ball tied up in back."

"We don't need the aggravation, Mark." Strickler bent and looked out the window, then back at Grant. "So, how are we going to handle this? Kick in the front door, or just walk up and knock."

Pulling on a hair just inside his right nostril, Grant seemed to ignore the question, but in fact was giving it serious consideration. Pulling on the hair he got a look of satisfaction on his face, then rubbed his nose back and forth to ward off a sneeze. "It would be easier to just knock and wait for someone to come to the door, but the fact is it would alert them. I don't think they get many people knocking on their door out here much. Especially after dark."

Grant looked out the window towards the house. "On either side of the front door they have glass set into the frame from top to bottom. I say smash the one nearer to the lock. We'll be inside in seconds."

Strickler nodded in agreement. "If we're fast enough, we can have them before they move very far."

"If I know how Fletcher thinks, he'll come to investigate what's happening, and walk right into my waiting arms," Grant smiled.

"Then it's settled," Strickler said, sitting down and pointing towards the television. "What's on that thing?"

"Would you believe not a damn thing? It doesn't work. At least I can't get anything but white noise and snow. No matter what I do, nothing happens."

Neither Strickler or Grant were familiar with recreational vehicles and did not realize that a panel inside a cabinet next to the television required the user to select either cable or antenna input, and that they had to activate the antenna booster. They missed the President's speech.

"Forget it. To tell the truth I'm as bored as you. This has got to be the quietest neighborhood in the world.

Grant looked over at Strickler, a serious look on his face. "Not for long my friend. Not for long."

• • •

Hugh Wong was half-way out the door when the telephone rang on his desk. He stopped and looked at it, debating inside, knowing that every call seemed to be nothing but bad news lately. Curiosity won out and he picked up the receiver. "Inspector Wong."

"This is Shepherd, I want to see you in my office."

Wong looked at the ceiling, his eyes rolling back in his head at his stupidity in answering.

"You hear me, Hugh? I want to see you in my office."

"Yes, I'm here... I was just on the way out... I'm running behind time and..."

"Well, I won't keep you long. Come to my office."

Shepherd hung up, and Wong stood there with the dial tone grinding into his eardrum. "You bag of fart wind," Wong said to relieve his anger, anger mostly directed at himself. He could have been in his car by now. Wong didn't get angry very often, and when he did, he usually kept it to himself. Lately he found himself outwardly displaying his frustrations, which came as a surprise to him, and to others around him.

What usually angered Wong was any intrusion into the cocoon he had woven around himself, the cocoon that prevented unpleasant decisions that could affect his career. His cocoon was being split open, however, and surprisingly, he found he had little difficulty in deciding what he stood for. One thing he knew, he detested Shepherd.

He entered the waiting area outside of Shepherd's office. It was deserted, and the lights had been dimmed allowing the light from Shepherd's partially open door to cast a long beam across the lush carpet. He looked at the stenciled name on the door, *Deputy Chief Fred Shepherd*, and rather than his usual tap, tap on the frame, he half knocked and half pounded on the door, causing it to swing inward.

Shepherd had his back to the door and was talking on the telephone behind his cherry wood desk. He appeared to be looking out at the skyline from his half reclined chair. Hugh Wong noticed there wasn't a scrap of paper on his desk.

Shepherd turned, saw Wong, and turned back to the window. He never got so much as a wave to come in, or an indication that he would be only a minute, and to please take a chair. Wong's resentment climbed another notch and his face altered in color.

Something changed at that moment, but Wong wasn't quite aware of what it was. Then, all of a sudden Wong did know what it was. He was finished worrying about what Shepherd wanted. He simply clicked Shepherd off as being important.

Wong walked into the office uninvited, feeling like a fool standing at the door, and sat down in the biggest chair he could find. Crossing his legs, he couldn't hear Shepherd's conversation as he spoke in low tones.

Shepherd hung up the phone and turned around, looking at Hugh Wong as he lounged in the chair. Saying nothing, Shepherd leaned back also, placed his hands across his stomach and locked his fingers together. Staring at Wong for a few seconds, he finally saw that there was no intimidation registering, and broke the silence. "I've got a job for you."

Wong uncrossed his legs, instantly alert. "What kind of job?"

"You've got a problem in your section, Inspector Wong, and you are going to deal with it."

Wong couldn't help himself, even knowing that Shepherd was referring to Fletcher as being the problem. "I haven't any problems; everything is running smoothly."

The lines around Shepherd's face tightened, his eyes narrowing into small slits as he slowly leaned on his desk. "Smoothly, you say. Smoothly! You've got a man on suspension, and you call that smoothly. That same man is facing criminal charges and a court appearance, and you call that smoothly. Smoothly my ass, half the United States Government is looking for your Mr. Smoothly, Inspector Wong, and *I* want him. *I want him!*" Shepherd said with a quiet hatred in his voice. "You, Inspector Wong, are going to go and find him and arrest him. I know for a fucking fact," Shepherd said, working himself up into an angry state, "That Fletcher is in this city, or at his home, or sneaking about somewhere involved in who knows what!"

"Okay," Wong said, getting up out of the chair, "I'll get at it first thing in the morning."

"You'll get on it right now! Is that clear? Right now!"

"Deputy Chief Shepherd, I have put in thirteen and a half hours today, and I am sitting in your office on *my* time. Are you prepared to pay me double time?"

Shepherd stood up, not feeling comfortable looking up at Wong. "You are not in the damn police union, Wong, and you'll work the hours I set for you." Shepherd's voice softened. "Look, Fletcher has gone bad on us, Hugh, and I am not taking any chances. Either you do what you're told, or you're relieved."

Wong looked at Shepherd, detesting the man, but knowing he had to keep on top of things for Fletcher's sake. "Okay. I'll see what I can find out and I'll call you, but may I remind you that he has already been arrested and legally released by a police department in the valley. You have no legal right to arrest him again."

"Those assholes let him go," Shepherd snapped. "Actually let him go, if you can believe it. Well, it won't happen again I can assure you..."

"He is still out on his own recognizance, and you nor anyone else can arrest him if he doesn't do anything wrong," Wong cut in.

"You let me worry about that! Now get out! You had better be booking on the air within the next few minutes with some men assigned to his arrest, or you'll find yourself suspended as well. Now get out!"

Wong looked at Shepherd and smiled, getting some satisfaction in seeing Shepherd's complexion darken even further. As he walked towards the door, he called over his shoulder, "When I find him you can damn well bet he'll be treated within the framework of the law."

"When you find him, you will notify me immediately. Before you do anything. Is that understood? Remember you work here at the pleasure of the Police Board, and your contract can be terminated without cause."

Wong reached the door and turned back to Shepherd. "Not as long as I do my job. By the way, you're on the same contract, aren't you?" Wong closed the door.

The loud bellow blasted through the closed door as Wong walked across the outer office and into the hallway. "You better do what you are fucking told, Wong! Your days are numbered."

Wong felt a little queer inside, and as the elevator descended, he tried to analyze it. By the time the elevator door opened, he still hadn't recognized the feelings of self-respect and dignity.

Hugh entered his office and punched in a phone number from his telephone index. "Hello, Mrs. Gifford? It's Hugh Wong at the office. Could I speak to Tom please?"

"Hello, Hugh. All of a sudden it's Mrs. Gifford?"

"I'm sorry, Jo-Ann, I'm not thinking. I just had a meeting with Shepherd, and..."

"Say no more, I'll go get him."

Wong only had to wait about ten seconds before Tom Gifford came on the line.

"Tom, listen to me– Shepherd's given me the job of bringing Craig in. I need your help here if we're going to save his ass."

"What's going on?" Tom asked.

Wong took a few minutes to explain the meeting with Shepherd. "I need you here, Tom, you're the only one who can arrange a meet."

"No way! I've got Craig's kid here and I'm not leaving her– or my wife for that matter. There have been some serious threats against Craig's daughter."

"Look, I'll have a car there with two good men in half an hour. They'll stay there, guaranteed, until you get back."

There was silence on the line for quite a while as Tom thought over his options.

"Tom, you want to help your partner, you can't do it sitting at home."

"Okay, sounds all right. I'll leave when they arrive and I'm satisfied you're not sending two goof-off's."

Flipping his telephone index, Wong stopped at 'F' and searched for Craig Fletcher's home number. The phone rang three times, then the answering machine kicked in. He was about to hang up, then changed his mind, waiting for the tone to vibrate against his eardrum.

"Craig, it's Hugh Wong, if you're home please pick up the phone. This is important, and I need to talk to you." Wong waited two heartbeats, and then continued. "Call me on my direct line, Craig, it's vital that you understand what's going down. Tom will be here with me."

Wong hung up and sat back, rubbing his eyes as exhaustion started to weigh down on him. After assigning two men to head out to Tom's house, he closed his eyes and waited for Gifford to arrive.

• • •

Craig and Jennifer were sitting in the kitchen nook with a coffee when Jesse walked into the room. "What's up?"

Jennifer reached for a fresh cup for Jesse, motioning him to sit down. "We got a message on the answering machine."

"And? What? Is it bad news?"

Craig put his cup back down on the glass surface, carefully placing it in the same ring that was already there. "Don't know. It was a call from my immediate supervisor, Hugh Wong, and he wants to talk to me right away. I don't know if I should call him because I said we wouldn't come near the house. 'PRECISE' is the main concern right now, and I've already set up a time to briefly talk to the radio host tomorrow about the interview."

"Anything I can do?"

"Not really, Jess. Tom is supposed to be with Wong, which indicates it's important, but if it is, why hasn't he called me? Tom said he wasn't going to leave Lorraine."

Jennifer placed the phone on the table. "Why don't you phone him and find out?"

"Yeah, why not," Craig sighed, picking up the phone.

Jo-Ann picked it up on the second ring. "Yes? Hello?"

"Hi Jo-Ann, it's Craig."

"Oh Craig, I'm so glad you called, we've been worried sick about you and Jennifer. There are so many stories in the papers and on the news, and..."

"I know, Jo-Ann. Only believe ninety percent of what you hear."

Jo-Ann laughed, continuing through her chuckles. "You'll never change. Does this mean I'm involved with a criminal now?"

"If Shepherd has his way, you are."

"Shepherd! He has Tom a nervous wreck at times. Does that man have any friends?"

"I don't know. How's Lorraine?"

"Now don't worry, she's just fine. She went to bed early, and I fed her so much chicken you'll not have to mention it for at least a month," Jo-Ann laughed over the phone. "Bev and I are just having a cup of coffee."

"I appreciate what you are doing. Hopefully I can pick her up tomorrow."

"I said not to worry, Craig."

"Thanks. Can I speak to Tom?"

"Tom isn't here. He was called in by Hugh Wong. He didn't have a clue what it was about, but Hugh sent two men to guard the house. They're inside right now. Tom said it has something to do with you."

Craig smiled. "What else? I'll try and get hold of him, Jo-Ann. Thanks for your help."

Turning to Jennifer, Craig explained, "Tom was called into the office by Wong. Something's going down, and I'm not going to find out unless I call."

Jesse, wearing khaki colored shorts, uncrossed his long legs as Rusty walked in and placed his long snout on his lap. "You trust, Wong, don't you?"

Craig nodded then picked up the telephone and punched in the number. While waiting for the phone to be answered, he turned to Jesse. "By the way, Bev's just fine. She and Jo-Ann have a police guard sitting on the place and..."

"Hugh Wong," the voice cut in.

"I got a message on my answering machine, Hugh."

"I don't even want to know where you're calling from Craig," Wong said without any preamble, "but you've got to meet with me and Tom somewhere."

Craig never replied, and Wong continued. "Look, trust me on this, Craig! Shepherd is weaving intricate little plans and will soon start to involve others. We have to meet privately. I'll guarantee your safety and your freedom."

"What do you mean, my freedom?" Craig asked, puzzled.

"Not over the phone, okay? Now what about the meet?"

Craig was really hesitant to meet Wong. Not because he didn't trust him, but because he would be leaving the house, and Jennifer. He looked at Jesse, making a quick decision. "Okay, but the downtown core is out. Meet me," Craig tried to picture a location in his mind, somewhere not too far away. "Meet me under the Port Mann Bridge on the west end. I'll be in amongst some of the sea containers and I'll watch for you."

"We'll be there as soon as we can," Wong said. "One car, just Tom and me." Wong hung up.

Craig got up and walked downstairs, returning a moment later with his Beretta semi-auto tucked into his belt holster. He gave an old thirty-eight revolver to Jesse. "Remember how to use it?"

"Point it, close your eyes, and pull the trigger. Right?"

"Yeah, right," Craig smiled, knowing Jesse didn't do all that bad on the range. "I'll be back soon. No one comes into this house while I'm gone, I don't care who they say they are. Got that?"

"Not without wearing a hole," Jesse said with bravado. "We'll be fine. How long do you think you'll be?"

"Couple of hours. I'll take the cellular and anything at all happens, you phone me." Craig pointed to the gun in Jesse's hand. "Don't take any chances, Jess, remember what's at stake. I wouldn't be going, but I have to tie up some loose ends. I have to make sure we won't have any interference with the planned media interview."

"Just go, will you!"

Jennifer got up and walked over to Craig. "You're not supposed to be carrying that," she said patting the Beretta. "We already have a lot on our plate."

"Yeah, well, as long as it's not my head. This is just some cheap insurance." Craig headed for the door, turning as he reached the door to the garage. "Put the samples out of sight somewhere, Jess. Jennifer will help you."

Rusty left Jesse and walked over to Craig, wagging his tail in anticipation. "Pay attention to Rusty, you two. He's got good ears."

Craig backed out of the garage, lowering the garage door as he eased the Grand Cherokee towards the road. As the rear wheels dropped from the driveway to the road, Craig lowered the driver's window and looked up and down the dark road. There was nothing out there, except for the neighborhood dogs talking to each other and the sound of frogs in the night.

• • •

The overpass took him over the railway tracks and he looped back and dropped into the industrial area of sea containers, flatbed trailers, and large cranes. It was dimly lit, with little in the way of cover until you drove further in and back towards the underbelly of the Port Mann Bridge.

The containers were stacked as high as a three-story building, and in the dim light they appeared to stretch to the horizon. Craig backed between two rows, facing so as not to reflect any light off of his vehicle. Shutting off the motor, he sat and listened, the motor making little ticking noises as it cooled. He was committed; now he only had to wait.

Getting out, Craig shut the door quietly and walked to the rear of the long corridor between the sea containers. He could hear the sounds of the river traffic from where he stood, along with the accompanying smells of oil, lumber, and water. Satisfied that there was a way out, Craig then walked three rows to his left, then three rows to his right, watching for any silhouettes in the adjoining rows. It was clear.

Finding an advantage point away from the Jeep, he waited fifteen minutes before he saw a single vehicle entering the complex, the lights on low and bouncing over the uneven roadway. The car slowed considerably as it moved closer to Craig's lookout point, and Craig recognized Tom's slightly battered vehicle.

Craig waited until they drove by, seeing only the two of them silhouetted against the dim light, then stepped out from his position between the stacks. If he let them continue, it would be another twenty minutes before they returned to his location.

Taking a small metal flashlight out of his pocket, Craig flashed it in the direction of the driver's mirror. There was no response for a full three seconds, then the brakes went on briefly and the small back-up lights illuminated as Tom backed between one of the rows. Craig walked over as the two men got out of the car.

Tom smiled in the darkness and offered his hand to Craig. "Fancy meeting you here."

"Yeah, how about that," Craig said, looking across the hood as Hugh Wong got out of the car. "Hi, Hugh. What say we get into a different row so I can keep an eye on the road."

Craig started walking without waiting for a reply, and walked into a very dark row, one in which he could see the entrance if anyone drove in.

Hugh patted Craig's shoulder. "I'd say you're looking good, but I can't friggin see you."

Craig laughed, "Just as well, Hugh, it's not a pretty sight."

There was silence and a slight awkwardness as the men shifted their minds to the business a hand. "Well, you called this meeting, Hugh," Craig said, watching the roadway. "What's happening?"

Tom spoke before Hugh had a chance. "You won't believe it, partner. Ol' Shepherd is even outdoing himself."

Wong leaned against something solid in the darkness. "I'm supposed to find you, and arrest you."

Feeling his anger beginning to rise, Craig asked, "Is that why you invited me here?"

"Don't be a horse's ass!" Wong said, offended and angry. "I asked you here for two reasons. One, to find out for myself what the hell *is* going on, and two, because Shepherd makes me want to puke."

"Sorry," Craig said, and meant it. "What are you supposed to be arresting me for?"

"Shepherd said he would worry about that once you are in custody."

Tom came closer to Craig. "Look, you want help, just ask. Okay? But I think you owe us an explanation of some sort, Craig. I mean, this is way out of character, the things we've been hearing. Never mind the bullshit complaint against you from Kaufmann. What the hell have you gotten yourself mixed up in?"

Craig sighed, looking from one man to the other and knowing that he really did need to offer an explanation. It was all going to be made public anyway.

A short blast from a far away tug reached them as Craig tried to think out some sensible answer. "It started out as simply trying to help a friend with a problem. His name is Jesse Harris, and he was winding up years of research on a drug he was developing. He discovered that the U.S. Government was going to use it illegally."

Wong asked what was on Tom's mind as well. "What kind of drug?"

Listening, Craig could hear the steady hum of overhead traffic high above their heads, the tires thumping the familiar click-clack on the bridge surface as they hit the road connectors. The darkness intensified both the smells and sounds of the night.

He walked a few feet, and thought of what he should say. Would they believe it? Hell, did he believe it? It was going to be one hell of a selling job now that he thought about it.

Craig started slowly, filling the two men in on the call he had received and of his going to Seattle. He then told them about 'PRECISE,' and about Jesse taking it and giving it to him.

"Com'on now! You telling me they have a drug that makes you tell the truth?" Tom laughed. "Hey, I'd never be safe around my house."

Wong didn't laugh. He was listening to everything Craig said, and was taking it seriously. "From what I know, and it isn't much, they've always had some form of drug like that over the years. What's so different?"

"Quite a bit, from what Jesse told me. It ... there's a vehicle coming in. No lights." Craig pushed Wong and Tom back into the shadows so light wouldn't reflect off of their faces. Looking towards the hidden cars, he was satisfied that they were well out of sight.

"Now who the hell is that?" Tom asked.

Wong inched towards the corner and looked around. "I was sure we weren't followed. Whoever it is, they're moving in real slow and quiet. Dark car, can't tell the make."

"I can't afford to get caught in a net now," Craig said as he moved backwards to the rear of the passageway so he could get to the Jeep. "I should be able to drive out from the other end of the rows."

Tom grabbed him and moved him against the hard container. "No! If they're working as a team, there's only one entrance and exit. Stay put."

The intruder was barely moving, only the occasional noise from a crushed piece of gravel giving him away. The interior was totally black as the car coasted to a stop a hundred feet away from the entrance to where Craig was standing.

The engine was cut and both doors opened. The interior of the car remained dark, and two men got out and stood leaning on the doors, the light from the upper bridge deck partially filtering down on them.

Tom leaned over and whispered in Craig's ear. "Can't quite make them out." Tom nudged Craig. "They're pulling out weapons."

"The passenger is." Craig whispered. "Can't see the driver."

Craig touched Wong's shoulder in acknowledgment. "You two stay here and back me up. I'm going to slide around to their rear and work myself closer."

Tom grabbed Craig's arm and moved along with him. "Not without me, you're not. Let's go." The two of them left Hugh Wong to watch the movements of the two other men, and moved swiftly towards the end of the long container row.

A few moments later they both glanced around the edge of a container.

The unidentified vehicle was less than thirty feet away. Both doors were still open but the driver was not in sight. Craig could make out the passenger as he leaned over the roof. His face was resting on his left forearm and and they saw what looked like the glint of a shotgun.

Craig and Tom stood very still. It was quiet except for the intermittent roar of the big rigs as they made their way across the bridge overhead.

Looking closely at the open door of the car, Craig noticed a green light shining from beneath the dash. "That's a police car," he said as he nudged Tom.

Tom was about to answer when a vehicle engine roared to life, and tires began to spin in the gravel. The guy at the car brought up his shotgun and turned on a powerful hand-held light. "Police. Stay where you are or I'll fire!"

The car came to a sliding stop only twenty feet from where Tom and Craig were standing, and the driver's door flew open. Wong jumped out and began to yell at the man displayed in the vehicle headlights. "Johnston, you asshole! What are you *doing* here?"

The driver showed up from one of the side lanes as Johnston lowered his shotgun, looking sheepish as he thought of an answer. "Look, Inspector Wong, I've got a job to do."

"Job my ass. What the fuck are you doing here? You're screwing up my operation!"

"I've got orders to...ah...assist you in finding Fletcher. Saw you come in here and thought you might need backup."

"Well you thought wrong." Wong said as he raised his voice and called over his shoulder. "Tom, you might as well come out. They've screwed everything up royally."

Craig gave Tom a poke in the ribs. "Get out there. You came together."

Tom stepped out from concealment and raised his voice. "Yeah, tell me about it. He'll never show up now." Walking up to the men, Tom looked at Johnston and the other man. "Semi-auto's, shotguns, what is this? You guys planning on helping or killing Fletcher?"

"Now you just watch your mouth. We heard he turned nasty."

"You know," Tom said, "you'd believe anything. Shepherd tells you to squat, you fart before you even move. You got your priorities all fucked up."

Johnston moved towards Tom Gifford in a threatening manner, bringing both hands up in front of him. "You little cocksu..."

"That's enough!" Wong commanded. "You've done enough damage for one night. You and your pal get back into the city."

"Seems awful strange that Fletcher's partner is on stakeout," Johnston stated, looking from one man to the other.

"You wouldn't know the word loyalty, Johnston, if it was tattooed on your dick," Tom said as he moved towards Johnston.

"I won't say it again! Into your car and move out," Wong said as he stepped between the two men.

Getting into the unmarked unit, Johnston leaned out of the window with a crooked smile on his face as the driver did a slow reverse turn. "You tell Fletcher we were asking about him."

Gifford and Wong watched the car move towards the entrance to the industrial park as Craig moved over to join them. "Good thinking, Hugh."

"Why the hell do you think I'm an inspector?" Turning to Tom he waved him towards their car. "Let's go, Tom. We're out of here. Now you see what you are up against, Craig. Give it ten minutes and leave. We'll be in touch later."

As the two men settled into their vehicle, Craig gently patted the roof and leaned towards the window. "Hey you two. Thanks, okay?"

Tom nodded. "Take care. I have a feeling you have more than a few people tracking you."

Craig moved briskly along the highway towards home. Traffic was non-existent and he was making good time. Punching in his home number, all he got was the answering machine. Expecting that Jennifer wouldn't answer, he spoke anyway, waiting for someone to pick up the telephone. "Com'on you guys, it's me. Pick up the phone."

No one picked up the receiver.

Making his way in the dark was easier as his eyes adjusted. He was on foot and had left the vehicle around a bend further down the road. Cutting across the rear of his property Craig did a careful scan with his eyes, removing his Beretta as he moved in. Every side of the house appeared secure, which may or may not be good, but he couldn't risk walking in unannounced. He might get a bullet for his effort.

Craig returned to the parked vehicle and drove it towards the house, hitting the garage door opener and rolling the jeep into the garage and cutting the engine before it came to a stop. As the garage door came down, Craig quickly looked underneath for any suspicious movement.

Easing the Beretta out of its holster he quietly entered the laundry room, taking in the alarm panel. It was in alarm mode and he shut it off. Looking around the doorjamb into the kitchen, he saw Jesse standing there with the .38

pointed in his direction, and shaking like he had a fever.

Letting out a deep controlled breath, Jesse lowered the gun. "Jesus, I'm not cut out for this."

"Where's Jennifer?"

"In the bedroom. Crying, I think. She let Rusty out a while ago and he took off around the side of the house. We heard a horrible howl and he hasn't come back."

Craig started for the bedroom, but Jennifer came into the kitchen. Tears were running down her cheeks. "Oh Craig, I think something's happened to Rusty."

"That's what Jesse was saying. I..."

The glass at the front door shattered, sending shards flying all the way down the hall to the kitchen nook. Craig could see an arm trying to unlock the inner tumbler, but whoever it was didn't realize that a dead bolt was set above the doorknob. "Downstairs," Craig said softly. "Quick!"

As they ran for the basement stairs, Craig slid open the patio door, hoping to draw them in that direction, then ran for the stairs himself. He barely hit the downstairs floor when the upstairs door smashed against the wall.

He knew he hadn't fooled them when he heard footsteps at the top of the stairs a few moments later.

···CHAPTER THIRTEEN

Tom Gifford looked over a Wong and remarked, "Any bets they'll head straight to Shepherd's office?"

"He won't be in at this hour. They'll already have called him from the car."

As Tom turned a corner and accelerated to keep the other car in view, the scent of the ocean filled the car as a southwest breeze worked it's way through the maze of downtown office buildings. It failed to invigorate their tired bodies.

"You know," Tom continued, "I wouldn't be surprised if he *was* in the damn office."

"Well, I intend to find out."

"What?" Tom looked over at Wong. "You planning on getting yourself in more hot water?"

"Noooo. But I do intend on doing a little snooping. I'm supposed to report to Shepherd, remember. If I time it right, I'm sure our boys will be in his office."

"Want me to come up? It would be perfectly normal."

Wong sat in silence for a moment, watching the closed shops roll by. He was about to answer when a car came along side, the womp, womp, womp, of speakers blasting against his eardrums.

"Fucking idiot," Tom remarked. "He'll be stone deaf in no time. Otta be a law."

"There is a law," Wong said, amazed. "You've been out of uniform too long."

"Yeah, well somebody should do something. Jerks keep going up and down my street with the god awful thump, thump, thump, banging away."

"You're a cop. Pull him over and give him a ticket."

"What's a ticket?" Tom asked with a smile.

"Yeah, right. I..."

"They're pulling into the garage now," Tom interrupted.

"Give them two minutes to get parked."

Tom pulled into the police garage and cut the engine. In the silence that followed, they both sat watching the elevator and the large empty garage. Nothing was moving.

Wong opened the passenger door and turned to Gifford. "I'll go up alone. This is my turf and I'll handle it."

"Are you sure? You may need a witness."

"No," Wong answered, as he got out and shut the door. "But I'm going up alone anyway. Talk to you later."

Tom sat in the car, unsure of his next move. He knew Craig could probably use some support. He was about to start the car when his pager went off, the beeper sounding overly loud in the confines of the vehicle. It was Craig's home number, but the numbers 911 followed it.

Moving quickly to the garage phone, Tom hit the nine button and upon hearing the outside tone, punched in Craig's telephone number. The phone rang twice, then there was nothing. It just went dead.

Tom had the car in gear and moving with a squeak of the tires before the engine settled into life. He aimed the car towards the freeway and activated the red and blue grill lights and switched the siren to *yelp*.

The traffic moved obediently out of his path. The speedometer touched seventy miles per hour as Tom forced oncoming traffic out of the way and the wigwag headlamp blasted the darkness ahead in alternate brilliance. Within ten minutes he was out of the core of the city and onto the freeway, his foot going further and further into the accelerator as traffic rapidly disappeared in the rear view mirror.

A few large drops of rain smashed against the windshield and ran off in different directions. Then a few more followed, rapidly increasing until a light shower turned into an all-out downpour that made visibility almost impossible.

About the time Tom hit the cloverleaf taking him towards Ridge Meadows he was frantic with worry and maintained his speed on the slippery hot surface.

A group of kids, all crammed together in a little Honda and playing their music at an ear splitting level, left the Westbound exit of the freeway and bounced into the merge area of the bridge, laughing with the rain and the music.

The packed car, the loud music, and poor visibility were some of the reasons the driver of the Honda didn't see the emergency lights or hear the high pitched siren on Tom's car as he bore down on them. Then again, maybe it was the fact that the sweet young thing next to the driver had her hand inside his pants and was keeping time to the speakers and the steady duh dum, duh dum, duh dum.

The Honda came in from the right at a speed faster than the inexperienced driver could handle, and the car rapidly drifted to the left and into the next lane at the exact moment that Tom came along side. The Honda smashed into the side of the police car and propelled it into oncoming traffic.

Reacting in alarm, the young driver overcorrected and sent the vehicle to the right and over the embankment in a shower of sparks as he made contact with a metal guardrail. If there was anyone there to hear, the young driver's scream would easily be heard over the blasting radio as he plummeted like a rocket to hell into the darkness below.

At the same moment that the front end of the Honda smashed into the asphalt below, Tom floored the car in an effort to return to his own lane. Unfortunately, this was the exact spot that the Department of Highways determined that a concrete barricade was needed to stop head on collisions.

The left front wheel of the unmarked police unit hit the slanted end of the concrete divider with enough force to flip it to the right in a continual role; the roof hit the curbside barricade as it continued its course down the embankment. Tom's head smashed into the side post with a sickening crack before the car settled onto the railway tracks in an upside-down position.

The last thing Tom saw from his suspended position in his seatbelt was the twin ribbon of steel running off into the distance, then blackness.

People jumped out of their cars and ran towards the Honda. The doors were jammed shut and screams of terror were emanating nonstop. Except for the driver who was unconscious with a head injury, most of the fear was claustrophobic, and due to everyone being pinned together.

As the first liberator arrived at the side of the little car he was taken by surprise at the sight of a young girl, blood running down her face and her knees jammed into the dashboard. She was screaming her head off as she squeezed the living hell out of the driver's dink.

It only took a few minutes to get Tom out of the wreckage using the Jaws of Life. He was leaving the scene in the ambulance when he woke up, a member of the emergency crew reassuring him that everything was all right. But everything wasn't all right; there was something he should be doing. Apprehension gripped him as he drifted towards unconsciousness. There was something...

• • •

Craig, Jennifer, and Jesse slid into an enclosed area under the stairs. Quietly pulling the door closed, Craig reached up and pulled a wire that released a rotating panel that revealed a space of about four feet by five feet. They all stepped in and Craig pulled it closed. Craig kept his guns here, hidden from prying eyes, secure in the knowledge that they were stored safely.

Motioning for both of them to be quiet, Craig watched as Jennifer slid down the wall and came to rest on her haunches, arms wrapped around her knees. Jesse was pressed against the wall with the .38 held across his chest. Sweat was beading his forehead and his breath was becoming short and shallow.

Craig heard a slight creak in the wood above his head, and looked through a small space in the stairs just in time to see a foot fill his vision. The feet grew into legs, and then hips and shoulders as the man quietly slipped into view. Looking through the crack with an intensity that was starting to make his eyes water, Craig finally saw what he was waiting for– the guy's face.

The guy was in his thirties and had an intense look about him. Craig found some comfort in the grip of his Beretta, but that soon disappeared as he looked into the hard blue eyes and the bulging arms that stretched the fabric of a short sleeve shirt.

The man remained at the bottom of the stairs and was carefully sectoring the room with his eyes. The automatic in his hands was held in front of his body in the combat position.

The second man appeared, and the two of them did nothing but stand and survey the room for exits and hiding places. They finally moved out of Craig's line of sight.

Ten seconds later the door to the underneath portion of the stairway crashed open with a bang, and Jennifer was barely able to stifle an involuntary cry. They could hear the man move into the enclosure, taking his time to inspect the small area. A few moments later he moved away. Both men could be heard in various parts of the basement as they checked the game room, bar, bathroom, and the storage area.

Rolling thunder could be heard outside of the house, and rain started to pelt the outside patio door with a vengeance. Taking advantage of the search taking place in the other part of the house, Craig quickly laid down his weapon and dialed Tom Gifford's pager number. When he got an answer, he quickly punched in his own telephone number. As an after thought he also punched in 911.

Craig turned and looked at Jesse. He received a smile in return, but Craig could tell he was way beyond his depth as the corners of his mouth twitched nervously. Jennifer hadn't moved. He bent down, his knees cracking loudly, and put his hand on her shoulder. She covered his hand with hers and gave it a squeeze. Man he loved this woman.

He was about to stand up when a voice shattered the stillness not more than three feet away. "I don't get it. Where the fuck are they? The basement doors are locked on the inside, and we've checked everything."

"Are you sure they didn't slip out the upstairs door?"

"No fucking way. There wasn't one footmark in the dew outside. They're here all right."

Craig could see Jennifer's and Jesse's face in the dim light. He motioned for them to be still and brought his Beretta up to line up on the voices on the other side of the wall.

He had all sorts of ammunition, as well as rifles, shotguns, and a couple of different handguns, but they would do no one any good if the three of them were discovered. With the walls being made of drywall and phony wood paneling, their chance of survival was very slim.

The gray haired one came into view at the bottom of the stairs, and as Craig watched him he carefully scanned the room again. The thunderstorm was getting closer, and Craig could see flashes of lightning play across the guy's face.

Grant scratched his cheek with his left hand, a large caliber semi-automatic with a silencer attached clutched in his right. "Maybe they didn't come downstairs. Could be hiding upstairs."

"Don't second guess yourself. Let's keep looking."

The two of them disappeared, and a few moments later the door on the other side of the false wall opened again. It seemed like ages before it was closed and the two men searched elsewhere. They reappeared suddenly at the bottom of the stairs and started upwards.

Craig turned and gave the other two a thumbs-up, a smile creasing the corner of his mouth. The smile froze in disbelief as his cellular came to life on the shelf next to his head. It warbled once more before he could grab it and shut it off. Looking at Jesse and Jennifer, he saw the same look of disbelief and fear.

Any hope that they were home free was quickly shattered as two bodies thumped back down the staircase. Grant turned to face the stairs and the room in general on his left, his gun raised and ready for action as Strickler disappeared into the room.

"You're all very clever," the unseen voice said, "but if you do not come out right now, I am going to start to shoot very large holes in every wall I see. Nobody will hear a damn thing, and I've got plenty of ammo. Now... do you want to be alive, and I take what I came for, or do you want to be dead, and I still take what I came for?"

Craig crouched very low, unable to see anything anymore. He was, for once, at a loss as to his next move. His choices were rapidly disappearing.

Grant's voice boomed through the wall a few feet away. "I say fuck it! I'm not screwin' around anymore!"

Grant began to methodically pull the trigger of his weapon, the gun jumping in his hand as pictures and glass exploded; numerous holes appeared in the wall above their heads.

Jennifer screamed as a cleaning rod took a hit and fell off of the wall and hit her on the head. Five more rounds immediately followed, with dust and debris falling all about them. Craig was about to return fire when the other man yelled out.

"That's enough! Now, come out of there now!"

Looking at his wife and his friend hugging the floor, Craig knew he couldn't take any more risks. Slowly he stood up and yelled through the wall. "Okay, hold it. No more shooting. We're coming out."

"Good decision. Now come out empty handed and nice and slow."

Jesse stood up, the .38 still in his hand, and helped Jennifer to her feet. He pulled on the wire next to the sloping ceiling and the wall moved to the right and opened. He started to walk through and Craig stopped him, a hand on his shoulder. Craig pointed to the gun in Jesse's hand, and Jesse looked at it dully, not realizing the significance of walking out the door. Craig took it from him and pushed him out the door gently.

Jennifer followed, and Craig placed the handgun on the shelf. He was about to follow suit with his own, when something stopped him. He quickly put the gun in the small of his back under his belt, and pulled his shirt over it. He followed Jennifer out of the small hideaway.

Grant had moved to the left of the opening, and Craig could see an empty cartridge clip on the floor behind him. The other man was to his right and on the other side of the pool table. This one looked like the one in charge, so Craig addressed his remarks to him.

"Okay, now what?"

"The first thing I want you to know is this is not some good guy, bad guy game I'm playing here. You know what I want, and if I don't get it now, you are all going to die."

"That wouldn't be smart," Craig replied. "You have been tracking us through four states and two provinces, and I'm sure you are well known. Besides, if you kill us do you really have time to look?"

"How about I just kill your wife?" Grant spoke up. "Or, for an appetizer, how about this?" Grant whirled and lined up on Jesse, firing the silenced weapon in one smooth action.

Jesse was flung to the wall, his large frame smashing with great force before he fell to the floor. Jennifer screamed, and without thinking ran to Jesse. Craig was about to reach for his gun, when he saw the same black tiny hole aimed at him.

"I'm not fooling. Now, your friend over there is only wounded, but I'll place a neat little hole in his forehead for all the trouble he's caused us if we don't get 'PRECISE' back. Now, where is it?"

Looking at the two men, Craig felt completely helpless. Everything seemed to collapse from within. Craig nodded and pointed to Jesse, "You'll get it. Let me see to him for a moment."

"You'll see to nothing," Strickler interjected. "Just get the goodies. The sooner you do, the sooner we are out of your hair."

Jennifer was busy with Jesse's wound; ripping a piece of bar towel, she was trying to stop the bleeding. He was very pale and breathing raggedly from the trauma. He needed medical attention, and in a hurry.

The shooting of Jesse had just proven to Craig what he already knew. These men were not about to leave three people alive to walk and talk. With Strickler and Grant back in the United States, it would end up as one cold trail.

"Come on, move it!" Grant demanded.

Craig indicated the rain splattered basement patio door that led to the backyard. "It's out there. It's in the equipment shed at the back of the yard."

"Bullshit!" Strickler cut in. "It's in this damn house. Now get it."

Craig was about to answer when lightning cracked overhead, immediately followed by a deep, rolling clap of thunder. Waves of water slashed against the windows, making it impossible to see outside even with the aid of the lightning flashes. "You think I want to go out in that? Look, you asked where it is and I'm telling you. I can't afford to screw around with other people's lives." Craig pointed with emphasis towards the patio doors and the backyard. "It's out there, in a briefcase."

"Okay, Mark, go with him and get the briefcase," Strickler ordered.

"We'll need a flashlight," Craig said, pointing towards a drawer. "I have to work a combination on the door."

Strickler opened the drawer and pulled out a large metal flashlight, and before he could give it to Grant, Craig nonchalantly took it from his hand and moved towards the door.

Excruciating pain tore through Craig's left ear as he unlocked the patio door. Doubling over, he waited until the agony subsided before turning to look at Grant.

Grant smiled wickedly as he brought his gun back to line up on him. "That was a love tap. You so much as take a step without permission and I'll turn you into a piece of useless rubbish. Got that?"

Craig nodded, lightning playing across his face as he opened the door and stepped into a wall of water. Thunder clapped so loudly he couldn't even hear the rain.

Turning the flashlight towards the shed in the corner of the yard he started walking against the heavy onslaught of water and wind. Lightning flashed again, and he turned and saw Grant about four steps to his rear watching his every move.

Reaching the shed, he played the light over the combination lock. He tried to turn the dial but he was unable because he was holding the flashlight and his hands were too slippery. Water was getting into his eyes and he had to keep wiping his arm across his eyes and forehead.

Thunder rolled across the sky, and the wind was building up and becoming bitterly cold. Craig brought the flashlight up and turned to his left towards Grant, at the same time reaching behind his back for his Beretta in the small of his back.

Craig yelled against the thunder and wind into Grant's face, shining the light partially into his face. "You'll have to hold the light. It's too wet and I need two hands."

He handed the light to Grant, momentarily playing the beam directly into his eyes. Bright blue light captured them both like two figures frozen in time, and then faded as Craig hit Grant full in the face with the beam again.

As Grant took the flashlight, Craig stepped to the left and whipped out his own gun. He brought it down with all his force on the other man's wrist. Grant's weapon fell from loose fingers as he cried out in pain, and Craig was about to step back and level his own gun when Grant turned on him in an unexpected charge.

Craig couldn't react fast enough. The grass was slippery under his feet. A fist exploded into the left side of his face as he desperately tried to hold onto his gun. A knee narrowly missed his testicles, and Craig knew he was dealing with a trained fighting machine. He was loosing ground rapidly.

Craig swung his gun in an arc, unable to see but feeling solid contact at once. Grant grunted and fell backwards, only to shake his head and lash out with his right foot, catching Craig squarely in the ribs, under his raised left arm.

Craig flew backwards, landing on his back and sliding in water four inches deep, his breath momentarily knocked out of him. Mark Grant was on top of him before he could move, and began smashing Craig's head into the ground while holding large handfuls of his hair.

Stars were forming behind Craig's eyes and his brain was producing a roar of sound from the first contact with the ground. He knew he didn't have long and he felt stupid; he was just lying there doing nothing.

Craig realized that he had lost his gun, and with an effort brought both arms off of the ground quickly and smashed his open hands against Grant's ears as hard as he could. The immediate pain was apparent as Grant let go of Craig's hair and let out a scream from the colliding pressure within his ears.

Craig's hand fell on his own weapon as he placed his hand on the ground to get up, and he brought it up and swung it sideways into Grant's head. Grant fell over onto the ground, blood running from a cut on his cheek and disappearing at once in the heavy rain.

Getting to his feet Mark Grant staggered uncertainly, trying to focus and locate Craig. Lightning illuminated them both and Craig got to his feet quickly and backed against the shed, the automatic held out in front of him.

"Your finished, asshole," Grant said as he moved towards Craig, a smile on his face. He flicked open a long pointed knife, the blade slim and gleaming in the downpour. "I love this shit! I really do! This is living, you know that, Fletcher? This is living." He suddenly sprang, covering the distance in a flash. "And this, you prick, is dying!"

Craig stepped aside as the knife came in low and fast, the point penetrating the side of the shed. He took another quick step to the side and his foot caught the edge of a boulder, sending him onto his back again.

Grant stood over top of him, one leg on either side of his body, and as a feeble flash of lightning framed him, Craig saw that he only had seconds to live. Distant thunder erupted again as Craig took aim and the Beretta jumped with a familiar feeling in his hands. Mark Grant disappeared from his vision as if a giant hand had yanked him from behind.

Craig got slowly to his feet, his legs barely supporting him. Looking down at Grant in the flickering light, he saw two side-by-side bullet holes just above Grant's left eye. He had a very surprised look on his face.

"*Good grouping,*" Craig thought stupidly, looking with a blank expression at Grant's open eyes. He started to shake uncontrollably, and didn't know if it was the cold rain and wind, or a reaction from just killing a man.

Looking towards the house and towards the warm lights, Craig walked the short distance and stumbled onto the patio. He tried to look into the room but the glass was steamed up on the inside.

Slowly, he moved the door to the right and looked into the room. Jesse was still on the floor, only he now had a blanket over him. Jennifer looked up from her position beside him, her face was ashen and she was shaking uncontrollably. Before Craig could look further, the cold hard steel of a gun was placed against his temple. Craig froze.

"Drop the gun and get inside. Now!"

Craig stepped inside, sliding the door closed behind him. He was immediately warmed by the inside temperature and started to control his shivering. Wiping his face with his wet upper sleeve, Craig looked over to his right and saw a young male with dark sandy hair holding a pistol on him in the ready position. The man was dressed in blue jeans, a light summer shirt, and a windbreaker. He looked as if he had just left his university class.

"Who are you?"

"RCMP. Now drop the weapon."

Craig looked down and realized that he still held the Beretta. "I don't see any identification; all I see are two guys who may want to kill me, and I've been shot at enough tonight."

Slowly, the sandy haired man produced his identification. "The names Ronald Edwards."

Craig let the Beretta slide from his hands. As it thumped on the carpet, Craig saw a man lying face down by the opening to his under-the-stairs gunroom.

It was Strickler. He was quite obviously dead, his eyes seeing nothing as his gun hand rested in his own blood.

Craig noticed a second man standing by the bottom of the stairs. He was dressed in casual pants. A maroon windbreaker half-covered a golf shirt.

The RCMP officer saw his look. "This is Agent McAdam, F.B.I."

Craig pointed towards Jesse. "My friend needs an ambulance. He's been shot."

Edwards turned and motioned to McAdam to use the phone. "911– Have a look at him."

While McAdam was using the phone and checking on Jesse, Edwards put his gun away and frisked Craig.

"Where's Grant?"

"If you mean the guy who tried to kill me, he's outside with his brains blown out." Craig pointed to the body on the floor. "That one, and the one outside, broke in here. They were going to kill us. It was self-defense."

"That's what it looks like to me, too," Edwards nodded. "For the time being."

Craig paused, pointing to the floor, "What happened to this one?"

"Strickler? He wouldn't listen to orders. Tried to throw down on us. I had to shoot him." Edwards walked closer to Craig. "Sorry we're a little late but you kept throwing us off and losing us."

Craig looked at Edwards, not comprehending what he was talking about. Then it struck him and he gave a small painful chuckle. "The car at the ferry. Sorry, there wasn't room for you."

Craig walked over and sat down beside Jesse and Jennifer, his wet hair dripping down the back of his neck. "You'll be okay, Jess," he said and leaned over and gave him a hug. At the same time he whispered in his ear. "What about 'PRECISE'?"

Jesse just gave a small shrug with his good shoulder in return.

Craig heard the patio door open and turned to see Edwards entering the house as he came back from checking Grant. "He won't be going anywhere."

Craig turned to the F.B.I. man. "Just what do you have to do with this? As far as I know, you're not supposed to be working outside of the United States."

McAdam smiled in a friendly manner. "I'm working in co-operation with the RCMP. I was keeping tabs on things until you all crossed the border. Then... well, it became a little more complicated."

"You look like you're targeting your own people," Craig said, pointing to Strickler. "What's going on?" Craig demanded.

"Let's just say that they had a different agenda, and along with the Secret Service, we managed to come across something that was very dangerous to the security of the United States."

Craig said, "If the U.S. Secret Service is involved, that means your President is involved somehow. Right?"

"I've already said more than I should have," McAdam answered.

The sound of running feet came down to them from upstairs, and a moment later two men from the emergency health service appeared with a stretcher and medical kit. Everyone stood back as Jesse was attended to.

McAdam addressed Craig from across the room. "Your buddy doesn't go anywhere, Fletcher, until we get the U.S. property you have."

Craig shrugged his shoulders, and looked back at McAdam.

McAdam stepped forward and hunched down beside Jesse as the medical team was preparing to check Jesse's vital signs. "Mr. Harris, I believe you have something we want. The game is over."

Jesse looked over at the RCMP Officer, and then turned to look at the FBI man squatted down beside him. Looking closely at the man, Jesse said, "I know you from somewhere. I've seen you... Yeah, you're the one I gave a ride to. Ah...ah...Ernie, yeah– you're Ernie, for Pete's sake."

McAdam chuckled and patted Jesse's hand. "Yeah, you've made me. Thanks for the ride."

"Why didn't you arrest me if it was that easy?"

"Believe me, Mr. Harris, there is more involved than you know, and to be frank, we needed you to lead us to 'PRECISE.'"

Craig spoke up, stopping Jesse before he could continue. "The motel rooms up country, it was you guys wasn't it? It wasn't this Strickler and Grant at all. You broke in, looking for 'PRECISE.'"

McAdam, 'Ernie', just smiled and looked at Jesse. "I want the property of the United States Government, Mr. Harris. Now."

Jesse pointed to the door that lead under the stairs, his hand shaking with the effort. "It's in a briefcase in a small room in there."

A small tear formed at the corner of Jesse's eye and rolled down his cheek. He was holding back emotions that he couldn't release and they were threatening to choke him. Everything they had been through, the running and all the worry suddenly came to the surface and was over. Jesse looked at Jennifer and Craig, but nobody could find any words to exchange.

As Jesse was taken away in the ambulance, Craig walked over and put his arms around Jennifer, feeling her quiet controlled sobs against his chest. Turning towards Edwards, he nodded towards the backyard. "It *was* self-defense with that guy outside. I didn't have a choice."

"That's the way we're treating it for now. I have the forensic people on the way. You *have* killed a man, Fletcher. We both did. All we can do is play it out. It appears, however, that you are a victim. A break-in in the middle of the night by two armed assailants looks like a home invasion to me." Edwards smiled, and pointed towards the stairway. "You and your wife go upstairs and rest. You'll have plenty of time to give your statements. You want to call for legal advice, go ahead."

"What's going to happen to Jesse?" Jennifer asked McAdam.

"I have no idea. He'll know soon enough."

"And the stuff in the briefcase?" Craig asked pointing to McAdam's left hand. "From what I know, that is a extremely dangerous drug."

The F.B.I. man held up the briefcase and agreed. "That it is. This little item could change the world!"

•••CHAPTER FOURTEEN

The door to the garage went slowly but steadily upward behind the Jeep. The other door, where they used to park the Mustang, remained closed. Craig stepped out under overcast skies and walked towards the waiting press, noting that some were too impatient and were gathering up their equipment to walk-trot towards him. He held up his hands, indicating they were to stop. "Okay, okay. I'll only give you a few moments, and I'm not answering questions that I haven't had an opportunity to talk to my lawyer about."

Craig kept walking towards the roadway, ignoring and evading cameramen and reporters and all their rapid-fire questions. Reaching the roadway, he moved to the right and away from the driveway, and out of Jennifer's way as she backed out.

"Detective Sergeant Fletcher, is it true you have been charged with murder?"

Craig looked at the young male reporter, obviously eager to ask the right questions. "Not that I'm aware of. I'm not in jail."

"You did kill a man though, isn't that right?" asked another man dressed in a horribly wrinkled brown sports jacket, and holding a microphone towards him.

"Doug, isn't it?" Craig said, looking the man in the eyes.

"Yes," the man nodded, pleased that he had been recognized, especially on camera.

Craig continued. "Doug, two men died after breaking into my home. The police are conducting an investigation at this very moment, and as I've already said I have not been charged with anything."

"You *are* the center of that investigation though, aren't you, Fletcher?"

Craig groaned inwardly, knowing the voice belonged to Georgina Farnsworth. *"Keep your cool, Fletcher,"* he told himself. "Naturally I'm involved, they broke into my home in the middle of the night!"

"My information is that you shot a man in cold blood, Detective Sergeant Fletcher, a man who was legally trying to get back top-secret documents stolen from the United States Government. Isn't that correct?"

"Are you making statements or seeking honest answers, Miss Farnsworth?" Craig asked.

"You have not answered my question, Sergeant Fletcher. The man you shot, was he trying to retrieve stolen government documents belonging to a foreign government? And did you have them in your possession?"

Craig looked directly into the camera, knowing this was the best tactic when dealing with T.V. news coverage. "As I've already stated, there is an investigation going on, and I'm not in a position to divulge any of the facts right now. The investigators are the ones who should be questioned. I have not been charged with anything."

Farnsworth stepped forward with the microphone extended further. "Is it not true that you have already been arrested for aggravated assault on a Vancouver citizen?"

"There are many things that have been alleged. That doesn't make them true."

Farnsworth continued to press. "The people of Vancouver are wondering..."

"No, Georgina, the people of Vancouver are not wondering. You are! If you want me to be up front with you, quit hiding behind the people of Vancouver. Besides, that's old news and you know I cannot discuss that case with you."

Another reporter stepped forward and Craig recognized him from the other news channel; he had always been honest in his reporting.

"One question, Gerry, then that's it for today."

"I think it's only fair to say that you have been involved, in some way, with the disappearance of highly secret information from a lab in the United States. This seems way out of character for you, what with your past record and years of service. How are you involved?"

"I'm sorry, I can't answer your question, Gerry. Some things are not always what they seem and I will do my best to clear this up after I find out what the authorities have planned. I may even call a news conference." Waving to them all, and moving away, Craig softly called out, "That's all I have for now. Thank you."

Craig jumped into the passenger side of the waiting Jeep and indicated for Jennifer to take off. Looking back, he saw that Farnsworth was facing the camera and talking up a storm.

"Well, how did it go?" Jennifer asked as she steered around a bend in the road.

"They all have their jobs to do. You can bet Farnsworth will put her own little twist on things, though."

"So what happens if Shepherd wants to arrest you when we get into the city?"

"We'll handle that if and when it comes. As soon as I see Tom, I'm heading to the lawyer's office. Jesse still wants the world to know about 'PRECISE,' and he's out of it for now. Thank God the bullet didn't hit any bones or vital nerves."

Entering the hospital, Craig led the way towards Tom's room. Lorraine was sitting in the waiting room by the nurse's station, reading a magazine and watching T.V. at the same time. She didn't see them until they quietly sat down on each side of her. When she looked up, her face lit up in total surprise and delight. She didn't know which way to turn first.

"Mom, Dad, I didn't even see you." She gave them each a hug and continued, "I've been positively bored sitting here. I hate hospitals."

"I'm sure all the sick people in here do too, sweetheart," Craig said, giving her a bear hug.

She groaned with pleasure and pounded him on his shoulder. "That's enough, Dad, I can't breath. Let's go home."

"We will, but first I have to see Tom if I can. Then I have to try and see Uncle Jesse."

"Uncle Jesse? What's wrong?"

"You sit and explain it to her, Jenn, I'm going to find Tom."

Jennifer gave Craig a pained look, as he turned and walked towards the nurse's station. "Can you tell me where Mrs. Gifford is?"

The nurse pointed towards a small area and Craig found her sitting alone and twisting a handkerchief. Upon seeing him, Jo-Ann got up and put her arms around him, not wanting to let go.

"How is he?"

Letting go, Jo-Ann sat down tiredly. "I just this minute talked to the doctor. He said he'd be okay. He's in the recovery room. They said that he had a good banging around and that he'll be sore.... but boy, is it scary," she said as two large tears rolled down her cheeks. Looking up at Craig, she shrugged her shoulders. "I'm sorry, I'm not very good at this sort of thing."

"You're doing great, and you're stronger than you think. It'll be easier with Lorraine out of your hair. I can't thank you enough for being there when I needed you."

"She's a doll, and no problem at all. She's been great company while I waited to hear from the doctor."

"Have you been told how it happened?"

"Yes," and she filled Craig in on all the circumstances of the car accident. "He has a concussion, broken ribs, and internal bruising."

"I don't know what's going to happen. He was on an emergency run and apparently he didn't let anyone know. The accident happened outside of the city limits and they say he was going very fast."

"These things sort themselves out. Don't worry. It was an accident, and he was trying to save my butt."

"You know damn well," she said taking a shaky, audible breath, "that they pick apart everything you guys do, *after* it's all over."

"Yes, that's part of the job. Don't worry, he'll have lots of people who will stand up for him. Who knows, maybe after everything is out in the open, nothing may happen. I guess seeing him is out of the question?"

"No, they won't allow you in right now. What's going to happen with you? From what Tom has said, you have a lot to answer for. Don't get me wrong, I'm not judging, it's just that nobody has any answers except what they read or hear from the news."

Craig took a seat and leaned back on the thick padded hospital chair. Looking at his partner's wife, he realized that the years had flown by and they went back a long way. He had to enlighten Jo-Ann a bit or she would continue to worry.

"Jo– " He waited until she looked up before he tried to find words to continue. "First of all, Tom's not involved in anything that I've been doing. Shepherd suspended me on a trumped up charge of assault. I was supposed to have broken a guy's bones, and whatever. I didn't. Then I got a call from a very good friend who needed help. I went to find out what was wrong and to help him out of a jam if he needed me. I didn't know what it was until I got there, and then I had to make a snap decision then and there. Whatever decision I've made, I'll have to justify it to someone down the road."

Graig was speaking very quietly, watching Jo-Ann's eyes as he spoke. Her gaze never left him. "Does it involve a very top secret U.S. project? Yes. Did I help take it? I suppose I did, after the fact, but not for espionage or self-gain or anything to harm the security of the United States. The project my friend was working on is for a good purpose I'm told, but... someone has turned it into a very dangerous drug for use on ordinary people. I couldn't refuse my friend when he said he wanted to turn it over to responsible people. He wants it out in the open."

Jo-Ann sat forward, rubbing her nose with her handkerchief. "What does it do, that it's so dangerous?"

"Jesse says it will make people tell the truth. The truth, and nothing but!"

"I'm worried for you, Craig. You can be put away for life for this sort of thing."

"Yes, I know. If I was in the United States it would be a different story, but I'm not, and I don't have the time to worry about it. I'm probably out of a job, but I have to concentrate on following through on this before there's a cover-up."

"That's quite a sacrifice for a friend."

"Not just for a friend. At least not now. I've thought this through, and it's gone beyond that. To me it's a simple path, with no other choice."

"Most people run and hide from anything threatening or unpleasant," Jo-Ann commented. "You're programmed different than others. I remember you going to bat for Tom a few times, and taking the heat when you didn't have to."

"Ahh! That's different! He's my partner, and a good friend. You don't... "

"You don't turn your back on a friend," Jo-Ann finished for him. She smiled and touched his arm. "Go on, get out of here. Go. Straighten things out while you can."

"Where's Bev? Has she been told about Jesse?"

"Yes, she's been to see him briefly. She will go back up this afternoon. They'll only allow family though. Now get going."

"Sorry about Tom," Craig said, standing up.

She squeezed his hand and smiled. "I'll be fine now."

Back in the Cherokee, Jennifer turned towards Craig. "There's something I don't understand."

Looking over at her as he pulled up to a red light, he waited for her to continue. Lorraine was busy reading a magazine in the back.

Jennifer looked back at Lorraine before speaking to Craig. They hadn't told her about Rusty yet. "I don't understand why they simply let us go after they got all that stuff back that Jesse took. It doesn't make sense! We should be in a..." Jennifer looked at Lorraine, and whispered to Craig. "A cell right now."

"I'm as surprised as you are. Someone is making decisions and it isn't like we weren't straightforward in our written statements. We did help Jesse take that drug, and we definitely should be behind bars. Someone is making decisions from on high, and it's probably for political reasons. Two U.S. operatives did cross an international border and break into our house."

Jennifer continued, "Yes, but they should be practically *dragging* us all back across that border. They have to answer for the loss of 'PRECISE,' and you and I know someone will want to unravel and dig into what's happened."

"Well, maybe they're just relieved to get it back."

Turning towards Craig, Jennifer asked, "Do you believe that?"

He looked at her and smiled his lop-sided grin. "No. I'm sure we'll be hearing from somebody, and soon."

Craig shifted lanes as he steered towards home. He knew Lorraine was anxious to be in her own home, and he knew Jennifer needed a lot of rest. He picked up his cellular and punched in the numbers.

"Who are you calling?" Jennifer wondered.

"It's too soon to visit Jesse, but I want to see how he's doing."

Amazingly, he was put through to Jesse's room. A nurse picked up the phone. After promising only to talk for a few moments, he found himself talking to his long-time friend. Asking about Jesse's condition, Jesse informed him that the slug had passed through muscle only, and he was feeling better than he had a right to.

Craig changed the subject. "What are you going to do concerning 'PRECISE?'"

"I've been laying here going through my options. If I'm to have a clear conscience, I have to tell my side of it. I have to go public."

"That's why I called, Jess, but it will have to wait until you are on your feet."

"Yeah," Jesse said over the telephone, "but it has to be soon. I've been thinking of some of the applications they could use the drug for, and laying here with nothing else to do, I couldn't believe how the list grew in my mind. Improper use could lead to manipulation of juries, or polls, or even elections. The Democrats could destroy the Republicans, or visa versa."

"That's a pretty sad picture you're painting, Jess," Craig said as he neared home. "There has to be some honest people out there besides you."

"Yes, Craig, but I've learned that they always justify their actions. It allows them to commit acts above and beyond the average person. It allows them to gain power, usually in the name of national security. Any government that has referred to atomic fallout as 'sunshine units' isn't to be trusted too far."

"I'll set up a way to bring this public, Jess, but you will have to be there. At least a lot of the pressure is off."

"Thanks, Craig. Once this is out, I may be able to do cross border interviews. Put the pressure where it belongs."

Craig promised to visit, and cut the call short. At least Jesse still wanted to expose the illegal use of the drug.

• • •

Jesse Harris didn't know it, but there really were a lot of hard working, honest, and determined people who were defending and protecting the citizens of the United States.

He couldn't know of all the arrests, the dismissals, and the investigations. He couldn't know, as yet anyway, that the President of the United States had been the subject of a direct attack.

The spray directed towards the President could have contained nerve gas, anthrax, or any lethal toxin. And that instead of 'PRECISE,' it contained plain oxygen. The intended application of 'PRECISE' on the President couldn't be made public, however, because of the secrecy surrounding the drug.

The FBI's Counter Intelligence Unit and the Intelligence and Security Command had everything well in hand long before Jesse Harris had made his rash move.

Funny thing though– the President came out with items on law and order that were a surprise to a lot of people, like more money, more police, and stricter gun control legislation.

Jesse Harris and Craig Fletcher were loose ends, however. There were those who wanted them in immediate custody. It was thought that they were about to do a lot of damage to the 'PRECISE' project. The White House Administration couldn't begin to handle the damage control that would be needed to fend off world condemnation.

They didn't waste any time. The two men left Washington, D.C. early in the morning. There was no thought of a motel, or anything else for that matter, as they rented a car and headed towards the city core.

Jesse woke up from a light sleep and saw the two men standing at the foot of the bed. They were dressed in suits and were immaculately groomed. Looking around the hospital room, Jesse suddenly realized that the other patients had been rolled out. He was alone. If it weren't for his drugged condition, his level of anxiety would have been much higher.

One of the men moved to the side of the bed, while the other man pulled the curtain from the wall to half screen the doorway.

"Who are you?" Jesse asked, feeling helpless.

A few moments later, he found out.

• • •

The ring of the phone jarred him out of a fitful sleep. Craig swore, then reached across Jennifer for the telephone, her soft body reminding him again of the sharp intrusion. "Hello," he said sharply.

"Craig, it's Brad Duffield."

"It's a little late to be calling, Brad, but good to hear from you."

"Yeah, well, I got something here maybe you should know about. Just picked it up from an RCMP source."

Craig didn't say anything, waiting for Brad Duffield to continue, but he finally had to prod him to continue anyway. "I can stand to hear some good news, Brad."

"Well, I don't know if it's good or bad, but it looks like your shit-rat friend, Kaufmann, has surfaced."

Craig sat up, instantly all ears. "Where?"

"Well, a little bird told me that the coroner in Chilliwack has him."

"He's dead?" Craig was half relieved and half pissed off. With Kaufmann croaking, the truth would always be just hanging there.

"Been dead for quite a while it seems. He was a floater in Chilliwack Lake, and it took the horsemen quite a while to I.D. him."

"When did the RCMP pull him out, Brad?"

"Middle of the week. Just got a positive I.D. today."

"Have they determined the cause of death, do you know?"

"Well he didn't drown, Craig. Seems he has this neat little hole dead center in the back of his head."

"Execution?" Craig offered, and felt Jennifer tug at his arm. He shook his head for her to wait and concentrated on what he was thinking. "Drug deal gone sour?"

"Could be. I have nothing more to give you."

"How about making a call for me, Brad? Call Chilliwack and find out about Kaufmann's car."

"His car? What for?"

"Because the asshole never went anywhere without his car. It was a year old dark purple Firebird, and he practically lived in it."

"Okay, I'll get back to you."

Craig hung up and turned to Jennifer. "It was Brad. Kaufmann, the one who said I beat him up. He's dead." Craig went on to explain what he had heard. Jennifer went to make them a drink. It was twenty minutes later when Duffield called back.

"Strange thing about that car. Chilliwack never found it but it was traced to a used car lot in Vancouver. They were hoping to gather some Intel from it because he was associated with the car on the computer."

"He sold it?" Craig said with some irony. "I don't think so."

"Me neither, Craig. I'll get back to you tomorrow after I nose around a little."

"Thanks, Brad, talk to you later."

Sitting with the phone in his hand, Craig knew that Kaufmann was as tied to him in death as he was when he was alive. He didn't like it. Now Kaufmann couldn't talk. No, he didn't like it at all.

···CHAPTER FIFTEEN

Craig said goodbye to Lou Maynard, leaving his lawyer's building a few moments later. Looking at his watch he saw that he had only three and a half hours before he had to pick up Jennifer from work. Being down to one vehicle was taxing them both.

Traffic was normal, and he used his skill in avoiding the usual clogs and tie-ups; he even managed to hit every other green light. The cell phone rang as he went through a yellow.

"Craig, it's Brad Duffield. Can we meet somewhere?"

"Name it. I'm on Granville right now."

Duffield was silent for a moment, and Craig shot into the curb lane and passed a truck on the inside.

"Park by the marina just before Stanley Park, then meet me in the bar at the hotel."

"Be there in ten," Craig said and broke the connection. Brad Duffield was turning out to be very helpful.

Pulling into the parking lot, Craig looked for the battered vehicle that Brad usually drove, but couldn't see any sign of it. That wasn't unusual, and he didn't blame Brad for not advertising the meeting.

The sky was very low, the dark gray clouds folding over and rolling into themselves as they moved rapidly towards the mountains like some gigantic, angry, living, rampart of energy. The water didn't look any better. Dark, and churning with the movement of the current and the tide, it was whipped up by the wind, causing white caps that left little tufts of spray hanging in the air.

Craig stopped inside the lobby, the warm air engulfing him as he straightened his hair and looked for the lounge. Tropical plants and well-used furniture pointed the way and provided a pleasing atmosphere after the strong winds of the outdoors.

Soft music played overhead as Craig scanned the bar looking for Duffield, unable to see him against the bright windows that showed the same white caps spewing forth their sodden plumage.

Duffield raised his arm, and Craig was able to see him silhouetted against the rear windows. He sat down a few moments later, noting that there was a glass of beer waiting for him on the table.

"Just about to order a chicken sandwich and another beer. Want one?"

"Might as well," Craig said, picking up his beer. "Haven't eaten much today."

Brad called the waiter over and completed the order, waiting until the man retreated before resuming the conversation. Looking at Craig he shook his head. "You aren't going to believe what I'm going to tell you."

"Give me a try, only make it nice. I'm so sick of rotten news."

"Well I have this friend, who has a friend, who knows a guy who happened to handle the transaction on the late Kaufmann's Firebird. It seems the car was brought into the lot by someone else you know."

"Who?" Craig couldn't help asking.

Kaufmann's tag-a-long," Duffield said quietly. "Jules Vincent."

"Come on!" astonishment lit up Craig's features. "He wouldn't let that jerk anywhere near that car."

"Yeah, well, be that as it may, he got nine big ones for it."

"Sold it kind of cheap, didn't he?"

Smiling, Duffield continued. "Not really. He appeared on the car lot and produced the papers, saying he needed cash in a hurry. From what I'm told, he made a profit of eight thousand, nine hundred, and ninety-nine dollars."

"You mean..." Craig paused as the waiter placed two fresh beers on the table and left. "You mean he only paid a buck for that car?"

"That's right, but that's not all of it. The guy Vincent got the car from, well... I find it totally stupid that the guy got himself involved in this. Would you believe your old friend, ex-councilor, Gordon Parrento?"

"He can't be *that* stupid, Brad. This ties him directly to the murder of Kaufmann."

"Maybe," Duffield said, scratching his chin while looking at the ceiling.

"The date of sale is one month prior to the discovery of asshole's body, and... I forgot to mention, Kaufmann was seen hoofing it around town a week before his disappearance."

"Which means he didn't have wheels. Specifically the Firebird," Craig interrupted.

"Exactly. Which means Parrento probably forced Kaufmann to sign over the car, and then he sold Vincent the car for a buck. Vincent would do anything to own that car."

The sandwiches arrived and both men dug into the meal, not saying anything until their initial hunger had been abated. It gave Craig time to think, but it hadn't provided any answers.

Taking a swig of his beer, Craig leaned towards Duffield who was devouring the second half of his sandwich with huge bites. "If Vincent wanted that car so bad, he sure sold it in a hurry."

"Drugs," was all Brad Duffield answered.

"I wonder why Kaufmann and Parrento had a falling out?"

"Who knows? But for sure, Parrento took the car before Kaufmann died. That car might have been a gift to Vincent for services rendered."

"Or," Craig countered, "about to be rendered."

"Exactly. Craig, I'll be honest; something fucking smells here. I mean, you've had your problems with Shepherd, but what the hell do Shepherd, Parrento, and Kaufmann have in common?"

Craig shook his head, "I've gone over this a lot. Believe me. He's involved all right. He has to be, especially when it comes to Parrento and me. That's how this thing started. How else do you think Kaufmann managed to complain so fast? Straight to Shepherd."

Brad Duffield leaned forward onto his two forearms, pushing the near empty beer glass into the center of the table as he asked Craig, "Have you any theories on the who, what, and the where of Kaufmann's involvement in all of this, Craig?"

Craig shrugged his shoulders, waiting to see where Brad Duffield was heading.

"I mean the man is, or was, a hothead who for the most part steered clear of the law near the end of his life. He was too busy selling. Except for the time at the convenience store, you really didn't see much of him. Right?"

Craig nodded yes.

"Kaufmann knew that you don't go around pissing people off in his type of business. So what happened? Why do him in?"

"I have a few ideas," Craig shrugged. "Trouble is, they don't make sense all the way to a conclusion. All I see is Shepherd and Parrento putting pressure on Kaufmann to complain about me. Something went haywire, though and I just haven't figured out what. A while back I heard a rumble from one of my informants that things weren't all that cozy between Parrento and Kaufmann. Apparently it was a private matter. Maybe he started making demands on Parrento or Shepherd."

"Blackmail? Can you see Shepherd giving into blackmail?" Duffield scoffed.

With a straight face, Craig looked back at Duffield. "No. Neither would Parrento."

Duffield smiled. "You think maybe Parrento got pissed off and took him for a swim?"

"Interesting, isn't it? I'll even go so far as to say Parrento acted without Shepherd's knowledge."

"Interesting stuff, Craig, but there is absolutely nothing in it to help you prior to the Hearing. I can't see one single thing you can use."

Craig looked out towards Burrard Inlet. A seaplane was touching down on the rough surface, coming in behind an incoming ship and throwing up a brief wall of spray before settling down to a rough crawl towards shore. Craig threw some bills on the table for lunch and got up from the table. "Thanks for your help, Brad, I'll call you soon."

"I'll keep scouting around," Duffield said.

Craig nodded and then walked out to the Cherokee. A sudden blast of wind caught the driver's door as he opened it, his hair whipping around as small drops of rain hit hard against his cheek.

It was getting close to the time he was supposed to pick up Jennifer, and he aimed the nose of the car towards police headquarters. Craig knew he shouldn't dwell on things he couldn't control, but there was so much too think about. Between Jesse and Tom being in the hospital and the up coming Hearing he sometimes felt overwhelmed.

• • •

Jennifer jumped into the Jeep and proclaimed, "We are going out for supper. Then, we just have to visit Jesse and Tom at the hospital."

Craig didn't argue. They had a relaxing meal and tried to steer away from unpleasant topics such as the Hearing. Craig did fill Jennifer in on Brad Duffield's investigation and on the now dead Kaufmann.

"Wow," she said softly. "This may be worse than you expected."

"It's probably why Shepherd has been pushing so hard to bury me. He may have his own problems."

Craig's cellular began its incessant chirping and he fished it out of his pocket. "Yes?"

"Craig, it's Brad again. I haven't got long to talk. Can you meet me down around the docks, around Main and Coal Harbor Road?"

Graig looked over at Jennifer, thinking about having only the one car. "When?"

"Not sure. I'm on a bit of a wait and see. Could be a couple of hours or it could be anytime. It could also be worth your while."

"You got it, Brad. I have to drop Jennifer off first. Thanks."

"What's Brad got?" Jennifer asked as he eased out onto the street.

"He has some information for me. Bev will be at the hospital and can give you a ride home."

• • •

The inside of the Jeep was damp and chilly from being so near the water. Parked in the dark next to a building, Craig had watched the brightly lit intersection for the past two and a half hours.

He needed a cup of hot coffee and couldn't believe how slow the time was passing. He could see his breath and was tempted to put a little heat on, but he didn't want the exhaust rising up behind the vehicle.

A car appeared at the intersection and stopped at the curb. The lights were shut off but the exhaust was still visible as it curled up over the back bumper.

"That's Brad," Craig thought, and pulled the turn signal lever towards him a couple of times, sending multiple flashes blazing across the distance.

The driver of the other car reacted immediately and moved, lights out, towards the darkened area where Craig waited. Duffield coasted to a stop and shut his engine off. Craig climbed into the passenger's seat and closed the door to the first click.

Craig turned to Duffield. "What's happening?"

The engine started instantly; the soft rumble seemed overly loud in the chilled night air. Duffield reached down and flicked a switch off, deactivating the daytime running lights. Two cars whipped past on the opposite side of the road, and Duffield accelerated along the edge of the roadway, guided by the glow of the city lights.

Duffield turned left and drove between two buildings towards the rear.

"What are we looking for, Brad?" Craig asked.

"I'll fill you in shortly. I want to make sure I have the right location."

The car was rolling slowly ahead in the darkness, a brick wall on the left the only guide to steer by. It soon gave way to a fence and what looked like railway tracks on the other side.

The building on their right was about twenty feet away, and as they reached the corner their visibility improved. There appeared to be no ground floor windows, or doors. Finding himself moving into the open, Craig felt the car roll to a stop and turned to Duffield. "Well?"

Duffield was busy looking out his side window, but shifted his attention to the right side of the windshield and towards a third building that was across a clearing about two hundred feet away. A single light bulb was burning near the corner of the building, outlining a stack of pallets and a couple of front-end loaders.

"Nothing moving," Craig said.

"Keep your eyes on that door. I'd better shut the car off, they might hear us."

It was quiet, except for the background sounds of the city. Craig cracked the window open to let the moisture out.

"I was lucky enough to spot Parrento's driver earlier on," Duffield said. "So I followed him to a restaurant in North Vancouver where he met some jerk I've never seen before. I managed to sit in the next booth, and from what I could gather, the driver's queer. The jerk was his girlfriend. Parrento has a meeting somewhere down here, and his driver didn't want to sit around and wait forever. I followed the car until he picked up Parrento, and then watched as it pulled towards the back on the other side of that building. Parrento got out and walked further on into the darkness, but I didn't see him open any door on that side."

"So the driver's still in the car?" Craig asked.

"He was when I backed out of there. I had to go around to meet up with you. Whatever is going down, it's not normal hours for Parrento."

A slight movement caught Craig's eye. "We've got company."

Duffield strained to see what Craig was referring to, but couldn't see anything out of the ordinary.

Craig inspected the area around the door and slightly to the left where it turned into blackness. "He's there. He stepped out then back again. Whoever it is, he's being very careful."

They sat very still, hunched down to blend in with the interior of the car. It was becoming difficult to see out, with the windows forming a light mist on the outside.

A man stepped out into the open and walked under the light. He was in silhouette, and the light cast a downward shadow across his body. He turned and surveyed the open ground before him, then turned towards the door and walked under the light.

"Well, well. I think our boy Jules Vincent is paying somebody a visit," Craig whispered.

"What's he doing here?" Duffield asked.

"Probably summoned by Parrento for last minute instructions. He's supposed to give evidence at my Hearing."

Vincent walked backwards, reaching behind and to the side as he pulled on a small door set into a large sliding bay door. He disappeared inside without any light showing.

"That is one nervous cat," Duffield stated.

"Now," Craig said as he quietly levered the door open, "time for a bit of scouting."

Neither of the two men spoke as they quietly made their way to the building and the door with the single bulb. Vapor from their breath hung in the air, and no noticeable breeze whisked it away. A train whistle sounded somewhere in the night, the mournful sound echoing off of the water and fading into the distance.

The large bay door was perched on rollers. Craig continued walking to the smaller door. He eased the door open a couple of inches, then wider when only darkness loomed in front of him. Moving slowly, he stepped inside and felt for the floor in front of him as he moved. He stopped to regain his night vision but it was pitch black.

A soft glow lit up the immediate area and Craig turned to see Duffield holding his hand over the end of a small pocket flashlight. His hand glowed red as he allowed a trickle of light to escape to reveal the interior of a loading dock. They were on the lower part of a ramp, with the platform about four feet higher. A ladder was evident to their left, close to a small shipping and receiving cubicle.

Duffield moved forward holding the flashlight, followed by Craig. A few moments later they had climbed the old steel ladder and were standing in front of a small door.

Craig motioned for Brad to extinguish the flashlight, then turned and pulled slightly on the door. It didn't budge. Craig pulled harder with no results, then reversed direction and pushed slightly. The door moved silently and easily under his hand, revealing another darkened area.

There was a light visible on the far side of the warehouse that was throwing shadows down the wide isles stacked high with merchandise. Moving to the right, Craig advanced silently beyond four of the isles until he could see the source of the light at the other end of the row.

A small office, probably a foreman's, was built against the far wall and close to the main entrance. The three large office windows were filthy and covered in years of grime and dust. Neon lights produced a jaundiced glow on the other side of the greasy windows, only allowing a general outline of the people within.

The rows appeared to be about fifteen feet high, and moving quickly they covered the one hundred or so feet to the office. There was no noise coming from inside as Craig looked through the side of the grimy window. Dust particles were threatening to make him sneeze.

A voice broke the silence next to Craig. It was so loud and clear that Craig felt himself jolt backwards from the window, his heart pounding from the unexpected shock. He looked at the window as the voice continued to speak, and finally saw why the man could be heard so clearly. There was a row of smaller windowpanes at the bottom of the large windows, and one was broken out. One small scrape or noise from them and they would be discovered.

Craig leaned forward slightly, placing his finger against his lips for silence, and peered through the window. The man who was speaking had his back to him and had the attention of the others in the room. Someone else was sitting just below and to Craig's left.

The man to his left spoke, and it sounded like Jules Vincent. "The RCMP was just nosin' around is all. They don't know nothin'. They was just askin' about the Firebird."

The man who was standing turned to address Vincent, but his features were blocked by a piece of tape on the dirty window. "Just nosing around! You stupid little turd! When are you going to realize that cops just don't nose around? They are paid to investigate everything you do, say, and think. What a dumb fuck you are!"

The man moved away from the window and turned. Craig saw his face; it was Parrento.

"What do I do about tomorrow?"

"Tomorrow you go like you're supposed to. God knows you've been in court enough times. Take a small hit to calm yourself, but if you show up spaced out or do not show up at all, I will personally throw the first shovel full of dirt over your body."

"I'll be there," a sullen voice answered. "I still don't see why it's so important. I mean, Kaufmann's dead and who gives a shit."

Parrento lit a cigarette and blew the smoke towards the lighting fixture, then sat on the corner of a desk while he studied Jules Vincent. His voice was calm but low with anger as he spoke to the small man. "I give a shit. You had better remember that."

A third voice intervened quietly, coming from the man with his back to the windows. "I don't mind you having your fun, Gordon, just so it doesn't interfere with our little business. I mean, Fletcher is one thing, but putting our venture at risk is out of the question. Too many people and too much money is at stake."

Gordon Parrento turned and spoke to the unidentified man. "I want Fletcher. Understand? I want him to know what it's like to have things collapse around him. He caused me major money and major contacts. Once he's out of the Department he'll think a fucking crime wave descended on him!"

"Like I said, Gordon, have your fun. Just don't mess up. You mess up, and well– you know how it goes. There are responsible people who dearly want this territory. It's prime real estate, Gordon, and nobody can be allowed to jeopardize it. We like things nice and quiet."

"Don't worry about it, okay? I know what I'm doing. This is just a little something on the side. It needs to be done. For me, it needs to be done."

"You just make sure we stay well clear of any difficulties with the Kaufmann murder investigation. We are here for one reason only, and that's to move the merchandise; everything else is secondary. I'm leaving for Toronto tomorrow, then New York, and I want to be able to insure everyone that everything is running smoothly. This *is* a smooth operation, is it not?"

"Of course it is, and everything will be fine," Parrento answered. "I'll talk to Shepherd to see what's happening. By the time you return I'll have a new boy in place. The Hearing is tomorrow, and..."

"I am not interested, Gordon. This is your little diversion, not mine."

A tug on Craig's sleeve jarred him from his deep concentration, and he turned to see Brad Duffield motioning him to follow.

Once around the corner, Duffield put his mouth next to Craig's ear and whispered, "They're about to wrap it up. Do you want to stay and snoop a little, or leave now?"

Craig thought for a moment, then whispered back. "I don't know if this place is alarmed or not, but let's do a little looking around."

Duffield nodded and at that moment they heard the door to the office opening. Moving to the end of the isle, they were able to peer through the end shelves and view the office. The man Craig had been unable to identify through the office glass had entered the warehouse proper. He looked to be about five-foot-ten, bald, and fifty-five to sixty years of age. He was well dressed.

The man took a couple of steps towards the exit, and then turned. "Why make our own shit when there's tons of it out there already? Personally, I think you're bringing too much attention to yourself and you may reap something you didn't count on."

The man left, walking away into the darkness as Parrento stood in the open doorway. The far door banged against the framework, and Parrento turned back into the office. "That smug son-of-a-bitch!" he said with quiet venom, turning and slamming the office door, causing the glass to shatter. "That old fart giving *me* ultimatums." He turned to Vincent and continued in anger. "No screw-ups tomorrow, Vincent. You get stoned or not show up and I'll fucking kill you. Now get the fuck out of here. I'll have someone pick you up at precisely eight o'clock in the morning. Be ready!" Vincent nodded and hurried into the darkness, followed a few minutes later by Parrento.

They walked into the small messy office. "Shit," Duffield said, shaking his head. "How can anyone work like this?"

"They say a clean desk is a sign of a sick mind," Craig joked.

Duffield moved out into the warehouse; the beam from his flashlight could be seen moving around as he maneuvered between the different isles.

The light moved back and forth impatiently as Craig stepped into the warehouse. "Somebody coming?" Craig asked as he walked up to Duffield.

"Uh uh. Come see what I found."

Rows of shelves gave way to an open space and another large, but open, bay door. Walking through the opening, Craig saw large shipping containers parked along the side walls. Most had iron cross bars with padlocks.

"Look at this shipping label, Craig. Destination: Mother Russia." In the light of the flashlight, Brad Duffield read out loud, "Instruments of husbandry."

Walking further into the area, Craig followed the light. Pieces of metal were strewn about everywhere but were unrecognizable in the darkness. Duffield stopped in front of a container and pulled on the unlocked steel bar. The door swung open easily, revealing the contents to the flashlight's glare.

A shiny black Mercedes gleamed within the interior. The tires were blocked, and heavy padding stuffed between the doors and the container walls.

"You can bet your next pay check, that baby is hot," Craig said.

"Yeah," Brad nodded, looking around with the light. "Direct shipping, from one organized crime group to another."

Craig took the flashlight from Brad and walked into the container. Easing onto the hood he slid towards the windshield and shone the light into the corner of the dash. "New rivets and a freshly painted VIN plate." Craig backed off the car and walked out. "How many containers here?"

"I counted twelve," Brad replied. "At twelve vehicles a week, that's six hundred and twenty-four vehicles a year! No wonder my insurance is so high."

"I think I see why our little bald headed visitor was so concerned. These vehicles must be coming in from all over. Probably in semi-trailers." Craig paused, shining the stream of light around the cavernous area. Moving quickly down the floor area, the two of them worked under the single light trying to identify discarded parts.

Stepping up to a discarded dashboard, Craig turned it over and revealed the metal strip of numbers they had been searching for. He quickly wrote them down in his notebook and stood up. Four more numbers were jotted down, as well as the numbers from vehicles sitting in the center of the floor.

"Looks like you'll have your work cut out for you tomorrow while I'm sitting around in City Hall," Craig said.

"Okay, let's get out of here," Duffield said.

"I don't have to tell you to keep this very close to your chest," Craig said. "We don't want any calls back to Shepherd."

"The J.P. doesn't have to know the name Parrento," Duffield instructed, as they got into the Jeep. "Just the type of building and the address. In fact, maybe I'll make a call to Mr. Parrento and find a way to get him down to the warehouse just prior to our little visit."

"You're an evil man, Brad," Craig chuckled.

"Yeah, and you're going to have an evil time tomorrow if you don't get some sleep for that Hearing. Let's get you home."

···CHAPTER SIXTEEN

Craig felt an irritating knot in his stomach as he walked out of the driving rain and into Vancouver City Hall. The main floor was crowded with people waiting for the elevators and he recognized more than a few. He couldn't help but notice the furtive glances in his direction, followed by whispered messages.

Deputy Chief Shepherd was standing on the other side of the large reception area, surrounded by three lawyers. High powered help. The only winners on this day were going to be the lawyers and their fat fees.

"Craig. Over this way."

Turning towards the voice, he saw Lou Maynard standing in the doorway of a small room. He had a huge grin on his face and was waving for him to come in.

Maynard closed the door as Craig walked into the room. "What the hell are you so happy about?"

"You're paying me big bucks, Craig, why shouldn't I be happy?"

"Funny. You're always so funny, Lou."

"Ah, perk up. I have to put on a confident face for all those morons out there. Keeps them off guard, wondering why I'm so gleeful. Anyway, whatever they throw at you today we should be able to counter it. We are only dealing with Discreditable Conduct, Abuse of Authority, Insubordination, and..."

"Only, he says. What are they asking for in the way of penalty if they find that I'm a bad boy?"

"Immediate dismissal, but we'll deal with that if and when it comes up. *Never* allow anyone hear you talk about penalty. Makes you sound like you are guilty."

The door opened and Jesse Harris walked in, a bandage and sling covering his arm and shoulder. "Sorry I'm late, traffic was heavy."

"What the hell are you doing here?" Craig asked, astonished. "You're supposed to be in the hospital!"

"What the hell do you think I'm doing here? You think I'm going to leave you in the lurch? I'm in a position to shoulder most, if not all, of the accusations against you."

"I appreciate this, Jess, but you look like hell. You shouldn't be out of bed."

Lou Maynard held up his hand, taking a pencil out from between his teeth with the other. "He'll give evidence. If required. I couldn't hold him back. Like it or not, you need him."

"Give evidence on what? This is between Shepherd and me."

"No, Craig, this has everything to do with Jesse and you and what you allegedly pulled off together. Even though it was outside the country, it brought the charge of Discreditable Conduct and Criminal Activity against you. You were supposed to be fleeing with a wanted fugitive. Remember?"

"Yeah, but..."

Maynard put up his hand again. "We need him. Anyway, from what Jesse tells me, it couldn't have been that bad, because he's going back to work for the same boss."

"Say that again!" Craig demanded.

Jesse laughed, wincing with the pain. "It's true, Craig. I had a visit from two men from Washington, D.C., right in the hospital. They said they had orders from the White House. They want me back! When I'm better they want me to attend a special debriefing in Washington.

Craig just stood there. He didn't know what to say. He had too many questions and no answers. Why would the U.S. Government *do* that?

Jesse came up to Craig, pulling him aside. "It's true, Craig. Honest. There is so much that we didn't know about. I am authorized to tell you that 'PRECISE' was going to be used illegally, in a big way. We helped to stop it."

"Are you sure?" Craig asked, concerned for Jesse.

"You bet! They even reminded me about the Official Secrets Act. It looks like I'm back being one of the good guys. So are you, Craig. Thanks so much."

"All right," Craig said, turning to Maynard. "So how can you use Jesse to my benefit?"

"He's going to get up there and, without breaking any oath, he'll tell them exactly how he involved you without giving you any warning, or much choice. In addition, the Government of the United States has recalled him to work on the same secret project. Therefore, he's not guilty, and neither are you." Anyway, leave it with me; we go in about five minutes. I'll call you."

Craig was about to follow Maynard out of the room when Brad Duffield walked in. "Brad!" Craig lowered his voice and leaned closer. "I thought you were setting things up for the execution of a warrant."

"Later. It's all set up, don't sweat it." Duffield smiled. "You think I'm going to miss this?"

A long conference table sat in the center of the large room with chairs lining the walls on each side. The room filled up quickly with spectators until there was standing room only along the walls. The doors had to be closed.

Craig sat next to Lou Maynard, a couple of chairs down from the Presiding Officer and his counsel. Maynard exchanged nods with the prosecutor. His name was Charles Jelinski. Craig made note of how Jelinski purposely avoided eye contact with him.

"I would like to call our first witness," Jelinski stated. "Please call Deputy Chief Shepherd."

Craig looked directly behind him and saw Bev, Jo-Ann, and of all people, Jennifer. Craig was pleasantly surprised; he hadn't wanted her at the hearing. He got up and walked the few feet to her chair. He stood looking at her for a few moments. "You always seem to do the right thing. I'm glad you're here."

"We had to pick up Jesse, and we didn't want to worry you. I'm sneaky, aren't I?"

"You might say that," he grinned.

Craig looked up as Shepherd walked into the room dressed in his best uniform, his rank emblazoned on his epaulets, and his long service medal glittering on his chest.

Craig returned to his chair as Shepherd sat down quietly and looked at everyone at the table with equal sincerity, including Craig. After he was sworn in, he smiled and turned his attention to Jelinski.

"Thank you for your time, Deputy Chief, we know how busy you are and..."

Lou Maynard laughed quietly and said, "Mr. Chairman, I appreciate all this politeness, but let's get one thing clear here. Deputy Chief Shepherd is here as part of his duties, not out of his good will."

"I withdraw my opening remarks," Jelinski said with exaggerated politeness. "May I continue?"

Turning to Shepherd, Jelinski picked up a piece of paper and waved it back and forth to draw attention to it. "As you are aware, we are dealing with some serious charges concerning one of your subordinates. One of the charges against Sergeant Fletcher, Deputy Chief Shepherd, is one of insubordination, is that not correct?"

"I normally like to stay out of these things," Shepherd said magnanimously, "and let my men handle this kind of unpleasantness, but this was far too serious in nature."

"Now," Jelinski continued, "I know you had to have *some* say in the various investigations involving the charges before this Hearing, such as those of Criminal Conduct, Abuse of Authority, Discreditable Conduct, and of course, Insubordination, but let's deal with the last one for the time being. Most people, including a lot of people in the police field, would tend to think that the charge of insubordination is a bit of a– well to put it bluntly, a chicken shit charge."

"Normally, I would agree with you," Shepherd said in a fatherly way, "but not this time. I have bent over backwards for Detective Sergeant Fletcher, taking him under my wing so to speak, to try and keep him out of trouble."

Craig shifted in his seat, the anger building up inside of him with nowhere to go. Maynard, sensing Craig's discomfort, placed a hand on his arm.

"Please tell this Hearing what took place when Detective Sergeant Fletcher attended at your office in answer to your summons so you could explore the legitimacy of the complaint against him."

"I must say I was very disappointed in him. It is standard practice when a complaint appears to be serious to suspend the individual for a period of time. Fletcher did not take it well at all."

"How was he insubordinate to you?" Jelinski asked, quite comfortable with his witness.

"What occurred was more of an out-and-out threat, rather than insubordination. Some wanted him charged criminally, but I don't go for that. Things happen in the heat of the moment."

Lou Maynard exchanged a look with Craig, and Craig looked over his shoulder at those sitting behind him. Brad Duffield sat shaking his head from side to side.

"Tell us what happened, please."

"I told him I had to suspend him. He told me to come outside and he would finish the problem once and for all."

"There's been animosity between the two of you in the past, hasn't there Deputy Chief? I am bringing this out in the open at your insistence to make sure, as you put it, that everything is open and above board."

Shepherd looked at Craig for the first time while giving evidence. He kept his eyes on Craig as he delivered his remarks in a reasonable manner, as if he was trying to convey a great deal of patience with a wayward child.

"Fletcher brought me some evidence quite a while ago, evidence about a former city councilor by the name of Gordon Parrento who was supposed to have been involved in illegal activity. His case was very weak and I suggested that he drop it until I could have it investigated at a higher level. We would be dealing with a major scandal and a possible law suit if we didn't have everything buttoned down tight."

"Bullshit," Craig whispered to Maynard, who looked back at him with disapproval on his face.

"Fletcher wouldn't listen and he went behind my back and was insubordinate at that time as well. Everything went well for the Department and the city at that time, but I must stress that Fletcher has a past record of not being a team player. The decision I had to make back then involving Parrento was made after consultation with the Chief of Police. We were involved in putting together a task force when all hell broke loose because of Detective Sergeant Fletcher. In fact I blame *him* for the case not going to court."

"Please tell this court about the charge of Criminal Activity brought against Fletcher."

"I fully expect to bring evidence before this Hearing before it is completed. Evidence that Fletcher was involved with a criminal, and was involved in criminal activity within the United States. Criminal activity is criminal activity whether it's at home, in the United States, or in Zululand. Fletcher was publicly involved with a suspected United States felon."

"Deputy," Jelinsky smiled, "this man Kaufmann we have been hearing about, he was due to appear and give evidence if he had lived, was he not?"

"Yes, he was. He was the man who Fletcher bea.... ah, who complained about Fletcher beating him."

"If he had lived, Fletcher might have found himself in Criminal Court. Is that true?"

"Yes, it certainly is."

"So... would you say that Fletcher, ah... benefitted from his death?"

Lou Maynard slammed his open hand on the table. "Mr. Chairman!"

"I withdraw the question," Jelinski said, cutting off any further discussion. "Deputy Chief, how did Kaufmann die?"

Shepherd looked directly at Craig and said, "He was murdered."

Jelinski turned to Maynard and said, "Your witness."

"Before we continue, we'll take a fifteen minute break," the Chairman stated. "The witness is reminded not to discuss his testimony with anyone."

"I'll talk to you in a minute, Craig," Maynard said. "I'm going to talk to Jelinski. I don't like where he's heading with this."

Jelinski, Shepherd, the Official Recorder, and the Chairman left the room followed by Maynard, who began to talk to Jelinski earnestly.

Craig got up and stretched, turning towards Jennifer and the others. "Doesn't seem to be going too well."

"My ol' worry wart," Jennifer said as she grabbed his arm with both hands and held on.

"That guy is enough to make me barf!" Duffield exclaimed.

"What bothers me," Craig said, pointing towards the last of the press as they squeezed out of the door, "is what they're saying. Win or lose, it'll never go away."

"Sweetheart, you are wrong," Jennifer smiled. "Bigger and better things will happen in the world, and you'll fade into the background." Jennifer turned to Jo-Ann. "Let's get to the ladies room. And I could do with some coffee."

Twenty-five minutes later, everyone filed back into the room, including Jesse. Craig was about to tell him he had to wait outside the room until he was called, when the Chairman turned to Maynard and told him to proceed with the cross examination.

Maynard reached into his briefcase and took out a different file folder before turning his attention to Shepherd.

Craig sat up in anticipation, wanting Maynard to wipe that smug smile off of Shepherd's face, to make him so uncomfortable that he would think twice before he ever smiled again.

"Let's see, Fred Shepherd, 28 years of service, age 54 and currently holding the rank of Deputy Chief. Is that correct?" Maynard asked coolly.

"Yes. Frederick Elwood Shepherd is correct."

"I want you to cast your mind back to the time and date in which Fletcher was in your office. Do you recall the incident?"

"Yes."

"It really was an unpleasant meeting the two of you had, wasn't it?"

"Yes."

"He really didn't invite you outside to, as you put it, to kick the shit out of you, did he?"

"Yes, he did."

"And he did this because he was mad at you? Because you suspended him?"

"I didn't suspend him, Inspector Wong suspended him."

"On your orders though. Isn't that right?"

"Yes."

"Did you feel anger towards Sergeant Fletcher?"

"At times. Yes."

"Craig Fletcher was arrested on a warrant out in Abbotsford. He was then released to appear in court at a later date. Is this a time that you got angry?"

"Yes. He should have been kept in jail."

"The records show that Kaufmann laid a complaint late in the evening. How did you hear about this complaint about Kaufmann, Deputy Chief?"

"I received a call."

"May we ask from whom?"

Shepherd sat quietly, looking back at Lou Maynard with confidence. "From a man by the name of Smitty."

"Smitty?" Maynard said in surprise. "This is the first that I've heard of this Smitty. Who is Smitty?"

"He is Gordon Parrento's driver," Shepherd said in a matter-of-fact way.

"Mr. Chairman," Jelinsky said. "I don't..."

"Overruled. Continue, Mr. Maynard."

"What did this Smitty tell you when he phoned, Deputy Chief Shepherd?"

Shepherd looked directly into Maynard's eyes and said, "He said that he was telephoning for Parrento, and that he was to tell me that Kaufmann had met with an accident at the warehouse. He said that this might be the time for me to clear up an old marker. He said that Kaufmann was going to lay a complaint at the police station and I was to personally handle it."

Craig could not believe what he was hearing. Several reporters moved about the room as Craig turned around to look at Brad Duffield, who was having an animated conversation with another police officer.

"What the hell is going on!" Craig thought.

"Order, Order!" the Chairman called.

The gallery quieted down and Lou Maynard forestalled an adjournment by asking to be allowed to continue. He was given the nod.

"I am, to put it mildly, stunned at your testimony here today, Deputy Chief. What kind of *accident* did Kaufmann have in the warehouse?"

Shepherd looked at Maynard for a few moments, then answered in a straight forward manner. He appeared to have a bit of a smug look on his face, but Craig looked a little closer, unsure of what it was that was different. Then he remembered a conversation he'd had, a conversation that now seemed so long ago. It fell into place like a ton of bricks and, shocked, Craig turned and looked at his friend, Jesse Harris. Jesse just looked back at Craig with a straight face, then a small smile inched up and played at the corner of his mouth nervously.

"Oh Christ!" Craig thought. *"He's given Shepherd 'PRECISE!'"* His heart hammered within his chest. Jesus, he couldn't believe it! He was actually watching it in action. Then it dawned on him; Jesse had turned around and used 'PRECISE' for the very reason that he had stolen it, to prevent its misuse by anyone. He felt humbled that Jesse would do this for him. He felt relief, anger at Shepherd, and extreme anxiety that someone was going to notice.

Craig looked frantically at Shepherd then around the room to see if anyone else had noticed. Everything was the same, except for the knowledge Craig now carried within himself. Craig sat back, his heart gradually returning to normal as he listened to Shepherd's answers unfold.

"It really wasn't an accident. I learned later that he was worked over by Parrento's crew after Parrento had heard of the incident with Fletcher. He saw it as a window of opportunity to get at Fletcher."

"The Chair will entertain a motion here, Mr. Maynard," the Chairman said.

"Please allow me to continue for a moment, Mr. Chairman. We need to get at the truth of these events." Maynard turned his attention back to Shepherd. "So, you knew all these charges pertaining to Kaufmann were a fabrication?"

"Yes."

"And the other charges," Maynard continued, "Did you personally launch a vendetta against Sergeant Fletcher?"

"Yes, I did."

"Let's talk about your association with this Gordon Parrento whom you mentioned earlier."

"I object," Jelinski interjected quietly, clearly shaken. "This has no bearing on the case."

"On the contrary," Maynard laughed. "This is the *whole* case."

"Objection overruled," the Chairman intoned.

"Deputy Chief Shepherd, how well do you know this Parrento person?"

"I have known him for many years."

"At the time of this so-called bungle by Fletcher, did you know him then too? When Parrento was forced to resign?"

"Yes, we were doing business together."

There was a slight gasp from people in the public seating area. As Maynard continued, Craig turned and looked at Jennifer. There was a smile on her face, and a definite twinkle in her eyes. She looked relaxed, and very relieved.

"What kind of business were you involved in with Parrento?"

"The import and export business," Shepherd answered.

"I see. What was your function within the company?"

"Nothing, really. I was a figurehead to help Parrento with his contacts."

"Parrento was involved in illegal activities at the time. Were you aware of that, Deputy Chief Shepherd?"

"Yes."

"I don't mean as a result of Fletcher's investigations, I mean prior to it ever coming to the Department's attention. Did you know he was involved in criminal activities?"

"Yes, I did."

Craig Fletcher felt sheer anger when he looked at Shepherd. He thought of all of the damage that had been done while Shepherd was Deputy Chief of Police. Other emotions were happening within him also, and a sort of euphoria and a feeling of sheer triumph and happiness was gradually replacing his anger. He felt the lifting of a great weight from his mind and body.

"Was it you, Mr. Shepherd, who created the media opportunities which involved Fletcher in controversy?"

"Yes."

"Did you leak information, Department information, to Georgina Farnsworth?"

Again, "Yes."

Craig sat back in wonderment as the Hearing was adjourned and all the charges were dismissed. He watched as Shepherd continued to sit in his chair, not moving and not looking at anyone. He watched as Brad Duffield approached Shepherd and stood there looking at him for a few moments.

Duffield took his handcuffs out and placed Shepherd under arrest. The look on Duffield's face was a mixture of pleasure and contempt.

Craig sat there as the others crowded around him to offer their congratulations. The others were also beginning to watch as Shepherd was ushered away. Craig turned and thanked Maynard.

Maynard laughed. "Either I am *really* good at what I do, or Shepherd is off his nut. Weird. I'll send you my bill," he said as he got up. "Then again, I think I'll send it directly to the city."

Craig turned and found himself looking into the eyes of Edwards, the RCMP officer.

Edwards shook his hand. "Just to let you know, it will be a while before everything is cleared up, but don't sweat it. The word is out, but we have to go through the motions."

After Edwards left, Craig looked over at Jesse and shook his head in disbelief. He walked over and looked at his friend closely, not saying anything for a moment. Then he said, "I think we have a few things to talk about, Jess."

"What...to be *precise*?" Jesse smiled.

• • •

"I can't believe how fast the time has gone," Jesse said, sitting in Craig's living room.

Craig looked at Jesse. "Yes, you have a plane to catch. It's going to be boring around here when you leave."

Jesse laughed. "Thank God! Right?" Jesse shook his head. "Think of all that's happened! Shepherd's out of your hair; you get a promotion..."

"Temporary promotion," Craig corrected him.

"You *get* a promotion, and just the other day, this Parrento guy commits suicide..."

"I can guarantee you, Jess, Parrento did *not* jump off of his penthouse balcony. Somebody was trying to teach him to fly." Craig paused, shaking his head. "*You* can't believe all that's happened! Man, because of you I actually feel free!"

"It worked out okay," Jesse smiled.

"I guess giving back 'PRECISE' wasn't really that difficult for you after all. Not when you mailed some to yourself when we were in Vernon. Why did you do that?"

"At that time," Jesse explained, "I needed some 'PRECISE' to back up what I was saying if they managed to grab it."

"Well, I'm glad you did, but my heart was thumping so hard I thought *you* could hear it. I was sure someone would see what was happening. It was absolutely unreal... no, that's wrong. It was so, ...so natural."

"That's why I got you involved in the first place. It's natural, and scary," Jesse remarked, getting up to leave.

"I still find it hard to believe that you are going to work for them."

"I agree– but we need each other, Craig."

Jennifer and Bev walked in from the kitchen, the puppy bounding awkwardly ahead of them. "Time to go?" Bev asked.

"Yes," Jesse agreed, pointing to Craig and Jennifer. "The two of you follow me."

Jesse walked to the front door, Craig and Jennifer looking at each other in puzzlement. At the door, Jesse turned and offered his hand to Craig. Craig shook it, and found a set of keys left in his palm.

"I hope it's the right color," Jesse said, and stepped outside to the driveway.

Craig was speechless as he looked at the dark cherry colored Mustang. It sat gleaming in the morning sunlight with a huge card attached to the radio antennae.

"For the one you had to get rid of, Craig. You can't say no because it's already registered in your name."

"It's beautiful," Jennifer sniffed, tears running down her cheeks.

Craig hadn't said a thing; he was too full of emotion. He went to Jess to offer his hand, and ended up hugging him. It wasn't the car; it was the thought of his friend giving it to him.

"Of course you had to wait until you were getting onto the plane to do this, didn't you?"

"No arguments that way," Jesse smiled.

"Thanks, Jess. The color's perfect. I accept it very gratefully," Craig said opening the door. "Shit! I won't be able to get into the thing without thinking of you."

"That's the idea," Jesse laughed.

Jesse looked at his watch. "We have a plane to catch."

Saying goodbye was hard for Craig, and he knew it was the same for Jesse. They looked at each other and shook hands, turning the gesture into an awkward hug. Then Jesse and Bev were gone.

"God, people come in and out of your life so bloody fast," Craig said, turning to Jennifer.

"Yeah? Well, not this babe, Mr. Fletcher," Jennifer said as she put her arms around him. "Not this babe!"

• • •

Bev was sitting by the window as she usually did, taking in the view of the passing mountains as they passed majestically beneath the aircraft wing. Jesse was engrossed in a Washington, D.C. newspaper left behind by a passenger. He was nursing his drink as he tried to learn about the D.C. local scene.

Turning to the world news, Jesse's attention was caught by a small headline in the upper right hand corner of the page. He almost skipped over it, but he noticed several key words that made him read on. Reading further, he found it hard to breath. The hair on the back of his neck began to stand up as his skin tightened, like it had not so long ago.

NORTH KOREA ADMITS TO NUCLEAR CAPABILITIES
In a surprise move today,, North Korea admitted that their country was in possession of a nuclear bomb.

The turnabout occurred suddenly during an early morning session as the two sides met along the hostile border. The South Koreans are at a loss as to what caused the sudden change.

The President of the United States says he is amazed at the turn around, and looks forward to a harmonious relationship between all naitons. The president also stated that there was no room in the world for further development of weapons of mass destruction.

THE END

THE FIRE THAT NASA NEVER HAD

by Colonel B. Dean Smith

This book is an account of Colonel B. Dean Smith's flying activities in support of research and development of the United States' Ballistic Missile program and the space exploration of NASA from Cape Canaveral (Kennedy), Florida. Included is a report of a test done for NASA that examined space suits for the Gemini project. During this project, the author and another pilot experienced a disastrous fire in a simulator containing 100% oxygen, nearly taking both their lives. Five years later, in 1967, NASA's Apollo I capsule was consumed by a similar 100% oxygen fire, taking the lives of three astronauts, Gus Grissom, Ed White and Roger Chaffee. The author takes the reader through an account of the preparations made before his test flight and fire. He then makes a comparison of the two fires and the subsequent NASA investigation report of the Apollo I incident and draws conclusions regarding the lessons learned.

Paperback, 270 pages
6" x 9"
ISBN 1-4241-2574-X

About the author:

Colonel B. Dean Smith graduated from the US Naval Academy in 1953, commissioned in the Air Force. After pilot training, he served numerous flying tours and administrative positions. He earned an MBA from GW University, and served a tour in Vietnam, retiring from the Joint Chiefs of Staff on July 1, 1974.

also available from publishamerica

THE BRIDES' FAIR
by Hal Fleming

A novel of international intrigue and terrorism.

The Brides' Fair, an annual folkloric event in the Mid Atlas Mountains of North Africa, serves as an exotic setting for a novel of international intrigue and terrorism. Americans, mountain Berbers, Moroccan Arabs and those of a rebel faction converge on the festival, and it soon becomes clear that their fates are interwoven. The plot is driven by attempts to forestall an act of terrorism, while sub-plots tell of the tangled love interests of the Americans; the frantic efforts of a young Berber girl to escape a forced marriage; the trials of local officials in dealing with threats to their country's national security; and the obstacles faced by a small band of terrorists in carrying out their mission to disrupt the fair. A major disaster is averted at the last minute with the revelation that one giving aid to the terrorists was an American of the diplomatic community.

Paperback, 212 pages
6" x 9"
ISBN 1-60563-706-8

About the author:

Hal Fleming has been a senior official with the Peace Corps, the Department of State, UNICEF and the US Mission to the United Nations. He has lived ten years in West and North Africa. Early on, he worked at Forbes Inc. and taught at the university level. He has published various works and holds degrees from Brown and Columbia.

available to all bookstores nationwide.
www.publishamerica.com

also available from publishamerica

HOVERDOWN
by Raland J. Patterson

Hoverdown is a revenge-driven thriller tracking the lives of three men. Beginning in Vietnam, a skilled helicopter pilot, Bill Dant, foolishly accepts an opportunity to deal drugs to his fellow soldiers. Platoon leader Captain Sam Wright is instrumental in sending him to prison. After three inmates crush his hand, ending any hope of flying again, Dant begins his trail of vengeance. Killing comes as naturally to him as breathing. Captain Wright is disabled by a gunshot wound and goes to work for Jim Coleman, a former self-proclaimed vigilante. After the execution of his wife for a murder he committed, Coleman seeks peace by becoming a lawyer advocating justice for juveniles. A strong-willed doctor, Amanda Hicks, knows she has found a man to reckon with when Coleman refuses to cater to her bossiness and throws her in the lake. The three men's stories merge into a conclusion of startling destiny.

Paperback, 276 pages
6" x 9"
ISBN 1-60474-283-6

About the author:

Raland J. Patterson is a retired Army lieutenant colonel with twenty-two years of active duty. He served in Vietnam as a helicopter pilot from 1970-1971. His awards include the Distinguished Flying Cross, Bronze Star, and fourteen air medals. His second career was as a financial planner in Europe.

available to all bookstores nationwide.
www.publishamerica.com